APR 1 3 2009

DUNDEE TOWNSHIP PUBLIC LIBRA

W9-AJN-587

3 1783 00380 5896

RENEW ONLINE AT
http://www.dundeelibrary.info
"MY ACCOUNT"
OR CALL 847-428-3661 X301

DATE DUE

THE BLOOD DEBT

Dundee Township Public Library District
555 Barrington Avenue
East Dundee, IL 60118-1496
http://www.dundeelibrary.info

Other Pyr® titles by Sean Williams

The Resurrected Man

The Crooked Letter,
Books of the Cataclysm: One

The Hanging Mountains,
Books of the Cataclysm: Three

THE BLOOD DEBT

BOOKS OF THE CATACLYSM **TWO**

Sean Williams

Dundee Township Public Library District
555 Barrington Avenue
East Dundee, IL 60118-1496
http://www.dundeelibrary.info

an imprint of **Prometheus Books**
Amherst, NY

Published 2008 by Pyr®, an imprint of Prometheus Books

The Blood Debt, Books of the Cataclysm: Two. Copyright © 2006 by Sean Williams. All rights reserved. No part of this publication may be reproduced, stored in a retrieval system, or transmitted in any form or by any means, digital, electronic, mechanical, photocopying, recording, or otherwise, or conveyed via the Internet or a Web site without prior written permission of the publisher, except in the case of brief quotations embodied in critical articles and reviews.

Inquiries should be addressed to
Pyr
59 John Glenn Drive
Amherst, New York 14228–2119
VOICE: 716–691–0133, ext. 210
FAX: 716–691–0137
WWW.PYRSF.COM

12 11 10 09 08   5 4 3 2 1

Library of Congress Cataloging-in-Publication Data

Williams, Sean, 1967–
    The blood debt / Sean Williams.
        p. cm. — (Books of the cataclym ; 2)
    Originally published: Sydney, Australia : Voyager, an imprint of HarperCollins, 2005.
    ISBN: 978–1–59102–694–5 (paperback : alk. paper)
    ISBN: 978–1–59102–493–4 (hardcover : alk. paper)
    I. Title.

PR9619.3.W5667B66 2006
823'.914—dc22

2006020965

Printed in the United States of America on acid-free paper

To KIM SELLING,
for reacquainting me with magic

"The Void Beneath is a horrible place. A ringing emptiness infuses it, an endless hum that scrubs the soul clean. Imprinted on this eternal drone are the minds of the lost, clinging to their memories like life rafts. Despairing and desperate, the Lost Minds smother new arrivals with pleas to hear their stories—for if they are forgotten, they inevitably die.

"Among the Lost Minds is one they call the Oldest. The Oldest One bade me listen to his story, and I did. Sometimes I wish I hadn't. If it is true, then even the most outlandish tales in the Book of Towers are based soundly on fact. If it is not true, then we are as much in the dark about our past as we ever were. Even now, years later, I am still unsure which of these two possibilities is the more terrible."

Skender Van Haasteren X

Seth remembered: the Flame imploding and the two Sisters being sucked into it; ekhi breaking into Sheol and Ellis escaping on a brilliant, hypnotic back; mountains closing in over a dark, hunched shape and three slender glassy towers entombing them all. Through the chaos, a green figure strode calmly toward him and whispered softly into his ear.

"Peace, Seth. This is neither our first meeting nor our last. In your future, the Goddess awaits."

The bubble of the world burst, and a new topography swept over the land.

"Remember us, Seth," Horva insisted from very far away. "Please, remember us . . ."

Sandwiched in the knot that had once been Bardo, the twins rolled and tumbled. They weren't in the First Realm; they weren't in the Second Realm; they were between, holding the worlds together like glue. A hum swept over them like the breathing of an ocean, smoothing them out and removing their sharp edges. The void pressed in until only echoes of their lives remained.

They had bent worlds to their will and travelled the darkest of ways; conversed with gods and with those who would be gods; walked in the company of monsters and angels. They had killed.

Time passed, and they knew it not.

THE WARDEN

"On the matter of the ghosts, we find that their presence comprises no direct threat to the citizens of the Haunted City. Only when summoned can they do any harm. In order to deter such a summoning, necromancy will remain a Category A crime, punishable by expulsion from the Haunted City.
"Therefore, on the matter of Shilly of Gooron, we find her guilty of necromancy and recommend that she be punished accordingly. She may live freely in the Strand provided she does not attempt to practise or teach the Change, or reenter the Haunted City. Any deviation from this course will result in exile beyond our borders."

JUDGMENT OF THE SKY WARDEN CONCLAVE IN EXTRAORDINARY SESSION, YEAR EIGHT OF THE ALCAIDE DRAGAN BRAHAM

The young man looked out to sea.

As far as days went, this one was almost perfect. The sky hung overhead in a marvellous blue dome, marbled with clouds. The sea sighed with easy, patient rhythms. An effervescent breeze blew directly into his lungs from the grey expanses of the ocean.

He should have been content. But he wasn't. His skin tingled from more than just the salty spray. He would have been sunburned hours earlier, but for the protective charms daubed on his shoulders and back. The smell of rotting fish came strongly on the breeze. The pounding of the surf was relentless, day and night.

A seagull cawed in the distance, and he looked up sharply, feeling eyes on him.

I'm not here, he projected. He imagined the beach as it would look from the air: a ribbon of cream-coloured land separating the blue from the brown; him alone along its length—shoulder-length dark hair waving in the wind, an oval face with unremarkable features, apart from his eyes, which were shades of blue mottled with white flecks. His mother's eyes; and his adopted father's hands, weathered and calloused from plenty of hard work.

The seagull cawed again. Sky Wardens sometimes used seagulls as spies along the Strand. Whether this was one of them or not, he couldn't tell, but it paid to be careful. The beach he stood upon was a part of their endless, linear empire, and for Sal the sea had never been a friend.

Gently, so as not to raise more interest than he might already have, he painted himself out of the picture.

Just a fisher. Not Sal Hrvati.

Wheeling and diving, the seagull resumed its hunt for lunch.

Sal was hungry, too, but that wasn't the source of his discontent.

Something's wrong, somewhere, he thought. *I've been feeling it for days. But what does it have to do with me? Now?*

He closed his eyes and let the world rush into him. He forgot the seagull and the wind and the heat on his temples and the sea's stealthy creep. He exhaled, then inhaled deeply. A vibrant buzz passed through his bones. The Change was powerful and raw on the beach, where earth and ocean met. He could feel it in everything around him, as wilful and nebulous as air. Sometimes he would sit for hours and let his thoughts drift beyond the ephemera of everyday life. In the ebbing and flowing of the Change, he felt vitality and vigour that was equally beautiful in life and in death.

But not any more. There was a tear, somewhere—a tripping of the cadences of the Strand. It nagged at him, maddening in its ability to pull out of reach when he tried to pin it down. He couldn't tell if it was a person or a thing, or something he feared to see in himself. As much a part of the Change as anything else, he knew he was far from infallible.

Sal glanced to his left at a grave marker on the edge of the beach line. The weatherworn post was inscribed with charms and encrusted with salt. *What would you tell me, Lodo? Am I imagining things or beginning to see clearly at last?*

He returned his attention to the sun and the sand and the sky. The wind danced fitfully around his legs, as though sweeping the way clean for a storm, but he could smell no rain, no thunder. The stone pendant around his neck, a weather charm called *yadeh-tash*, was silent.

Then it struck him—at once both physically and mentally. He cried out at a fierce stab of pain between his shoulder blades, and spun to look behind him. The beach was empty, except for him and the birds, but his eyes saw beyond them, through the rough fringe of scrub and into the gracefully towering folds of sand dunes that marched effortlessly inland. In the long moments he had been gawping at faraway fractures, he had completely overlooked something nearer and infinitely more precious. Close to home someone had tripped a trap.

"Carah." He called the name as loudly as he dared. "Carah!"

His toes clenched in the sand and he began to run.

Carah!

The sound of her heart-name propelled Shilly out of a deep sleep she didn't remember entering. She had been dreaming of an outline of a face, or something very much like a face, although it seemed to have too many eyes and maybe an extra mouth. It belonged to something buried under the sand, something that was trying very hard to surface. It frightened her, and with her hands she had tried to sweep the impression of it from the sand. But sweeping the grains away only brought it to the surface faster than ever . . .

She sat up with a jerk. Sal had called her, and he had sounded panicked. It had been a long time since the last false alarm. Although they knew theoretically that they could be found at any time, it wasn't possible to live in a state of perpetual dread. Their jitters in the early days had settled down to a constant, low-level vigilance. Hiding was second nature to them now.

She didn't dare take the chance that he was jumping at shadows. Struggling free of her rabbit-skin coverlet, she shook off the lingering veils of sleep. The underground workshop, their home, was warm but not stuffy, ventilated by a chimney leading up through the compacted sand to fresh air far above. Kidney-shaped and high-ceilinged, the workshop had been fashioned decades earlier by a renegade Stone Mage who had come to Fundelry in search of new ways to master the Change. Instead of peace and quiet he had found Shilly, a girl with a knack for the Change but without the talent to use it. He had taken her as an apprentice and, on his death, left Shilly all his possessions. The workshop contained the trinkets he had made or gathered to himself down the years. Some she understood perfectly, grasping their purpose the moment she studied them, even though she didn't have the spark that would make them work. Others remained a mystery despite many hours of contemplation.

A flawed metal mirror caught her in its depths as she shrugged into the cotton dress she had worn the previous day and slipped on her sandals. Her dark hair stood in total disarray, bleached at the tips by sunlight. The same light had burned her skin deep brown, darkening what nature had given her still further. A series of thin white scars marred the skin of her right leg. The mirror had been dropped and was now warped on its left side, giving her a compressed, foreshortened aspect, as though she was walking into an invisible barrier. She didn't linger.

She grabbed the workshop's pole-shaped latchkey from its usual place and hurried through the tunnel which led her from the main room to an antechamber. There was a wicked hook at one end of the latchkey and, on reaching a cave barely large enough for her to stand upright, she poked this into the sandy soil and twisted. Half of the latchkey vanished into the wall, as though tugged at by hands on the far side. She hung onto her end and firmly twisted the pole again. The charm had come with the workshop, one of those she hadn't quite fathomed, but she understood its operation well. Something clicked under her hands, and she raised her eyes to look into the dull, sandy wall.

A faint echo of the dunes outside the entrance to the workshop came to her, as misty as a dream. She didn't see the shape of the dunes so much as the *form* of them: the lines they made against each other, against the spindly grass that grew in their shadows, against the blurred horizon. She swept her attention along those lines, looking for any recent change. Birds appeared as swooping vortices, dimples in the sky; crabs were asterisks leaving complicated ellipses in their wakes; humans stood out like giant, dead trees on a fallow field.

There. She focused on a new feature of the dunes: a line of footprints marred the smoothly changing symmetry. Past them, just touching the low hills beyond the sand, were several parallel tracks that looked hauntingly familiar. *Made by wheels*, she realised. No hoofprints, horse or camel. Self-propelled, although she couldn't see the machine itself.

A chill went through her. The view flickered. While the reservoir in the latchkey lasted, she followed footprints into the dunes, seeking the person who had made them. Her gaze skidded over a discontinuity and lost the trail. She backtracked, and skidded again. The person making the tracks was deliberately hidden from her sight.

She had just enough time left to see Sal hurrying from the beach. His trail was hidden, too, subtle and barely visible but as familiar to her as the dunes themselves. He angled around the interloper, coming up from behind.

Be careful! she thought, even though she knew he couldn't hear her.

The latchkey gave out, the store of the Change within it consumed by the wall's charm. She was left on the wrong side of the exit, anxious and blind. What to do? She couldn't just sit in the workshop like a rabbit in its hole waiting for the trap to spring.

She had seen enough, though. The interloper was approaching from a point near the outer edge of the dunes. That left him or her, most probably, with no line of sight to the workshop's entrance. If she was quick, she might just get through without being spotted.

She took a deep breath and withdrew the latchkey. It slid freely from the sand, unhindered by the arcane mechanism it operated. Turning to another section of empty wall, she outlined a figure eight in the soft soil. With a sigh and a shower of sand, the wall collapsed, leaving a metre-wide hole in its wake. On the other side of the hole was the back of a bush. Beyond that, sunlight and the dunes.

Shilly hurried through, carrying the latchkey with her. The white sand glared bright in the daylight. The smell of salt and spear grass was sharp in her nostrils. She squinted to check around her before running away from the exit, erasing her footprints with her free hand as she went. She ducked out of sight at one end of a wide dune-valley just as a flash of blue fabric appeared at the other.

A Sky Warden? So far from the Haunted City? It wasn't Selection time for months, when the young of the village were examined for Change-sensitivity or talent. There was just one other conceivable reason for a warden to be in the area. Shilly forced herself to confront the awful truth: that she and Sal might have done something to give themselves away.

She held her breath and hoped Sal would stay out of sight. The last time Sky Wardens had come to the dunes, her life had been turned upside-down. Pain shot along her right leg, from hip to ankle, and with a worried look she reached down to rub at it.

Unnatural silence had fallen over the dunes. Sal's hearing seemed muffled as he moved to catch up with the person who had triggered the early warning charm on the dunes' northeastern perimeter. Just as thick fog could dampen sound, so, too, could sufficient skill deaden the Change.

That thought sobered him. The chances were that this person was better trained than himself; not someone from Fundelry, then, or a wandering weather-worker, foraging for driftwood. For all the natural talents he possessed, subtlety was not one of them. He couldn't just rush in and hope for the best.

He inched around the outstretched limb of a dune and caught his first glimpse of the person he pursued.

A thin young man with black, curly hair and ebony skin strode confidently towards the workshop entrance. He wore the bright blue robes of a Sky Warden. A crystal torc hung around his neck—a sign of rank, Sal remembered. Over his right shoulder drooped a black bag shaped like a teardrop. Its contents swayed heavily from side to side.

Whoever he was, he crossed the sand with long-legged strides, making no obvious attempt to conceal himself.

The bush camouflaging the entrance to the workshop stood out against the wall of sand behind it, a suddenly pathetic hiding place, even though it had served Lodo well for many years. Sal had felt the entrance open and Shilly scurry for freedom, so he was spared the worry of her being trapped inside. But that wasn't the limit of his concerns. If the Warden found their home and reported it to the Syndic, they would be forced to run again. And he wasn't ready to leave the one place he had felt at home—not yet.

Sal reached out through the Change, fighting the interference radiating from the trespasser, and touched the second line of defence. The buried traps stirred, awaiting his command. They had grown in the years since he had placed them in a series of concentric semicircles around the entrance to the workshop. They throbbed with readiness, swollen and angry like bees ready to defend their hive.

The Warden stopped in his tracks and looked around.

Sal ducked out of sight and slithered to a new position. The Warden turned his head from side to side, as though seeking the source of a faint sound. His expression, when Sal got his first good look at it, was one of intense concentration.

Sal went to duck again, but froze. There was something familiar about that face, those long features and dark eyes. He had seen them before. Or *had* he? He'd met only a few Wardens during his ill-fated stint at the Novitiate, five years ago, and none since. Would he remember any of them from that far back, even if his liberty depended on it?

The Warden straightened upon one last inspection of the dune valley. He swung the pack off his shoulder and put it on the sand by his feet. By accident or not, he had stopped just before the concealing bush.

The Warden raised his empty hands and turned in a full circle.

"Come out, Sal and Shilly," he called, speaking slowly and loudly. "I know you're here."

Sal rolled over and flattened himself hard against the sand, staring desperately up into the sky. Sky Wardens didn't necessarily need their hands free to cast charms any more than he did. The Warden's gesture of peace was purely symbolic and therefore meaningless, but symbols had power. So Lodo had tried to teach him years ago, and Shilly had reinforced the lesson many times since.

Silence choked the air over the dunes. The wind had died completely; not even the seagulls dared brave the sudden stillness.

Sal didn't know what to do.

"Who are you?" came Shilly's voice from the other side of the Warden. "What do you want?"

Sal peered over the dune, alarmed by the thought that Shilly had put herself in danger. He reached out for the buried traps as the Warden turned to address the area that Shilly's voice had come from. It wasn't too late. She was far enough away not to be hurt.

"What's the matter?" the Warden asked, his words echoing from the walls of sand. "Don't you know who I am?"

"I know *what* you are. That's enough."

"No, it's not." The Warden made no move, except to sag a little. "I dreamed last night that you and I were riding a ship of bone up the side of a mountain, into a cave of ice. Something dark and ancient lived there, under the ice, and it knew we were coming. It had slept for an eternity, but was waking now, and it was hungry. We had to stop it, you and I, before it ate the world."

Sal listened, hooked by the same odd sense of familiarity he had felt on seeing the man's face. The Warden's voice had changed while talking about the dream; it was higher pitched, and had a childlike rhythm. Sal had heard someone talk like that before, under very different circumstances.

For the first time, Sal noted how dusty the Warden's robe was, his scuffed and worn boots.

The name, when it came to him, was as unbelievable as it was a relief.

"Tom?" Sal stood up on the crest of the dune. "Is that really you?"

The Warden turned away from Shilly's hiding place to look at him. Now that Sal knew the truth, he could see the resemblance. Gone were the awkward ears and lack of height. Gone were youthful uncertainties and baby fat. In their place was a lean, almost ravenous, sense of concentration that hit Sal like a physical force as Tom's gaze fixed on him.

The teenager Sal had last seen as a boy didn't smile. "Who else would I be?" he asked, appearing genuinely puzzled.

A surge of relief carried Sal down the side of the dune. "It's been such a long time," he said. "I didn't recognise you."

"You look the same."

"Thanks, I think." Tom's equine features took on a younger cast as Sal neared him. Under the dirt, he had pimples. Sal held out his hand. Tom's grip was uncertain, fleeting.

"What in the Strand brings you here?"

Tom looked over his shoulder as Shilly came out of hiding. She didn't look as relieved as Sal. Favouring her weak right leg, she leaned on Lodo's latchkey in lieu of a staff.

Tom turned back to Sal. "It's your father," he said.

The heat of the day vanished at those three words. "What about him?"

"He needs your help."

"He sent you to find us?"

"No." Tom shook his head emphatically. "I came here of my own accord. No one knows."

Shilly looked from Sal to Tom when she joined them.

"A cave of ice, huh?" she said. "That's not a prophetic dream; it's the sort of nonsense normal people have."

Tom opened his mouth to respond, then closed it. Sal could practically hear his mind working. Brilliant in the ways of the Change, Tom struggled when it came to everyday matters.

"It will happen," he said. "That's the way it works. I thought you'd remember, after the golem and Lodo and—"

"Easy," she said, a look of sadness clouding her features. "I remember. I just don't understand how it could ever be possible. I haven't seen ice in my entire life, let alone a *cave* of ice. The nearest mountains are half the world away, and I'm in no hurry to get there. As for hungry things wanting to eat you and me . . ." She put her hand on his shoulder. "Be assured that this is one fate I'll try my level best to avoid."

Tom didn't argue, although her answer obviously didn't reassure him.

"Why don't you come inside?" asked Sal, indicating the bush and the entrance to the workshop behind it. The deadness over the dunes had faded; the wind had returned. "You look like you could get out of the sun for a while."

"Yes," added Shilly, "I'll get you some water, make you some tea."

Tom nodded, but stayed where he was. "Tell me," he asked Sal, his dark eyes very serious. "What would you have done if I hadn't been me?"

Sal looked at the ground around them, wondering how much Tom had sensed. Woven in a thin layer just under the surface of the sand was a pattern of interlinked charms designed by Shilly and willed into potency by Sal. The charms—resembling insects with circular bodies and crosses for heads—caught light filtering through the grains above them and held it there, the pattern growing increasingly powerful with every day that passed. At a word, Sal could release the stored energy in the light-traps and send it flooding back out into the world. He didn't know how much energy, exactly, there was in the traps, but definitely more than enough to kick up a dense sandstorm, allowing Shilly and him to escape under cover. Probably enough to blow a person standing on the light-traps to pieces . . . There was only one way to find that out, and fortunately he had been spared such a decision this time.

"Don't worry about us," he said. "We know how to look after ourselves."

Tom's dark eyes took him in with one long glance. Sal's assurance was one thing Tom clearly understood.

Shilly tugged Tom forward, her sun-bleached hair dancing. He allowed himself to be led up the slope of the dune, first picking up the heavy bag and draping it back over his shoulder, then dragging his leather boots through the sand.

"Come on down," said Shilly, waving their old friend ahead of her along the secret passage into the workshop. "Tell us everything you know."

"That could take days," he said. "I've been dreaming a lot lately, and not just about you. I think Skender might be in trouble, wherever he is."

Shilly glanced over her shoulder at Sal. He rolled his eyes. Nothing had changed.

"What we *need* to know, then. Let me get you a drink, and then you can get started."

Sal came last, ignoring the sensation of being watched as he closed the door behind him. The birds on the dunes were the last things he had to worry about now.

THE MINER

"It is clear that the ground subsided after the Cataclysm, but before the making of the Divide, so the city endured not one but two separate and unrelated catastrophes. The first lowered the city into a depression several kilometres around, with sloping sides and a roughly flat bottom. The second split the depression and therefore the city into two sections of unequal size. The inhabitants of the larger portion took shelter behind a sturdy wall designed to keep the Divide at bay. Some speculate that the creators of the Wall were the same as the creators of the Divide, suggesting the riving of the city was accidental, and that architectural triage on a massive scale was both called for and delivered."

LAURE HISTORICAL SURVEY

S kender Van Haasteren the Tenth was stuck. It wasn't the first time he had been in that situation. His home, the Keep, an ancient cliff-face refuge deep in the heart of the Interior, was riddled with secret passages and unnoticed cracks, most of which he had explored during his childhood. Only on becoming a teenager had he realised the screamingly obvious: that such illicit expeditions were a form of escape that would never lead anywhere. All they did was annoy his father.

The one time he genuinely escaped, he had ended up on the other side of the Divide, fighting golems and worse. It had come as quite a shock that the outside world he had always dreamed of might actually be dangerous. He had gone home with a feeling of relief, his youthful rebellion out of the way nice and early. Time to settle in and do some safer work. No more adventures for him, thanks.

But now, here he was, out in the world a second time and finding himself caught in a crack he would once have slithered through with ease, distressingly deep underground.

I'm too big for this, he told himself as he reached for a handhold just out of reach, *obviously*. He was curved like a hairpin; if he could only obtain some sort of leverage, he could easily wriggle around the bend, but his fingers were flailing about like a newborn's and his feet kicked uselessly at air. He flexed his entire body, hoping to shake things up, but succeeded only in banging his knees and scraping his spine even more. He tried twisting in a spiral fashion and brought his skull into sharp contact with stone. He saw stars.

For the first time in years, he truly feared for his life.

"Help!" he yelled, even though he knew it would be futile. He was deeper than few in Laure ever went, surrounded on all sides by heavy, ancient stone. Thinking him mad and possibly dangerous, the guides whose experience he had tapped had all warned him about the dangers of going down into the caves. Not one of them offered help, but nevertheless he had had to try. His mother was down here *somewhere*, and she needed rescuing.

Hands gripped his ankles.

He yelped in fright and kicked out. His foot struck something soft.

"Hey!" came a muffled voice past the plug of his twisted body. "I'm trying to help you, you idiot!"

"Sorry." He forced himself to relax and let the hands clutch him again. Whoever they belonged to used their body weight to pull at his legs. Skender yelped as he shifted suddenly in the bend, losing still more skin to the rough, dry stone. His spine complained and his face was rammed hard against rock. For a moment he thought he might lose his nose.

"Ow! Be careful."

"You want to stay down here forever?"

"No, but—"

"Then stop whining!"

The weight dragging at his ankles dislodged him from the hairpin. He tried to grab the walls to slow himself down, but he had been taken by surprise, and so had the person pulling his legs. He shot out of the crack to freedom in a rush and they tumbled together to the floor of the cave. One flailing limb caught his rescuer solidly in the abdomen. He heard a sudden exhalation of air, then pained wheezing.

"Bloody—hell!"

"I'm sorry. It was an accident." He fumbled to lift his fallen pack off the glowstone he had been holding when he became stuck. Its reservoir of stored sunlight was strong enough to make out the person who had popped him from his early grave like a cork from a bottle.

He saw a young woman, around his age, with black hair and almond eyes. Her skin was neither white nor brown, but something in between. A dirty boot print stood out on the front of her chest.

"That's—gratitude—for you," she said, casting him a dark look. Wheezing, she climbed painfully to her feet and dusted herself off. She wore a faded black leather uniform that had seen better days. Patched and piecemeal, it had obviously belonged to many other people before she had acquired it; tight-fitting, with padding around the shoulders, elbows, and knees, there were two dull purple lines crossing at the front in a large X. The motif was repeated on the upper arms, in miniature.

"I *said* it was an accident," he repeated, although his mind was already moving on. "Hey, I remember your face. You were in the crowd at the coffee stall, and at the hostel." Facts clicked belatedly into place. "You've been following me!"

"You don't sound very glad about it," she said, glaring at him and picking up a short, fat tube from the rough ground. Tapped once, hard, against her thigh, it emitted a beam of weak blue light that she shone into his eyes. "If I hadn't come along, you'd be another squeal closer to dying down here."

"But . . ." Although there was no denying his gratitude at being rescued, he couldn't leave it at that. "Who are you?"

"My name is Chu. I'm a miner."

Understanding dawned. "So *that's* what you're doing down here. This is where you work. You weren't following me at all. You just heard me yelling."

She laughed. "You're an idiot, Skender Van Haasteren the Tenth."

"Huh?"

"You have no idea how Laure works. That's why I'm following you. Someone's got to keep white folks like you out of trouble."

Stung by her tone, he turned away to check his robes for rips. Vivid afterimages cast by her lightstick danced across his vision. "Look, thanks for helping me, but if you're not going to tell me anything useful, don't bother sticking around. I can find my own way back."

He felt her staring at him, and turned to find her examining him quite seriously, all trace of mockery gone.

"You're a strange one," she said. "It's not just your pale skin. I watched you taking directions in the hostel last night. The place was full of people. Once the word got around that a Stone Mage with money was looking for information about the caves, every guide and scrounger in town came running."

"I'm not a Stone Mage," Skender protested. "I haven't graduated yet."

"So? If you dress like one, people will naturally assume. I followed them out of curiosity, and there you were, listening to everything everyone was saying, taking it all in. You never asked twice; you never drew any maps. People thought you were having them on. Some of them started giving you bogus directions, trying to catch you lying, but they never did. If what they told you was inconsistent, *you* caught *them* out. It was as if you knew the way already."

Her intense regard made him feel uncomfortable. "I don't know the way," he said, quite honestly. "I just have a good memory. A perfect one. Once I see or hear something, I never forget it."

"Really? And here I was thinking you remembered me because of my good looks."

The beginnings of a flush made his ears redden. "That's not what I meant—"

She laughed again. "You're such an easy target, stone-boy. Don't you ever get teased back home?"

He certainly did. He'd lived his entire life in a school full of older students. That his father was the headmaster didn't protect him from regular ribbing; in fact, that encouraged it.

His defences were normally excellent, but there was something about Chu that put him off-balance. Something about her eyes, quite apart from their unusual shape. He blinked and told himself to remember what he was supposed to be doing.

"You were at the hostel," he said, "so you know why I'm here. My mother is missing."

"And you're looking for her down here." She nodded. "That was the part you weren't very clear on. Why down here? Why the caves of Laure?"

It was a long story, and the air in the cramped cave was beginning to grow musty.

Skender indicated the crack behind him. "Looks like I'm not going to get much further this way. Why don't we go up and I'll tell you then? Maybe you can help me work out what to do next."

Her teeth were white in the light of his glowstone. "I'd better not make a habit of doing that," she said. "You couldn't possibly afford my rates."

"Rates? If I could afford hired help, I wouldn't be lost down here in the first place."

Her laugh was rich and echoed back at them from a hundred rock faces as they began their ascent into the daylight.

◣ ◣ ◣

Some five weeks earlier, Abi Van Haasteren had left on her latest expedition, departing the subterranean city of Ulum with a caravan full of
Surveyors, porters, camel riders, cooks, and grunts. She even had a
man'kin with her for advice on esoteric matters. The stone intelligence, a high-templed man-shaped bust called Mawson, was a free
agent who helped her willingly, not because he was bonded into service
as many of his kind were. Still, from the position where he would ride
out most of the journey, lashed firmly to the back of the leading caravan, his expression had been disdainful.

"*Dignity*," he had told Skender, his voice like the buzz of bees at a
great distance, "*is in short supply among the living.*"

"But you are alive," Skender had responded, "aren't you?"

"*In a manner of speaking.*"

"Which manner?"

"*The one that matters.*"

"Is this boy bothering you?" asked a voice. Skender felt a big hand
come down heavily on his shoulder. "Move along, Skender. Mawson
has important cogitating to do."

Skender turned and looked up into a broad, pale face. Kemp was
the largest person he had ever met, and albino with it, so he stood out
in any crowd. A refugee from the Strand, he had taken up with the
Stone Mages and was by now a regular traveller with Skender's mother
through the Interior.

Skender didn't respond to the good-natured ribbing. "You'll keep
an eye on everyone. Won't you?"

"An eye and an ear," Kemp had assured him, grinning and moving
off to help the baggage handlers. "Don't worry about it. We'll be back
before you know it."

Skender had come to see them off via the space-bending Way

leading from the Keep to Ulum, which allowed him to cross hundreds of kilometres in a few paces. Why his mother didn't use such means to travel to her destinations was beyond him. The charm took its toll and wasn't entirely safe, but travelling across the Interior for weeks on end had the same disadvantages. He had tried both, and knew which he preferred.

"At least take the buggy," he pressed her as she checked the last of the provisions to be loaded. "You know Mawson prefers to travel that way."

"He's the least of my concerns," she said, lashing a crate into place with a deft knot. Her long brown hair hung to her waist in beaded strands and swung with every movement. Lines of delicate, tattooed characters framed her face and lined her arms. She was striking and mysterious, even to Skender, her son. He had inherited her hair and skin colour and his father's memory, but the height of neither.

"What about Dad?" he pressed her. "Couldn't you at least have gone to say good-bye to him?"

"Couldn't he have come here?" She adjusted a camel's harness a little too abruptly. It snorted and eyeballed her warningly. She sighed and turned to Skender. "Your father doesn't approve."

"He never does, but that doesn't stop you two getting along."

"Not this time," she said. "He doesn't like where we're going, or why."

"Where is that again?" he asked, trying to sound casual. "I don't believe I've heard."

She tilted her head to one side. "If you'd heard, you'd know. And that's why you *haven't* heard. I'm keeping this one close to my chest, in case someone else beats me to it." She put a hand to the rust-red material of her travelling robe where it covered her heart. "Don't worry, my Skender. We'll be okay. And when we come back, we'll have found something wonderful. Just you wait and see."

She had hugged him tightly then, and he had hugged her back, even though her words did little to reassure him. The caravan had trundled with a rattle and clatter of wheels out of the staging area, with the dour ex–Sky Warden Shom Behenna bringing up the rear, his black skin a vivid contrast to Kemp's and the others' around him. His mother had waved at him as her wagon mounted the ramp leading to the surface, then turned her eyes forward, to the long journey ahead.

Skender returned to the Keep and finished his assignments for that week, then climbed out of his bedroom window and scaled the cliff as high as he dared without ropes or harness, relying solely on the strength of his arms and legs to hold him firm against the sun-warmed rock. He knew he was taking a risk—but why shouldn't he? If his mother was allowed to throw herself headlong into some unknown venture his father disapproved of, he didn't see why he should be any different, in his own small way.

Five years earlier, he had stowed away on a caravan similar to hers, one headed south for the Haunted City. He had hidden in a chest until his bladder forced him out, and he, too, had thought that his adventure was going to be wonderful, that he would come back with riches and wisdom. Instead, he had seen a woman murdered in front of him and barely escaped with his mind intact from the Void Beneath.

Ever since his return, he had had a keen appreciation of what his mother was risking every time she left him. He didn't want to lose her to the dangers of the world. He wished she could be more like his father, who seemed perfectly happy confined to the Keep, where he taught his charges in the way of the Change. Why wasn't his mother, like him, content to stay *home*?

Skender told himself that he worried too much. His mother was a supremely capable Senior Surveyor. She had a good team. He climbed back down to his room after the sun had set, feeling his way by moon—and starlight. The smell of roast potatoes drifted up from the kitchens and his stomach rumbled.

◣ ◣ ◣

A month later, when word had come that Abi Van Haasteren and her party had been given up for dead by their caravan porters, he confronted his father and demanded that something be done to find her. He railed and ranted, expecting an argument in response. His father normally defended his mother's right to do as she willed. This time, however, all Skender received was worried agreement.

"I am concerned, yes," said the Mage Van Haasteren, settling heavily into a chair and resting his head on one hand. His rich red robes, trimmed with gold thread, sighed with him. "Abi normally makes contact once a day when she's away. It takes a significant amount of strength to call so far, especially among the Ruins, but she does it to ease my mind. I haven't heard from her for two days, now."

Skender's father stared at him with a long, lined face and helpless eyes.

"Two days—and you didn't tell me?" Skender paced the room, needing an outlet for the vague anxiety that had just transformed into a very specific concern. "We should raise an alarm, send another party, do *something*!"

"You know the Surveyor's Code, Skender. I can't ask them to break it."

Skender did know the Code. He could even see the sense in it. Ruins were dangerous places, filled with power from ancient times. Some of that power was inimical to humanity. If a Surveyor met with disaster inside a Ruin, sending a rescue party might see more people injured or killed. Such disasters were written off as bad luck, and those Ruins never visited again.

But this was his *mother* . . .

"Tell me where she went," he demanded.

The Mage retreated. "No. If you don't already know—and I'm certain you asked—then I will not break her confidence."

"*Tell me*," Skender insisted, leaning over the table to confront his father nose to nose. "I'm not leaving this room until you do."

"And if I *do* tell you? What then?"

Skender was startled by the alarm in his father's voice, but he didn't let that deter him. "You know what I'll do. And I know you want her back as badly as I do. So let's just get it over with. If we're both wrong and she turns up safe and sound tomorrow, I'll never let on."

The Mage had capitulated then, looking older than Skender had ever seen him. He also was trapped, pressured by law and custom and plain good sense to abandon his wife to her fate, yet hating the thought of it as much as Skender.

"A city called Laure."

"Where?"

"On the Divide."

His stomach clenched. "Don't tell me! She wouldn't be so stupid. Would she?"

His father neither nodded nor shook his head. "Your mother may be many things, Skender, but stupid isn't one of them. She claimed to know what she was doing. All I could do was believe her."

Skender couldn't credit what he was hearing. Many dangerous things had walked the Earth since the Cataclysm and the early days of the Change. Most of them came from—or had been herded into—the Divide, a vast crack across the landscape separating the underground desert cities of the Interior from the coastal villages of the Strand. Deeper and wider than an ordinary canyon, the Divide had been made centuries ago for purposes unknown. Many people had died in the attempt to plumb its mysteries. Their ghosts, legends said, wailed in despair from the cliff faces, echoing from one side to the other. Trapped forever.

He tore his mind from the image of his mother caught in such a trap and found himself standing in the middle of his father's chambers with his hands hanging limply at his sides. He felt as though he had woken in the middle of sleepwalking.

His father's hand came down on his shoulder. He looked up into the Mage's face, for once not resentful of the fact that their heights weren't equal. It felt good to be towered over. He longed to be held, as though that alone would solve everything.

"You'll need these," his father said, pressing something cold and sharp-edged into his hand.

He looked down at a ring of keys. "The buggy?"

"I can't give you anything else. The Synod won't support a rescue mission; I've tried to make them, and they won't listen."

"But—"

"Go now. Forget about your homework. Some things are simply more important."

More important than homework? That the idea had ever occurred to his father, let alone issued from his mouth, impressed on Skender just how serious the situation was. He hurried to his room, threw everything he thought he might need into a satchel, and ran to where the buggy rested in its makeshift garage. It was fully fuelled and provisioned for a long journey. The smell of fresh oil was testimony to the fact that it had recently been serviced.

As he swung himself into the seat and started the engine, he realised that his father had been thinking of going himself.

"I'll bring her home," he whispered over the roaring of the motor. "Don't worry."

That promise had kept him going for two thousand kilometres, across desert and ancient hills, to where Laure crouched like a child playing hide-and-seek in a corner of the Divide, with only the tips of its tarnished towers peeking into view.

"So you followed her trail to where the porters left her," Chu said over the lip of a tiny, porcelain cup. Coffee as black and potent as any Skender had tasted left black grains on her teeth. Around them, the walled New City bustled and blustered its way through the day. Robed traders hurried back and forth along constricted alleyways, their heads wrapped in white cloth. Animals clucked, brayed, or hissed through bars, muzzles, or harnesses. Cockroaches scuttled. Spindly, four-legged creatures with curling tails scampered up drains and through windows; some of them wore embroidered vests, signalling that they were pets. The sky above, visible through rips in the canvas shade angled over them, was a faded pale blue. Laure didn't appear to have seen rain for years. The air was dry, the cobbled road beside them parched; with water strictly rationed the stink of spices was strong in the air, covering the smell of unbathed humanity.

Behind the general hubbub, Skender could hear the wailing of the city's ruling guild of red-robed weather-workers, the yadachi, as they exhorted the wind to bring relief. They sat on thin, vertical poles high above street level, distant from everyday concerns. Skender knew that on certain days, when significant winds blew, giant pipes caught the superheated air and turned it into notes so low they were felt as much as heard. That music was silent for the moment. The only other melody he could detect in the city's babble was the mournful lay of a *duduq*, a double-reeded instrument that in skilled hands could make of every note a lament.

"Then what?"

"She went into the Divide," he said, "at a natural pass called the Devil's Elbow, which is protected by charms against things trying to come up, not down. They camped at the top, and that's obviously where they argued about who was going to go and who wasn't. I found signs suggesting that the porters stayed for a while after she went down the pass. Maybe they genuinely waited for her to come back; maybe they waited barely as long as was decent. Either way, they left no tracks to suggest that they went after her, or that she came back that way later."

"Did you go down the pass?"

He shook his head. "Her trail was old, and I didn't know what I'd be walking into. I followed the top of the Divide instead, heading northeast along the Interior side." Even from the relative safety of the escarpment, he had felt on edge during that daylong journey. The far side of the Divide was kilometres away, and the yawning emptiness had tugged relentlessly at him. The buggy bounced over rough ground, following a faint track that hadn't been used for decades. Every bump seemed to twist the wheels toward the Divide. He gripped the steering wheel and concentrated on keeping his heading straight.

At the same time, he looked for any sign of his mother and her expedition on the parched valley floor, dozens of metres below. The earth was pitted and scarred down there, as though an ancient battle had churned the soil and split the bedrock in thousands of places. Dust devils and heat distortions danced in the air above gaping rents, as capricious as ghostly birds. Fleeting glints of light drew his eye to shadowy clefts, but disappeared before he could see what made them. He was reminded of descriptions of the Broken Lands, where the earth lay in endless disorder, terrain of all sorts jutting into each other like a jigsaw puzzle dropped by a giant.

Between the rents were sheets of startlingly smooth sand dunes, white, grey, and red. Some of them were hundreds of metres long, stretching like melted caramel along the centre of the Divide. On these sheets he saw tracks that might have been made by a reckless Surveyor and her party. Nowhere else did he see a single sign of human life.

Then he had seen Laure, the walled city, and her destination had become obvious.

"I don't know much about your home," he said to Chu. "Laure is mentioned only briefly in the *Book of Towers*. Fragments three hundred and ten to three hundred and twenty-four tell of a town sundered by a great rending of the Earth. The story goes that each of the city's two halves thought the other was responsible, and they fought for years, causing still more damage to what remained. The war was won by the northern half, and the southern half soon fell into ruin."

"We call it the Aad," said Chu. "It's an old word that means 'disease' or 'bad luck.' No one goes there. It's inhabited by creatures from the Divide now."

Skender nodded. That matched the *Book of Towers*, too. "What the book *doesn't* say about Laure is that it rests on a cave system—I could see the openings from further up the Divide." The geography of Laure was complex, belying the simplicity of the tale. Laure cowered in a triangular dogleg of the Divide like a mouse backed into a corner. The ground it rested on had subsided in the distant past, most probably during the Cataclysm, so that the remains of the original settlement now clung to its sloping fringes. A new city had been built in the gutted centre of the hollow, the matching piece of which rested on the far side of the Divide—the Ruin Chu had called the Aad. A steep, forbidding wall cut a stark line around the side of Laure not protected by the steep slopes of the dogleg. Massive symbols painted on the outside of the Wall added to the protection granted by the sheer mass of stone. No one knew who had built it, but without it the city would be completely exposed to the Divide.

To the left and right of the Wall, dotting the sheer cliff faces, gaping holes led deep underground. "I think my mother was heading for them, or was forced to hide in them by something unexpected."

"They're not just caves," said Chu. "There are artificial tunnels, too. I've never seen them myself, but I've heard stories. They're bigger than anything we could've made, and were full of old metal a long time ago."

A shiver of dread mixed with excitement rushed through him. "I don't understand how you could be a miner and not have seen them. Isn't using the old tunnels and caves the obvious thing to do if you're digging underground?"

"Right." Again she smiled knowingly.

"There's something you're not telling me," he said to her, pushing his empty cup aside and leaning over the table. "You know where my mother is, don't you?"

Brushing an errant strand of perfectly black hair from her eyes, she also leaned forward until they were less than a hand's span apart. "I think it's time we came to an arrangement, Skender Van Haasteren," she said in a conspiratorial whisper. "You say you don't have much money, but that's not a problem. We can still do business. Agree, and I'll tell you why me being a miner doesn't have anything to do with old tunnels and caves. I'll also tell you why you're probably looking in the wrong place for your mother. Okay?"

Skender was automatically suspicious. He thought of all the material things he had brought with him: the buggy; a small amount of money; an ornate metal clasp his mother had salvaged from a burial site excavated three years earlier, which he was too afraid to wear in the city in case it was stolen. There was nothing he would willingly part with.

On the other hand, he needed to know where his mother might be, and he found that he enjoyed the company of this strange young woman. He could live with the risk of being screwed over in order to keep her around a little longer.

He scratched his arm where his Blood Tithe had been taken on entry into the city. The small wound itched.

"What do you want?" he asked her.

"Something you take completely for granted," she said. "And if you do it right, it won't cost you a thing."

"*What?*"

"Freedom, Skender Van Haasteren." Her dark brown eyes were bottomless. "You're my ticket, and I'm not letting go of you until you've delivered."

THE HOMUNCULUS

"Through the Change, we can connect far-flung places. We reach out with our thoughts and our senses; we send our bodies along Ways from one end of the Interior to the other. But where are those thoughts, minds, and bodies when they are in transit, if not in the actual world? They are in the Void Beneath."
THE BOOK OF TOWERS, FRAGMENT 242

"We don't know exactly what happened," said Tom, perched awkwardly on a squat driftwood chair, periodically swigging from a second bottle of clear water. The first had gone in one long draught, as though he hadn't drunk properly for days. He had removed the outer layers of his robes, exposing a knee-length sky-blue tunic that looked almost new, and taken off his leather boots. His toes were long and clenched at the sandy floor of the workshop with instinctively sensual motions.

Shilly listened to the story of what had happened to Highson Sparre, Sal's genetic father, with acid pooling deep in her stomach.

"This is what we do know. Highson left the Haunted City one week ago. He chartered a ferry to the town of Gunida, on the coast. The captain of the ferry remembered Highson, even though he travelled under a false name. He brought a large amount of matériel with him, so the ferryman assumed he was a trader. In Gunida, he unloaded the boxes with the help of a local by the name of Larson Maiz. Maiz was known to be a member of the underground economy, a shady type who would do anything for money."

"Was?" repeated Sal. "Would?"

Shilly had noticed the ominous use of past tense, too.

"Maiz was found dead the next morning. He'd been killed several hours earlier, after meeting your father."

Sal nodded, his face closed tight as it always was when he was most upset.

"Go on," he said. "Tell me why you think my father killed him."

Tom looked startled. "We don't think that at all. That is, we don't think Maiz's death was deliberate. It was an accident, a side effect. He was unlucky, probably."

"Do you know where Highson is now?"

Another shake of his head. "Those who know him best have looked, but we can't find him anywhere. He appears to have vanished."

Vanished. The word dropped into Shilly like a stone down a well.

"Just tell us what you know," she told Tom, catching Sal's eye and making sure he understood. "You've come a long way to give us this information. We won't interrupt any more. I promise."

Sal nodded. Tom looked relieved.

"At the second hour of the morning, one week ago," he said, as though he had rehearsed it many times during his long trip to Fundelry, "Gunida was woken by the sound of the world tearing open."

Sal listened to Tom's account with mounting alarm. *A tear in the world* was exactly what he had been feeling on the beach. Not an explosive event, as Tom described it, but as a growing feeling of wrongness. It seeped into him from the edges of his life and crept slowly to his heart.

The residents of Gunida had staggered from their beds that night a week ago, terrified. The western sky was bright with light—a flickering, perfectly white glow so bright it cast shadows from chimneys, trees, and outstretched hands. A few brave souls dared to follow it to its source, thinking it lay on the outskirts of town, but it was in fact much further. Barely had the intrepid group travelled two kilometres through dense scrub and low, anonymous hills when the light went out. A thunderclap rolled across the land, shaking trees, knocking off hats, and sending dogs cowering under verandahs. A terrible silence fell in its wake.

The night was utterly black. The stars and moon hid behind clouds. The group had little hope of finding the source of the explosion, but still they tried, spreading out and beating through the bushes, hoping to flush out more than the occasional startled rabbit.

Only one more event marked the stillness of the night: a distant scream that could have come from a man's or a woman's throat. One witness described the sound as the most awful thing he had ever heard, a cry so full of fear it melted all resolve to find its cause. The group immediately turned back to Gunida, there to wait for dawn before recommencing the search.

By daybreak, a party of Sky Wardens had arrived. The pyrotechnics of the previous night had not gone unnoticed by those of the Haunted City. Crossing the choppy waves on *Os*, the mighty ship of bone, the party included Alcaide Braham—the Strand's highest authority—and many other senior Wardens. Tom was among them.

By then, Highson Sparre's absence had been noted and every available Warden summoned to help shed light on a very mysterious situation. Sal's father had left the island with a large number of arcane artefacts, formerly housed in the depths of the Novitiate's storerooms. Many of them had no known use, although their potency was undoubted. They fairly crackled with the Change and had been interred more for safekeeping rather than because of any sense of value. That Highson had apparently made off with specific items and not a random swagful suggested that he had something in mind for them.

"Highson was a lot of things," agreed Sal, "but he wasn't a thief."

After a deep draught of water, Tom's story continued.

The search party followed Highson's trail to Gunida. They listened to the testimonies of town residents and put together their own expeditionary party. Before the eighth hour, this new force journeyed on foot from the harbour town, following the fading spoor of the event that had shaken the world that morning. They found the source before long: a clearing set in a hollow between three low hills with a ring of flattened trees surrounding a scorch mark blacker than anything Tom had seen before. The crater at the centre of the clearing was a metre deep.

They approached it cautiously.

"People perceive the Change in different ways," Tom said. "Some smell it or see it, or even taste it. I hear it, like a ringing in my ears. Highson's work had a distinct sound to it, a mix of harmonics unique to him. His signature was so powerful in that place that I could hear it hours later, still vibrating in the soil and the trees—and the body."

There went Sal's last hope that Tom and the Wardens might have been mistaken, that his father's connection to the death of Larson Maiz was tenuous, perhaps even completely circumstantial.

"How did Maiz die?" asked Shilly, taking Sal's hand in hers. He was grateful for the gesture.

"Maiz's heart failed," Tom said. "Some say he died of fright."

"He saw something? Was attacked by something?"

"We don't know. There were several tracks in and around the scorched area. Maiz made some of them before and after the burning took place; the patterns of the prints match the soles of his boots, so we have no doubts there. There was a second set of tracks that we presume belonged to Highson, as they, too, preceded and postdated the thing he came there to make. The procedure involved a lot of unpacking and preparation; various empty crates and containers scattered around the clearing testified to that."

"What about the thing itself?" Sal asked. "Did you find it?"

"Not in the clearing. Not exactly."

"What do you mean by 'not exactly'?"

"We found a third set of footprints." Tom drained the last of the water from the bottle and put it on the ground beside him with a hollow thud. "I'm not a tracker; I'm an Engineer. But even I could tell that something walked out of that clearing that didn't walk into it, and it didn't walk on legs as we know them."

Sal didn't want to know what sort of legs they were. Not yet. Strange screams and holes in the world were enough for now. "Where did it go?"

"It tore a path through the scrub wider than a person. There are signs that Maiz tried to stop it, but obviously wasn't successful. Markings suggest that Highson himself was knocked unconscious for a time, at least several hours after Maiz's death. We do know that shortly after awakening, not long after dawn that terrible night, he set off in pursuit."

Chasing the thing he made, thought Sal.

"They had quite a head start," Tom went on. "It was a day or more by the time we returned to the Haunted City and a fully equipped search party set out to follow them. Alcaide Braham is quite determined to get to the bottom of what happened."

"I'll bet," said Shilly. "Something like this, right on his doorstep . . ." She shook her head. "Do you have any idea what it was that Highson made?"

"Master Warden Atilde took a closer look at what he stole. That, combined with what we found at the site, led her to suspect that Highson created a Homunculus."

"A what?" asked Sal.

"An artificial creature designed to house a disembodied mind, like a ghost or a golem."

A chill went down Sal's spine. "Does Atilde think he succeeded in giving it a mind?"

"Yes. But what it was physically, she doesn't know. It's obviously *something*, something that walks."

"This doesn't make any sense," said Shilly, frowning deeply. "Highson knows how dangerous ghosts and golems can be. Why would he want to make a home for one?"

"Did anyone notice *anything* about him before all this happened?" asked Sal. "Was he acting strangely? Was he still himself?"

Tom knew what question he was really asking. If a Change-worker strained too hard, their minds could be pushed out of their body and stuck in the Void Beneath—the empty nonspace underpinning the real world. The vacant body left behind could then be inhabited by a golem. The three of them sitting in Lodo's old workshop knew from grim experience what horrors such a being could unleash.

"He was still Highson," said Tom, with quiet surety. "No one doubts that for a moment. He wasn't something other than himself."

Sal believed him. Golems weren't known for their subtlety.

"So where does everything stand now?" he asked. "This all happened a week ago. Has anyone heard from Highson since? What happened to the search party? When did you leave?"

Tom blinked under the barrage of questions. "The search party hasn't returned. The last I was told, they were still following the trail. No one's heard from Highson or been able to find him through the Change. I've looked, too, but he's either hiding or being hidden by something."

"Or he's dead," put in Shilly.

"I don't think so. I left two days ago. My dreams have been unsettled since Highson disappeared. It's hard to tell what's real and what isn't. There's only one thing I'm sure of: you two are involved. Your faces keep coming up, over and over. There's only one way you *could* be involved, and that's if someone came and got you. So I did. I requisitioned a buggy and set off. I stopped to refuel and rest in Samimi, but apart from that I drove straight through."

That explained his haggard appearance, and reinforced something that had unnerved Sal ever since Tom's unexpected appearance. Tom wasn't interested in being a hero or standing in the spotlight; he was normally content to watch from the shadows as people played out their roles. He only acted when he felt he had to—when his dreams told him that something was important.

This obviously was.

"How did you know where we were?"

"Where else would you be?" Tom reacted as though Sal had asked why the day had begun that morning. "When you escaped from the Haunted City, you went through a Way to the workshop."

"But you weren't there," Shilly said. "No one was supposed to talk about it."

"They didn't need to. It was perfectly obvious what had happened."

"To you, perhaps," said Sal. "You're the first visitor we've had in five years."

"And a very welcome one, too," Shilly added, "although the news you've brought is less than cheerful."

"Did you tell anyone where you were going?" asked Sal, unable to hide the worry in his voice.

"No. I—uh." An alarmed look crossed Tom's face. He stood up suddenly, knocking over the empty bottle of water.

"I'm sorry," he said, performing an awkward hop on one foot and turning pink. "I need—uh."

"Through there." Shilly realised before Sal did what Tom required and pointed to a curtained alcove. "I was wondering how much you could drink before you started to overflow."

Tom vanished behind the curtain. Sal grinned at the sustained splash and sigh of relief that followed, but his mind was too full of images old and new, of golems and midnight detonations, of Highson Sparre and dead Larson Maiz, of hiding places and family ties, to be distracted for long.

Shilly caught his eye and held it. Her expression was very serious. He could tell that she had already decided what she wanted to do.

"What do you think?" she asked.

"I'm trying not to."

"He's your father." Her voice held a hint of reproach.

"My father died in Fundelry before I ever met this man."

"Highson married your mother; he sired you. *And* he helped us escape from the Syndic."

Sal nodded. All true and relevant, especially the latter. Highson Sparre's aunt, the most powerful woman in the Strand, had locked horns with Sal on more than one occasion. If she had had her way, he would still be studying in the Haunted City, fuelling her plans for advancement.

"You know it's the right thing to do." Her hand found his. "And besides, Tom dreamed we were involved. There's nothing we can do about it now."

"If he'd left us alone, perhaps we wouldn't be." He heard the petulance in his tone and hated it. The truth was that he didn't feel ready to leave Fundelry, the fishing village he had lived in for five years after a life of constant travel. Part of him wondered if he would ever be ready to leave. Fundelry was safe: the dangers were known and familiar. He had no control over the outside world and the threats it contained; out there, he might have no control over himself, either.

Only twice had he let his wild talent consume him. The eruption of rage he had set free had almost killed a man. Then, later, he had killed an ice-creature deep in the bowels of the Haunted City. Even though that had been in defence of Shilly, the potential for violence contained within him frightened him even more than the first time. His wild talent was like a large animal blundering about in a city; by its very nature, it was dangerous. But that wasn't the *fault* of its nature. It was just out of place. In the right place, it wouldn't be a problem. Sal simply hadn't found out where that was yet.

In Fundelry, with Shilly, he had learned to balance the wild talent and bend it to his will, but it was a truce he feared could be easily broken.

"All right," he said. "We have to help. But I don't like it. What's Highson doing mucking around with a Homunculus in the middle of the night? What's he brought into the world? What are we getting ourselves caught up in now?"

She didn't say anything, just leaned her head into his shoulder. He put an arm around her and held her, tasting an uncertainty he had thought long swallowed.

A bell rang at lunchtime, apparently of its own accord. There were twelve strung in an elaborate mobile from the ceiling's highest point. Each had a unique pitch and timbre, and each had an identical twin to which it was subtly linked. When one rang, no matter how far away, so would the twin.

"That's Thess," said Sal, looking up from the chart he and Tom were studying. "Do you want me to go?"

Shilly shook her head. She had been laying out their clothes and other possessions in preparation for packing, finding herself amazed by how little they actually owned. Discounting the workshop and everything Lodo had left them, plus the occasional trinket the townsfolk insisted they take, they had only a few personal effects to call their belongings. Part of her found it sad that they could have left so small a mark on their world that no one would notice its absence.

"I've got it," she said, grateful for the opportunity to think about something else. Rummaging in a closet, she wrapped up two small vials in a leather bag and tied her hair in a short pigtail. She picked up her favourite walking stick, one which Sal had carved with simple but potent charms for strength and endurance out of a piece of near perfectly straight driftwood. The charms sparkled with the Change irrespective of how the light caught them. "I'll be home soon."

Outside, the sun had begun its lazy drift across the westward quarter of the sky, and she walked with it at her back. Tom had moved the buggy into the dunes, where it would be less conspicuous, and she gave it a wide berth, even though she had no reason to be afraid of it. Buggies were rare in Fundelry; few travellers used them, and the town's mechanic spent most of his time repairing fishing boat engines and water pumps. This one was an efficient Sky Warden machine, made of black metal and brooding like a disgruntled spider on wheels. Big enough to hold four, it seemed to glower at her as she passed.

"Be patient," she told it. "You'll be on the road again soon enough."

Then she was hurrying through the dunes to the rendezvous point, a dry creek bed halfway between the workshop and Fundelry. She went into town only when she absolutely had to, and made sure Sal charmed her appearance thoroughly before she did. Her and Sal's friends knew how to find them, but no one else did. Or so she had preferred to think.

Long-limbed Thess and her young son sat under the shade of a spreading eucalyptus, playing a game involving Thess's hair and the boy's small fingers. The sound of Gil's laughter brought a smile to Shilly's face. Gil's father had drowned in a fishing accident the year before. The five-year-old had been uncommunicative since.

"I hope you haven't been waiting long." Shilly kissed Thess's cheek and sat next to them, stretching her bad leg out before her. Gil looked up at her, wide-eyed, then shied away. They were as dark-skinned as herself and Tom; on the Strand, Sal's light skin was the exception. "It's been a complicated morning."

Thess beamed. "We've had fun. Haven't we, Gil?"

"Mmm," said the boy, discovering a sudden interest in the ants exploring stringy bark on the far side of the tree.

"I have some of the sand I told you about," said Shilly, putting the first of the vials into Thess's lap. "Put this in little Gil's shoes and the itching will go down in a couple of days."

"Thank you. I—"

"And this one's for you." The second vial contained a yellow powder that shifted smoothly, like a fluid. "Half a teaspoon in water every morning and I promise you'll notice the difference. I tried it last week, and—" She mimed an explosion of energy.

"Shilly, thanks, but—"

"It's the least I can do. I know it's been a long haul for you." She pressed Thess to take the vial. "I'd advise against taking this forever, but it'll help get you out of this rough patch."

"I think I might already be out of it." Thess dropped her voice. "That's actually why I called you."

"Oh?" Thrown off giving the spiel she had memorised from Lodo's notes, Shilly stared at her older friend, really looking at her for the first time. Gil wasn't the only one of the pair sporting a more cheerful demeanour. Understanding suddenly dawned. "Not that fisherman!"

Thess shushed her so Gil wouldn't overhear. "Yes."

"What was his name? Boone? Boden?"

"Booth. Last night—" Thess's voice dropped even further in volume. "He stayed all night. I haven't woken up with a man beside me for an awfully long time. It felt good."

Shilly gripped her friend's hand. "I'm glad for you. I am, truly."

Thess affected a measure of nonchalance. "Oh, things will be complicated. Gil doesn't know yet, and I don't know how he'll take it. His father's family, too, could be tricky. But I'm not doing this for them. It's for me, and I want it to work."

"I'm sure it will." Even if it lasted no more than one night, Shilly would regard it as worthwhile. The glow surrounding Thess was palpable.

"Well, that's why I wanted to talk to you. Aunty Merinda gave me a tonic, but it's been giving me terrible headaches. She said that you might know something better, to keep any, um, awkwardnesses at bay, until I'm ready."

Thess glanced at Gil, who was engrossed in the antics of a gecko he'd disturbed. Her meaning was obvious. Aunty Merinda, the local weather-worker and fortune-teller, was also the chief dispenser of contraception to Fundelry's womenfolk. She had taught Shilly everything she needed to know long before Sal came to town, and provided valuable advice after the fact, when they had been two young people flung together by circumstances as well as by the bond growing between them. Shilly had been glad for someone trustworthy to talk to, if nothing else.

"I think the headaches relate to the dose, not the substance itself," she said, thinking carefully. She didn't feel entirely comfortable dispensing advice of this nature, when a single mistake could change the course of a person's life. But she was flattered that Aunty Merinda thought her capable of offering it. "I'll look into it tonight."

"Thank you."

"There could be a problem, though," she went on, the words hard to come by because the notion was still so new to her. "Sal and I are leaving. I don't know how long for. You'll have to do without us. Can you tell the others?"

"Of course." Thess examined her closely. "Is everything all right? You haven't been found, have you?"

"Oh, no," she lied, hoping her uncertainty didn't show. "Everything's fine. We just need to help someone. It won't take long, I hope."

Thess looked barely mollified. "We'll miss you. We've been spoilt, having you so close for so long. The town won't know what to do when your charms wear off and all our chimneys block again."

Shilly felt a rush of affection for her friend, and found herself spontaneously embracing her, clutching her as tightly as she would the mother she had never known. Thess's warmth was soothing, as was the rich, womanly smell of her. Strong hands gripped Shilly's back; silence enfolded them, and she was somewhat reassured that all *would* be well.

On the way back to the workshop, Shilly reflected that, although their packs might be light, she and Sal were rich in other ways. They had friends and accomplices all through the town; they helped out in myriad small ways, from purifying water to treating minor ailments; they were making progress in working out how they fitted into the world. They *would* be missed, just as she would miss her home.

The greatest treasure they owned lay in their heads and their hearts. Nothing could take that away from them, no matter where they went or what they did. Golems and ghosts had tried in the past, and failed; Highson Sparre's Homunculus—or whatever it was—would fare no better.

▚ ▚ ▚

Later that night, when Tom had fallen into a heavy sleep broken by the occasional snore, Sal removed himself to a dark corner of the workshop and squatted on the earthen floor. Their evening meal—rabbit fried in local spices with a side dish of seeds and nuts marinated in honey, washed down with a glass of clear white wine that had been given to them a year ago by a grateful customer—roiled in his stomach like surf on the sands. He had to try something before giving in to his fate.

Shilly had been busy all evening, rummaging through Lodo's recipes and old notes; some last-hour concoction, he presumed, that they would deliver when they set out the next morning. Even now she fussed and bothered among Lodo's tools.

Sal closed his eyes and blotted her out. She was still there, but he wasn't paying her any attention. He did the same to Tom and the rest of the workshop, until he was just a point of awareness floating in the blackness behind his eyes, breathing slowly and deeply.

When he had the rhythm right, he began to visualise.

He stood on the boundary between sea and land, but it was no ordinary beach. The sea glowed like the sun and the land was molten with power. The air crackled. He breathed deeply of it, and strength filled him. His skin felt as transparent as glass, as hot as a lantern left burning too long.

Highson Sparre, *he called,* where are you? *He pictured his true father's face as he had last seen it: brooding eyes, broad features, skin as warm as dark honey. He took the lines of those features and bent them around a simple charm. The world was seeping into him with every breath. Wherever Highson was in the world, the charm would help him to know of it. He poured all his energy into the effort.*

Highson, save me the trouble of leaving and answer me!

A fluttering of wings distracted him. The face dissolved. A burning bird with bones of charcoal circled him, trailing flames. A sea creature made of stone surfaced from the fiery ocean and landed with a crash. He irritably waved them away with a flex of his will. They were symbols: the sea of the Sky Wardens, so familiar to him in his everyday life but always a reminder of his fugitive status; the bedrock of the Stone Mages, who had sent him back to the Strand rather than shelter him from his enemies. That he routinely bypassed the usual teachings and went straight to the source, the borderland of stone and water, fire and air, proved that they were conventions only, and neither essential nor dangerous to cross.

They had, however, successfully distracted him. No matter how he tried, he couldn't quite reassemble Highson's image. It eluded him. Or the charm refused to accept the image, and he could only think of one reason why this might be so: if his father was no longer in the world, then the charm would never work no matter how hard or often he tried.

A black sun rose over the burning sea, casting rays of darkness across the land. Burning bird and stone sea creature fled before a rolling hum that grew louder the longer Sal persisted. He knew that sound. He had heard it too many times to ever mistake it. It came from the Void Beneath, and it meant that he was trying too hard. He retreated immediately, unravelling the illusion as he went. The hum faded back into the ebb and flow of his breath, and the darkness of the black sun became the red-tinged oblivion of his closed eyes. The charm dissolved.

It was odd, then, that the feeling that he had been getting close to something remained. Not to his father, but to the tear that had opened in the world, somewhere . . .

"No luck, huh?"

He opened his eyes to see Shilly watching from a position directly in front of him. Time had flown. The glowstones she had been working by were yellow and dim, almost depleted.

"No," he said, unfolding his legs.

"Worth a try."

He sighed. The thought of leaving made his insides tremble with both excitement and fear. And now he was tired, too. He should sleep. They would get precious little of it over the next few days.

"I keep remembering Larson Maiz," he said. "How must it feel to die of fright? I don't want that to happen to anyone I know. To you."

She reached out to cup his cheek. "We all die someday, Sal. Yesterday's people are tomorrow's ghosts. And we can't stay hidden here forever."

"I know, but . . ." He stopped, unable to find the words to express what he was feeling. "We'll have to be very careful."

"Don't worry about me, Sayed," she said. "Or yourself. I'll be so terrified nothing will get within a hundred metres of us without me noticing."

Her face was just visible in the yellow warmth of fading glowstones. Her words did reassure him, even though he knew that, like himself, she had little idea of what they were heading into.

"I love you, Carah," he said, knowing that she returned his love as fully as it was offered. Whatever happened, he could depend on that.

When he finally slept, he dreamed of the road moving under him as rapidly as the wind, as it had for most of his life before coming to Fundelry. Dafis Hrvati, the man he had thought was his father—who had raised him and loved his mother; who had protected him when she was taken from them by the Syndic and imprisoned in the Haunted City; who had brought him to Fundelry in a vain attempt to save him from his wild talent; who had died at the hands of the Alcaide in order to set him free—rode alongside him. His tanned, weathered hands firmly gripped the steering wheel. He smiled at Sal, and winked.

Sal woke with tears on his cheeks. The feeling of loss lingered, and grew stronger as their journey began.

THE MAGISTER

"There is power in blood, just as there is power in air and fire, water and stone. No one would deny it, but only the most desperate would use it, and even then not willingly their own."
THE BOOK OF TOWERS, FRAGMENT 195

Chu led Skender up a staircase that circled a central column no wider than his head. It was difficult to talk, and he had plenty of questions. His knees and back were getting stiffer with every turn around the spiral. As a result, his frustration levels were high and rising.

"What does this place have to do with mining?" he called to her.

"Wait and see," returned her muffled voice.

He ground his teeth together and kept climbing, trying to work out the solution to the puzzle. Her reticence on the subject of his mother was almost total. Apart from sly hints and digs at his ignorance, she had very little to say at all, even about their deal and the so-called freedom he was supposed to help her attain. She wandered the streets of the walled city without restriction and no one questioned her or got in her way; she seemed, on the face of it, to be as free as he was.

"You've been down in the caves," she had said to him as they left the coffee parlour and headed off through the winding streets. "Did you notice any sign of digging?"

He hadn't, but he'd been looking for signs of his mother, not evidence of the city's mineral wealth or lack thereof.

"You're lucky you didn't stumble across one of the sewage channels," she told him with a malicious chortle. "Then you'd have seen firsthand what we normally use the old tunnels for."

For that much he was very grateful. "So you mine elsewhere, away from the city?"

"Look up," she had said. The usual patchwork of drying clothes and banners briefly allowed a glimpse of the sky. "What do you see?"

"Birds," he'd replied, noting numerous gliding shapes against the bright pale blue, circling and looping in mathematical spirals. "Were you expecting something else?"

She'd laughed again and told him to stop dragging his heels. "You're about to see something stone-boys like you only dream of."

He bit his tongue. Since then, he'd seen little more than her backside as she preceded him up the stairwell. Attractive it might be, but that wasn't what he had come to Laure for.

Just as his patience reached its limit, she stopped. A creak of wood and inrush of air followed. He breathed deeply, not realising just how close it had become in the narrow stairwell. She moved again, climbing two more steps then suddenly lifting her legs upwards, out of sight. A trapdoor. Her hand thrust down at him. He brushed it aside and hauled himself through the square hole without assistance, ending up on his hands and knees on a roof high above the city. The sky was brilliant around him. A steady wind blew, as fresh as a draught of clear water.

"Almost there," she whispered in his ear. One hand pressed him down when he tried to stand. She crouched next to him, peering around a nearby chimney. Her full lips were so close to his ear that he could feel her hair brushing his neck. "You have to be quiet for this last bit. Can you manage that?"

He nodded stiffly.

"Good. Follow me."

She scurried off, moving in an awkward crouch from chimney to chimney, keeping her head low. He followed her lead, noting that they were atop one of several tall thin buildings at the heart of the New City. Just visible in an intersection two blocks across was a yadachi perched on the top of a pole, red robes trailing beneath him like a flag.

To the north, east, and west, sprinkled with the yellowing remains of the Old City, sloped the sides of the depression Laure occupied; to the south was the smooth blankness of the Wall, as brooding as a thundercloud. Beyond that, invisible, lay the eerie chasm of the Divide.

He noted that birds flew over the Divide as well as the city, circling all along the length of the mighty chasm to either horizon. What they hunted and ate was a mystery to him . . .

Except they couldn't be mere birds. For them to be visible at such a distance, their wingspan had to be *huge*.

"Down." Chu squeezed him beside her in a niche between attic wall and ventilation shaft. She peered through a hole made by a missing brick, then, moving aside, gestured that he should look, too. What he saw left him breathless.

On the next building across a young man stood strapped to a crescent-shaped canvas wing spread out above him. Several others in various stages of preparation waited nearby, adjusting buckles or checking struts, dressed in brightly coloured uniforms bearing stark geometric patterns, none of them identical. They congregated on five separate platforms stacked one on top of the other, each one sticking out further than the last. They were close enough that Skender could hear their voices coming to him in snatches on the wind. Their words, diced with the chopping blade of the wind, were meaningless.

As Skender watched, the boy wearing the wing took a running jump for the edge of the platform and, with a cry, plunged headlong into empty air.

Skender gasped, then mentally kicked himself. He'd read about gliders and balloons in the *Book of Towers* and other texts—books he doubted his guide had heard of. He should have had some inkling of what was coming; now he looked like a hick from the deep desert.

As the boy fell, the wind caught his wing and twisted it. Skender admired the skill it took to bring it into line, to angle his glide into a tight swoop so he wouldn't crash headlong into the unforgiving face of a nearby building. Gusts tugged him to and fro until he managed to ascend above the nearest towers, then his flight levelled out. From below, Skender could see that the wing was covered with hand-drawn charms that rippled and flowed like shadow clouds in fast motion. The wing tilted, and the boy swept away over the city.

What Skender had seen from street level—and from a distance, while approaching the city—weren't birds at all. Neither were the things over the Divide. They were all people, gliding aloft on wings and will.

"Amazing."

If Chu was amused by his surprise, she didn't rub his face in it. "It *is* pretty cool." She pressed in close to peer through the hole with him. Her leather outfit creaked. "You should try it up there. The air is clear and fresh. There's no smoke, no stink. You can see forever."

"You—?" He turned to look at her, startled for the second time. "You're one of them?"

Her face twisted. "Used to be. Crashed my wing. Couldn't afford to pay for repairs, or for my licence when renewal fell due. Now I'm stuck here on the ground, just like you. I'd give anything to be back out there."

"Ah," he said. "So *that's* what you meant by freedom."

"Yes. And you're going to help me get it."

"How?"

"We'll work on that. I have a few ideas."

I bet you do, Skender thought. "You have to keep your side of the bargain first."

"Haven't I already?" Chu shook her head. Her deep brown eyes held immense reservoirs of amusement. "I assumed you would have worked it out by now. Oh well. See those gliders over there?" She pointed to the Divide. He nodded. "Watch them for a while and you'll find your answer."

He did as he was told, simmering at her tone. He wasn't an idiot— far from it. He was just a long way from everything he took for granted. The time would come, he swore, when he would turn the tables on her, and then she'd know how it felt. She'd be the one to feel embarrassed and stupid. She—

He stopped in midthought when something about the distant gliders penetrated the thick mire of his anger.

They were swooping like gulls snatching fish from the ocean. But there was no ocean, no fish. There was just the Divide, a deep wound gaping in the surface of the world, from which all manner of strangeness had been observed to emerge . . .

Suddenly, in a flash, it all made sense. It was insane, but it did fit the facts.

"The people in the gliders," he said, choosing his words with care as he thought it through, "they're scavenging for artefacts in the Divide."

"And?" Her nod was purely probationary.

"And when they find something, they dive down to check it out." His mind reeled at the skill required for such missions. First, the pilots had to spot items of interest on the surface of the valley floor, far below. Then they had to negotiate unreliable air currents and approach closer to see if it was something genuinely valuable. Finally, since voyaging out into the Divide on foot was generally considered foolish, the most daring might try to snatch the bounty off the ground and whisk back up into the air. "I can't believe so many people would be willing to risk their lives like this!"

"It's a matter of economics," Chu said. "This area has always been rich in artefacts. The foundations of Laure were laid a thousand years ago, and the city was once full of metal and ceramics and other trinkets. Long since picked clean, of course, but there are deposits outside the city. And the Divide is full of such things if you know where to look. Now, I know you haven't been in Laure for long, but I'm sure you've noticed that we don't have much of anything else here. We can't grow crops because the water table is too low and what the yadachi can summon doesn't leave enough for irrigation. The ground is empty of any metals that weren't left behind by the ancients. Cattle live barely long enough to breed outside. So our only export is what we can find in buried ruins and the Divide. That means the people out there—" she indicated the flyers with a thumb, "—the *miners*—they're very well paid for what they do, and they play an important part in keeping the city alive. You see, now? It's not just for kicks, Skender, if that's what you're thinking. Next time you're using a fork or admiring a jewel, consider that it probably came from the Divide or somewhere similar, and ask yourself if you wouldn't do the same thing, in our shoes."

Her speech was impassioned. He could see that this really mattered to her, that she wasn't showing it to him just to make an out-of-towner feel small. But he still couldn't see the relevance. "What does this have to do with my mother?"

"It's all to do with timing. Rogue man'kin and other creatures too weird to name are often sighted along the Divide, moving back and forth as the will takes them. We leave them well alone; some of them can be extremely dangerous. Just lately, though, there's been an increase in foot traffic along the Divide from the Hanging Mountains. What they're doing here, I don't know, but they're mean and they're in a hurry. And they're dropping things as they go." She indicated the flyers again. "Normally there'd be just a half-dozen of them out there at this time of day. Not now. Every able flyer has been called in to take advantage of the situation. There's lots of stuff out there just waiting to be harvested. All you have to do is pick it up."

She sighed. "Of all the times to lose my wing, it'd have to be now."

There was a look of yearning in her eyes that reminded Skender of how frustrated and stifled he had been before his adventures outside the Keep. He felt for her, but his mind was simultaneously working on his own problem. He'd assumed that his mother's party had headed for the tunnels of Laure to look for the thing they sought. But if the tunnels were mined out, that was exactly the wrong place to look.

A dark smudge on the far edge of the Divide drew his gaze and held it. Laure was half a city. Before the Divide had come along, it had been whole. Therefore, the tunnels that now gaped into empty air once connected to matching tunnels on the other side—under the forbidden Ruin called the Aad.

Right idea, he told himself; *wrong place*. All he had to do was get across the Divide and under the Aad to see if he was right.

However, Chu's description of the Ruin was still vivid in his mind. *Disease; bad luck; inhabited by creatures of the Divide . . .*

"Judging by your face," she said, "you've just worked out where your mother is."

He nodded despondently. "And a fat lot of good it does me. How in the Goddess's name am I going to get over there?"

"There is a way, but it's going to be tricky. When a miner finds something big in the Divide, too big for her to carry herself, she flashes for a heavy lifter from the city."

"Flashes?"

"By mirror." She waved that explanation away. "The heavy lifters are dirigibles with ropes and hooks designed to pick up just about anything from above. They're slow but reliable. Although they don't usually go that far, we could get across the Divide and return with your mother, and whoever she has with her."

"That sounds good," he said. "How do I go about organising it?"

"That depends on whether you have enough money to charter a lifter."

"I might have, depending on how much it costs."

She named a figure that made his head spin. For a brief moment he considered selling the buggy, which was locked securely in an empty camel stall under the hostel he'd booked into. But that was a mad idea; he had to get home somehow, once all this was over.

"Okay, so that's out." She looked through the gap at her peers hurling themselves boldly into the sky. "There are only two other ways to go about it. The first and most obvious is to petition the Magister."

Skender nodded. The Magister was the head of the yadachi, and had ruled Laure for thirty thirsty years.

"Do you think she'll help us?"

"That old vampire? Given my record and where you're from, she's more likely to throw us in the brig just for asking."

"Great. So what's the second way?"

"We steal what we need and worry about the consequences later."

"Are you joking?"

She shook her head. "I'm renowned for two things: the ability to fly and the inability to stay out of trouble. Neither requires much of a sense of humour."

"You could've fooled me," he muttered. "Looks like you're having a great time at my expense."

"Hard though it might be to believe, watching you squirm isn't what I was put on the Earth for. It's just a consolation prize."

He had to admit that she'd stopped smiling some time ago.

"Okay," he said, resigning himself to the situation. "We try the Magister first. Whether you say it'll work or not, we have to give it a go. And if she doesn't see it our way—"

"We renegotiate. Right." She took one last look at the other miners and their wings before making moves to leave the niche.

"Wait," he said, gripping her forearm. "I can't believe you're seriously thinking of doing this—stealing a balloon and helping me rescue my mother. Aren't you in enough trouble already?"

Her eyes moved restlessly as they focused first on his left pupil, then the right, then back again. "You don't get it yet, do you? This isn't about you. I expect to be compensated. Handsomely, too. Otherwise you're right: there's nothing in it for me but more hot water."

He didn't know what he'd expected, but her words disappointed him. "I'll make sure you get what you deserve," he said. "Don't worry about that."

"Good. Then let's get going. The air is thin up here. It's making me thirsty."

➤ ➤ ➤

Street-level frontage in Laure was at such a premium that most shops performed two or more functions simultaneously. Food vendors also sold
coffee and tightly rolled cigarettes, and provided venues for wiry old
people to play complicated-looking games involving tiles and dice. They
served alcohol as well, as Skender discovered half an hour later—although
he received the distinct impression that most of the business in the narrow
bar Chu had taken him to was conducted out the back behind the kitchen,
where money changed hands over flat paper packets whose contents he
didn't want to know anything about, beyond a quick glimpse as they
passed through. The black market thrived in Laure, which had laboured
under strict rationing for as long as anyone could remember. Traders visited regularly, but never frequently enough to satisfy the populace.

"I suppose I'm paying for this as well as dinner," he said as a waiter
brought two stubby glasses and a bottle of milky liquid to their table.
Chu muttered something in reply, then nodded thanks to the waiter
and started to pour.

"What did you say?" he asked. It was hard to hear over the racket
of the band. The instruments were unfamiliar to his ears, as were the
tunes, but there was no denying the musicians' enthusiasm.

"I said, shut up and enjoy." She handed him a glass. The weathered
leather of her jacket hung over the back of a chair. Under it she wore a
grey tank top that revealed light brown skin covered in a fine patina of
sweat. It was stifling in the tavern.

He loosened the neck of his robes and took the glass somewhat
nervously. Personal experience had taught him that the alcohol content
of a drink was inversely proportional to the size of the glass it came in.
These glasses were *tiny*.

Chu knocked hers back with one gulp. Skender took a deep breath,
and followed suit.

For a brief moment, he thought he might die. His tongue curled up and his throat burned. Water sprang from his eyes. His gut clenched.

"Do you like it?" she asked with a gleam in her eye.

"Wonderful," he managed. "A couple more of those and getting across the Divide will be the least of my troubles."

"That's the idea." Chu refilled their glasses, revealing as she did so a procession of fine pink cuts up the inside of her left wrist. She didn't explain them. "We've made it known that we want to see the Magister. Now all we can do is wait for her to contact us."

"How long will that take?"

"Could be a day or two." She burped with enough gusto to drown out the band, then downed the second shot. "Might as well relax in the meantime."

"On my savings."

"You know you're getting your money's worth." She indicated the glass in front of him with her chin. "Going to drink that, or are you hoping it might evaporate?"

He tossed it back with a grimace, fuelling the fire already burning in his belly. She filled the glasses a third time.

"Tell me something, Skender Van Haasteren. Tell me what your mother was looking for."

"I don't know."

"Oh, come on. You don't have to keep secrets from me."

"No, really. I have no idea."

"It must be something pretty important. Flying over the Divide is scary enough; going down into it takes a special kind of crazy."

"She's not crazy," he bristled.

"To most people, she'd have to be. You think the Wall is there for aesthetic reasons?"

The liquor was already making him feel dizzy. He could smell it over the stink of smoke and heavily spiced vegetables. It was coming out of the woodwork.

"Are you trying to get me drunk?" he asked.

"No. I'm trying to get *me* drunk." The contents of a third glass disappeared down her impervious gullet. "And I'm curious about your mother. Surveyors come through Laure every now and again. They're a quiet lot, for the most part. They do their thing and we do ours. Some of us—not me, of course—call them Ruin Rats because they're always scrabbling around in the dirt."

Skender's taste buds were sufficiently numb to make a third hit bearable. "That's not very nice."

"You know what people are like." Chu rested her elbows on the table and her chin in both palms. "Scumbags for the most part, and those who aren't are complete bastards."

"I'm sensing some negativity, here."

She sighed. "Seagulls are rats of the sky. Isn't that what they say? Give someone a wing and that doesn't make them better."

"And taking the wing *off* someone doesn't make them worse," he said, hoping he was keeping up.

"Obviously," she said. "I'll drink to that." She poured them another round, spilling a substantial portion on the rough wooden tabletop. She didn't seem to notice. "Not everyone agrees."

Her head tilted back, exposing a long, elegantly muscled throat. Skender caught himself staring, and covered it up by drinking from his own glass.

"Is your father a Surveyor?" she asked him.

"No. He's a teacher, like his father before him."

"Well, good for them. A teacher and a Surveyor. Some people might think that odd. Some people might say that like should stick with like, or else you're asking for disaster."

Skender thought of his parents and their separate lifestyles. "Some people might be right."

"Some people are arseholes, as well as scumbags and bastards." Chu's sudden vitriol made him blink. "You shouldn't try to defend him."

"Who?"

"Don't play the innocent. He knew what he was doing. It became clear once I'd lost my wing that I wasn't good enough for him any more. And why is that? I was good enough *before*, wasn't I?" She sniffed. "He's just an idiot. A rat of the sky. I'm better off without him."

For a second, Skender was hopelessly confused. Then the mental clouds parted. "Oh, I get it. 'Some people' is someone specific."

"And he could be very specific, when he wanted to be. Here I was thinking he helped me out because he liked me." She blinked down into her empty glass. "God, I'm such an idiot."

Skender stared at the crown of her head, at the whorls and flows of her rich dark hair and the paler skin beneath. He wanted to reach out and take her hand, or at least touch it, but the world was swaying alarmingly around him and he couldn't trust himself not to poke her in the eye by accident. He felt as dizzy as he had after his Blood Tithe had been taken. "I don't think you're an idiot."

"Yes, but you're drunk. You'd say anything right now."

"That's not true!"

"Then you aren't drunk *enough*." She looked up and reached for the bottle. "Hey, this is almost empty. Let's get another one."

She turned around to hail the waiter.

"I drink," he protested, "that I've had enough to think."

"Really?" Her laughter was pure and unrestrained.

"I mean—"

A hand came down onto his shoulder, startling him, and a rough voice spoke in his ear.

"The Magister will see you now, Mage."

"I'm not—"

"Do as the man says, Skender." Chu had turned back. Her expression was suddenly very serious. "Come on."

She shrugged into her jacket and helped him to his feet. His legs were wobbling and he was grateful for her support.

"Where are we going?" he asked the man, a tall, triangular-faced yadachi with a beard that covered most of his face. His robe was as red as blood and he carried with him a heavy scent of cloves. Cold blue eyes regarded Skender with naked disdain.

"I've told you once," was the only reply he got. "And I'm in a hurry."

"Lead the way," said Chu, gesturing to the door. "I assure you we'll keep up."

The man turned his back on them and pressed through the crowd. The music continued unabated as they left the heat and stink of the tavern and entered the night.

Laure was a desert city, but one very different from the underground metropolises of the Interior. Its position right on the Divide left it technically part of the Interior but facing a raft of problems unique to such border towns. Skender hadn't had very long to research the history of the walled city before he left, but he did know that the yadachi weren't indigenous: they had originally been a roaming sect of Change-workers, struggling to survive in a world where neither sea nor stone were very strong and where most of the available reservoirs were already taken. Their particular solution to that problem had found fertile soil in Laure, so they thrived where both Mage and Warden would struggle.

Their yadachi guide took them at a brisk pace through winding streets, without once looking back. Skender and Chu walked one pace behind, catching each other when they stumbled. He was surprised to realise that she was exactly the same height as he. In the bar and on the rooftop, she had seemed much taller.

"He called me 'Mage,'" he hissed to her. "What was that about?"

"Assumptions, remember?" she whispered back. "It doesn't hurt to encourage them, sometimes."

"But I'm not—"

She put a hand to his mouth. "Don't argue. Being a Mage still means something here, and it's getting us to the Magister sooner rather than later. Every hour we save is one less your mother languishes in the Divide. Right?"

He couldn't argue with that, although he disliked her methods. Twisting his head to free his mouth, he glared at her and told himself to sober up, fast. It was all very well to be seeing the Magister, but it wouldn't do him much good if he couldn't string a coherent sentence together.

Being a Mage still means something here. He supposed that made sense. The rest of the Interior might ignore Laure's existence, for the most part, but the artefacts they sold had to be bought by *someone*.

Slowly, the architecture improved. Slumping walls and drifts of sand that had been allowed to build up in corners gave way to clear, bold lines and well-maintained sidewalks. The city's tapering minarets strained for the stars in the crisp evening air. Frosted circular windows glowed with warmth and light. Voices filtered faintly through thick stone walls. By dawn it would be very cold. Skender hoped to be safe in his bed well before then.

Their guide passed through a heart-shaped gate with a wide, sharp-tipped portcullis above their heads, and led them into a fortified building with no windows. Their footsteps echoed off ceramic tiles that gleamed by stone-light. Brass shields hung on thick chains from hooks all along the wide corridor they followed. It doglegged to the right and terminated in two broad white doors.

Their guide knocked twice, firmly. The doors opened. Skender and Chu were ushered into an antechamber larger than the tavern they had just left. Its walls were featureless, polished stone, except for the one facing the door, where hung a gleaming glass mural of restless blues and greens—colours rarely seen in the city's desert environment. Guards in yellow and black uniforms stood stiffly to attention in each corner. A single tall-backed chair rested between them on a square dais. Seated slightly askew in the chair was a striking woman with no hair at all and the biggest hooknose Skender had ever seen. Her eyes were a deep, potent green. She wore a black robe with red trimmings and rested gnarled white hands on the globe of an ebony walking stick. Her lips were broad and expressive, but only ever smiled on one side.

The incision on his left arm still itched but he refused to scratch it.

"It's late," said Magister Considine. The room barely contained the rich harmonics of her voice, "and much demands my attention before I am allowed to retire. Be brief, I beg you."

"Th—thank you for seeing us," Skender stammered, affecting an awkward bow. "I'm not familiar with your customs here, so I hope I haven't offended—"

"Customs are for the lazy-minded." She waved his apology away with one hand. Her fingernails were long and unpolished, like claws. They clicked against the knob of her walking stick as she brought her hand back down. "I prefer to get right down to business. I will not ask again, young Van Haasteren."

"You know who I am?"

"Of course. I know everything in this city."

"Then you know I'm looking for my mother."

"I know she had business near Laure. All Surveyors declare their intentions when they encroach upon my territory. They learned the wisdom of doing so long ago, lest I mistake them for thieves." Her eyes hardened. "The fate of your mother is no concern of mine. If the Divide has taken her, so be it."

"I don't believe she's in the Divide," he said. "She's in the Aad. If I can get there, maybe I can help her."

"Maybe you can. I am not stopping you."

"No, but I need more than your permission." The liquor in his belly made him bold. "I need your help."

"Is that so?" Magister Considine shifted her sharp stare to Chu. "And no wonder, with this one swinging from your robe."

Chu looked indignant. "He doesn't know our ways, ma'am. Someone has to guide him."

"You both stink of smoke and araq. In your eyes, perhaps, you are making satisfactory progress."

"We've been waiting for you," said Skender, not liking the way the Magister belittled Chu in front of him.

"Close your eyes," the Magister ordered him.

He blinked, blindsided by the request. "I'm sorry?"

"You heard me." The Magister crouched over her stick like a predatory insect. "Do as I say, or this conversation is over."

He closed his eyes.

"Now, tell me how many rings I have on my fingers. You have five seconds before my guards throw you out of the city."

Skender thought fast. He hadn't consciously noticed any rings, but the image of her hands was impressed on his memory as clearly as if he was seeing it for the first time. There were thick black bands on the two longest fingers and a silver coil on her left thumb.

"Three," he said. "You have a matching bracelet on your right hand, in silver and black, and a pin at the throat of your robe in the shape of a crab. On the—"

"Enough. You are who you say you are, then." She clicked her fingers and he opened his eyes. "Now, tell me exactly what you want."

"A dirigible," he said, "a heavy lifter so we can travel to and investigate the Aad."

The Magister nodded. "I thought as much. Perhaps you aren't aware that this city labours under unusual circumstances. A growing stream of man'kin pours down from the east; rumours of unrest come to us from our furthest boundary riders. We must take advantage of the opportunities this presents, yes, but we must also be vigilant for threats. Were these more usual times, I might have had an aircraft available for you to commission. Presently I do not."

"But it wouldn't take long." He glanced at Chu for guidance, nervous of how far he could push the Magister. Her face was expressionless. "We could be there and back in no time at all."

"Or you could be delayed, or shot down, or captured. These are risks I must contemplate for the good of the city. I cannot allow your natural desires—with which I completely sympathise, believe me—to jeopardise those in my care. Find another means to rescue your mother. Perhaps I will be able to assist you then."

The Magister raised one hand to dismiss them.

"There *is* another way," said Chu, stepping forward. "Renew my licence. Give me access to the armoury so I can fix my wing. I'll fly him over myself."

A-ha, thought Skender, realising now how he fitted into her plans.

The Magister raised her left eyebrow. Her hand remained upraised. "The moment I give you your licence back, you will abandon this young man to his fate. Your intentions are transparent to me."

"How can you say that? You don't know the first thing about me!"

"No?" The Magister clicked her fingers a second time and a robed lackey appeared from a subtly concealed panel. He handed his mistress a thick paper file then disappeared again. Taking it with the hand that had been about to dismiss them, the Magister opened the file and flicked through it, glancing from the pages within to Chu's reddening face.

"Improper use of safety equipment, wilful defiance of aerial regulations, felonious acquisition of material and labour, trafficking in illegally obtained artefacts . . . You've been a busy girl these last two years. Do you sincerely expect me to believe that your momentum has been checked overnight by some young fellow and his mother's plight?"

Chu's lips were set in a tight line. "I expect nothing."

"Good. That way you will never be disappointed."

"It's just . . ."

"What?"

"So *unfair*."

"There is no such thing as fair or unfair, girl." The Magister's stare was intense. The folder lay closed in her lap, but clutched so tightly in one hand it almost bent in two. "The world owes you nothing—neither a father nor a friend nor an opportunity to redeem yourself. We dig our own pitfalls just as we make our own fortunes."

Skender stared from one to the other. The two women, although separated by age, rank, and experience, had almost identical expressions.

"You're not going to help us," said Chu. "Is that what you're saying?"

"Not at all. I am going to give you one last chance, lest anyone call me unfeeling. You may use the armoury. I will instruct the quartermaster to lend you such assistance as you need, within reason."

"And my licence?"

"That I will not restore. You have yet to earn my confidence in that regard."

"Oh, that's just great. How are we supposed to get to the Aad without a licence? Are you telling me to break the law and steal a heavy lifter?"

"I'm not telling you that. A licence you will have. *His* licence." One knobbled finger pointed at Skender.

"Mine?" he said, alarmed by the high-pitched voice he heard coming from his own mouth. "But I don't know the first thing about flying!"

"Then you had better start studying. The paperwork will arrive tomorrow morning. And be warned: the guards on the heavy lifter hangars have been tripled. Don't even consider trying to steal one."

"But—" The thought of being suspended over thin air by a sheet of canvas and a set of unreliable charms made Skender's head spin. He glanced again at Chu, prepared to argue the point that giving him a licence was as useless as giving them none at all—but her expression was furious, and it appeared to be directed at him as much as at the Magister.

"You can thank me later." The Magister settled back into her seat with a smug expression. "Leave, now. My generosity is quite exhausted."

Chu turned on her heel and stalked out of the room. Skender, left standing on his own, froze for a moment before executing a short bow and hurriedly following. The door slammed shut behind them, cutting off the beginnings of an amused chuckle from the ruler of Laure.

He caught up with Chu outside. Grabbing her arm, he spun her around.

"I'm sorry," he began.

"*You're* sorry? Great. That makes me feel a whole lot better."

"It's not my fault!"

"Well, it's not mine, either." She spat into the gutter. "I should never have expected that bitch to help me."

"But she has," Skender protested. "Hasn't she? She's letting you fix your wing for free."

"A fat lot of good a wing will be if I'm not allowed to fly it."

"One step at a time, Chu. You can't have everything at once!"

"Why the hell not?" She turned and stalked away, a palpable wave of gloom travelling with her.

"Does that mean our deal is off?"

She didn't answer. Skender let her go. There was no point pushing her, although he hated the thought of ending it like that. If she didn't come around, he supposed he would just have to find another way past the problem.

With the beginnings of a headache throbbing in his temples, Skender waited until Chu was out of sight before retracing the route back to the tavern. In the hostel that was his temporary home, he climbed under the mosquito net and tried to sleep. He wasn't strong enough in the Change to reach out and touch his father's mind, but part of him wished strongly that he could. In a city full of strangers and their unfamiliar ways, he felt very alone and very much at the mercy of those around him, all of whom had their own games to play. The quest to rescue his mother had taken some surprising twists and turns, and he still didn't know how close he was to achieving that end. If Chu didn't reappear the following morning, he would be right back where he started.

THE WAKE

"The occurrence of wild talents is undeniably rising in all parts of the Strand. Ordinarily, one instance a century would be remarkable. Records indicate that three have emerged in the last fifty years alone. Of those three, the first spontaneously combusted while swimming in a Ruin water tank; the second overreached even her considerable talent and was consumed by a golem; the third remains at large, a threat to everyone around him. The reasons behind the increase are presently unknown."

REPORT ON ANOMALOUS PHENOMENA
YEAR FOUR OF THE ALCAIDE DRAGAN BRAHAM

For Shilly, the journey was both a respite and a chore. The old north road from Fundelry to Gliem was rutted and full of detours, so their progress was slow at first. They drove in shifts, two awake while one slept, stopping only when they needed to refuel. Once they hit the paved stretch leading to Kittle, their pace improved dramatically. Landscape flew by, becoming browner and hillier as they headed inland. The feeling that she was leaving her home was strong, but she wasn't as panic-stricken as she had been years before. Then, she had had very little say in the matter; now she was coming because she wanted to. Rushing headlong to someone's aid felt very different to running away.

That feeling sustained her when they reached Kittle. Instead of continuing north as they had on that previous journey, following the Old Line into the hills, they turned east along an ancient thoroughfare that snaked as wide and flat as a giant serpent's skin across the undulating landscape. Skirting foothills that never truly amounted to much, through low scrub and abandoned pastureland, the road took them the five hundred kilometres to Moombin, directly north of the Haunted City. There they paused to rest. Tom's rank saw them well looked after by local merchants. In exchange for repairing a seized-up tractor, he earned them a hearty meal and an offer of accommodation. Although grateful for the latter—Shilly could easily have been tempted—they opted to press on.

From Moombin, the road continued east for another three hundred kilometres before angling gradually northwards. They passed four horse-drawn caravans and one trader from the Interior, her camels loping steadily behind her with heads held high. Apart from that, the old roads were empty. The second night fell in a wash of rich red. Cloudless, the sky melted into a star field as rich and varied as any she had ever seen. With her hands on the wheel and her attention firmly ahead, she tracked the moon's steady progress across the heavens. The buggy's headlights sent yellow, dancing light across the road ahead of them. Beside her, in the forward passenger seat, Sal maintained a watch for any animals that might cross their path. He held her stick across his lap, tracing its charms with his fingertips. Tom sprawled across the back seats, dead to the world.

Sal kept her awake by singing songs he had picked up during his travels as a child. She didn't understand the words to all of them; many dealt with notions and quests quite at odds with her experience. Ghosts of dead people, gods, angels, other worlds—they were kids' stories, not to be taken seriously. She liked the songs with rolling rhythms and lyrics that made her want to put her foot down harder on the accelerator.

"*Over the Mountains*
Of the Moon,
Down the Valley of Shadow,

Ride, boldly ride,'
The shadow replied—
'If you seek for Eldorado!'"

She handed the wheel to Sal when her stiff leg could no longer work the brakes. Sleep came to her in fits and starts as they bounced along the weatherworn tarmac; her dreams were of storm-tossed fishing boats and giant, purring cats. Every time she awoke, the relentless throbbing of the engine had numbed a new part of her. The Change sparked along the buggy's many wires and cylinders, just centimetres from where she lay. The principles by which it worked were familiar in theory and mysterious in practice. The engine ran on alcohol fuel, but not just by burning it. It needed the Change as well as fire. Mages and Wardens had been trying and failing to store the Change for centuries—since being static ran against its nature—but alcohol made from organic material, when combusted, *did* change, and the essence, the so-called chimerical energy, of that reaction when bled off via pipes and wires to engines could be turned into mechanical force.

Loudly.

When Sal stopped two hours before midnight to relieve himself and to give Tom the wheel, her head hummed like a gong in the blessed silence.

"How much further?" she asked, hugging herself to keep the chill of the wind at bay and stamping her feet to restore their circulation.

"That depends on how far the search party has progressed," said Tom. His focused gaze alighted on her, then slid away into the night. "At the speed they were travelling, they should be about an hour or so from here."

"I don't think I can sleep any more. Do you want me to drive?"

Tom shook his head. "There are Broken Lands ahead. I'd rather be behind the wheel for them, if you don't mind."

"Not at all." She had vague but deeply imprinted memories of bouncing through a different patch of Broken Lands on the way to the Interior, after the accident that had left her thigh shattered. The leg had been strapped and splinted, her mind fogged by powerful painkilling tablets. "That's a job I'm happy to leave to you."

Sal returned from the darkness as wind moaned softly through the endless scrub. "Spooky," he said. "What would happen if the Homunculus got away from the search party and found us here?"

"That would depend on its nature," said Tom. "Why Highson made it, and for what purpose."

"Or for whom."

An artificial creature designed to house a disembodied mind, Tom had said, *like a ghost or a golem.* What exactly had Highson summoned, and why?

"We'd better just hope," Shilly said, "that it's not in a bad mood if we come across it."

The feeling that they were finally closing in on the search party kept all three of them awake as the landscape became ragged and disjointed around them. The road turned back eastward and became increasingly unreliable, and their pace slowed as a result. The road disappeared completely on occasions, giving way to wide stretches of sand, naked stone, or gravel, only to reappear some tens of metres on. Wheel ruts or milestones marked the long, empty stretches, evidence that the road was still used, despite its patchwork nature.

They came to a T-junction and turned right along a south-southeast heading.

"Is this the right direction?" asked Shilly from the front passenger seat.

"There's a north turn fifty kilometres ahead," said Tom, his eyes fixed forward as he navigated the irregular terrain. "If we haven't come across anything by the time we reach it, we'll stop there and wait for dawn."

"Sounds good to me," said Shilly. All thoughts of sleep were completely banished as the eerie thrall of the Broken Lands took a strong hold on her. The temperature seemed to drop even further.

Sal leaned forward from the back seat, perching between Shilly and Tom with an elbow resting on each of their seats. His eyes scanned the Broken Lands ahead of them.

"I sense," he said, "*something.*"

"So do I," said Tom.

Feeling left out, Shilly put her hand on Sal's arm. She had no talent herself, but she was acutely sensitive to the flows of the Change around her. No small blessing—as she had come to realise—it allowed her not just to read the world in ways others could not, but also to tap into the strength of those who *were* talented. With Sal's permission, she could share his perception and use his strength. For the time being, she just wanted to look and see what he and Tom saw.

By the light of the Change, the Broken Lands were full of strange eddies and truncated fluxes. The usual patterns of life were disrupted along with the landscape, frozen in an attitude of chaos and confusion. Wind and water didn't know where to flow; animals lost their bearings. A sense of wrongness pervaded everything. Legend told that such regions were wastelands left over from a cosmic battle.

And there was something else. She immediately sensed what Sal and Tom were referring to: a concentration of the Change, a knot of vitality that lurked in the tangled web of the Broken Lands directly in their path.

"Is it the Homunculus?" she asked.

"I don't know," said Tom. Through Sal she could sense his nervousness. "It's definitely on the road, though."

His foot edged off the accelerator. The throbbing growl of the engine dropped back a notch.

"I don't know what to do," he said.

Sal's jaw muscles bunched. Shilly tightened her grip on his arm.

Before either of them could suggest anything, a bright light exploded high up in the sky. Shilly shielded her eyes against the sudden glare and squinted between her fingers. A miniature sun transformed the world into a realm of stark black and white. Harsh details leapt out at her: a jagged shelf of rocks to the left of the road; the bitten roughness of Sal's fingernails where his hands gripped her shoulder; the strange way the shadows moved as the new sun sank towards the Earth.

"It's a flare!" said Tom, pulling the buggy to an ungainly halt. Another sun blossomed to one side of the first. "Two of them!"

"Who's firing them?" asked Sal.

"And whose attention are they trying to attract?" Shilly added. Movement in the stark landscape caught her eye. "Look!"

Something was running towards them along the road, waving its arms. A surge of adrenaline gripped her.

Sal stood up in the seat. She felt the Change stirring in him, gathering like a thunderhead. The hairs on the back of her neck stood up.

"No!" Tom grabbed Sal's leg. "Wait!"

The figure ran into the light cast by the buggy's headlights. *Blue*, she thought, and her heart anxiously tripped a beat; old habits die hard.

"A Sky Warden!" exclaimed Sal. The thunderhead receded slightly. "We've found the search party."

Tom was the only one who didn't seem reassured. "What are they doing?" he asked, his frown deeply etched in the shadow cast by the flares. "Why are they giving themselves away like this?"

Shilly didn't say anything. The Warden was almost upon them. She figured that, in a moment, they would have their answer.

"You're a sight for sore eyes, young Tom." The woman was in her middle years, round-faced and heavyset with short brown hair and good-humoured eyes that never stopped moving.

"Warden Banner?" Tom's expression was still one of puzzlement. "I didn't expect to find you here."

"Glad to see the universe can still toss you a surprise or two. We heard the sound of your buggy but didn't know who you were. That's why we sent up the flares. You might have run into us in the dark, or worse. Only when you got closer did I recognise the cadence of your engine and decide to head you off."

Sal wanted to ask what she meant by *worse* but was struck temporarily dumb by the blue robe and the torc. Banner motioned that he should make room for her in the back seat. He did so, taking Tom's acceptance of her at face value, for the moment. "I was dragged along for the ride when you went missing, Tom. They needed an Engineer, and Marmion would only have the best."

"Warden Banner was my first tutor at the Novitiate," said Tom, almost shyly.

"Not for long." She mussed his hair with genuine fondness. "This one has taught me a thing or two since."

"You're not here alone, I presume," said Shilly, bringing the conversation back to the immediate.

"Goddess, no. The others are up ahead." She pointed past Tom's cheek. "Take us onto the shoulder up there, by that outcrop. We're parked just over the hill."

Tom revved the engine and put the buggy back into gear. Sal was glad they were moving again; he felt dangerously exposed being stationary in the Broken Lands.

"So, Tom," the Warden said when they had travelled a short distance, "are you going to introduce your friends or are they going to have to do it themselves?"

Sal and Shilly exchanged a quick glance.

"They're Sal and Shilly," said Tom without hesitation. "I asked them to help."

"You did, did you?" Banner's sharp gaze examined them in detail. Her warmth didn't ebb, but the lines around her eyes drew together. "Well, this should be interesting."

Sal felt his teeth beginning to clench in a familiar anticipation of conflict and forced himself to relax. He wasn't a child any more. The

Wardens had no claim over him or his talent. At the first sign of overt hostility, he could just leave.

Or could he? Despite the long, exhausting drive, he felt as if they had caught up to the search party with great suddenness. He had no idea what he would do if they did reject him and Shilly. Would he go back home or continue searching on his own? How much *exactly* did he owe his real father?

Banner's eyes flicked forward as Tom reached the outcrop. "See that track? Follow it to the bottom. Flash your lights twice."

Tom did everything she said without hesitation. The buggy bounced down the side of a shallow hill, jolting in and out of potholes and ruts, shaking the last dregs of sleep from Sal. They found themselves in the middle of a petrified forest. Grey tree stumps, as rough as bark but as solid as stone, surrounded them like silent spectators. Out of the darkness between them emerged the shapes of two angular open-frame vehicles large enough to hold a dozen people each, and a domed tent. A faint tang of smoke hung in the air.

Tom flashed the lights as instructed and a small group of people emerged from their hiding places. Eyes and crystal torcs glinted in the glare. Sal's shoulder muscles ached from tension.

"Stop here." Tom brought the buggy to a halt and killed the engine. "All clear!" Banner called to the rest of her party. "Looks like we picked up some stragglers."

One of the Wardens said a short, sharp word, and light blossomed from three mirror-finished cylinders on spikes, anchored in the ground around the impromptu campsite. By the stored starlight, Sal made out more than a dozen men and women moving in to get a better look at them. One of the men was the tallest Sal had ever seen, a rangy giant with thick black hair crowning a deeply lined face. The only one not wearing a torc or a blue robe, his attire consisted of practical leather pants and an open-necked shirt.

It was this man who spoke first. "Stragglers, eh? I suppose that fool Braham sent you. Doesn't he trust us?"

One of the other men hissed. "Show some respect, Kail. The Alcaide knows what he's doing."

"Not out here he doesn't." The rangy giant spat into the dirt and stalked away.

Banner alighted from the buggy and whispered quickly into the ear of the second man who had spoken. Shorter, with a receding hairline and a soft, oval face, he looked more like the Wardens Sal was used to than the hard, abrupt Kail.

Whatever Banner said, it provoked an instant reaction. "Why would he do that?" he asked, looking at Tom, then Sal and Shilly, in alarm.

"They say they're here to help." Banner stepped back in deference to the balding Warden. She looked relieved that they were no longer her problem.

Sal didn't need Tom's prophetic dreams to tell him what was going to happen next. They were about to be told to go home without being given the chance to speak.

"I'm Sal Hrvati," he said, standing up in the back of the buggy and dismounting. "This is Shilly of Gooron. We're here to find my father."

A whisper went through the Wardens. The balding Warden nodded as though accepting a challenge. "I'm Eisak Marmion, the leader of this expedition. Alcaide Braham gave us the task of locating Highson Sparre, and us alone."

"Have you found him yet?" asked Shilly, coming to stand with Sal.

"We know where he is."

"That's not the same thing."

"I'm not required," said Marmion, moving closer, "to explain myself to you."

"Well, we're here now," said Sal, "and we're willing to help. It'd be easier if you did explain."

"We don't need your help."

A bark of laughter came from the shadows. Kail's angular silhouette reappeared. "What are you going to do, Marmion? Force him to leave?"

The balding Warden shot Kail a cold glance. "The best tracker in the Strand has assured us that we'll have the fugitive within our grasp sooner rather than later. Isn't that right, Kail?"

"We would've had him now if you hadn't got us stuck here like pigs in a bog," replied the rangy tracker. "While we twiddle our thumbs, he's slipping further and further out of our reach!"

An old argument was gathering momentum between the two men. To forestall it, Sal said, "Highson Sparre is not a fugitive."

"No?" snapped Marmion, turning on him. "Then why is he running from us?"

"He's not running from you. He's hunting the Homunculus, as you should be. That's the important thing."

Marmion fumed. "Your father may not think he's a fugitive, Sal, but he is a thief. His actions have resulted in the death of at least one man. Until he deigns to explain himself, I am justified in seeking him *as well as* the thing he summoned. Since he's following the Homunculus, finding him will find the other. Does that make the situation clear to you?" His gaze swept the circle of Wardens. "Would any of you like to question my judgment while we're at it?"

Shilly raised her hand.

"I wasn't asking you," Marmion said.

"I know, but I'd still like to know. Why *are* you sitting here twiddling your thumbs? Why aren't you doing what you set out to do?"

For a moment, Sal thought she had pushed Marmion too far. His eyes bugged and his face went red. He raised one finger and pointed it at her like a weapon. A whisper of the Change rustled through the campsite like a fitful breeze. Sal tensed, ready to defend her if she needed it.

Then a switch seemed to trip inside the Warden, and the pressure eased.

"All right," he said lowering his hand. "We might as well put you to use. Banner, get Tom under the hoods of the buses. I want them

ready to roll before midnight. Kail, check the course Sparre is following and make sure it matches the one on our charts. You two," he
pointed to Sal and Shilly, "come with me."

He turned and headed off into the darkness, robe flapping between
his legs. Sal hesitated a second, then followed. Shilly came with him,
leaning heavily on her stick when the terrain became rough underfoot.

Marmion led them unerringly away from the parked vehicles. He
had obviously walked this way many times. Sal tried to discern any
details out of the darkness, but his eyes had adjusted to the mirror-
light: the absence of landmarks was profound. He took Shilly's hand to
steady her, and was glad of *her* support when he tripped over a stony
tree stump and almost went sprawling.

"Where are we going?"

The silhouette of Marmion looked over his shoulder. "Let's make
one thing absolutely clear, Sal. I'm under no obligation to tell you anything. You're here without invitation and without my approval. That
may be your father out there, but Alcaide Braham put me in charge of
this search party, and I will not bow to your threats or manipulation."

The Warden's persistent defensiveness surprised him. "We're not
trying to manipulate you," he started to say, but Shilly interrupted him.

"Warden Marmion, are you afraid of us?"

"Of course not," Marmion responded immediately. "Why would I be
afraid of you? You're just a couple of young idiots off on an adventure."

But Sal could hear the fear loudly in the man's voice, underlying
the anger it disguised. The understanding dismayed him. There had
been incidents in the past, yes, but they were forgotten now—or so he
had hoped. What did Marmion think they were? Monsters?

"Don't mistake us for something we're not," Shilly said. "We're
not kids, and we're not completely ignorant. Someone we care about is
in trouble, and we're trying to help. The past is irrelevant. If we work
together, we'll do a much better job than if we work separately or
against each other."

Sal smiled in the darkness. Shilly was good at getting what she wanted. The fact that they had lived in Fundelry for so long without anyone giving them away was testimony to her diplomatic skills.

Marmion, however, was no hick Alder or Mayor.

"No one knows exactly what happened five years ago," he said, his voice less strident than it had been, "when you escaped from the Haunted City. You defied the Alcaide, the Syndic, and the Conclave with suspicious ease; someone must have helped you do it. Although he denied the charge, Highson Sparre is commonly assumed to be that someone. So don't give me any empty rhetoric about wanting to help your father out of the goodness of your heart. You're two fugitives helping a third—helping him get away *from me*. That's how I see it. Yes, you can stay, but be assured that at the slightest sign you're betraying those I serve, you will suffer the consequences."

"We understand," said Shilly, her voice grave. "And now we've got the posturing out of the way, are you going to tell us what we're doing out here? Or is stumbling around in the dark the way you usually go about your business?"

Marmion drew a sharp breath.

Without warning, all sensation of the Change fell away, as though a heavy veil had been drawn over the world.

Shilly and Sal stopped dead and looked around in alarm. Superficially, the night seemed no different from a second ago: there was no sound apart from the sighing of the wind; the multitude of stars still twinkled above. But something essential had been taken away from it. The Change was as important a part of the world as light, and without it Shilly felt like someone suddenly struck blind.

"What did you do?" she heard Sal ask Marmion. His words fell flat and lifeless on her ears. "What have you done to us?"

"Nothing," said the Warden. He had stopped walking and turned to face them. "You feel it, then."

"Of course we feel it." Sal looked around. "This spot is—" He struggled for words. "—*dead*."

"Is it a Change-sink?" she asked.

"No, and it's not just here," Marmion said. "The deadness extends all the way from here back to Gunida, to where we started. What you're feeling is the wake of the Homunculus."

The night seemed to close in around her, full of suffocating silence. She shivered, thinking of Larson Maiz, frightened to death by the thing Sal's father had brought into the world, whatever it was. "It came this way?"

"And recently, too. The wake has been getting stronger the closer we come to it. We've been measuring the width and the way it varies depending on the landscape and vegetation it passes through. It seems to spread further when there's less around it—the earth and living things interfere with it, reduce its strength. We had no idea how strong it would become in the Broken Lands, and that was our mistake. While Kail followed the wake on foot, the rest of us were using the roads to cut in front of it, head it off. We must have just missed it. We crossed its path without warning, just over that hill. The buses died immediately, sucked dry of the Change. We lost contact with Kail. We were stuck."

"Did you see it?" asked Sal.

"No." Marmion shook his head. With his thoughts focused on something other than the two of them, the Warden seemed much less defensive, although never truly comfortable. "Nor did we see your father. We could only sit and wait for Kail to find us, in the hope that he could get the buses going again. He couldn't. He's never seen anything like this before. Neither has Banner. Hopefully, she and Tom can get us moving again soon, otherwise we'll have to continue on foot, thereby losing our only advantage."

His voice was full of frustration, which Shilly could understand. To have been so close to the Homunculus and then have it snatched out of his grasp must have been galling. And now she and Sal had appeared, adding to his problems.

"Who is Kail, exactly?" asked Sal.

"Habryn Kail is a tracker from Camarinha. They get a lot of strange things spilling over from the Divide up there, and he knows the spoor of most of them. Or so he says. Seems to me there's not much skill in following something that leaves a trail two metres wide and travels in a perfectly straight line." Frustration turned querulous. "You two, travelling on your own, would probably catch it quicker than we would with all our impedimenta."

Shilly took pity on him. "But what would we do when we caught it? I presume you have some sort of plan."

Marmion, barely visible against the stars, bent down and picked up a stone. "You're still feeling the wake, right? This is several hours old. Can you imagine what it must be like standing next to the Homunculus?" He issued a sound that might have been a snort. "None of us are keen to jump uninformed into that situation. Until we can see it, even from a distance, and maybe work out what it wants, we're as much in the dark as you are."

The Warden threw the stone into the blackness. It clattered and skittered away.

Shilly could appreciate his position. No living thing could get rid of the Change entirely as, by definition, that which didn't change couldn't be alive, but it left the exact nature of the Homunculus still very much in question.

"No plan, then," she said.

"Not as such," he said, as sombre as the dead night around them. "Still want to help us?"

"Sounds like you're going to need it."

The revving of an engine came from the impromptu campsite. Light spilled across the rugged ground, catching Marmion for an instant then sweeping elsewhere. An afterimage of the Warden remained frozen in her eyesight briefly. He didn't look especially relieved by the latest development.

"Let's get back," he said. "I want to follow Tom's progress."

They followed him out of the Homunculus's wake. The background levels of the Change swept over them again and she felt Sal physically relax beside her.

She wasn't so easily reassured. The little they had learned about the Homunculus only served to make her more worried, not less. What else could it do, if it put its mind to it? Where was it going, and why? What would they find waiting for them when they caught up with it? And where was Highson amongst all this craziness?

The only thing she was certain of was that they were caught up in the world again. She thought of Fundelry, and her heart ached.

THE QUARTERMASTER

"The Age of Machines never ended; the magic that drove it simply stopped working. Since then, Humanity has learned a new magic and built new machines— and so we will do again, should the Cataclysm strike a second time."
THE BOOK OF TOWERS, FRAGMENT 129

A heavy pounding at his door woke Skender from a deep sleep. At first he thought the sound came from inside his head, and he rolled over with a groan, cursing himself for drinking too much the night before. Memories of Chu and Magister Considine faded in and out of focus. He was unsure how much of it was real. Perhaps he had dreamed the whole thing.

The hammering persisted. Staggering to his feet, he crossed the tiny room and opened the door.

"For you." A dark-skinned youth thrust a thick envelope into Skender's hand.

"Uh, thanks." The messenger didn't wait for a tip. Skender shut the door and retreated into his room, turning the envelope over in his hands. It was marked with a large, important-looking seal in red wax and had his name written in ornate fashion on the front.

He didn't need to open it to know what it was. Its prompt arrival suggested that his memories were as accurate as ever.

"Curse it," he muttered, collapsing back onto his bed and wishing he were dead. His eyes felt hot and heavy. The leftovers of dinner—aromatic meatballs and spicy vegetable wraps—formed an acidic, oily residue in his stomach that simply didn't bear thinking about.

There came another knock at the door.

"Go away!" he said. "Haven't I suffered enough?"

"Hardly," returned a familiar voice. "I've barely started on you."

He groaned and hauled himself up. Chu stood outside his door clad in her flying uniform. Her bright, laughing eyes took him in with one up-down sweep.

"Nice underwear. And skinny is good for flying. You could use a bit of muscle, though. We'll work on that this morning."

He retreated from her relentless energy and fell face-forward onto the bed. "I'm not planning on doing anything this morning, except quietly dying."

"Nonsense." She followed him into the room and shut the door behind her. "You've got a mother to rescue."

"She can wait."

"What about me, then? Don't you want to show me what you're made of?"

"You already know. I'm a stone-boy, and I'll drop like a stone if you push me off that tower."

"Maybe, maybe not. There's only one way to find out."

He could feel her looking at him, and pictured her with hands on hips, lips pursed in prim amusement. All trace of the previous evening's gloomy backlash had apparently vanished.

"Why are you so bloody perky?"

"I'm a morning person. And I figure that if I do right by you, it'll look good on my record. How could the Magister turn me down then?"

He groaned. Nothing had changed. He was still a pawn; a means to her selfish end.

She hauled him back onto his feet. "Come on. Brush your hair and clean your teeth. Fill a water bottle. We'll rustle up some breakfast and then start training. It's not like we have forever, you know."

He gave in. She was right, and unstoppable. The chance of getting any more rest with her around was nonexistent. He might as well submit and get it over with.

And maybe, he told himself, he'd feel better after one of those noxious potions the locals called coffee.

"Is this what I think it is?" she asked, picking the envelope off the bed as he struggled with the lacings of his robe.

"Open it and see."

She did so with one deft swipe of a fingernail and withdrew the thick sheath of papers, flattening them out on her lap. A corner of something black poked out of one side.

"'Name: Skender Van Haasteren the Tenth. Address: the Keep. Age: sixteen.' Hey, that's the same as me. I thought you were younger."

"Just naturally immature," he said. "Look, why don't you take it? I've got no use for it."

"It doesn't work that way." Her eyes scanned the rest of the form. "Excellent. I was hoping they'd do that."

"What?"

"They've given you a standard miner's licence, probationary for three months. You're subject to the same regulations I was."

"So?"

"That means you're rated to carry a passenger." She folded the papers and put them in the envelope, which she stuffed in a pocket at the back of her pants. "Ready? Good. Let's use some of that Interior coin of yours to fill our bellies. And then, my friend—" she clapped his back loud enough to make his head ring, "—you and I are going to soar like birds."

The first stop after breakfast was a small storage facility near the base of the Wall. Skender was acutely conscious of the fact that the Divide was just a stone's throw away as he followed Chu down steep staircases and along circuitous lanes, angling further and further downhill. The memory of sky retreated until barely a glimmer of natural light filtered down through the layers of awnings, overhangs, and walkways.

Laure, he was beginning to realise, was a city that had been built over, over and over, since the Cataclysm. Once the Wall went up and protected the land inside it from the depredations of the Divide, reconstruction had been vigorous and long-lasting as people moved from the tilted buildings of the Old City and created the New. Bridges and ramps overlapped streets, which in turn wound around stairwells and buried accessways. The air was thick and heavy down there, drenched in many different scents, perfumed and pungent both. They were headed for the very bottom.

"I know it doesn't look like much, but it is secure," Chu said as they came to a series of small, locked metal doors, none of them matching, at a dead end that looked like it was a home for stray cats. The ancient cobbles were buried under years of accumulated grime and rubbish.

Chu pulled a key from a pocket and used it to open the third door along. Inside was her wing, neatly folded and collapsed like a moth in a cocoon. She told him where to grip, and together they lifted it up. It was as large as a person, yet surprisingly light. One person could have lifted it easily, but two definitely made the task easier.

He carried the rear end as they retraced their steps through the city. The light grew brighter, and the wing seemed to come to life. Faint traceries of colour appeared on the thin fabric, shifting and blending like oil on water. Its many struts and control surfaces were a translucent amber colour and flexed smoothly under his fingers. What he had assumed at first to be wood and canvas turned out to be something very different indeed. It looked organic rather than human-made, as if its many pieces had assembled naturally. But as well as its beauty, he saw where it had been damaged. The skin had torn away from the struts in several places; the central, largest strut was kinked in the middle, like a hunchback. Instead of a newborn butterfly waiting to inflate its wings and take to the sky, it seemed more like an injured bird, huddling around itself for protection.

"Where are we taking it?" he asked Chu.

"The armoury."

"Is it far?" Although lightweight for its size, the folded wing was growing heavier with every step.

"Remember that tower we looked at yesterday? The one you reckon you'll drop like a stone from?"

Skender rolled his eyes. "Yes."

"The armoury is on ground level."

"Why is it called the armoury? Do you carry weapons when you fly?"

"Why would you? When you're above someone, all you really need is a rock and a good eye. And you're usually too busy flying to fight anyone. We've just always called it the armoury. It's where we go to be kitted out for mining."

"Will I have to wear a suit like yours?"

"Don't you like the look of it?"

"I didn't say that." On her it looked good, but the thought of wrapping all that tight leather around himself made him sweat in advance.

She laughed. "You only have to wear it if you want to; otherwise, we can tie your robes to your legs so they won't tangle. That's sure to impress the girls."

"You know that's the least of my concerns."

"I doubt it. You *are* sixteen, after all."

"So are you."

"No argument there. I'm wearing the leather, aren't I?"

He shifted his grip uncomfortably. "Tell me how you damaged your wing."

"Ah. Well, it was a dare. Someone said I couldn't steal an egg from the nests at the top of Observatory Tower, and obviously I had to prove him wrong."

"Obviously. What was his name?" he asked, wondering if this was the same "some people" she had been complaining about the previous night.

"Kazzo Niclais. Do you know how high Observatory Tower is?"

"Not exactly. I've seen it, though." There was no way he could miss it. The tower speared upward from the centre of the New City and stood at least twice as high as any of the other buildings. It was circular, externally featureless, and tapered slightly as it rose. Just below the top was a fat sphere, like a fish egg impaled on a pin, which he assumed contained the instruments that earned the tower its name. What the yadachi did with them he didn't know; bent the weather to their collective will, or tried to, he assumed. "Bird's nest up there?"

"Safest place for hundreds of kilometres," she said. "Safer than the mountains. The only predators are each other. The eggs are supposed to be particularly potent, medicinally, *masculinely* speaking—if you know what I mean."

"I get the idea."

"Even the broken shells that fall naturally from the nests fetch a fair price on the black market. So there were sufficient incentives to give it a go."

"You don't have to justify yourself to me."

She glanced at him, sharply, perhaps wondering if he was mocking her. He wasn't. "We're a competitive bunch, miners. There's hardly anyone over twenty, for a start, and there are a lot of boys, because they're stronger and have a natural advantage. That's a bad mix. When you're a girl trying to make her way, you have to take these things seriously because everyone else does—even if it's completely stupid. Even if it means trying to capture a stationary target at speed in high winds, when the slightest mistake would mean falling a horribly long way to your death."

"Sounds worse than the Divide."

"Exactly. At least there we don't have eagles pecking at us for trying to steal their eggs." She shrugged. "Anyway, that was the problem. I got the winds right; I managed the ascent perfectly, spiralling from updraft to updraft until I was level with the nests; I dodged the worst of the turbulence around the big ball and found a nest with eggs in it that I could reach okay. I even got my fingers on one of them—a big blue egg with brown spots, as wide across as my palm. It was so warm against my skin; I can still feel it.

"And that's when it happened. This giant bird attacks me from above—the one direction I can't see. Puts holes all along my dorsal stabilisers and sends me crashing into the tower. Next thing I know, my wing is almost useless and I'm falling. Not a good position to be in."

"I can imagine." And he could, all too well. It wasn't the sort of thing he wanted to think about prior to his first attempt.

"Luckily, the safety charms caught in time, giving me a measure of control. I crash-landed through the roof of a water tower. Hurt like buggery and tore the wing up a little more, but at least I wasn't dead."

"And the egg?" he asked.

"I must've let it go when the bird attacked, so I had nothing to show for my efforts except a bunch of scratches and broken wings— and then a maintenance bill for the water tower, fines for polluting a city reservoir, repair costs on the wing, and a licence renewal final notice. It really wasn't my week."

"What about Kazzo?"

"If you listen carefully," she said sourly, "you can still hear him laughing."

Skender felt for her, knowing the power of peer group pressure. He had seen and been involved in many foolish pranks at his father's school. One boy had been lucky to escape with his life after a similar stunt went wrong: slipping down a barren cliff face while searching for a rare type of beetle supposedly imbued with supernatural powers. In his case the goad had been unrequited love, not prestige, but the effect was the same. People pushed themselves to the limit for no good reason, and in the process either got themselves killed or learned a lesson about their limitations that would stop them getting killed the next time.

Skender had a perfectly good reason for going out on his particular limb, but he still didn't feel happy about it.

"So we go to the armoury and get the wing fixed," he said. "Then what? You're not seriously suggesting we fly across the Divide together, are you?"

"Well, that's the obvious plan. I'll admit I'm having trouble thinking of another one. How about you?"

"I'll let you know if I do."

"Don't take offence, but I'm not holding out much hope of that."

"I won't," he said. "Neither am I."

The Magister continued to be as good as her word. The armoury had received the authorisation to proceed with whatever repairs Chu required, at the city's expense. The quartermaster—a hairless giant of a man with bulging muscles and elaborate tattoos—instructed them to bring the broken wing into his workshop. Skender brought up the rear as they wound their way past steaming vats, glowing forges, straining bellows, and heat-blackened anvils. It looked more like a smithy than the sort of place where fine workmanship could be performed. But Skender was to be surprised on many points. Not only was the quartermaster astonishingly skilful at the most delicate of tasks—his blunt fingers cradling instruments that looked as though they might snap at the slightest touch—but he did so with a sure and certain knowledge of the Change.

The first thing the quartermaster did when they reached his workshop was lay the wing on a broad table and stretch it out to its full extent. It unfurled with a soft sigh. Five metres across and three long at its deepest point, tapering to slender points at either trailing edge, it didn't look strong enough to hold a person, but the harness of soft leather straps and clasps was clearly designed to do so.

The quartermaster then ran his hand along a line of tuning forks hanging from the wall, ranging from the minuscule to one as large as his forearm. Making a selection from the smaller end, he tapped it against the table and placed its base on the nose of the wing. Two slightly different notes sang softly through the workshop, crystalline in their dissonance.

"A little flat," observed Chu.

"Not good," said the quartermaster, wrinkling his broad face as he concentrated on the fading tones. His words were clipped and to the point. "Structural damage. You've been careless."

"I know," she admitted. There was no attempt to bluster her way out of the situation. "It's a mistake I won't make again."

The quartermaster nodded. "I can fix her."

"Thank the Goddess. How long?"

"Five hours. I will need your help."

"You've got it." Chu glanced at Skender. "My friend here is Skender Van Haasteren. He's a Stone Mage, if that's of any use."

"I'm not—"

She shushed him as the quartermaster's surprisingly small eyes studied his face. He felt as though he was being appraised by a walking mountain.

"Van Haasteren, eh?" The quartermaster nodded. "It doesn't matter. Stone and air don't mix."

"That's what I think," he said, "but no one else seems to agree."

"He'll be the pilot," said Chu, clearly unhappy at having to admit such a thing. "I'm just going for the ride."

"He'd better stay, then." The blunt head nodded. "Watch. Learn. Don't interfere." The quartermaster turned back to Chu. "Wash your hands and we'll begin."

She did as she was told without question. Skender took a seat on an empty bench, from where he watched the quartermaster's dexterous fingers move over the wing's injuries, testing the wounds and determining the best means of repairing them. Skender couldn't tell what was going on half the time. The quartermaster employed a unique mix of drawn and sung charms: the former were applied with a series of bizarre-looking tools; the latter he hummed as he worked. The gently exotic melodies tugged at Skender's concentration and made his thoughts drift. Rhythms drifted in and out of synchrony with his heartbeat. He felt dizzy, then sleepy, then anxious and on edge.

He was on the fringe of powerful yet subtle Change-working—which did not involve, he was relieved to note, bloodletting of any kind. Before his eyes the torn fabric healed, the damaged struts straightened. Chu took off her jacket and attended the quartermaster's every wish as morning became noon, and noon became afternoon. She never complained of hunger or fatigue while being ordered to hold down firmly here, to prise apart there. She was obedient in complete defiance of her character—or so it seemed to Skender. Only as he watched for some time did he realise that her behaviour was in fact perfectly consistent with her love of flying. This was the means by which she would get back into the air. She wasn't going to make it any harder for herself than it had to be.

Her smooth hands moved from place to place with the grace of birds. She brushed her hair back behind her ears and wiped sweat from her eyes. She was as lithe as an acrobat and as wiry as a camel trainer. He had never met anyone like her before. The Goddess only knew what she thought of *him*, but he was trying not to worry about that. It was too distracting.

Time passed and Skender's eyes drifted closed. He dreamed that he was being sewn into a giant seagull costume with translucent, dragonfly wings. But his arms were tied to his sides so he couldn't reach the controls, and when he tried to explain the problem he found that he couldn't open his mouth. The bird suit became a coffin, a stone sarcophagus with a tight-fitting lid. The lid swung shut as his mother and father tipped it over the cliff. Then he was falling and falling and he didn't know when he was going to hit the ground . . .

He was woken by the crash. The pain came an instant later. He had slumped off the bench and toppled to the floor.

"Ow!" He sat up, rubbing his head.

"When you're done catching up on your z's," said Chu, "I need a hand here."

He clambered gracelessly to his feet. His eyes were as thick and heavy as his thoughts.

"How long was I—?"

"Irrelevant. Come hold this." She waved him closer and placed his hands under the left wing. He cradled it as gently as he could while she peered along the leading edge.

"You snore," she observed in an aside.

"I do not."

"Are you calling me a liar? And stop wobbling. I'm trying to make sure it's straight."

Skender's face felt as red as an overripe apple. "Where's the quartermaster?"

"He went to get some straps to finish the harness."

"You mean . . ." He cast his eye along the wing. All the rents were mended; all the struts curved just right. "So fast."

"The Magister isn't paying him for his time. She's paying him for his knowledge—and that's substantial. What he can do in a day would take anyone else weeks to accomplish." She shrugged. "Luckily for us, the major charms hadn't dissipated yet and the bulk of the structure was sound. If I'd left her too much longer, she would've needed a complete refit."

Chu ran a loving hand along the smooth top of the wing. It gleamed under her fingertips. "It's good to see her whole again."

The quartermaster returned and attached a second harness to the first. Even repaired, the wing didn't seem strong enough to support one person, let alone two people in tandem. But the quartermaster insisted.

"Two at least, Change willing." He washed his giant hands in a bucket of water and splashed the grime from his face. Droplets trickled into his eyes unheeded. They stared at Skender with something like regret. "You will fly. It's up to you for how long."

"You told me to watch," Skender told him. "Watch and learn. Was there anything I missed that's particularly important?"

"It's all important," the quartermaster said, folding up the wing so they could carry it again, "but the most important is to know what it takes to undo mistakes. Crash her again and even I might not be able to fix her. She'll be ugly junk, fit for nothing. So take care, young Stone Mage. Listen to your friend, and to your heart. And fly well."

It was a surprisingly long speech for someone who had barely spoken a dozen words in sequence before now. His rough sincerity moved Skender sufficiently that, for once, he didn't object to the persistence of Chu's shameless exaggeration of his rank.

"I'll try," he said.

"We'll bloody well do better than that," Chu said. "Come on. Don't wait for him to give us the bill. Let's get out of here and up into the sky."

The quartermaster turned to the next wing awaiting repair. He didn't watch them work their way to the door. Only at the last moment did Skender briefly glance around and notice that the quartermaster's left leg terminated in a wooden prosthetic.

When he raised the matter with Chu as they were lugging the wing up the long, winding staircase to the launching platforms, she nodded grimly.

"I don't know exactly what happened," she said, "but he lost it in the accident that ruined his wing. He's been grounded ever since."

"Couldn't he just fix the wing, or build a new one?"

"He could've yes, but there wasn't much point. Not without his leg."

"Why not? Wouldn't it make *more* sense to fly when you're crippled, not less?" He pictured the quartermaster soaring through the clouds, unencumbered by one less of his heavy, muscled limbs.

"It doesn't work like that," she said again. "You'll see."

"Not by crashing and losing a leg, I hope."

"No. Here's hoping, anyway."

It seemed to take them hours to reach the top. The stairs were steep and they took turns at being fore or aft to preserve their backs. Rest stops came with increasing frequency. Only as they neared the end of the stairwell did Chu explain that there was another way to get there, one involving counterweights and pulleys that took no more energy than crossing a room.

"So why are we bothering with all this? Why nearly kill ourselves when it's not necessary?"

"I think it's necessary. Consider it an initiation. You need to be acutely aware of how high you are before you take off. Otherwise you might get careless. I want you nice and primed before I put my life in your hands."

"I thought it was the other way around."

"You're the one with the licence, stone-boy."

"But you'll be doing the actual flying, right?"

"It doesn't work like that," she said a third time.

He felt like a kite on a line, tugged and jerked about by her slim hand. "Isn't it about time you told me how it *does* work?"

"Much easier to show than tell. Be patient. We'll be there soon."

He didn't clarify the point that he wasn't so much impatient as terrified. It seemed a perfectly appropriate response to his situation.

Fading sunlight greeted them when they reached the top. He staggered out of the stairwell and put his end of the wing down on the ground to catch his breath. They were standing at the rear of the uppermost platform, looking south. To his left, nightfall turned the sky orange over a forest of spires, chimneys, and onion-shaped roofs. Observatory Tower out-reached all of them, giving the skyline a focus and the flyers a ready point of reference. Silhouetted against the sunset were a number of gliding shapes as miners returned to the city from the Divide, sweeping in to land on their level or one of the others below. The air was full of the sound of voices, the rattle of wings, and the clatter of thin, hooklike tools with which he assumed they snatched prizes from the Divide floor.

"It's going to be dark soon," he said, feeling the wind stiffen around him.

"The best time to fly." Chu secured the straps of her uniform. "Less traffic."

"We won't see much."

"That's not our intention, this first time. It's just a practice run. Tomorrow we do the real work."

If we're still alive, Skender thought. Marginally rested, he bent down to pick up his end. "Let's get this over with."

She punched him on the shoulder. "Not exactly the spirit I'm looking for, but it'll do."

Together they carried their awkward burden to a clear area of the platform well away from the other flyers. There the two of them unfurled the wing and made sure everything was secure. Chu checked the repaired struts and fussed with the harnesses. As the sky grew darker, her adjustments became progressively finer until he could barely see what changes she was making.

"Well, well," said a voice from behind him. "This is an unexpected development."

Skender let go of the wing and turned to see a leather-clad flyer standing nearby. He was a full head taller than Skender and elegantly muscled with it. His blue uniform hugged his body, except where it hung open down his chest, revealing an extensive network of angular black tattoos crisscrossing his skin. His hands were also tattooed, as was his face behind the beginnings of a reddish beard. Skender had rarely seen such extensive work, even on the most charm-mad Stone Mages. His eyes were a deep, impenetrable black.

Chu looked up from her work, then glanced pointedly back down. "What do you want, Kazzo?"

"Nothing, Chu. I'm just concerned for your well-being. The last time you went flying, you ended up impersonating a drowned cat being pulled out of a reservoir. Looks like you've landed on your feet. Does this mean you're back for good?"

"Only so long as it takes me to get out of your face."

Kazzo laughed. "Perhaps you should try the mountains, if you're looking for easier nests. Do send us a clutch of eggs when you get there."

"You need them that badly, do you?"

"That's not what Liris says."

Skender could only see Chu's face in profile, but the effect Kazzo's remark had on her was pronounced. She froze in midmovement and her jaw muscles worked.

"I think you should leave her alone," said Skender, hearing the words as they came out of his mouth but not believing he was actually saying them.

"You're a long way from home, stone-boy," said Kazzo with a scornful glance. "What you think isn't relevant."

Skender had seen Kazzo's type plenty of times, but had yet to find a good way to deal with them. Standing up to them would only start a fight, while backing down would set a dangerous precedent, one the bully would call on every time they met.

Skender wiped his hands on his robes and didn't look away.

"That's Stone *Mage* to you, Kazzo Niclais," he said.

The tall miner performed a barely perceptible double take. Skender could practically hear the cogs turning as Kazzo considered calling his bluff. Laure might be a long way from the deeper deserts, but a Mage was not someone to lock horns with lightly. The Interior possessed considerable political weight even where the Change was weakest.

A young woman on the far side of the platform called Kazzo's name. The tall miner broke their stare and flashed a diffident wave at her. Skender wondered if he saw a hint of relief in his eyes.

"Yes, well," Kazzo drawled, "I'll leave you two lovebirds to get better acquainted. You won't have long before the ground takes you. Better make it count."

He swaggered away, affecting utter unconcern. Skender let out the breath he was holding and wiped a hand across his forehead. *Lovebirds?*

Then Chu was standing next to him, watching Kazzo's retreating back.

"I can fight my own battles," she said, "but thank you, anyway."

He looked at her, and was surprised to see something very much like tears in her eyes.

"You're welcome," he said.

"Whatever. Now, come here," she said, tugging him to the far side of the wing. "The waiting is finally over."

She forced him to stand still while she raised the wing into position at his back. As the leather straps of the harness fastened over his shoulders and around his waist, he was dismayed at the thought of his own weight. How he and the wing—and Chu—were supposed to stay aloft for even a second was beyond him. He felt tired and irritated. And very, very heavy.

Some things are simply more important, his father had said. Finding his mother was more important than his fear, he told himself. Even if he died trying.

They didn't talk about Kazzo. They didn't talk at all.

When the harness was in place, she stepped back to look at him. With a water bottle tied around his neck he felt like a very ugly moth. The wing extended in a rigid sheet behind his back, vanishing to the periphery of his vision when he looked directly forward. His arms hung at his sides. He had expected them to be lashed to the underside of the wing in a grotesque parody of bird-flight, but he was spared that indignity. As promised, his robes were firmly strapped where they wouldn't get in the way. A cool breeze trickled up his left leg.

"Remarkable," she said. "You look almost convincing." Someone whistled from the far side of the platform. Laughter smattered. "Ignore those idiots. Here's where you find out why I can't fly you in this wing." She reached into her back pocket and produced the envelope she had stashed there. "This is your licence. Only you can use it."

"What difference does it make whose name is on the piece of paper?"

"It's not just paper." Chu pulled the papers out, selected one, and put the others back in her pocket. She held up the one she had kept so he could see. It was black, not white, and looked more like cured hide than paper. "This is what matters. The rest is just bureaucracy. Hold still."

She came closer and pulled the neck of his robe wide. He tried not to flinch, realising then how naive he'd been. Flying wasn't as simple as sticking on a wing and jumping into the air. If it was, people would be doing it whenever and wherever they felt like it. They would be launching in droves from the stone windowsills and verandahs of the Keep, swooping like eagles among his home's stony crags.

He turned his face away as she pressed the black sheet to his chest. It was cool and moist against his skin. A tingle of the Change rushed through his veins. Chu stared fixedly at him, at whatever transformation began in him.

The tingling became stronger. He felt as though ants with red-hot feet were crawling out of his chest and spreading across the rest of his body, burning him where they passed. His muscles tensed. Breath hissed between his teeth. Chu gripped his shoulders and held him steady. He couldn't make his arms work properly to hold her in return.

One glimpse of his hands told him what was happening. Sinuous black lines spread down both wrists, wriggling and twisting like streamers in a gale. They crossed and recrossed on his palms, coiled around his fingers, flexed like mathematical grids on his knuckles.

Something black slid across his vision, snuffing out the world. He cried out at the sudden blindness, giving in to a subtle, insidious terror: that he had been too trusting; that Chu meant him ill; that his mother would be lost because he was trapped in a malevolent web that he had willingly walked into. He cursed himself for letting the yadachi take blood from him so easily. Surely he could have found another way into the city. Who knew what dreadful hex they had placed on him as a result?

Then Chu's breath was in his ear. "Relax," she whispered. "Almost there."

Despite his doubts, he believed her. Whatever she had done to him, it had to be for a reason. She needed him to fly in order to get her

THE TRACKER

**"Warden and Mage have ever been at odds.
Their natures demand it. Sea pounds at stone, wearing
it down, while fire boils water, dissolving it in air.
The alchemical war is as old as the world,
as old as the elements themselves."**
THE BOOK OF TOWERS, EXEGESIS 15:7

"There's only one way to catch the Homunculus," Habryn Kail said, unfolding a map on the dirt and pinning it flat with rocks at each corner. "Following it won't work. Get much closer than we already have, and we'll be caught in the same trap that killed our buses. We have to get in front of it—and we have to do it right, this time. No splitting up; no hedging our bets. We have to be completely committed to the attempt or we might as well give up and go home."

Sal watched the reactions of the wardens to this bald declaration. The ring of dirty faces, lit from below by the glowing mirrors, watched the tall tracker in exhausted silence. The emptiness of the Broken Lands was a fitting accompaniment to the grimness of Kail's opinion.

"I haven't the strength to argue with you," said Warden Marmion. His eyes were sunken. What hair remained on his head hung limp and greasy. "What do you suggest we do?"

"We prepare a trap. Something that doesn't rely on the Change to spring or stay shut. Something it won't anticipate."

"Do you have anything in mind?"

"I have an idea. It depends on where we set the trap, though."

"You have some thoughts in that regard, too, I presume."

"I do." Kail took a stub of pencil lead and drew a line on the map from the Haunted City across the Strand. "This is the path the thing is following. We know it hasn't deviated more than a few degrees throughout its journey. I feel confident in assuming that it won't change its habits in the near future. I propose, therefore, that we can make a guess at its ultimate destination. There or nearby I hope to take it by surprise."

Sal leaned over the map, the better to see what the tracker was driving at. The bold straight line of the Homunculus's path sliced across empty landscape until it crossed the old road they themselves had followed from Moombin. They had been far enough behind it to avoid the effect of its wake, otherwise they might have suffered the same fate as Banner and the others. Their paths crossed again when he, Shilly, and Tom had turned north on the approach to the Broken Lands, and they would have crossed again had not Banner waved them down.

Projected ahead, the line exited the Broken Lands and continued over vacant countryside until it hit the Divide. The Divide zigged and zagged from west to east like a lightning bolt through earth, unmistakable for anything natural. The Homunculus's path struck the great rent just west of a sharp one-hundred-and-thirty-degree bend. Marked on the map, on the northern flank of the bend, was a small dot. There was nothing else for hundreds of kilometres in any direction.

"What's that?" asked Shilly, leaning on Sal to point at the dot.

"According to the map," said Kail, "it's a city called Laure."

"Never heard of it."

"I have, but I've not been there. It has an ill reputation."

"For what?"

"Isolationism. And other things."

"And you think that's where it's headed?" asked Marmion before Sal could press for more information.

"Its path is too direct to be a coincidence." Kail looked down at him. "Whether it's going there of its own accord or following some obscure directive from Highson, that doesn't concern us. As long as we know *where* it's going, we can make an effort to head it off on this side of the Divide."

Sal felt eyes turn to him, perhaps waiting for him to elaborate on his father's motives. He was unable to. Highson and he had exchanged not a single word for five years. His father's state of mind was as unknown to him now as it had always been.

"That sounds like a plan," he said.

"A plan that hinges on our ability to travel," said Marmion, turning to Banner.

"The damage is fixed, for the most part," the Engineer said, her face smudged with grease. "We're recharging the reservoirs from Tom's buggy. That shouldn't take long—an hour or so at the most. We'll have enough to get to Laure."

Tom agreed with a nod.

"Good." Marmion stood for a moment with his hand on his chin, considering the map. "I don't really see that we have much choice but to try. Get us ready to roll as soon as the buses are charged. Habryn and I will work out the details of the trap as we go."

"Can we call ahead?" asked Shilly, leaning on her cane to Marmion's right. "There might be someone in Laure who can help us."

"Wrong side of the Divide," said the Warden, dismissing the suggestion without giving it even a second thought. "We're on our own out here."

Sal opened his mouth to protest.

"Yes?" said Marmion, noticing the movement.

A moment's reconsideration convinced Sal that there was no point arguing. From Marmion's point of view, they *were* on their own. The ideological divide between the Strand and the Interior was as deep and wide as the actual Divide. Wars had been fought over it—and people like Lodo and Sal had been exiled or worse for defying it. It was simpler sometimes to go with the flow, even if that meant ignoring a potential source of aid.

"Would you like us to be part of this?" he asked instead.

"I assume you will be, whether I want you to or not." Marmion's expression was unreadable. "Don't worry. I'll call on you when you're needed."

"Gee," said Shilly, "it's nice to be appreciated."

Marmion didn't respond. "Tom, Banner, you know what to do. The rest of us will make sure we're packed and ready to go in one hour." He turned away.

"Do you believe this guy?" Shilly muttered to Sal as the group dispersed.

"I don't have any choice." Sal put an arm around her and sighed. The closed-mind attitude of the Sky Warden brought back familiar frustrations: from the outside, a school of thought might appear to be an immovable mountain, but its very inflexibility meant it could evaporate into thin air if challenged the right way. From the inside it looked like there *was* no outside.

"I suppose we could just cut ahead and get to Laure ahead of them," he said.

She looked up at him. "Is that what you want to do?"

"Well, it would give us a chance to get Highson away before Marmion finds him. That might be his only chance."

"But . . . ?"

"But if we get tangled up with the Homunculus, we might make things worse for everyone. Whatever it wants in Laure, we have only one chance to stop it. Do you know how we can do that? I don't. Unless Marmion comes up with a plan we really hate, I think our best bet is to stick with him for now."

"It's Kail *I'll* be listening to," Shilly said, poking a hole in the dirt with the tip of her cane and tipping a small stone into it.

Sal watched the tall tracker as he moved from vehicle to vehicle, checking supplies and testing ropes. The buses rested on six chunky tires with a low centre of gravity and looked hardy enough to weather any sort of terrain; battered black paintwork suggested they were frequently required to. The other Wardens cleaned up the remains of a hasty meal and stowed their utensils with the rest of their equipment. Tom was already busy under the frame of one of the buses, scribbling charms and making arcane mechanical adjustments. Sal could sense the flow of the Change through the engines as a strange buzzing underneath the rhythmic thudding of their many parts. Although Sal had once known how to strip and clean the engine of his adopted father's buggy, he lacked the real mastery of an Engineer. He could tell the buses weren't working properly, but he had no idea how to fix them.

Shilly stepped closer to Sal and embraced him. He relished her warmth in the chill of a desert night. "You told me I was bossy, once. I hope you don't think I'm as bad as Marmion."

Sal kissed the crown of her head, where her hair was darkest. "If I did, I would've left you at home."

"And hated every moment of it." She smiled up at him. "I know you, Sayed. You'd have blown someone up by now, if I wasn't here."

"That's still a possibility." The remark came out less wittily than he had intended it. Being around Sky Wardens again put him on edge. Cooperating with them went against every instinct in his body.

You'd better truly need help, Highson Sparre, he thought as they walked back to the buggy, *or there'll be a reckoning between us.*

As they waited for the Sky Wardens to be ready, Shilly and Sal had little to do. Shilly rested her leg on the back seat of the buggy and closed her eyes.

She felt Sal withdraw from her as he sat in the buggy's front passenger seat. His posture didn't change, but his mind had gone elsewhere. She sensed him looking for his father through the Change, reaching out beyond the Broken Lands and across the open countryside; looking for the man who had not just given him life, but had also given him a chance to live that life in freedom. She wished she could help him, but she didn't know Highson well enough to have a hope of finding him. Looking for an unfamiliar mind in an unfamiliar place was like searching for a sliver of soap in a murky bath with gloved hands. She was more likely to find a rock that looked like him, or a lizard that smelled like him, than she was to find the real thing. Possessing a biological connection to Highson, only Sal had a chance.

He sagged after half an hour, giving up the quest. He was as tired as she was; as all of them were. The thought of setting off in rapid pursuit at any moment made her feel wearier than ever.

A shadow fell over her, blotting out the stars. She looked up at the towering silhouette of Habryn Kail.

"I'd like a quiet word with you two," he said, "and I'm guessing you can spare the time."

She sat up. "Sure." Sal turned as Kail folded his elongated frame into the seat next to Shilly. The buggy shifted on its suspension under his weight. His long, craggy face was close to Shilly and she was surprised by the smoothness of his skin. She had expected him to be as weathered as Aunty Merinda, whose face looked like a pear that had been left in the sun too long. Kail's face was a well-worn but well-oiled boot, flexible and far from infirm.

His eyes were violet, a colour she had never seen before.

"Where we're headed," he said, "it's dangerous."

"We know," said Shilly. "We're still going."

He raised a hand. It looked as long as her forearm. "I'm not trying to talk you out of it. Having you along, Sal, is only going to make things easier when we do find Highson, since he won't be so likely to run if he knows you're with us. I want to talk to you about something else—about the Homunculus, and what's inside it."

"Do you have any idea what it is?" Sal asked.

Kail shrugged, his broad, bony shoulders lifting under his cotton shirt. "I'm keeping my mind open on that one. As you should, too. All we really know is that it's heading for Laure and it can somehow neutralise the Change. In forty years of patrolling the Divide, I've seen a lot of things. Some of them have names; others defy any attempt to define them. While I can't say I've seen anything quite so driven as this, I *have* encountered creatures that ate the Change as easily as we'd breathe air."

"Golems," said Shilly, thinking of the horrors she had seen in the Haunted City.

"Yes, and others. They'll take any charm you cast and twist it back on you like a snake. Or they'll suck you dry and make merry with what's left. I don't," he said, leaning forward for emphasis, "want to see either thing happen to you two."

"You don't have to worry about us," she said. "We've learned that lesson the hard way."

"I mean it," Kail said, looking mainly at Sal. "No matter what danger your father appears to be in, I don't want you throwing your weight around. That might only make it stronger. Understand?"

Sal was grim-faced. "You can trust us."

"Good." Kail sat back. "I do believe you. I just think it needs to be reiterated, and Marmion is too chickenshit to do it himself. Like, if he ignores what happened to Lodo, it'll all just go away."

A strange sensation swept through Shilly at the mention of her mentor's name. Five years ago, she had thought Lodo dead when he summoned an earthquake to help them escape the Alcaide, but the effort had only emptied his body. The creature that had taken Lodo over had later perished with it, dragged down into death by the last vestiges of Lodo's will. He had died in her arms on the beach at Fundelry, and lay buried there still.

"You know about Lodo?" she asked, her heart racing.

"Of course."

"Did you know him?"

Kail smiled. It didn't sit comfortably on his rugged features, but the emotion behind it was pure. "I wish I could say I had. He was quite notorious in his day. I was in my final year of the Novitiate and not doing quite as brilliantly as I'd hoped when he defected to the Interior. He provided a welcome distraction from my own problems."

Shilly hid her disappointment. The only thing Kail and Lodo had in common was their age. Even if they had been the best of friends, that didn't mean he would owe her any loyalty or friendship.

But she couldn't help that momentary twinge of hope. Her parents had abandoned her as a toddler, unable to cope with a brief flash of talent she had displayed before it burned out forever. She didn't remember them or know their names. She had, therefore, no family apart from Sal. Any connection to her past, even if it was secondhand, through Lodo, was something to treasure.

"He was unique," said Sal, "and he didn't deserve what happened to him. We'll be careful."

But Kail's eyes were on her, now.

"Did Lodo ever talk about his past?" he asked.

"No," she said. "It only came out when Sal arrived in Fundelry."

"What about family?"

She shook her head.

"Lodo had an older sister," Kail said, "and his sister had a son. I can tell by the look on your face that you're not aware of this."

"A sister?" Her mind momentarily baulked at the revelation. "A son?"

"They spurned him for casting shame upon the family, for being different. They behaved stupidly and heartlessly, without a doubt."

"What happened to them? Where are they now?"

"These days, Lodo's nephew likes to think he's leading this expedition. There are, however, plenty who disagree."

Shilly twisted in her seat to stare at Marmion. The balding warden was berating one of the younger Wardens for knocking over a box of supplies. She looked back at Kail, unable to suppress a stunned gape, and shook her head in denial.

"*Marmion?*" hissed Sal.

"Is a hapless peacock who would rather die than admit any disloyalty to the Alcaide. Look all you like, but I doubt you'll see any family resemblance."

"I don't believe it."

"You don't have to, and I'd rather you didn't tell anyone I told you this," Kail nodded sagely at Shilly, "but I thought you ought to know, all the same."

She just stared at him as he eased himself out of his seat and loped away.

They barely had time to assimilate the information Kail had given them when Marmion whistled and announced that the Wardens were ready to move. Tom and Banner had recharged the buses and added a barrage of protective charms in the hope of preventing a recurrence of the breakdown. Shilly stared at the balding Warden as he issued orders. Sal could tell that she was confused.

He wasn't sure what he thought, either. Marmion owed them no allegiance or enmity, regardless of how he was related to Lodo. But the existence of a blood connection did change things, if only in the way they perceived him. That he had failed to bring it up suggested that he didn't want to acknowledge it. Where did that leave Shilly, who wanted to know more about the man who had raised her? Should she ignore her new knowledge, or ignore Marmion's obvious, if unstated, wishes?

Tom returned to take the wheel of the buggy with Banner in tow.

"I'm riding with you three again," she said, swinging a small satchel into the back seat, "if that's okay with you."

Shilly made room for the Warden next to her. "No worries." Her tone was wooden.

Tom started the engine and awaited further instructions.

Marmion sauntered over. "You'll be our vanguard," he told them. "You're smaller and more mobile, so you can scout ahead."

They were also expendable, Sal thought. If the Homunculus's wake was still powerful enough to affect them, the Wardens would lose little.

"At the next junction," Marmion went on, "just before the end of the Broken Lands, take the left turn, north. Head westward off the road when you see the lights of Laure across the Divide. There'll be no chance of encountering the Homunculus on the way, since we'll be looping around from the east. Should it change course or do anything else unexpected, don't tackle it head-on. Let us overtake and deal with it. Understood?"

Tom and Banner nodded. Sal refused to commit himself. Shilly stared at the man as though trying to peel back his face and expose the connection to Lodo beneath.

Unaware of her scrutiny, Marmion hurried back to his bus and took the forward passenger seat. Habryn Kail sat behind the wheel of the second bus. At a signal, Tom dropped the buggy into gear and they trundled out of the hollow, back to the road.

The dirt surface showed no sign of either Homunculus or Highson Sparre. The only disturbances were skid marks where the Sky Wardens' buses had come to a sudden, dead halt in the Homunculus's wake. Sal held his breath as the buggy crossed that point, but either the wake had dissipated or Tom's new charms successfully repelled it. The engine didn't miss a beat.

Sal sank back into his seat as Tom accelerated through the Broken Lands. They were back on track, hunting Highson Sparre and the creature he had created. That was a good thing, but still not easy. Driving through the Broken Lands was difficult enough in the day; at night it could be deadly. Tom seemed to manage well enough, but Sal still felt a duty to be vigilant, too, watching out for potholes, cracks across the road, or odd patches of colour that might indicate quicksand and other hazards. Having now joined the quest to find Highson, the last thing he wanted was to be left behind with a broken axle.

Shilly slept, or pretended to. Banner's restless eyes took in the scenery, while the wind flattened her curly hair. Sal wished he could sleep, but apart from keeping Tom company, he also felt off-balance and ill at ease. They were rushing headlong to a collision with so many unknowns he could barely keep track of them all. He rotated Shilly's stick in his hands, finding comfort in its familiar textures.

"What do you know about Laure?" he asked Tom.

His friend shrugged. "A lot of artefacts come from the city. It's a great source of Ruin fragments and old machine parts. The people who live there scour the Divide and trade what they find for salt, coffee, spices, and so on."

"I thought the Divide was dangerous."

"It is, and there's no bridge across like there is at Tintenbar and the Lookout. Trade isn't, therefore, as commonplace as we'd like. That keeps the prices high."

"Do you think that's what the Homunculus is heading for, then? Something they found in the Divide?"

Warden Banner joined the discussion. "There was some talk a few weeks back of a major expedition in the area, but word hasn't come through of what they found."

"Maybe they disturbed something," Sal speculated, "and it's connected somehow to the Homunculus."

"Or to your father. Anything is possible," she said.

"What did Kail mean when he said the town has an ill reputation?"

Banner hesitated. "I've heard of Laure," she said over the engine noise, "but until last week I couldn't have pointed to it on a map. It was certainly somewhere I never wanted to go. Like a lot of border towns, it has to deal with things we can't imagine. Finding a safe way to explore the Divide is just part of it. People can be very resourceful when things like water and food are in short supply."

"What are you hinting at?" he pressed.

"Laure is ruled by bloodworkers," she said, bluntly. "'Yadachi' they call themselves. Unlike Mages and Wardens, they use the energy in blood to keep the city alive, and they take a Tithe annually from every citizen and every visitor on entry to make sure they have enough. They're not vampires and they don't kill people. But the method is—distasteful."

Sal stared at her for a long moment, wondering if she was being serious. Her expression left him in no doubt. "Why do people put up with it?"

"They don't have any choice, Sal. These are the borderlands. Everyone is weak here, so far from stone and sea. Don't you feel it? Are you really so immune?"

He knew what she was asking, but didn't know how to answer. The Change radiated from living things and flowed through the landscape. Some places possessed more background potential than others, and those particularly rich in the Change were frequently tapped into by practitioners living nearby. Different reservoirs had different flavours, and just as with food, people sometimes preferred one flavour to another. He himself had a natural tendency towards the teaching of the Stone Mages. Only a natural wildness and half a decade of study had taught him to see reliably beyond those inclinations.

This knowledge is more important than it sounds, Lodo had told him, an age ago. *In it lies understanding of the great rift that divides the Stone Mages and the Sky Wardens. It explains why the Strand and the Interior are the way they are—and why, even though skirmishes are common between both nations, one has never succeeded in taking over the other.*

We can't use each other's reservoirs. It's that simple, at the base of it. The Stone Mages draw forth the background potential from bedrock and store it in fire. Sky Wardens, on the other hand, weave into the air what they take from the sea. The sea, in short, is their reservoir. It may not obey their will, but it is theirs nonetheless. They can tap into it and read its humours; when they bathe in it they absorb some of its vitality; and when they die, they are cast back into it, to sink slowly into its depths and become one with the water again.

The further Banner was from the coast, the less potential she could access. On the northern side of the Divide, should she go that far, she would be powerless. The same would happen to a Stone Mage removed from the bedrock bones of the deep desert. The Divide marked the furthest extents of both Strand and Interior. The political reach of each country was therefore sharply delineated by the alchemical powers employed by their rulers—and that was partly why, Sal was sure, Marmion didn't want to call ahead to Laure for help.

But these were just conventions, conveniences, even contrivances. Sal had taught himself to follow his own instincts, and he had seen what both Wardens and Mages could do if they had to, no matter how far from home they were. Shom Behenna, the Sky Warden sent to capture him when he had escaped from the Syndic the first time, had been stripped of his rank for using the Change on the wrong side of the Divide. The last Sal had heard, he had been heading for the Interior with Mawson— the man'kin that Sal had set free from bondage to Sal's family—and Kemp, the albino bully who had helped them in the Haunted City.

The bloodworkers, the yadachi, were another alternative, another system of thought, albeit one that made him feel slightly squeamish.

Banner was watching him, waiting for an answer, her round, brown face more curious than hostile.

"Lodo taught me," he said, "that eventually the Change comes from one single source, no matter who's using it. Wardens and Mages have their differences, yes, but those differences are irrelevant. Someone who doesn't buy into either method of using the Change won't be limited by them. So no, I don't feel any different here than I would on the coast or in the desert, because I don't think the same way as you."

Banner nodded. "I've heard of wild talents and what they can do. They flare up and die out fast, breaking all the rules. And I'd heard of you, of course. It just seems so strange. I mean, water and stone are complete opposites. They can't be the same thing."

"So where does blood fit in? It's all in the way you're taught. If two people speak different languages, the words they use to describe the world can be very different. They won't understand each other, even if they're talking about the same thing. But the physical world remains the same. Language doesn't alter it. Why should it be otherwise with the Change?"

"Because the Change connects us to the world. It's not just a way of talking to each other. It binds us, shapes us, just as we bind and shape it in turn."

"We also bind ourselves. If you could look past your training and see the world as I do, you'd be free, too."

"I don't feel trapped." His choice of words clearly unnerved her. "Do you think of me as trapped?"

"I know you can only live on this side of the Divide. There's half a world beyond it that you're not likely to see, because of what you believe. I don't know if that's the same thing as being trapped, exactly, but it's definitely a shame."

Banner absorbed that for a while, frown lines creasing the skin between her eyebrows. She was clearly becoming keen to change the subject from Laure and its rulers and her own, perhaps fallacious, assumptions.

"What's the most beautiful thing you saw in the Interior?" she asked.

"The most beautiful thing . . ." He thought about it. "There was so much. The lights of Ulum; sunset over the mountains; the Nine Stars at midnight. It was all incredible. But you know what? Places aren't important. That's the problem with what you Sky Wardens have been taught—and the Stone Mages, too. Places are irrelevant to the Change. It's us who matter—us and the people around us—the inhabitants of the world that the Change makes possible. That's what we should concentrate on connecting with. And in those terms, the most beautiful thing I saw in the Interior is the same as the most beautiful thing I saw in the Strand. And it's not *Os*, the bone ship, or the glass towers of the Haunted City. It's not even the Change itself."

"I know what it is," said Tom, breaking unexpectedly into the conversation. "I know *who* it is."

Sal glanced rearward at Shilly. Her eyes were open, watching him with liquid intensity.

"It should be pretty obvious," he said, "although I managed to miss the point for a depressingly long time."

She laughed softly and shifted to a more comfortable position, half slumped against the side of the buggy. "Very smooth," she said, closing her eyes again.

Sal felt a familiar warmth spread through him as he turned to Banner. "I don't care if I never travel again. As long as Shilly is with me, the Change is everywhere around me. Wouldn't you rather feel that way than be tied to an ocean, far away?"

Banner was smiling. "You make a convincing argument, Sal," she said, "when you put it like that."

He tilted his head to look at her sideways. "I'm not trying to convince anyone. You just asked, and I told you."

Banner sat back into her seat. "That's the best sort of argument."

"No," he said. "The best is when you don't have to ask at all."

They hit the open road and accelerated north for Laure.

THE WIND

"Flight is not for the fainthearted. Or the heavy."
THE BOOK OF TOWERS, FRAGMENT 379

Skender gaped in wonder at a sight he had never imagined. He felt as though a blindfold had been removed from his eyes. All the wealth of the visible world lay before him. Bulbous plumes of hot air rose from the sun-warmed buildings, expanding and overlapping as they hit cooler layers high above the city. Complicated eddies swirled around towers, forming knots and tangles. Directly off the edge of the platform, a strong plane of wind swept up and to his right. He could see, now, how miners coming in to land angled their wings to take advantage of that steady stream. Beyond them, vast edifices of air rose and fell in waves over the disrupted geography of the Divide. The earth itself seemed to be breathing.

"You see it?" said Chu into his ear.

"Goddess, yes. I see it."

"Good." She pulled away for a moment, then turned her back to him. "Let me strap myself in. You're going to be my eyes. We're going to fly together."

He tore his mind away from the magnificent vistas before him to concentrate on her words. The harness jingled as she slid into it and pressed tightly against him. The arrangement felt cramped and clumsy on the ground, and he wasn't so sure it would be any better in the air. They would be awkward compared to the other miners, who sliced through and skipped across the wind like stones on water.

But they didn't need to be graceful. All they needed was to remain airborne. For the first time he began to see how that might be possible.

"We give the winds names here," she said. "There's the Smoker from the north in summer, and the Twister that comes down the Divide late autumn. The Cocoa Express is brown with dust, while the Braid is cool and sweet. The one running by this tower at sunset is called the Red Lifter." She fastened the last strap across her chest. "Right. I'm ready. Which way is the Red Lifter heading?"

Skender pointed.

"We need to find a thermal that'll take us up above the city. It'll look like a big mushroom. Once we get up there, we can work out what to do next."

"I understand." And he did. He could see the necessity for elevation as clearly as he understood the need for paths and roads on the ground. Thinking in terms of up and down as well as forward and back, left and right, now felt as natural as breathing. The licence had made him a creature of the sky more surely than had merely strapping a wing to his back.

The Change-rich fabric that would support them in the air flexed organically as they shuffled to the edge of the platform. He spared no thought for the ground below, or for the other miners watching, hooting their derision. His attention was firmly focused on the wind. The sky was no longer a void. It was full of potential. He was a fish yearning to swim in the ocean. He was going home.

"Are you ready?" she asked.

He nodded.

"Hold me."

His arms slipped around her waist. Every muscle in his body tensed, ready, and she was no less poised. He felt her balance shift slightly, leaning outwards in a way that would have panicked him just a few moments earlier. Her knees bent.

They jumped, and the Red Lifter caught them.

With a cracking sound, the wing snapped taut, filled with air. The harness wrenched at him, digging deeply into his heavy, earth-yearning flesh. Downward the ground pulled them; he could feel its power clearly, even though the streets below were hidden in shadow. For one dizzying moment, the world became a spinning kaleidoscope of buildings and rooftops; Observatory Tower pierced the sky like a dagger. The platform blotted out the stars and threatened to swat them from the air.

Chu wrenched her horizontal body to the right, shifting their combined centre of gravity. He felt the wing instantly respond, shifting to a new tack. He and Chu didn't plummet to their deaths. They were, for the moment, holding their own.

The wind broke around them, trailing streamers and short-lived vortexes behind his legs. He ignored the details and concentrated on the flow.

"Up there!" He let go of her long enough to point to her right, then grabbed back on. Just below the leading edge of the wing was a strong up-welling of air. He could see its edges roiling powerfully against the clear night sky. The crimson sunset was fading fast, but he didn't need light to see the wind. His awareness of it came through entirely new senses.

With his eyes he saw red glowstones on every building roof and tower, visible only from above: navigation lights to ward off those in the air.

He didn't stop to sightsee any further than that. The scenery was relevant only if it came too close. Chu shifted, swinging them in a new direction. He kept the bulk of his attention on the noise and feel of the wing.

"Are you all right?" Chu asked him, her words barely audible over the wind rattling around them.

"I'm fine."

"Are you sure? You're hanging on very tight. Here." She took his arm and folded it diagonally across her chest, so his right hand was in her left armpit. "Hold me like this and let go with the other hand, so you can point. Does that feel better?"

He was, for a brief moment, completely distracted by the sensation of her body against his. Her breasts were soft under his arm and her hair whipped into his face. Her head angled back into him. Their eyes just met.

Then the world dropped out from under them, and they were tumbling downward.

"Which way?" she cried, twisting the wing's control surfaces wildly in an attempt to check their descent.

"There!" He pointed at the nearest thermal. "No—*that* way." A bigger one lurked just around the corner of a clock tower. "Can we make it?"

"We can try." She dipped their nose and used gravity to accelerate them into the hot up-welling. His body seemed to hang heavier in the harness as the wing lifted them upward, curling in tight circles in order to maximise their lift.

Their joint effort began to pay off. Slowly and not always surely, they crept higher over the city. The navigational glowstones grew fainter. The lights of taverns and homes took on a hazy, distant feel.

Another miner circled them, watching their progress with some concern.

"We're okay!" Chu yelled, waving. "Don't worry about us!"

The other miner dipped her wing in acknowledgment and descended gracefully to the landing platforms.

Circling within the thermal became a familiar chore. He found that he had time to look around. Stars appeared in the eastern sky over a land still hot from the day. Buoyant air formed a substantial cladding over the earth, and he knew that he could have flown indefinitely in any direction he chose. The wing thrilled through the air, its charms humming and crackling. When they reached the top of the thermal and circled lazily at the summit of the sky, he felt confident enough to let go of Chu and spread his arms.

Air rushed between his fingers, stealing their heat. But the cold didn't concern him. The wind rattled in the wing and rushed up the inside of his robe. They were rocketing to the edge of the world. He gave himself completely to the experience, and whooped for the joy of it.

He was flying!

"So," said Chu over her shoulder, "was it worth the effort?"

"Yes!"

"You know, I hope, that you're getting off lightly. At the moment, I'm doing all the work. If we're going to keep this up, you'll have to help out."

He sobered. "Of course. Show me how."

"Try shifting your weight from side to side. See what happens. Don't worry about making a mistake. We're relatively safe up here. Unless we come out the side of the thermal, there's not much you can do wrong."

He nodded and took a grip on the straps leading to the wing's control surfaces. Shifting his body from the way it wanted naturally to hang, flat in the harness, was surprisingly difficult. Giving up on subtlety, he wrenched himself violently to the left. The wing instantly banked to the right. He swung awkwardly, trying to regain control. Momentum and gravity warred over him, and he lost.

Chu tipped them onto a level heading with a gentle nudge.

"It's not as easy as it looks," she said. "Is it?"

He agreed wholeheartedly. It was as hard as rock climbing for a beginner. "You make it look easy."

"Thanks to a lot of practice. Try moving just part of you, rather than all of you at once—a leg, your upper body, your arms. Get the feel of the wing and work with it rather than against it. It's a partnership, like you and me. If we're working against each other, we won't get anywhere. You can't *make* the wing do what you tell it to. You have to make it *want* to do it."

He could appreciate what she was saying, but putting it into practice was difficult. The wing wobbled from side to side as he experimented with moving his weight around. He found it very difficult to maintain an even keel; the slightest nudge sent them angling left or right, up or down, and the odds of overcorrecting were high. It was better, he soon discovered, to give in to the nonlinear nature of flight and allow the wing to travel in graceful curves. Straight lines were strictly for the ground.

Before long, his muscles begged for a respite from the strain of tugging backwards and forwards, over and over again. Not a single limb was spared, and he could see why missing a leg might hamper the quartermaster's ability to fly, and why strength was an advantage.

Finally he managed a complete circuit of the top of the thermal without losing control. That was a long way from attaining mastery over the wing—and the thought of landing already worried him—but it was progress.

"Tired yet?" Chu asked him.

"Yes, but I don't want to stop."

"Good. Let me take over for a bit and you can rest. All you'll have to do is tell me where the wind is going."

He sagged gratefully into her, breathing heavily. "Where are *we* going?"

"Over the Divide."

A chill deeper than the wind swept through him. "I thought we weren't going to do that until later."

"I said we wouldn't do any real searching until tomorrow. It won't hurt us to make a quick pass, just so you know what it takes."

He nodded, hiding his nervousness. A fall would be fatal no matter where they came down, in the city or in the Divide. The thought wasn't terribly comforting, but it did put things in perspective.

He studied the flows of the wind. "There's a current over there," he said, pointing with his free hand. "Catch it and it'll take us halfway."

"Excellent." Her spine flexed under him, and the wing responded smoothly, tilting steadily nose-upward. "Hold on tight. You're about to see some *real* flying."

She flexed again and the nose came down. The wing surged forward as though released from a cage. Skender clung to Chu with both hands and hoped for the best.

They dropped out of the thermal with a lurch. Chu banked hard and fast, skidding through the air with consummate skill even though she couldn't "see" it. Moments of free fall alternated with sudden jolts upward. Skender swung back and forth like a rag doll in a dog's mouth. He concentrated on the city far below, studying the layout of its streets and the angular shapes of its roofs and towers, not thinking at all about the solid stone, bricks, and mortar waiting for them should they make a mistake.

The navigation lights looked like stars reflected in a still, red-tinged lake. Their distribution was uneven, forming odd constellations, matching none in the sky. Skender thought he saw the road they had followed the previous night to the Magister's chambers, but everything looked different from above. The usual landmarks—windows, doors, street signs, graffiti—were invisible. He couldn't decide if the city looked bigger or smaller. Certainly he had never been able to see it from end to end while inside it, so his appreciation of it had been confined to those few areas he had visited. Above, he could see every tower and building, from the smallest to the very large. There was no avoiding the vast mass of industry and humanity it contained. Only one section was dark, a bulging triangle far away from the bustle of the New City; he recognised it as the boneyard, the chimneylike structure in which the bodies of Laurean dead went for disposal. Birds fed on the flesh before it desiccated completely, leaving anonymous, sun-bleached skeletons behind. He was heartily glad the sun had set.

Gradually he became aware of a severe chord cutting into the city: they were flying over the Wall protecting the inhabitants of Laure from the Divide. The Wall curved gently inward, like a dam. Beyond it was nothing but darkness. That, in a way, was worse than the many lethal details of the city. There was no way to tell what lay beneath them. All manner of creature could be slithering across the distant ground, waving sharp-tipped limbs at them.

He pointed Chu towards another steady stream. The wind seemed colder over the Divide, and moved more quickly, as if in a hurry to distance itself from the wounded earth. Turbulence became commonplace. Skender hugged Chu more tightly, for comfort as well as warmth, and she didn't object.

"It's eerie out here, isn't it?" Her voice was just loud enough to hear over the snatching wind. The city was a blur behind them, the only source of light for many kilometres. He wondered what it would be like to fly without any sort of navigation at all. On a moonless night, he wondered, it might be possible to fly right into the ground without realising.

His only reassurance was the wind, which he could still sense through the licence's charms. Its restless flow warned of sudden disturbances. He was reasonably certain they wouldn't crash into the far side of the Divide without fair warning.

"Have you ever done this before?" he asked. "Flown out here on your own at night?"

She shook her head, sending a gentle vibration through the wing. "Too scared."

That simple admission made him feel a little better. "And there's not much point, I guess. It's not as if you can see anything."

"There are ghostlights out here sometimes," she said. "Occasionally, if they come too close to the Wall, someone's sent out to check. Usually older, more experienced flyers, or one of the heavy lifters with a Survey crew aboard. One mission brought back a man'kin in the shape of a giant gargoyle; chained, of course. It had lost a wing and couldn't speak. They tried to fix it, but it fell apart, and the bits were laid down in Slaughter Square. Some say that if you go there at night you can hear the pieces whispering to each other."

"What's Slaughter Square?" he asked, ignoring for the moment the image of a man'kin with wings.

"You haven't been there? I'll have to take you. It's a charming place. Centuries ago, a disease killed hundreds of people. The only way to stop it was to kill the sick and their families and the rodents who spread the disease. Once a year there's a festival celebrating the Year of the Plague. Rats and mice are killed and left on every street corner; their blood is poured in Slaughter Square. It's very charming. We get lots of tourists."

"You're joking, right?"

"Only about the tourists. If you stick around long enough, you'll be the first."

Skender had no intention of staying in Laure any longer than he had to. Once he found his mother, he could go home and return to his ordinary life. But when he tried to remind Chu of that, the words caught in his throat.

You haven't been there? I'll have to take you.

Had she just asked him out on a *date?*

Before he could respond, she pointed into the deep darkness away from the city.

"Look. There's something."

He craned past her, sending the wing wobbling from side to side. "Where?"

"There." She pointed again. "See it?"

Their flight levelled out. He peered into the darkness, squinting but unable at first to make out any detail.

Then, at the very limit of his vision, he saw a light.

"Yes, got it now," he said. "Any idea what it's coming from?"

"None at all. Want to check it out?"

"Uh—" The night was impenetrable in that direction, the Divide gaped wide, and the cold had seeped into his bones. Only the front of him, where Chu's body gave him protection, retained any heat at all.

He thought of his mother and what it must be like to be in the Divide at night, alone.

"Okay," he said, "but we're not stopping unless we absolutely have to."

"Goddess, no. I may be reckless, but I'm not an idiot."

He searched the sky for an appropriate stream. "Bring us up a bit, then across that way." He indicated a heading slightly to the right of the light. "There's a nice strong current running through there."

She glided them along the correct trajectory. He felt the stream grab them and pull them forward. Skender had never been swimming, but he had read about it in books. When writers talked about being swept up in powerful currents, he imagined it would feel something like this, with the pit of his stomach suddenly hollowing and all control wrested from him.

Chu sniffed. "I know this wind. It's called the Dark Bellows; it flows along the Divide from the mountains. Can you smell the trees?"

He took a lungful but could smell nothing but her. "It's good," he said.

She sniffed again, tilting her head back until it bumped his. "There's something else on the wind. A new stink. Man'kin, I think," she mused. "They're out late."

"I can't smell them. Could they be behind the light?"

"No. Look at our heading. The light isn't in the Divide, it's on the far side."

He peered over his shoulder to get a fix on the city glow—now a less-than-brilliant haze far behind them. Looking forward again, he could see that she was absolutely right. The Divide floor was obviously a very long way beneath them. The light she had spotted was only just below their height.

"Where's the Aad?" he asked, worried they might be heading to Laure's ill-favoured, haunted half.

"To our left, a kilometre or two away."

"You're sure?"

"Absolutely. The only thing out there," she said, pointing directly ahead of them, "is dirt and scrub."

"Not any more." The light was faint but not an illusion; more yellow than a star and too fine to be a fire. As they flew closer, it resolved into two lights, not just one. They were spaced evenly apart and seemed to be moving, rocking from side to side.

"What is that?" she asked. "Some sort of vehicle?"

"That's what it looks like." Skender pictured a buggy or truck bouncing across uneven ground with headlights on.

"Could it be your mother?"

He shook his head. "She travelled by camel. And even if she hadn't, how would she get up here?"

"There's an old road cut into the side of the Divide not far from here. It's steep but not impassable."

He watched the lights moving nearer, curious about their origin. They probably belonged to an isolated traveller whose presence had nothing to do with him and his mission, but they still piqued his interest. Why would someone be driving so close to the Divide in the middle of the night? Where man'kin, dust devils, and ghostlights walked, worse creatures no doubt followed.

They flew directly over the vehicle, too high up to make out any details but close enough to see that it was a buggy large enough for four people. An additional two sets of lights glimmered to the south: more vehicles out on a midnight journey.

Then the wing caught a rising gust from the edge of the Divide and they banked sharply around, losing forward momentum. Skender mentally kicked himself for neglecting his duties as wind-watcher. He reminded himself that staying aloft was much more important than the identity of the people in the vehicle below.

"Take us left and down," he said. "We can pick up speed and head back, if you want."

"Getting tired?" she asked.

He didn't bother lying. "You better believe it. It's been a long day."

"And we've got a longer one tomorrow." She reached over her

shoulder to pat his face. "All right. I'll take pity on you. Back we go for a nightcap, then some shut-eye."

"A *quick* nightcap," he said.

"Sure. That seems to be all you can handle."

She chortled to herself as they glided silently over the buggy, far below.

THE FATHER

"Humanity is a fearful species. For every fear we know, it is said, there are a dozen monsters who prey on it— and all of them, at some point or other, have called the Divide home."
THE BOOK OF TOWERS, EXEGESIS 17:7

Shilly stirred in her sleep, dimly aware of the buggy bouncing over rough ground, its engine growling and rhythmic through the seat's thin cushioning. The dream had her in its grip and wouldn't let her go.

She was standing in a wide expanse of yellow sand, a vast basin that seemed perfectly flat at first, but was in fact rising up around her. She felt like a grain of wheat in a vast, empty silo. The sand began moving, shifting and tumbling as though blown by a breeze. The breeze grew steadily stronger, sweeping in circles like the currents of a willy-willy. Sand danced higher and higher, then rose in a funnel, getting in her eyes and nose. She felt the ground being sucked out from under her feet, giving her the impression that she was sinking. Blinking and coughing, she crouched down and put her arms over her head.

Then a clear space opened around her. Thinking the maelstrom of sand had eased, she opened her eyes and peered out between her fingers. She huddled in the calm centre of the whirlwind, surrounded by rushing sand. The funnel extended upwards in a sinuous cylinder, flexing and writhing as it vanished into darkness far above her head. She stood slowly, incrementally, ready to bunch up again if the vortex collapsed.

It didn't. The sand-laden wind hissed at her like a thousand snakes and kept its distance.

When she reached her full height, she realised that she wasn't standing on sand any more. Under her feet was stone as black as the summit of the storm. It felt rough and warm against her soles, fresh from the heart of a volcano. There were three lines carved on it, deep gouges she could have stuck her thumb into, had she a mind to. The lines formed a triangle as wide across as her outstretched arms. She stood in the exact centre.

The eye of the storm widened and the sand retreated with it. More lines appeared, forming interlocking symbols of fiendish complexity. The wind picked up in volume and lightning flashed overhead. Thunder boomed so loudly it hurt. She swung her head from side to side, trying to memorise the pattern hidden under the sand. To her left was a series of spirals that interwove and overlapped to form an eye-bending illusion full of sharp angles and multiple intersections; to her right an infinite variety of rectangles somehow combined to form circles and sweeping curves. She despaired, knowing she couldn't possibly hold all of that in her mind at once. She wasn't Skender. She needed more time!

Time is running out, said a woman's voice. Her own voice, but withered and dry as if from the throat of an ancient crone. *Do it now, or not at all.*

It's too much.

You have to!

But I can't!

Shilly fully woke with a jerk. The sound of the storm became the sound of the buggy's engine. For a long moment she was disoriented. Rough ground sent her rocking from side to side. The stars were brilliant, barely dimmed by the moon. She stared up at them as she tried to gather herself, the cool air in her eyes evaporating the last shreds of sleep.

Something black and crescent-shaped slid in front of the moon.

She gasped and sat upright, pointing. "What the Goddess is that?"

Sal, behind the wheel of the buggy, slammed on the brakes. "What? Where?"

Shilly stabbed at the sky, following the black shape with difficulty across the starscape. "Up there! Something flying!"

"Where?" Warden Banner climbed onto her knees on the front passenger seat. Her eyes swept the sky. "I can't see it."

"There!"

Tom, slumped over on the buggy's rear seat, made a clumsy attempt to sit up. "What?"

The blackness of the sky confounded her. For a moment, she saw it again, silhouetted perfectly against the starscape. Then it disappeared and she couldn't find it.

"A bird?" asked Sal. "An owl, perhaps, or a bat?"

"No," she said, "its shape was all wrong. Bigger."

"Are you certain of that?" Banner was looking at her. "Where is it now?"

"I—I don't know," she said, turning her head in increasing arcs. "It really was there. I swear it."

But even as she said the words, she realised how they sounded. She slumped back into her seat.

"You were asleep," the warden said, touching her arm reassuringly. "You were dreaming."

"I *was* dreaming, yes, but that was about sand and a voice, or something. But then I woke up and I saw—that." She gesticulated helplessly. If they hadn't seen it themselves, she would never be able to convince them. In their shoes, she would have thought the same. "Hell, maybe I did dream it."

"No," said Sal. "There is something there." His eyes were closed; she could feel him searching the sky with senses other than sight. The engine chugged patiently in neutral. *"Something . . ."* He opened his eyes and looked at Shilly, then Banner. "It's going away. I don't know what it was, but I think we should wait here for the others to catch up. Just in case."

Banner didn't argue. "Whatever you say. How close are we to the Divide now?"

"Very," said Sal. "We would have had to stop soon anyway."

"Is it the Homunculus?" Shilly asked, feeling nervous in the empty, cold night.

"I don't know." He reached diagonally across the buggy to grip her arm. "But I think we're safe. Are you sure you're feeling all right?"

His warm hand and the concern in his voice soothed her somewhat. "I'll be better when this is over and done with. Can you feel Highson nearby?"

Sal shook his head. "Not even faintly."

"That's either a good sign," she said, standing up to stretch her legs, "or it's not." She stuck out her tongue to take the sting off the sarcasm. "If we're stopping, I'm going to find a bush."

"Don't wander too far," warned Banner.

"I won't," she said, thinking with a frisson of fear how awful it would be to take one step in the wrong direction and topple into the Divide. Sal returned her stick with a worried look. Parched pebbles crunched crisply underfoot as she stepped out of the buggy and hurried into the darkness, keeping one eye on the sky as she went.

The headlights of the search party glowed over the southern hills. While they waited for the others to catch up, Tom checked the engine and chassis to make sure the buggy had weathered the rough journey intact. Sal, feeling restless, unfastened the second headlight and swept its beam across the barren landscape. The light was firm and steady, sending back tiny, gleaming reflections. Chips of quartz, Sal assumed, or the eyes of desert-dwelling wolf spiders. He walked a short distance away from the buggy, and stopped to take his bearings.

The road they had been following had kinked northeast two kilometres earlier. Rather than head in that direction, they had aimed west for the Divide across country, in accordance with Marmion's instructions. How far they were from reaching the edge of the Divide, Sal didn't know, and he was curious to find out.

No one protested at his leaving the buggy, so he turned and kept walking. Whatever it was Shilly had seen, the last vestiges of it were long gone. He felt completely safe in the darkness with the light to guide him. He kept the beam moving, covering every direction ahead of him. The landscape was blasted and flat. If the Homunculus *had* somehow gotten in front of them and was lying in wait for him, it was either invisible or coloured exactly like dirt.

He walked in a straight line until the ground ahead of him fell away sharply. He slowed and checked his footing more thoroughly. How steep the drop-off was, he couldn't tell. There was no point taking unnecessary risks. Still, he approached as close as he dared to the edge of the Divide and played the beam of light out into the darkness, imagining that he could see the distant oval it cast on the ground far below. It probably wasn't a good idea, advertising their presence like that, but he was keen to see their destination. As it was, the only thing visible was the faint glowing smudge of Laure, far away, like dawn on a dead land, almost directly north. He thought of blood and the yadachi. Banner's statement that they weren't vampires held little currency in the blackness of night.

"It doesn't seem to worry you," said the warden from behind him.

He jumped at the sound of her voice, then laughed at the fright she had given him. He had been conscious of what lay ahead and to either side but he hadn't been paying attention to what was behind him.

"Goddess, you startled me."

"I guess that sets me straight," she said with a small laugh. "It worries me, too. When I was a girl, my mother used to tell me that the desert mice near the Divide never died. They'd live on and on, jealously guarding their territory, until they were so withered they looked like tumbleweeds. They haunted their territory for eternity, scratching and biting anyone who trespassed. She said that people couldn't live near the Divide for the sound of the mice clicking their teeth at night and scratching at the door to get in." She looked around her and shuddered. "I know it's probably nonsense but part of me will always be the little girl she told that story to. It kept me awake in bed every time a branch tapped at the window."

"And now here we are."

"Yes. Here I am."

Sal turned back to the apparently endless gulf before them. The night was silent and still, but somehow he could *hear* the emptiness of the Divide. There was no echo at all.

"I travelled a lot with my father," he said, "when we were on the run from the Syndic. We spent most of our time in the borderlands, going from town to town, although we never came this far east. The Divide was always close. Dad told me that it's like a brown snake: if you leave it alone, it won't harm you."

Banner looked puzzled. "You did this with Highson? I had no idea."

"Not Highson. The man who raised me as a father." *The man who loved me and taught me,* he thought, *and who died for me in Fundelry. Remember him?*

"Ah, yes, of course." She nodded. "Dafis Hrvati. I never knew him."

Sal forced down his acrimony. She didn't deserve it.

"Let's go back," she said as a horn honked behind them.

Sal looked over his shoulder and saw the two Sky Warden buses pull up to the buggy. Their headlights cast long, insectile beams through the dusty air. Sal raised the glowstone in his hand and flashed it at them. He could just make out Shilly in the buggy, waving back.

Marmion was pacing between the two buses when they returned, issuing orders and overseeing the unloading of their matériel from the covered rear trays. Kail stood to one side with his arms folded and eyes closed, as immobile as a statue. Tasting the night, Sal thought.

Shilly's expression was vexed. "See if you can find out what's going on," she said. "Marmion won't talk to me."

Sal strode up to the Warden and confronted him. "What can we do to help?"

"Nothing," Marmion replied. "You're not trained for this. Just keep your heads down and let us do our job."

Sal spoke softly so his threat wouldn't be overheard, but loud enough that it couldn't be ignored. "You'll make us part of this or I'll yell so hard every Stone Mage and yadachi for five hundred kilometres will come running."

Marmion looked at him with cold and calculating eyes. "We're building hides," he grated. "Camouflage shelters. Between us we can cover two kilometres of the edge. Kail thinks that will be enough. You and Shilly can take the northern end, if it'll make you feel better."

"It will. If we see the Homunculus, what do we do?"

"You'll let us know and we'll handle it. The same if you see your father first. Understood?"

It sounded a flimsy plan to Sal, but he didn't want to push any harder. He nodded. "If you show us how to erect the hides, we can help with that."

"I'd rather you stay here for now, to watch the buses. Tom says Shilly saw something. I don't want to take any chances on losing our only way home. Will you do that?"

Sal nodded again. That made sense, despite his conviction that the thing Shilly had seen was long gone.

"Good. Then let me get on with my work." Marmion turned away and went back to yelling orders. Sky Wardens scurried around him, building piles of yellow tarpaulins and frames. Sal watched them for a moment, feeling impotent, then went back to sit with the buggy.

The Wardens worked into the night. Shilly was glad that she hadn't been called on to help. Her leg wouldn't have lasted long under the burdens Marmion's lackeys hurried off with. No one was entirely sure how far ahead of the Homunculus they were, but the lights were dimmed to prevent giving away their location. It wasn't possible to dim them entirely—they needed the light to work by—but Kail hoped the creature would assume any faint glow belonged to Laure, if it caught sight of them.

Shilly marvelled at the complete ignorance of the Wardens as they laid their strange trap. The thing inside the Homunculus could have been blind for all they knew. It might have smelled or heard them already, from kilometres away, and altered course to miss them completely. But she could appreciate the position they were in. They had been charged to catch a thing they knew nothing about—not even its shape—before it killed anyone else, and they would do that to the best of their abilities. What would happen if it evaded them again she didn't know. Would Marmion be as desperate as Shom Behenna had been, years ago? Would he cross the Divide and enter the Interior just to follow orders?

She couldn't tell. Lodo's nephew kept himself carefully at a distance from her and Sal, and she didn't push anything. It wasn't the dismissal of *her* that bothered her most. It was the dismissal of Lodo, the man who had been Marmion's mother's brother. Wasn't Marmion interested at all in his uncle's life since he had been exiled from the Haunted City? In his death? In the years in between? She couldn't imagine not wanting to know about the fate of a family member. She didn't know how Sal and Highson had stayed sane the last five years, knowing each other was out there, somewhere, and doing nothing about it.

The only time Marmion spoke to her was when he came to assign them their hide. After a brief explanation of how the pieces went together, he told them that they had been allocated a position almost a kilometre away.

"So, if you carry the canvas and struts to that location and—"

"We'll take the buggy," Sal interrupted him, "and Tom."

Marmion was obviously tempted to force the issue, but let it go. "We have a cover for the buggy. You'll need to take that, too. I want you out of sight before dawn. If you see or hear anything suspicious before then, use this." He handed Tom a small glass sphere. "You'll find flares bundled up in the canvas as well. Either way, we'll come running."

They nodded their understanding. Tom gave Shilly the sphere for safekeeping and helped Sal load the collapsed hide into the back of the buggy. Kail looked up from his examination of a chart as the engine caught, and saluted farewell. With a slight spin of their wheels, they headed off into the night, heading northwards parallel to the Divide.

"I don't suppose you've dreamed what's going to happen," she said to Tom.

The young Engineer shook his head. "Something about this place looks familiar, but I don't know why. I think I'm seeing it from the wrong angle."

"From Laure, perhaps?" asked Sal.

"No. From above. I think I was flying in the dream."

"I'm usually flying in my dreams," said Shilly. "Except when I'm falling. And just lately it's been nothing but sand, sand, sand."

"I still dream of drowning," said Sal.

"Sometimes," said Tom with a shrug, "a dream is just a dream."

By the dimmed light, the route was difficult to make out. Tom drove slowly, skirting wide cracks that led to their left into the depths of the giant canyon. They passed four hides in various stages of assembly. More than one warden was sleeping while the others worked on the construction of the hides, intending to swap roles later.

Tom kept a close eye on the odometer. When they reached the required distance, they chose a hollow in which to park the buggy. Shilly tied the canvas over the buggy while Sal and Tom worked on the hide's framework.

The night was cold and quiet. With the black emptiness of the Divide at her back, seeming to watch her, and the memory of the mysterious black crescent in the sky still strong in her mind, she worked as quickly as her stiff leg would allow.

With barely an hour left before dawn, their hide was ready. Tom took both headlights off the buggy and turned them down to mere glimmers. The three of them assumed crouched positions behind the low, dirt-coloured shield and settled back to wait. They were right on the lip of the escarpment, tucked behind the first of several rough steps leading down to a very long fall. The chances of taking a tumble were small, but Shilly was acutely aware of the drop so close at hand. Whether she would feel better or worse at dawn, with the awesome expanse of the Divide revealed, she didn't know.

"So how does this work?" she asked, producing the glass sphere from her pocket. It was as wide as her palm and perfectly clear. She could see through it without distortion.

"You hold it like this," said Tom, taking it from her and gripping it tightly between both hands, one on top of the other, "and you twist." He mimed the motion. "All the balls will glow in response. Each of us has a unique colour. Marmion and the others will know if we're the ones who sound the alarm."

"Assuming the Change is working when we try it," said Sal.

"That's what these are for." Tom gave the globe back to Shilly, and picked up one of the two flares Marmion had assigned them. "These couldn't be easier. You just break the seal on one end and point it at the sky. You might want to cover your eyes while you do it."

Shilly was in no hurry to test the theory. "I don't suppose Marmion told you who has been assigned what colours for the spheres."

Tom and Sal shook their heads.

"Of course not." She sighed and leaned against the dirt and rock. "He wouldn't want us to know who else got lucky. That would make too much sense."

"I could go and ask," said Tom, already moving to stand up.

Sal grabbed the back of his robe before he could take a step. "Don't worry about it. I'm sure we'll hear if something happens."

Shilly thought of the scream Larson Maiz had let out when the Homunculus had frightened him to death, and hoped the rest of the night would go undisturbed.

◣ ◣ ◣

Dawn came, daubing the world with yellow and orange hues. The Divide gaped behind the hides, achingly ancient, scarred by the relentless passage of time and weather. There was no sense to be found in its geography. Deep creases pockmarked its steep sides. Strange, wandering gullies traced almost-legible lines across its edge-most floor, where water running down the cliff faces during monsoon rains pooled and spread. Its heart was cracked and parched. Relentless winds carried red sand in waves over features that could have been ruins, or just slabs of tilted, baked clay, broken by unknown forces in the distant past. Dunes taller than a house made their way down the centre of the great rift valley, their stately progress measured in decades.

Heat haze made details dance crazily in the distance. Sal saw movement everywhere he looked. He turned his back on the view, interested in neither illusions nor the Wall and towers of Laure. He failed to make the connection between the dots circling those towers and the thing Shilly had seen in the night. He had more important things to consider.

If Kail was right, his real father was approaching. That possibility—and his conversation with Banner about the Divide and the man he had thought was his father—brought back numerous memories. He knew of Highson's existence and the truth about his parentage just a few weeks before meeting the stranger who claimed him as a son. Their first encounters had been terse and full of unspoken emotion. Sal had never been able to see Highson as more than the focus of his loss and grief, of his anger and frustration, until on a dark night in the Haunted City, when every hope seemed lost, a subtle transformation took place, and Highson Sparre suddenly became a real person.

"You'll never win, Sal," he had said that night. "You can hate me as much as you like, but you'll never defeat me. Do you really think you could, with all the might of the Conclave and the Alcaide and the

Strand itself behind me?" The words were burned into Sal's mind, so tightly bound up in anger and grief that he could never possibly forget them. "You can try to escape again if you want to, and I have no doubt you'll find another way, in time, with similar consequences. But you'll never truly succeed. I will always haunt you, as long as you live. As you burn out in a blaze of something that might have been glory but ends up stifled and turned back on itself in frustration, you'll remember this moment, and you'll wish you'd listened."

Sal's real father had stared down at him crouched on a cobbled street, his gut aching and his mouth burning with bile.

"Hear me out, or die fighting me. For that is surely what will happen. The decision is yours."

"All right," Sal had said, knowing that Highson was the haunted one, not Sal. "Let's finish this. Tell me what you want me to hear and get out of my way."

Something like relief appeared in his real father's face, mixed with fear. The resemblance between them was slight, but their voices were identical. So was their stubbornness.

"I didn't kill your mother. I loved her."

"You keep saying that—"

"Because it's true, Sal. She was so easy to love: so beautiful, so full of life. When she said she wanted to leave me, I was grief-stricken. I'll admit that I didn't know what to do. I had hoped that she would come to feel the same about me, in time, but her betrayal made me see that this would never happen. I couldn't live with a woman who was in love with my friend's journeyman, no matter how discreetly we maintained our affairs. But how could I let her go when her family and mine forbade the divorce?"

"So you hunted her down when she escaped, and you dragged her off against her will. You're not telling me anything I don't already know."

"How do you know it was me?"

"What? Of course it was you!"

"But how do you *know*?"

"Lodo said you led the sweep across the Strand when they first escaped. He was there, he said, when it happened."

"That's right; he was. And what else? Did Dafis tell you anything about me?"

"He said that you took my mother from me."

"Unless he actually saw me do it, how could he be so certain?"

"What difference does it make?"

"All the difference in the world, Sal, because it *wasn't* me. It was my aunt. The Syndic."

"So? That's the same thing."

"It's not. Don't be an idiot, Sal! Think!" Sal remembered the urgency and hurt in Highson's voice. It transfixed him, kept him listening when every instinct had screamed that he was being lied to again. "Seirian and Dafis loved each other, as much as I loved Seirian. I could see that clearly. They were determined to be together despite the ruling of everyone involved. Such defiance was destined to cause trouble. It was always going to end in disaster, whichever way it went. I decided that I wouldn't contribute to it. I wouldn't put her through hell on my account. My happiness was secondary to hers.

"I heard about their plan to escape. They had friends who stole a buggy and planned to smuggle them out of the city on a supply ferry. I aided them without them knowing, using my contacts to make sure they weren't seen at either end. I *helped* them, Sal. I didn't get in their way. The search party: yes, I led that—but I had to in order to hide my complicity in their escape. I did everything I could to lose the scent. I let them get away. I allowed them a life together.

"Or so I thought. That should have been the end of it. I didn't reckon on the power of revenge. My aunt was humiliated by the whole affair; that I had lost the taste for politics only rubbed salt in the wound. She maintained the chase, and she succeeded where I had deliberately failed. She snatched Seirian from the man you call your father, and robbed you of a mother. She brought back to me the woman I loved—the woman I had hoped never to see again, although I longed for her with all my heart.

"You can probably guess the rest. Returned against her will, Seirian never believed that I willingly let her go, although I think she knew at the end how I felt for her. Seirian's death was a tragic accident I would happily give anything to undo, including my own life. She died alone, with neither the man she loved nor her child by her side. My part in that tragedy wasn't as great as the Syndic's, but guilt still consumes me. I am trying to atone for it now, Sal, if you'll only let me."

Stunned by the revelation, by the pain he saw naked before him, Sal could only say, "I don't believe you."

"Still? What do I have to do to convince you?"

"If it *was* true, you'd let me go."

"Exactly."

And he had. He had helped him and Shilly escape the Syndic and hide in Fundelry, where they could live their lives together in peace.

"It's stupid, I know," Highson had said. "You're my chance to redeem myself. If I can't—*couldn't* save your mother, then I can at least save you."

But that wasn't all his real father had told him that night. The rest of it ached in him like a wound—like the Divide ached behind him in the vast brown land. A part of him had never come to terms with the revelations and rifts in his life five years earlier, and he was afraid to probe too deeply into that torn and empty space. Who knew what had festered in there all this time? Who knew what new surprises might emerge?

After years of solitude and a wild race across the Strand, Sal was about to come face to face with Highson Sparre again, and with Highson's *other* dangerous creation . . .

Shilly shifted into a more comfortable position beside him, her dark skin soaking up the sunlight. At some point in the dawn light she had doodled in the dirt a fair representation of Kail and Marmion arguing nose to nose; Marmion's wispy hair became a prideful comb-over and Kail's nose possessed a menacing angle Sal had never noticed before. Tom was obeying orders with single-minded determination, but Shilly was clearly bored, and Sal had quickly grown tired of staying alert. He was relying more on the Change than his material senses to tell him if something was approaching.

Flies stirred, bothering him only when they crawled across his mouth. What they fed on so close to the Divide he didn't know—or want to know—but as long as they didn't bite him, he could tolerate their presence. They appeared to be the only living thing for dozens of kilometres, although Sal knew that wasn't true. Even the deepest desert was full of life; sometimes dormant, like seeds waiting to blossom into flowers after monsoonal rain, but often as active as any-where else. Hunters hunted; prey fled; scavengers prowled the grey areas in between. The Change flowed through them all.

The Change told him what he needed to know.

He felt the same as he had on the beach, only three days earlier. Something was on its way. The earth shuddered at its step, and the air recoiled from its skin. What it was, he didn't know, but there was no avoiding it—or the person accompanying it.

A nagging sense of familiarity touched him. He raised himself up onto his elbows and peered through the slit in the hide. Low brown clouds billowed to the northeast. A lone squiggle danced on the horizon; he couldn't decide if it was a dead tree warped by heat haze or someone walking towards them across the desolate landscape.

The feeling of imminence grew stronger. He reached out to touch Shilly, and she shivered wordlessly. She felt it, too, through him. It didn't feel like Highson as Sal remembered him, but time had passed and the strange Change-eating effects of the Homunculus could have interfered with his signature. There was no one else who knew Sal for hundreds of kilometres. It had to be him.

The anticipation became acute; he felt as though a twisting cord was about to snap inside him. He tensed, ready to spring in any direction, and didn't take his eyes off the landscape.

A bird wheeled high above the stony ground, circling gracefully in the rippling air. It caught his gaze and held it. He wished he could soar over the earth like that. It would, he thought, certainly make looking for the Homunculus that much easier.

When the bird suddenly twisted in midair and dropped like a stone, he realised his mistake. It wasn't a bird, and it wasn't his father he had been sensing.

With a cry of alarm, he leapt to his feet and burst out from cover.

THE SEER

**"All life is composed of three basic elements—
flesh, mind, and the Change—balanced to varying
degrees and in varying ways. Humans consist of minds
that live in bodies of flesh; golems are minds composed
of the Change. We use the Change to alter the world;
golems and other creatures use vessels of flesh
to become part of the world,
to wreak their havoc and mayhem upon us."**
MASTER WARDEN RISA ATILDE: NOTES TOWARD A UNIFIED CURRICULUM

He'd had better days, Skender thought. The previous night, after a landing he preferred not to remember, and a shot of araq that was even worse, he and Chu had quickly parted. There had, however, been the tiniest of hesitations at the hostel as she left. He had frozen solid while saying goodnight, thinking that she might be waiting for him to kiss her. And part of him had wanted to. The exhilaration of flying together was still thrilling through him, even in his exhausted state. His heart pounded.

But he had never kissed anyone before and didn't know what to do. What if he had misjudged the moment? What if she wanted nothing more from him than a chance to get her licence back? What if she thought he was nothing but a geeky *kid*?

The moment was gone as soon as it came. She wished him sweet dreams, inscrutable as ever, and he had kicked himself all the way upstairs to his room.

Over the araq, Chu had extracted a promise that he would meet her at the launch tower half an hour before dawn. Urtagh the landlord pounding on Skender's door at the appointed hour showed him just how much faith she had in his promises. But that was fair enough, he thought, as he'd been dreaming of the Keep's winding corridors at the time, and probably would have slept all day given the chance. He had leapt into his clothes and run to the tower, pausing only to wash his face and clean his teeth. His hair simply wouldn't flatten, no matter how he tried.

She had been waiting on the second platform with the wing extended, looking exactly as he had last seen her, minus the bags under her eyes. The last vestiges of sleep fell from him.

"Do you ever wash that uniform?"

"Are you *ever* on time?"

Her crotchetiness made him wonder if he'd imagined her hesitation the previous night. "I presume you have the licence."

"Of course." She waved the tattered-looking envelope. "Let's get it on you and into the air."

She had showed him how to apply the charm, letting the black skinlike sheath slide against chest and throat. It did the rest of the work, melting onto him like chocolate into hot milk. Again he experienced a strange blindness as the licence interfered with his normal sight. Then his eyes had cleared and the wind had returned.

It was strange, he thought. When taking off the licence the previous evening, it had come as a relief to see the world properly again, and overnight he had almost forgotten what it was like to see the city and its atmosphere as intertwined things, one wrapped around the other. As soon as the charm took root, however, the new sense it provided felt as natural as breathing. He was a creature of the air again.

They had strapped each other in and moved stiffly to the edge of the platform. Skender's muscles ached from the previous night's exhaustion, and the thought of more exercise wasn't a pleasant one, but his mother was out there somewhere, lost in the Divide, and he had to find her.

They launched in unison out into the crisp dawn light, accompanied by a yadachi's wailing exhortation for rain. The winds of the morning were turbulent and fresh. His cheeks instantly numbed in the cold, but the growing strength of the sunlight soon thawed them. Together, with his eyes and her skill, they negotiated the towers of the city and swooped over the Wall into the giant canyon.

It was very different during the day. Skender couldn't decide if the vastness of the Divide increased or decreased with the ability to see it, and if he was more scared or less. It was difficult to grasp the size of it. Hanging over its jumbled middle, either side was blurry and indistinct.

"Where do you want to start looking?" Chu asked him, all business.

Skender hadn't truly appreciated just how big a task he was taking on. He could discern nothing in the ravaged landscape to indicate where his mother might have gone.

"The Aad," he said, clutching at the only clue he had. "You said there were tunnels under the other half of the city. Let's try there first. Maybe we'll see some sign of their passage."

"Maybe." She tilted the wing and they tacked against a steady stream of air to approach the Ruin from the north. The sky seemed infinite above and around them. He was hanging over an enormous bowl with a V-shaped crack in it. The arms of the V diverged southwards, ahead of him, into the hazy distance.

"What are they?" he asked, pointing at a white line on the very limits of visibility.

"The Hanging Mountains," she said. "My family came from there, generations ago. They say people there fly all the time, gliding from tree to tree on wings made of spider web. Balloon-cities hang tethered from the branches, swaying in the breeze. Fog forests hide in the mist, only fully visible at noon."

"Sounds amazing."

"Perhaps *too* amazing. None of it could be true. I've always wanted to see for myself."

"Why haven't you?"

"Money, time, other stuff." She was quiet for a moment. "The last couple of years have been complicated."

He was about to ask why when she banked sharply and took them down lower. Taking the hint, he directed his eyes forward. The Aad, at a distance, had none of the clear, sharp lines of Laure. There was no wall, no concerted effort to keep the Divide at bay. Exposed on three sides, its dome-roofed buildings and truncated streets lay open to the elements, both natural and supernatural varieties. The outermost layers were uniformly rundown, with walls collapsing into rubble in numerous places and great rents in the sidewalks. At the heart of the Ruin were buildings that still retained some of their white paint and doors that at least appeared intact. A single, defiant watchtower, four-sided and broad, stood near the city's furthermost point from the Divide. Round black windows dotted its sleek planes like flies on a stick of salt.

Skender recalled everything written about old cities in the *Book of Towers*. There were only a few; most, like the Divide, had come into being relatively late in the history of the world. The truly ancient cities—the Nine Stars; the Haunted City; a dead city that moved of its own accord around the Broken Lands; and two others he had glimpsed during his adventures with Sal and Shilly—were dangerous, beautiful, Change-rich places. Strange creatures congregated or were confined there, and to stray into their territories was to invite disaster.

The Aad looked disreputable and had undoubtedly become home to creatures from the Divide through the years, but it didn't possess the same air those ancient cities did. His gut didn't recoil at the thought of setting foot there. It didn't resemble Laure, either. Laure had the benefit of continuous habitation and a good, solid wall.

The wind billowed above the ruined buildings, piling complicated shapes on top of an already jumbled topography. It was still too far away to make out much detail and his eye soon wandered, studying the cracked surface of the Divide's heart beneath him. Tracks of many different shapes and sizes crisscrossed in all directions. There were no obvious paths or destinations, just the marks left by unusual feet in dirt and dried mud, possibly years ago.

A gleam of reflected light caught the corner of his eye, and he turned to his right to see what had cast it. The sun was piercingly bright, baking the land under a strengthening yellow glow. Skender couldn't immediately pin down the source of the glint, but he did see something else strange.

"Are they the same people we saw last night?" he asked Chu, pointing with his free hand at three distinct clouds trailing a small train of motorised vehicles heading southwest from the ruined town.

"I don't know, but if they are they're heading in the other direction." She shrugged. "What does it matter? They can't be your mother's expedition. You said she didn't use buggies."

"I know, but—" He was about to confess to a nagging sense of curiosity when a second glint came from the edge of the Divide. "Something's going on down there," he said instead. "Take us right and up. There's a thermal that'll lift us higher, so we can see better."

"Make up your mind." The wing dipped, then rose into the cloud of hot air billowing up from the wasteland below.

Another glint. It originated in a shallow notch on the uppermost edge of the canyon wall, a fair distance from where the three vehicles were located. Again, Skender had trouble gauging the scale of what lay below. The inside of the notch was invisible. The vehicles looked like beetles. He couldn't tell how many people occupied them and what else they carried.

"When you're quite finished gawking," said Chu, "can you tell me how the sky looks ahead?"

"It's fine," he said. "Keep on this heading."

"Are you certain of that? The air is unpredictable near the edge of the Divide. You can't take it for granted."

Underscoring her words, the wing lurched a metre downwards.

"See?" she said.

"You did that deliberately."

"I did not!"

"Well, take us right. There's another thermal. We'll get some more altitude and then we'll be safe."

"I shouldn't have to say this," she said, "but the higher we go, the harder we'll hit the ground if we fall. Aren't you in the least bit afraid of heights?"

He shook his head. "Where I come from, you get over that sort of thing pretty quickly. Spiders, now, are a different story."

"Really? Then I should tell you about the time I was cruising down to pick up a lovely piece of flotsam on the bottom of the Divide. Just as I was about to grab it, a huge spider dropped off the leading edge, right up there." She pointed to the wing just above their heads. "It was as big as my hand, I swear, and must've been there the whole time. The speed of my descent dislodged it. I—"

"Enough!" He put a hand across her mouth, unable to repress a violent shudder. "You didn't crash and you didn't go mad with fear. That's all I need to know. Keep the details to yourself."

She nipped a finger and he hastily withdrew his hand. "I hope you washed that this morning."

"I did, for what it's worth. Laure water isn't much better than mud."

"On a good day," she agreed.

The wing reached the top of the thermal, and they were cruising again. Skender peered from a surprising height at the edge of the Divide as it crept by below, feeling better now that Chu was more her old self. The three vehicles, still moving, were now ants, and the source of the glint was little more than a dot on the cusp of the yellow dry land. As he scanned the edge of the escarpment, he spotted similar dots strung out in a long line at the edge of the Divide.

"This is getting stranger and stranger," he said. He explained what he thought he could see, and she squinted for herself.

"Either your eyesight is a lot better than mine," she said, "or your imagination is working overtime."

"Perhaps we should drop lower and take a closer look," he said.

"I don't know."

"Why not? The air is perfectly clear."

"You're clutching at sand," she said.

"I know, but it's something. I haven't seen much of anything else happening around here."

She shrugged and said, with a hint of asperity, "All right. You're the one with the licence." Angling the wing to her left, she began a slow, lazy spiral downward.

Skender knew that he was taking a risk, but the worst he could imagine happening was wasting a little time. And it seemed reasonable to him to connect the strange behaviour below with the disappearance of his mother in the area. She herself had suggested that the artefact she sought was valuable and that competing teams might be looking for it.

Although distracted by thoughts of camel chases and rogue Surveyors, he was ever mindful to check the ways of the wind as they descended. The occasional bump and jitter didn't scare him; he was over his early nervousness, when the slightest deviation from true had sent him into a panic. The licence hadn't lied yet, and it told him that the air between the wing and the ground held no surprises.

The notches along the edge of the Divide became clearer, to the point where people within them were now visible, lying spread-eagled on the dirt.

"They're in hides," Chu said, "waiting for something, or someone."

Skender glanced northeast, at the approaching vehicles. "They don't seem to be looking the right way."

"Maybe they're about to be surprised, then."

He slitted his eyes, trying to make out what object the glints of light came from. The people in the hides were wearing shiny decorations around their necks. It seemed likely that they were necklaces, although that struck him as odd. Change-rich collars designed to protect them from prying eyes? If so, they weren't working very well—not from above, anyway.

A more down-to-earth possibility occurred to him. The sunlight could be reflecting off crystal torcs. But that posed a whole new mystery. Why on earth would a couple of dozen Sky Wardens be hiding on the very edge of the Strand, as far away from the sea as they were allowed to go?

"There's someone else," said Chu, pointing inland.

He didn't take her seriously until he saw the morning shadow stretched long across the flat land. It was cast by a single person, possibly a man, walking with steady paces over the sand, holding something in his arms.

"Who the Goddess is that?"

"Your guess is as good as mine."

"What's he doing out here? What's he carrying?"

"This is weird," said Chu. "I don't like it. I think we should get out of here."

Skender shook his head. "Just a little longer." He projected the paths of the approaching vehicles and the walking man. They intersected not far from the line of hidden Sky Wardens. "I want to see what happens."

"Why? It has nothing to do with us, and it could be dangerous."

"How? We're perfectly safe up here."

"My bones disagree."

"Your bones don't have a licence. I do, and I'm telling you that the winds are clear. It's smooth sailing all around here."

"Maybe that's what I don't like. How can the air be so calm? We're over open land and the sun is up. It should be like the inside of a kettle!"

"Then we got lucky. Chu, I don't know what's going on, but I think we need to find out. It probably has nothing to do with my mother, but that doesn't mean it isn't important."

"All I care about is my own skin."

"Fine," he snapped, "so remember that your skin wants to fly, and helping me will convince the Magister to help you. Do we still have a deal or don't we?"

She didn't respond immediately. They continued in slow wide circles over the walking man and his burden, and over the people in the hides, descending further with every complete circuit. The figure striding with the regularity of clockwork across the parched land was as black as anyone Skender had ever seen. The object in his arms could have been a sack, or a person. It was impossible to tell.

"Okay," said Chu, taking a deep breath. "But if anything goes wrong, I'm going to—"

That was as far as she got before the wind emptied out of the wing and they were suddenly falling.

Skender's stomach leapt to his throat. He let go of Chu and clutched at the straps for support. They were spinning, tumbling.

"What's happening?"

"I don't know!" she yelled back. "You said the air was clear!"

"It is!" He tried to orient himself against the swinging horizon. He could see no chaotic flows gripping the wing, no miniature storms or hurricanes invisible to the naked eye. The air was as clear as it ever was.

And that, he suddenly realised, was the problem. It wasn't just the air around him he couldn't see. He couldn't see the air *anywhere*.

"The charms!" he cried. "Something's killed the charms!"

She looked around her, at the wing and at him. His tattoos had faded, and so had the black marks normally adorning the wing. Her knuckles whitened where they gripped the control straps.

"We're falling free!" He heard panic in her voice, barely hidden behind an iron determination to remain in control. "But it's okay! I trained for this. There are ways to ditch without getting hurt."

"With a passenger?"

She didn't waste energy answering the question. Wind whipped around them, blinding him. No longer his ally, it was both tenuous and as treacherous as a gale. Chu's arms wrenched at the wing, brought their graceless descent under a measure of control. He tried to help her, but feared that he was only making things worse.

They were falling like stones. It struck him abruptly that they could both die. *The higher we go, the harder we'll hit the ground.* In that instant, every other concern became insignificant: his mother, the identities of the strangers below, what Chu's plans were, and what she really thought of him . . .

"Hold on," she said. Her hands yanked at the wing's slender control surfaces. "This could be rough."

The ground ballooned in front of them. Chu threw herself backwards, trying to bring the nose up. The wing resisted. Skender could see them smacking hard against the ground if he didn't do something fast, so he wrapped both arms around her and wrenched their centre of gravity higher. The nose jerked and skewed to the right.

"Not the wing!" she cried, kicking outwards. "Don't damage the wing!"

The blur of the ground resolved into dirt and stones, rocks and stumps of trees, and then Chu's legs were running, trying valiantly to match their velocity. Skender covered his face with his hands, unable to do anything more than ride it out, feeling the heat of the sun reflected off the ground at him and the sudden lurch of impact, and hearing the awful scraping of leather against dirt, as a landing even worse than the one the previous night unfolded beneath him.

"Sal, wait!"

Shilly was three metres behind him and falling back, unable to match his pace. His reasons for bursting from the hide and running out into the open were a complete mystery. He was blowing their cover. Marmion was going to skin them alive!

That this was her first concern appalled her. She cursed herself as she tried her best to keep up with him. Behind her in the hide she had left Tom with the glass globe and the decision whether to use it or not. She had kept one of the flares, just in case. Not knowing what Sal had seen or sensed in the heat-dancing landscape around her made it difficult for her to know what to do.

Sal was running as though all the creatures of the Divide were after him. But he wasn't looking behind him. He was looking ahead and up.

That was when she saw it: a shape that could have been an enormous golden swallow dropping out of the sky. It angled in from above her and to her right. That it was the same thing she had seen the previous night, blocking the moon, she had no doubt. It was a flying wing of some sort, carrying two people below it. But what was it doing *here* and *now*, she asked herself, and why was it plunging at such a steep angle into the ground? If it hit, as it was bound to at any moment, its passengers were certain to be killed.

It levelled out at the last moment, turning a fatal drop into something more controlled. Lurching from left to right, it skidded across the dirt, raising a cloud of fine, dry dust into which Sal unhesitatingly ran.

"Sal!" she shouted, trying to make her stiff leg move more quickly. "Sal, be careful!"

He didn't seem to hear her. Not caring about discretion any longer, Shilly pulled the flare from her pocket and did as Tom had instructed her. The top cracked with the sound of breaking chalk, and she held the base well away from her face as it ignited. With a bang and a fierce whizzing sound, the firework shot up into the sky, trailing a line of black smoke behind it. It exploded high above her in a multicoloured cloud. Seconds later, another, much fainter bang came in reply from away to her right.

The dust had settled enough for her to see Sal again, and the wide scar the flying wing had carved into the yellow ground. Sal was bending over the wing, trying to get at what lay underneath.

"Don't touch her!" called a muffled voice. "She's hurt!"

"I can see that!" Sal said, pitching his voice reassuringly but loud enough to penetrate. "We have to get her out of the harness. Hold still. I see the latches."

Shilly could hear the concern he was trying to hide. There was blood on the ground where the flyer had skidded to a halt.

The wing wobbled.

"Easy!" Sal said more firmly. "I've got her. Can you get the wing off us? I need to look at her."

Shilly limped to a halt as the wing lifted up and away. She reached out a hand to help the person underneath. As the wing swung upright and the face of the person attached to it became visible, she took a step backwards.

"*Skender?*"

The name registered, but Skender didn't seem to see her at first. He looked at her and his gaze skidded away. His eyelids fluttered. Then he put a hand to his head and sank to his knees under the weight of the wing.

She forgot her surprise and moved in to help him. He was filthy and his robes were torn. The way he moved suggested that he was in shock.

And no wonder, she thought. After five years, he had just literally dropped out of the sky upon them.

"Is she . . . ?" Skender's concern was solely for the person stretched out on the ground between them. A young woman, Shilly saw; about her age or a little younger. Sal had turned her over and bunched a wad of fabric from his tunic in both hands and pressed it to her forehead. It was turning red fast.

"Head wounds bleed a lot," Sal said, gritting his teeth. "It's hard to tell what's going on underneath."

"Help her." Skender reached out with one badly grazed hand and gripped Sal's shoulder. "Like you helped Shilly when she broke her leg. *Heal* her!"

"I can't," Sal said. Shilly noted that their identities seemed to have sunk in, even if he hadn't acknowledged them in any other way.

"You have to!"

"I would if I could." Sal looked up at Skender with desperation in his eyes. "But I'm telling you—I *can't*."

In the dust and the heat of the moment, with an unknown woman's blood pouring through Sal's fingers onto the ground and an old friend pleading for the woman's life, Shilly felt a powerful chill, as of a cold, iron blade sliding down her spine.

"He's not lying," she said, turning to peer around her. Sal looked foggy-headed, as though trying to see through a veil. Skender's eyes were still not quite focusing. She herself felt no different—but being only sensitive to the Change, not naturally talented in it, she supposed she wouldn't.

Out of the weirdness of the heat haze to the southwest, a man walked towards them, carrying someone in his arms.

She let go of Skender and stood up. Despite the dread she felt, she would not confront that moment on her knees in the dirt. She would meet it face to face, and she would not scream like Larson Maiz.

The Homunculus stepped out of the wilderness. It *looked* like a man, but as it drew closer that first impression faded. Shilly was unable to bring it into focus; its outline constantly shifted, making its precise form difficult to pin down. Its skin was a deep, textureless black and it seemed to have too many arms. Its pace was even and unhurried.

The body in its arms hung as limp as a sleeping child, although it belonged to a full-sized man. The Homunculus carried him without strain. Dark hair with wide grey streaks framed a face she almost didn't recognise. Shilly knew it could only be one person.

"Stop right there," she said as the Homunculus came within a dozen paces of them.

Much to her surprise—and no small amount of relief—the creature came to a halt.

"Who are you?" it asked. The words issued fluidly from its mouth but, like its features, the sound possessed an odd distortion, as though simultaneously heard from a great distance and near at hand. Its mouth stretched far too wide. At odd moments it seemed to have four eyes.

"I'm Shilly," she said. "Who are *you*?"

The creature's oversized head blurred. "You don't need to know. Will you help this man?"

It stepped forward, offering her the body in its arms.

"What's wrong with him?" she asked, conscious of Sal watching the exchange closely from behind her. "What did you do to him?"

"Nothing. He needs water and food or he'll die."

"We can help him, but—"

"Good. It's been a long journey. He couldn't keep up, and you're the first people we've encountered. This land is so *empty* . . ."

The Homunculus's voice was full of sadness as it squatted and put the body of Highson Sparre on the ground at its feet.

"We'll take care of him," Shilly said. "Thank you."

The Homunculus didn't respond. It simply stood and looked around, getting its bearings. Shilly and the others stood between it and Laure. It turned, clearly intending to walk around them.

"Wait," Sal said, speaking at last. "This man is my father. Why did he summon you?"

"His summoning wasn't successful." The face turned to look at him, its expression unreadable. The strange eyes swung to focus on Shilly, then moved on. "You—" The Homunculus stared at Skender. "Your name is Galeus. We've met before, but you won't remember. We weren't part of this world, then."

Skender's mouth hung open in stunned surprise at the use of his heart-name. He shook his head.

"But I remember everything," he protested weakly.

The Homunculus stood frozen for a moment, staring at them all with intense concentration. Through the peculiar distortion, Shilly thought she saw the features of a young man, not much older than them, coalescing out of the chaos. The details of his face weren't completely stable; they came in and out of focus as though she saw them through ill-matched glass lenses. But there was definitely something trying to get through. Some*one*.

Shilly couldn't take her eyes off that strange face.

"Who *are* you?" she asked again, caught in a very strange dream.

For an instant, she thought the Homunculus might answer.

Then a shout from the south put paid to that possibility.

"Sal! Shilly! Get down!"

Shilly turned and saw Marmion and the other Wardens converging on the scene. Habryn Kail swung an arm over his head, and something whizzed towards them with a loud, singing noise.

She dropped her cane and ducked, recognising the bola for what it was, albeit one much larger than any she had ever used to catch rabbits or dune hens. The weighted rope spun over her and wrapped itself around the Homunculus's chest. It went down with a cry of pain in a furious tangle of limbs. Its form dissolved. She saw at least two heads and far too many arms and legs as the creature tried to right itself. But the bola had tied itself tightly around the Homunculus's torso. It was effectively pinned.

Then the wardens were among them. Skender gaped as the new arrivals helped Shilly to her feet and stood guard over the writhing creature.

"What the Goddess do you think you're doing?" Marmion asked her, his face white with fury. "I told you to stay down!"

"What's *your* problem?" she said, facing his challenge squarely. "You got what you wanted, didn't you?"

"I need help here!" said Sal, where he was still quenching the flow of blood from the injured woman's head. "Highson does, too. Argue later!"

"Eitzen, Rosevear," Marmion barked at two wardens, "help them!" He turned away from Shilly with a look that told her there would most definitely be a *later*, and went to study the Homunculus where it struggled on the ground, shouting its frustration.

"Misbegotten creature," Marmion said with a sneer. "We'll soon have you back in the earth, where you belong."

The Homunculus replied with a babble of words too fast to understand.

Through it all, Skender simply stared in shock. He didn't react until Tom joined the throng. Shilly watched the young Engineer as he checked on Highson then came around to Skender. Tom ducked under the wing and whispered rapidly into his ear.

Skender snapped out of his daze and stared at Tom with a matching intensity. "My mother?" he said in disbelief.

Tom nodded and stepped away. He put his right hand under his robes. Shilly watched him closely.

What's he up to now? she wondered.

The two wardens Marmion had named had taken over from Sal, checking the injured woman for broken bones then gently rolling her over so they could inspect her head wound properly.

Two more wardens examined Sal's father, lying ashen between them. Highson Sparre's lips were cracked and swollen. When they poured a trickle of water between them, he coughed weakly but didn't wake.

Tom crossed to where a tight knot of Sky Wardens stood over the flailing Homunculus. Marmion snapped his fingers and one of them handed him a long, thin staff that tapered to a wicked-looking point. Marmion raised it, whispering words under his breath.

Shilly realised then that there would be no careful probing into the Homunculus's nature, no exploration of why it had come into the world or what it wanted. Marmion had been sent to dispose of the creature, and he wasn't about to waste any time obeying his orders.

"You can't do this!" she exclaimed, remembering the Homunculus's concern for Highson. It hadn't seemed dangerous in the slightest. It had seemed simply *different*, and that was no reason for anything to die.

It was too late. The staff came down, and she was too far away to stop it striking home.

"No!" she shouted.

Sal was watching over Skender's friend, liberally covered in her blood, when Shilly cried out. He summed up the situation instantly. The

Homunculus lay sprawled before its executioner, hopelessly struggling. There was no way, especially without the Change, to intervene in time.

At the last moment, Tom shoved Marmion to one side. The point of the staff buried itself in the dirt. Marmion overbalanced and fell. Before any of the wardens could stop him, Tom bent over the captive creature and cut the bola with his work knife.

The Homunculus sprang to its feet and pushed Tom away. The wardens fell back as four arms spread in anger, like a spider about to strike. With one of its arms, it pulled the staff out of the ground and pointed it at Marmion, where he lay sprawled on the dirt. Their positions were now completely reversed.

"Don't!" called a weak voice.

The Homunculus's strange head turned to stare at Highson Sparre, who had raised one hand in warning from where he lay cradled in the arms of a Sky Warden.

"Don't," he repeated.

The Homunculus hissed in anger, but said, "No. You're right." It threw the staff to one side. "There has been enough death."

Then, without another word, it turned and ran for the edge of the Divide. Its manifold limbs moved in a blur, propelling it with inhuman speed.

"Stop it!" screamed Marmion. "Don't let it get away!"

Kail produced another bola and swung it over his head, picking up speed with each flex of his wiry muscles until it became a shimmering, humming disk. Sal didn't dare interfere for fear of losing a hand.

Kail set it free an instant before the Homunculus reached the precipice. The bola hurtled through the air with the speed of an arrow, flying swift and true. The Homunculus didn't slow as it ran out of space. It simply ran right off the edge. The bola sailed over its shape-shifting head as it dropped out of sight.

In that instant, the Change returned. The world, flat and dead in the Homunculus's presence, suddenly regained its usual life. The creature's wake had vanished, as though leaving the Earth's surface, however temporarily, caused the effect to evaporate. Sal could feel Shilly's anxiety and alarm where she stood near Kail. He could feel the buzzing of the pointed staff as Marmion recovered it and stuck it angrily in the dirt.

"*Idiots!*" the warden snarled. "*Now* what are we going to do?"

"We're going to keep tracking it," Shilly said, her anger a match for his. "And this time, when we find it, we're going to keep *you* well away from it!"

Marmion raised an arm to strike her, but Kail grabbed his hand.

"Don't do something you'll regret," said the tracker in a low, threatening voice.

"My only regret is surrounding myself with fools." The warden pulled free. Seething, he rounded on Tom next. "Do you intend to explain yourself?"

"What you were doing was wrong," Tom said without a hint of fear or remorse.

"That's not your concern!" Marmion yelled into his face. "The Alcaide sent us to do a job, and you just got in the way of it. Consider yourself warned. One more stunt like that, and I'll see your torc smashed into pieces."

Tom shrugged, his expression one of utter disinterest. Shilly went to him as a gesture of solidarity in the face of such vehement criticism. Marmion shook his head in exasperation. His gaze took in the severed bola, the discarded staff, Highson Sparre—who had fallen unconscious again—and Skender's injured friend. He seemed to be disbelieving his own eyes.

"Would someone like to tell me what *he's* doing?" he asked, nodding past Sal.

Sal turned. Skender was walking in the direction the Homunculus had taken, moving with difficulty under the weight of the wing still strapped to his back.

"I'll find out," Sal said, wiping his bloody hands on his robe and setting off in pursuit. Marmion turned to someone else and shouted at them.

Skender didn't look up when Sal came abreast of him just metres from the edge of the Divide. He was bent almost double and concentrating on carrying the wing.

"Going somewhere?"

"I have to. Tom told me that if I follow that thing it'll lead me to my mother."

"Your mother?" Sal was confused, realising only then that he knew nothing at all about what Skender was doing in this place. "What has happened to your mother?"

"I don't have time to explain, Sal. I have to go now. If it gets away from me, I might never find her."

"Is that what Tom said?"

"Yes!"

Sal came around the wing and stood in front of his old friend, forcing him to stop. Skender's face was lined with black markings that hadn't been there before.

"I can't let you fly like this," he said. "That's what you're going to do, right? Fly over the edge and chase it?"

"I don't have much choice."

"Sure you do." Sal looked at the fragile-seeming wing. Its flying surfaces were intact, and the delicate struts holding the wing-shape hadn't buckled or broken. Numerous fine glyphs and charms had appeared on its surface, indicating that it flew by more than natural means.

"You could take someone with you," he said, following his heart, not his head.

Skender's response was immediate. "No, Sal. I'm not going to take a chance with you. Chu and I were grumpy with each other; I talked her into flying over here; I didn't want to get her hurt, but she did. It was all my fault."

"It's not that simple. You flew into the bubble around the Homunculus. That's why you crashed. If you just keep away from it, we should be okay."

"But I *wasn't* flying it. Chu's a miner from Laure; she was doing the work. I was just telling her where to go."

"So what makes you think you can do it now, with or without me?"

"I remember what she did." Skender looked sick at heart, but he was weakening. No one wanted to go chasing monsters on their own.

Finally his eyes came up. They were completely black; all colour had vanished under the effects of the charm possessing him.

"Just tell me she's going to be okay. I couldn't bear it if—if she wasn't."

Sal put a hand on Skender's shoulder. "She's got a nasty gash on her head and plenty of bruises, but I think she'll be all right. I'm worried about *you*. How are you feeling?"

"I'm fine. Just shaken. Look, you can't stop me from trying—and I won't stop you from coming, if you really want to, but don't tell me I didn't warn you."

Sal took a deep breath. "That's settled, then," he said. "Show me how to strap myself in and let's get going."

Skender worked hurriedly to ensure that Sal was harnessed securely to the wing. Sal could hear his friend's laboured breathing in his ear, and quashed any visible sign of nervousness. Skender needed his support, not his doubts.

Sal only hoped that he was doing the right thing. With Highson found, there was no reason to stay behind—and if he went with Skender now, there was every chance he could track the Homunculus to Laure more quickly than Marmion and Kail.

His mind reached out for Shilly. *"Don't say anything, Carah,"* he told her through the Change. *"I'm going with Skender to help him find his mother. We're flying down into the Divide after the Homunculus."*

Sal knew that Shilly didn't have any natural source of the Change, so technically she couldn't reply, but a moment later her voice burst loud and clear in his head.

"What? Are you crazy?"

Sal could tell from the flavour of her thought that she was Taking from Tom—using their friend's natural talent to do what she could not do alone.

"Don't worry. Tom dreamed it, apparently."

"Well that makes everything *all right."*

He forced himself to ignore her anger. There wasn't time to deal with that. *"Look after Highson while I'm gone. And Skender's friend; her name's Chu, I think. Get them to Laure if you can. I'll meet you there afterwards."*

"Are you serious?"

"Okay, finished," said Skender in his ear. For better or for worse, they were now strapped together under the wing. "This is going to be hard, but we have to get right to the edge and jump off as far as we can. From there, just hang on. I'll do the rest."

"Okay." They walked awkwardly forward.

"I have to go now, Carah," he sent to Shilly. *"Sorry to leave you with Marmion. He's going to pop."*

"I can handle him. You worry about yourselves," she said more evenly. *"Just don't fall, Sayed. Come back to me in one piece."*

"Be sure of it."

Her concern came loud and clear over the link in the seconds it remained open. He was glad when it closed, because he was able to concentrate solely on what he was getting himself into. Before him, the vast gulf of the Divide looked very deep and very rugged. There were far too many jagged rocks on which he and Skender could be dashed to a bloody pulp.

But Skender's hands were covered with marks that weren't tattoos. He could feel the Change flowing through them. If Skender trusted the charms, so would he.

"I'm ready," he said, gripping the harness with sweaty, blood-stained hands.

Skender's knees bent and Sal bent his, too. Then they were jumping outward away from the safety of solid rock. A wall of wind hit them. The world flipped upside-down. Sal closed his eyes and hoped Tom had dreamed him surviving, too.

8

First the shadow had taken flesh and come to life. That had been bad enough. Then more shadows had come out of the darkness and pressed in around them, yabbering at them, forcing them to connect. It was too much all at once. Flight was the only solution.

But for a moment the connection had been pure and powerful. Anger was a white-hot stream pouring through the body they inhabited, washing away accumulated grief and confusion in a wonderful torrent. The air had been pure and the taste of iron-rich dust sweeter than any feast. Memories of life flooded back in. The world had been within their grasp, just for an instant.

And death. So long had they lived in the shadow of the void that the deepest shadow of all had seemed to forget them. Their beginnings stretched so far back as to be almost forgotten; their endings, likewise, had seemed an infinite distance away.

But even infinity had a way of drawing close, if stared at for too long. They were standing in it now, and death had almost reclaimed them.

Their new life had started with the light. It blazed like a sun at midnight, blinding them. They had woken, quivering and disoriented like a newborn, inside a body that wasn't designed for them, couldn't possibly contain them, and yet somehow held them, trapped together like twin yolks in an egg. They had panicked.

Then the light faded to black and a shadow had confronted them. Substance had overwhelmed them. Sensation flooded through nerves as new as dew. They felt air on their conjoined skin, heard sounds that might have been words, staggered on ground that felt as solid as the bedrock of eternity. They were in the world again. They were standing. They were alive!

But something was obviously wrong. The shadow hollered and fell away. Darkness pressed in again, and their panic deepened. The sense of wrongness grew stronger, took on a clear if distant form. It tugged at them, giving them purpose even as it sickened them, undermined any joy at being back.

They weren't the only things stirring in this strange, scarred world.

Their new body took some effort to coordinate, but it wasn't capricious. It possessed a strange internal logic that woke distant, disturbing memories.

One leg swung in front of another. Then another, and another.

They walked, and the cold, hard ground moved beneath them.

Darkness walked with them. Not the darkness of the void, but of predawn gloom waiting in anticipation of a sun that never came. Light seemed to radiate from their new body, illuminating the ground around their feet and anything that came within arm's reach. As they walked, they trailed a glowing path behind them. They imagined sometimes that they could see all the way back to where they had started, as if looking along an underground tunnel lit with phosphorescent mould.

All was not completely dark outside their elongated cocoon. The sun and moon shone wanly through the murk, and strange shapes brushed by them, unidentifiable but definitely there. Trees were skeletal cracks in their vision. Cliff faces and occasional ruined walls came into focus as the bubble of light touched them. Occasional glimpses of life stirred as creatures scurried out of their path, diving into undergrowth or under rocks as they approached. The new world was frightened of them, but why that might be they didn't know.

They walked on, never growing tired or hungry or thirsty. Their new body didn't need to sleep, and neither did they: they had slept an eternity already, and might never need to again. Entangled, they found it difficult to think separately, and remained that way as night and day rolled on around them. They felt they could walk from one side of the

Earth to the other. Even in its strange state, the world and its sensations were a wealth of riches compared to the poverty that had preceded it.

Eventually they realised that they were being followed. Down the corridor of light behind them, a shadow had appeared, distant but definitely there. It haunted them like the ghost of their past, never quite coming into focus, never quite within reach.

They knew that there was much they had forgotten, or buried in memories that had lain stagnant for an age. Pieces were coming back to them—faces, names, and places that had once been important to them. With those fragments came a growing sense of dread at the thought of their destination. The wrongness seeped into them, sucking at their resolve like a whirlpool.

Their pace ebbed, although they made no conscious decision to slow down. The shadow behind them held less creeping horror than the wrongness ahead.

When the shadow came closer, it resolved into a man, a man with dark skin and greying hair, whose lips were cracked and whose eyes saw right through them. He was staggering, exhausted. They had to force him to stop and look at them, although what he saw they couldn't tell. They had no mirrors to see their new face, and they had passed no standing water.

The man's lips moved, but his words made no sense. *Why not her?* he whispered urgently, his voice as ghostly as the world around them. *Why not her?*

They recognised him. That was the most startling thing. They knew who the man had been searching for and why his quest had failed. His desperation was naked before them, writ deep in lines and tear tracks.

He had delivered them into the world, and they supposed they owed him for that.

Many days had passed since their awakening; a great distance had passed beneath their implacably plodding feet. No other people crossed their path until a great gulf yawned before them, and they sensed a changing in the texture of the world. They were getting closer to their destination. Things were becoming increasingly strained.

Then—outrageously, unexpectedly—more shadows appeared. Things fell out of the sky. Fireworks. If their new body had had a heart, it would have been racing.

People they couldn't possibly recognise, but did, assailed them. Fractured memories coursed through them: *one of three who were caught in the Way; one of three who escaped; darkness pressing in on every side; a hum that threatened to stamp their minds flat under the heel of eternity . . .*

A hint of loneliness had kept them talking when they knew they should be moving on. As a result, death had almost caught them. What did death mean in this strange new world, in their new body? What would it mean for the world if they were to die before their job was done? Would all their sacrifices have been for nothing?

There has been enough death. They knew *that* with a cold certainty that cut through their fear like a knife. And anger, sweet and pure, had fuelled the thrust.

They ran. They sensed the lip of a cliff before them as they fled the shadows, and jumped over it without hesitation. The glowing path winked out behind them as they plummeted to an invisible ground below. For a moment, they were back in the void, with no point of reference, tumbling and turning, limbs a-flailing.

Then the ground hit them, and the light returned. Ahead of them, unseen but deeply felt, lay their destination. Nothing would stop them from reaching it. Not the shadows, not death, and not the fear that gnawed at their insides like time's teeth at stone. The wrongness awaited them.

Unharmed, but not untouched, they climbed to their feet and resumed their journey.

THE DUTY

"What do we mean when we say 'destiny'?
What is this thing called 'fate'?
A succour for the lazy-minded.
A balm for the weak of will."
THE BOOK OF TOWERS, FRAGMENT 83

With no small sense of misgiving, Shilly watched Skender's flying wing drop over the edge of the Divide. Just like that, Sal was gone, and the Goddess only knew if he would ever come back. So much had happened so quickly that she despaired of ever coming abreast of it all.

Deciding to head off at least one potential tirade, she explained the sudden change in events to Marmion.

"Sal and Skender are going after the Homunculus," she said, stating the fait accompli baldly. He would just have to accept it. "They'll call us if they find anything."

Marmion stared at her with fury in his eyes, but he didn't say anything at first. When he did speak, his voice was carefully controlled.

"And who is this Skender? Where does he come from and what is he doing here?"

"He's from the Interior," she began.

"I could tell that by looking at him. Was his arrival here planned? Were you expecting him?"

"No," she said with perfect honesty. "I haven't seen him in years. Apparently he's looking for his mother," she added, remembering something Sal had alluded to.

"Here?"

She shrugged, knowing nothing more about the situation. "I guess when Chu, his friend, wakes up, we can ask her."

"I guess we can," Marmion said with acid sarcasm.

Kail whistled for attention. "Company!"

Heads turned. The tracker pointed at a billowing cloud on the northeastern horizon. The sound of chimerical engines thrumming in the distance came dimly to her, now she knew to listen.

Shilly's pulse beat a little faster, wondering who would be driving so close to the Divide. A delegation from Laure, perhaps, or further abroad? There was no way of knowing until they arrived.

The wardens turned their attention outwards, forming a protective cordon around the injured as the vehicles approached. Marmion held his pointed staff at the ready. Kail regarded the scene from his lofty perspective, showing no emotion at all.

As the vehicles drew closer, they resolved into open-frame buses, smaller than the Wardens' buses but no less rugged. Their engines roared and gouted clouds of white smoke. Men and women clung to the frames, shouting words Shilly couldn't quite make out. They seemed to be jeering.

The buses fanned out, tracing a noisy circle around the wardens. There was no mistaking the threat. The new arrivals were sizing the wardens up, testing them.

Marmion refused to be provoked. He simply waited, a haughty cast to his round face.

Eventually one of the buses broke away from the others and angled inward. Spraying dirt behind its wide, corrugated wheels, it slid to a halt not far from where Shilly stood. Its engine growled noisily. Fumes billowed from its exhaust.

The driver, a heavyset, bearded man with the broadest shoulders Shilly had ever seen, stood up behind the wheel, his expression hostile. His passengers hung from the frame of the bus, silent for the moment but with an air of readiness. Some scowled; others grinned. Shilly saw the metal of weapons visible through their robes.

Marmion took two steps away from the rest of the wardens towards the driver—clearly the leader of the newcomers. The two men sized each other up from a distance, radiating indignation.

Before either could speak, a loud boom came from the Divide, as of a giant thunderclap. Heads turned. Lightning flashed down from an empty sky, the object of the strike invisible over the cliff edge. Black clouds boiled upwards out of the Divide, blotting out the sun. A cold wind rushed over them.

Shilly covered her eyes. The wind grew stronger, making her stagger. Around her, wardens fell to their knees, clutching their robes and covering their eyes. Lightning flashed again, and the earth itself seemed to rumble.

Alarmed, Shilly peered through her fingers at the newcomers. This had to be a trap. The wardens would be attacked while they were startled by the sudden squall. She found, to her surprise, that the people on the nearest bus were just as startled as she was. Voices raised in alarm, shouting words that the wind snatched away. The driver regarded the unnatural atmospherics with a respectful wariness that seemed to be directed at Marmion, the only one of the wardens left standing.

They thought we *did this!* Shilly realised.

The driver dropped back into his seat and, with a roar of engines, powered away. The other two buses broke their endless circling and fell into its wake. Without a rearward glance, the newcomers accelerated back the way they had come and vanished in a cloud of dust.

The storm ebbed quickly. The thick, black clouds became grey, then white, then blew themselves out with one mighty rush of wind. Shilly felt cool dampness on her cheeks and forehead, and was amazed to find moisture condensed there. The dry, desert air suddenly tasted sweet.

Static electricity crackled from her fingertips as she took Tom's arm. He had let her Take from him before, so she felt comfortable doing it again.

"Sayed, was that you?"

Sal's reply was faint and fragmented. "*—didn't want to give you a fright.*" He sounded a thousand kilometres away. "*Sorry—rough—*"

Although she was concerned for him, she didn't want to distract him from his immediate situation, whatever it was. "*Save your strength,*" she said. "*I just wanted to make sure.*"

His thoughts slipped from her mind, but the niggling sense of him remained. While that tickled at the underside of her mind, she would know that he was alive, somewhere.

Marmion turned to face the rest of the search party. He looked unsettled rather than angry. The latest twist in events had temporarily overwhelmed his predisposition to outrage.

"That's our cue to get moving," he said. "We need to uncover the buses and get them over here. Our immediate priorities are the injured people in our care. We'll either have to treat them here or find a way across to Laure—and it looks like we're going that way anyway, if we're to retain any chance of heading off the Homunculus. Whoever *those* people were—" he indicated the ruts left by the newcomers' wheels with a jerk of his head, "—I think we'd be best served by avoiding them in the future."

"You'll get no argument from me," said Shilly.

"I presume that was Sal," he said to her, lips twisted as though he had tasted something particularly noxious. "That little *display*."

She explained what little she had learned about Sal and Skender.

"Well, next time you hear from him, tell him to tone it down. We're not a carnival."

Shilly choked back a comment that she didn't care what Sal did or what it looked like to others; he could stitch the Divide back together from end to end, just as long as he was safe.

Tom accepted her thanks for using his talent. She could tell he felt the drain of it, and resolved to let him recover before trying again. Pale around the cheeks, he hurried off to collapse the hide and fetch the buggy, while she checked on Highson and Skender's friend, fighting exhaustion of her own.

Sal's father lay limply on his side, protected by a makeshift sunshade. His skin was peeling from long exposure to the sun and his eyes had retreated into their sockets. Consciousness seemed to have fled for good after his brief awakening, but his pulse and respiration were steady.

Skender's friend had the more obvious injury, but she was already beginning to stir. Shilly joined the warden caring for her, ready to offer help if needed. Her leather attire had been torn and scraped through to the skin in several places, but it had undoubtedly saved her from more serious injuries. Her face and throat were splattered with dried blood. It was hard to see what she would look like without the cloth wadded against her right temple, but Shilly made out thick black hair, almond eyes, and a proud nose. Full lips and warm, light brown skin suggested that her ancestry belonged to neither the Interior nor the Strand. Shilly remembered from years ago a taxi driver telling her about a yellow-skinned people who lived in the tops of giant trees.

Missing mothers, Shilly thought, *flying wings, and strange girls from the East . . . what have you got yourself mixed up in this time, Skender Van Haasteren?*

The young woman moaned and tried to brush away the hands at her head. Her eyelids fluttered. "What . . . ? How . . . ?"

"Take a deep breath," said Shilly, leaning close. "You're in safe hands. Your name is Chu, right?"

Her eyes flickered open, revealing irises so brown they were almost as black as her pupils. "Yes," she said, wincing. "Who are you? Where am I?"

"My name is Shilly."

"What happened to . . . ?" She sat up, eyes widening in alarm as she looked around. "My wing! Skender!"

"They're both okay," Shilly soothed her, hoping she was telling the truth. "Skender's gone after his mother. We're meeting him later."

"But I had everything . . ." Chu looked at Shilly, crestfallen, then at her torn clothes. "It was all going . . ." Without warning, she burst into tears.

Shilly did the only thing she could think of: she took the girl into her arms. Chu didn't resist, and Shilly brushed away the warden—a young man whose name she had forgotten—when he tried to hang on to the dressing still pressed to Chu's head. She held it in place as Chu wept into her shoulder.

Around them, the wardens assembled an impromptu camp, positioning the two buses and one buggy in a triangle around the two patients. The sun had crept higher into the sky and burned down with growing force. Two of the wardens took the raw material of the hides and reassembled it into a temporary sunshade. Shilly was heartily glad of it when its shadow fell over them. The dry, ovenlike heat was getting to her.

Finally Chu eased off. She sat back and wiped her nose, unable to meet Shilly's eyes as she assumed responsibility for the wadding at her head.

"Does it hurt?" Shilly asked her.

"Like anything," she said. "I'm sorry. I've no idea who you are, but you must think I'm a total freak."

"I've seen much worse." Shilly shrugged. "And besides, any friend of Skender's is a friend of mine, freak or otherwise."

"You know him?"

"Used to, years ago."

A flash of something very much like jealousy passed across the young woman's face. "How?"

"He helped Sal and me in the Haunted City," Shilly reassured her. "Sal's with him now, making sure he's okay."

"The Haunted City?" Chu winced and held the wadding tighter to her scalp. Her jealousy intensified, if anything, and Shilly realised that she had misinterpreted where the emotion was directed, and at whom. "He really does get around, doesn't he?"

"Those were exceptional circumstances." Shilly wondered how much Skender had told Chu about the old days. "I really don't know what he's been up to since then. Life has been—well, complicated."

Chu was beginning to take in more of her environment, looking around in confusion. "Seems like it still is. Are these Sky Wardens?"

"Yes."

"Are *you* a Sky Warden?"

"No way. You're from Laure?"

Chu nodded, and winced. A look of dismay crossed her fine features. Shilly thought she might cry again. "I don't know how I'm going to get back if Skender has my wing."

That problem had occurred to Shilly also. It was all very well for Sal and Marmion to talk about going to the distant city, but getting there wasn't going to be easy.

At least Chu didn't seem angry about Skender's actions. Concerned, yes; hurt, even; but Shilly was spared having to justify the actions of someone she hadn't seen for five years.

"We'll take you home," she said, "if you show us a way across the Divide."

Chu looked cautiously hopeful. "There's a road. It's pretty old, though, and supposed to be unsafe."

"Our rides have come a long way. They're pretty tough."

"That wasn't what I meant."

"Oh." Shilly didn't know what lived on the bottom of the Divide, and she was in no particular hurry to find out.

"We saw other vehicles out here," she said. "Three of them. They've gone now. Do you know anything about them?"

Chu shook her head. "Skender and I saw them from the air. He thought they were coming from the Aad, but I don't see how that could be possible."

"The where?"

"The other half of the city, where the Divide cut it in two. The Aad's a Ruin, and a dangerous one. No one goes there."

"And if the road to Laure isn't used very often, that means they probably didn't come from there, either."

"I guess so."

Shilly took a moment to collect her thoughts. Things weren't quite adding up right.

"Excuse me," she said, waving for the young warden to resume his ministrations, "I have to talk to someone."

Chu nodded wearily as Shilly went to find Kail.

The tracker had wandered off to peer over the edge of the Divide. During daylight hours he wore a wide-brimmed hat that kept his face in permanent shadow. A spreading patch of sweat darkened the back of his cotton shirt.

He looked up as Shilly approached.

"No sign of them," he said, pointing down into the baked rip in the land. "Look for yourself."

Shilly followed the direction of his finger. On the wide, cracked plain below, she saw nothing that looked like a road leading to Laure, and not the slightest trace of Sal and Skender.

She could read the latter evidence, or lack of it, two ways: that they were lying low as they tracked the Homunculus, or that the storm Sal whipped up had propelled them well out of sight. Either option left room for hope. She had no reason or inclination to consider other possibilities.

"I think you're wrong," she said.

"Really?"

"Not about this. I think you're wrong about the Homunculus."

Kail placed one leather-booted foot on a boulder and put both hands on the raised knee. "In what sense?"

"Let me ask *you* a question, first." She dug the tip of her cane firmly into the dirt. "Were you really going to stand by and let Marmion kill the thing you've travelled a thousand kilometres to catch?"

"It's not my place to wonder what he wants with it," Kail drawled. "I'm just the tracker."

"But you intervened when he went to hit me. Why did you do that?"

"Because if I hadn't, that would've been wrong."

"Can you understand why I'm a little confused?" she asked him. "Obviously I'm grateful to you for stopping things from getting out of hand, but I'd be happier if you could extend that charity to other creatures as well."

He regarded her for a long moment. "If that was the sort of stuff Lodo taught you, no wonder they kicked him out of the Haunted City."

"Was *that* why you did it," she persisted, "because he's Lodo's nephew? Are you afraid that Marmion might do something he'll feel bad about later? Well, I've got news for you. After this, he and I are never going to be friends, no matter who we have in common. Not if the Divide swallows the world and we're the last people left alive."

Kail smiled crookedly. "I can assure you, completely, that when I acted it was not for Marmion's benefit. And if I were you, I'd never suggest to him that it was. I guarantee you it won't go down well."

She imagined it wouldn't. The odds of her mentioning Marmion's connection to Lodo were growing remoter by the hour. She would be happiest to forget the whole thing entirely.

"I want an assurance from you," she said, "that the Homunculus won't come to any unnecessary harm the next time it's in Marmion's custody."

"Why should I agree to that?"

"Because we still don't know why Highson made it. Until he explains his motives, I'm prepared to give both of them the benefit of the doubt. Don't forget that he'd be dead now if the Homunculus hadn't carried him here."

"He might wish he *was* dead when he wakes up and Marmion starts questioning him."

"Either way, the truth will come out. Wait until then before judging. Okay?"

He nodded wearily. "All right. I'll do that. Any other requests?"

"Yes. I want you to help me convince Marmion to give up on going to Laure."

Prior to that moment, Kail had listened to her with a faintly amused air, as though nothing she said could surprise him. Now he straightened, and his long features creased into a frown.

"Why would I want to do that?"

"Because that's not where the Homunculus is going. And I think I can convince you."

"Go on then." His tone spoke more clearly than his words. It said: *This should be interesting.*

"Have you heard of the Aad?"

He shook his head.

"It's not on your map. It turns out that there are two half-cities here, not one. The half on the north," she said, pointing into the hazy distance, "is Laure. The other is the Aad, a Ruin. Chu, the girl in the flyer, says no one goes there."

"If no one goes there, doesn't that invalidate your argument?"

"Hardly. For starters, the Aad lies in the Homunculus's path, too, making it just as likely a destination as Laure. And I'd hardly call the Homunculus *anyone*, would you? There may be something in the Aad that you or I wouldn't recognise as important. The Homunculus may be looking for somewhere to hide."

"So it's shy. Do you really think that?"

She shook her head. "I think that our new friends, the ones who buzzed us before, are from the Aad, and that they were coming to meet the Homunculus. Unfortunately for them, we got in the way. Now it's on the run, and they've gone back to where they came from. I don't have any doubt that they'll try again."

Kail nodded slowly. "Interesting," he said, "but you're forgetting one thing. Just because these people have come from the Aad doesn't mean that that's where they'll end up. It could just be a staging area. Their real destination could be somewhere further afield. Like Laure."

That was true. "Even so," she said, "if the staging area is there, at the Aad, and we're quick, we might catch them."

"We've got wounded to think of. We'll need to get them to Laure."

"But not all of us would have to go. In fact, the fewer of us there are, the more likely we are to go undetected. Say we took the buggy. Me, Tom, you, if you wanted—"

Kail laughed at her, full-throated and long. There was no maliciousness to it, just broad amusement. A flush crept up her throat nonetheless; her mouth shut into a determined line.

He clapped one large hand on her shoulder, sending a shockwave down her weak thighbone.

"Shilly, you're amazing. You've seen what this thing is and what it can do; you don't know how many of its friends could be waiting for you in the Aad; yet still you want to charge on in with barely an ally beside you. Don't you think you're being a bit rash?"

"I think this is an opportunity we'd be rash to dismiss," she said, shoving his hand aside. "With Sal coming one way and us coming the other—"

"We might find ourselves holding nothing but air."

"So we do nothing?" Frustration flared into anger. She felt that he was dismissing her suggestion without properly considering it. "We expect Sal and Skender to do it all on their own while we twiddle our thumbs in Laure?"

"That's not what I'm suggesting in the slightest. Yes, we go to Laure, but don't think I intend to leave it at that. Remember: get there and we'll have the resources of a small city behind us. Doesn't that sound a little more appealing, my friend?"

She stared at him, trying to tell if he was fobbing her off with empty words. His deeply etched features seemed sincere enough.

"I am duty bound to do the Alcaide's will, as channelled through his loyal representative." Kail's nostrils flared. "But I can promise you this: I'll also do my level best to ensure that Sal and Skender—and the Homunculus, if it matters to you so much—aren't left in the lurch out here. Do you believe me?"

She did, although she didn't want to admit it. It unnerved her that he could so easily turn her around when she had been so sure of herself. There was something about him that made her believe him.

Maybe, she told herself, *it's just because what he says makes sense. If only Marmion had half his brains . . .*

"Very well," she said. "I'll take your word on this. But if you let me down, you'll regret it."

Without a trace of irony, he said, "I'm sure I would." His gaze left her and took in the distant smudge that was their destination.

Shilly reconciled herself to the change of plans and did her best to swallow the worry she felt for Sal. She was still angry at him for leaving so precipitously. Why couldn't they have gone to rescue Skender's mother together? What was the big rush? The temptation to turn her frustration back on herself or those around her was very strong.

We'll be back for you soon, she called to him, although she knew her mental voice went no further than the inside of her skull. *Be safe until then, my love.*

THE DIVIDE

**"Of all the new creatures contending with Humanity for dominion of the Earth, the man'kin are the worst.
Fashioned after us, yet owning none of our civilisation, they deserve only the hammer and the chisel.
Talk to one at your peril,
for lies spill from their lips instead of breath."**
THE BOOK OF TOWERS, FRAGMENT 177

*J*ust don't fall.

Simple words; an even simpler instruction; but surprisingly hard to obey when strapped to a wing that seemed to have a mind of its own. Sal opened his eyes a crack and instantly squeezed them shut again. The ground was spinning around him. He didn't think it was supposed to be doing that—and he was *certain* he didn't want to be so close to it while it happened.

"Can I help?" He yelled the words over the sound of the wind flapping and snapping past the wing.

"I don't know," Skender yelled in his ear, flinging his weight from side to side. "This is harder than it looked." Sal heard his old friend's desperation as clearly as he heard the wind. Each movement seemed to overcorrect a previous mistake. It was impossible to find an even keel.

Sal hung on to the straps for all he was worth. The Change thrummed through the charms on the wing, sending a strong vibration up his spine. He sought a way to shore up the charms, since he couldn't do anything for Skender at the control end. If it had been a case of brute force alone, he might not feel so useless.

But that route proved futile. The charms were elegantly fashioned, intricate things, relying on balance and delicate synergies to keep gravity at bay. His blunt intervention might unravel them all and send him and Skender to their deaths. If Shilly had been there, maybe . . .

He dared another glimpse. The Divide cliffs were horrifically near. Skender avoided colliding with an upthrust stone spar by bare centimetres, and then only to plunge even closer to the ground. They lurched upwards like a drunken bee, almost tipping over in the process.

Sal had to think of something, fast. He could assist neither Skender nor the wing itself, but there had to be another way. The Change was in everything; surely there was something else it could act on to help them out of this predicament.

Of course. He took a deep breath and gathered his thoughts.

It was hard to ignore the chaotic tumbling—or the fear that they might be dashed to the ground at any moment—but he did his best. He needed to focus on the world in a less emotional way. He needed to become part of it, to insinuate himself into it as he had insinuated himself into the mind of the seagull over the beach in Fundelry, days ago. He felt the sun's warmth beaming down on him, the bluff solidity of the Divide's southern wall nearby, the erratic snatching of the wind at his hair . . .

The wind.

He imagined being back on the vivid beach, down in the core of himself where ocean and bedrock met, and took what he needed. It was more than he had taken for many years, and he bent it to his will in ways he hadn't attempted since leaving the Haunted City: the Change came with seductive ease, fuelled by a desperation as strong now as it had been then. Power crackled through him like a bushfire through scrub.

The world responded instantly. The wind stiffened around them, filling the wing and lifting it higher.

Skender took advantage of the sudden development. The wing stabilised and its movements became more confident. Sal dared to open his eyes and found himself almost level with the top of the Divide, wobbling over the pitted, scarred ground below. He was far too high to feel comfortable, but at least they weren't about to crash headlong into solid rock. Giving Skender breathing space in which to recover his wits was the important thing.

Sal's old friend gasped in his ear. "Did you—?"

He got no further. The air temperature suddenly dropped. The sun vanished behind a cloud that blossomed out of nowhere directly overhead, as deep and black as night. Lightning flashed, blinding Sal and deafening him with its thunder. The wind that had so welcomingly filled the wing now blew at gale force, threatening to smash them from the sky.

Yadeh-tash, the tiny stone pendant around Sal's neck, quivered violently, telling him that a storm was coming.

Too late, thought Sal, cursing the unpredictability of the elements. *It's already here!*

Skender sent them sharply downwards, out of the roiling vapour. Lightning flashed a second time. Freezing droplets of water materialised out of thin air, instantly soaking them. The boom of thunder pursued them as they dived for the relative safety of the ground. Sal felt the fury of the storm at his heels, and remembered then why he only attempted such things when driven by the direst of need.

The weather became less choppy away from where the black clouds pressed like billowing sails at the edge of the Divide. Skender didn't keep them aloft any longer than they had to be. Once they were level and a suitable place to land appeared, he dipped them lower by increments until they were barely skimming the sand. A sharp tug brought the wing up, catching the air and delivering Sal and Skender to a stumbling, awkward landfall.

One last rumble, as though from a giant's belly, saw the unnatural storm unravel. *Yadeh-tash* became quiet as the threat of rain passed. By the time Skender pulled Sal free of the harness, the sun had come out again.

Sal collapsed gratefully onto the sand and wiped the water from his eyes. He was glad that their impetuousness hadn't resulted in injury or death, but he was bone-weary from the effort. The core of him was drained.

"Sayed, was that you?"

The voice came from Shilly, through Tom again. A sheet of imaginary "I" and "H" shapes rained down behind his eyes as the charm took effect. The touch of her mind brought home the fact that they were far apart, and that without her things always seemed to go wrong.

Sal clutched at the last dregs of his wild talent to reply.

"I didn't want to give you a fright. Sorry about that. A bit of a rough landing, but we're okay now."

"Save your strength," she replied. *"I just wanted to check."*

Then she was gone and he was able to relax—in a manner of speaking. He was stuck on the bottom of the Divide with no easy way out, no clear destination, no supplies apart from the water bottle slung around Skender's neck, and with no clear idea of exactly what he was chasing. But it wasn't all bad news. The ground beneath him looked perfectly ordinary; the dirt was dry and fine-grained, a greyish yellow in colour. He sniffed, and noted that the air smelled oddly of ancient ashes. A constant tingle of the Change surrounded him, but none of the legendary creatures for which the Divide was famous were in evidence, and nothing inanimate seemed likely to devour them in the next moment or two. He figured he could pause to catch his breath.

"Are you okay?" asked Skender. Somehow the wing had collapsed down to a roughly person-sized bundle. It lay on its side while Skender leaned over him, looking concerned. The black lines that had covered Skender's face and hands had vanished. His eyes had returned to normal.

"I'll be fine," Sal said, knowing it to be true. The blood on his tunic belonged to Chu. "Just give me a sec to recover."

Skender did that, although he was obviously restless to get moving. Sal watched him as he took his bearings and climbed a nearby mound to seek the Homunculus. Skender tested moving his shoulder and winced.

In his youth, Skender had been round-faced and crazy-haired. Some of that baby fat had burned off in his teens, but his features remained broad and homely and his dark locks rioted with the same lack of discipline as ever. His skin was even paler than Sal's, marking his Interior origins. He didn't seem to be much taller than he had been when Sal last met him.

Skender performed a minor charm to test which direction he was facing. Sal wondered about the tattoos he had seen on Skender's skin. Skender was well trained and educated but lacked the depth of talent Sal possessed. Where had he found the capacity for such powerful Change-working as flying the wing? However, these questions could wait. There were more important mysteries pressing for Sal's attention.

"Tell me about your mother," he called.

"She went missing around here somewhere," came the reply.

"Surveying, I suppose."

"Yes. I don't know what for. I came to find her, but haven't had much luck yet. I presume you haven't seen her."

Sal remembered Abi Van Haasteren from his journeys in the Interior. A tall, proud woman in ochre robes, she had been with Sal and Shilly before the Cold Moon Synod in the city of the Nine Stars.

"If I had seen her," he said, "I wouldn't be looking for her now."

"Right." Skender descended from the mound and came over to join him. The sudden wash of moisture in the air had made the dust on his face and robes streak. He looked like he had been roughhoused by mud monsters. "Thanks for that," he said. "I don't think I would've got even this far on my own."

"You never know. You were always pretty resourceful." Sal held out a hand, and Skender took it with both of his. "It's good to see you again."

They gripped each other for a moment, and Sal wondered where the two kids they'd been had got to. When had they grown up and started rescuing their parents, not the other way around? The years between then and now didn't seem numerous enough to account for the transformation.

Yet it was still Skender standing before him, and he was in just as much of a hurry as he had ever been, although for different reasons. He was bruised and his clothes were ragged. The dazed edginess Sal had seen in his eyes on the lip of the Divide was quite gone.

Sal allowed himself to be hauled to his feet. "Okay," he said, brushing himself off and trying to get his breath back. "Where to?"

"There are tracks heading towards the Aad," Skender said, pointing northeast along the Divide. "That's the other half of Laure, where I think Mum was headed when she disappeared. It's a Ruin of some kind."

In the distance, he saw that the mighty cliff wall on his right had subsided down to the level of the valley floor before abruptly turning southwest. There, where the shattered slope met the plain, Sal saw a field of tumbled masonry. That, presumably, was the outskirts of the ruined city.

"Off we go, then," he said. "Easy."

"They're not human tracks."

Sal followed Skender to the marks and saw instantly that he was right. The imprints were perfectly triangular and deep. Whatever had made them was very heavy. Three lines did indeed lead towards the Aad.

"Well, it's a start. Something went there. We might as well, too." When Skender didn't seem reassured by his reasoning, Sal added, "And we'll look for more concrete clues along the way. Don't worry. If we cross the Homunculus's path, we'll know about it."

Slightly reassured, Skender nodded and indicated that Sal should pick up one end of the collapsed wing. Sal didn't relish the thought of carrying any more than his own exhausted body weight, but understood that leaving the wing behind wasn't an option. Weary and covered in dried mud, the two of them set out across the surface of the Divide.

Skender did his best not to let his thoughts range too far ahead, or too far behind. As he and Sal followed the strange impressions in the blasted soil, he concentrated solely on the present, on what he needed to do. *Find the Homunculus*, Tom had said, *and you'll find your mother. If you don't, you'll never see her again.* The instruction was perfectly simple, even if the reasoning behind it eluded him. Doubting it soon saw him debating the wisdom of leaping off the edge of the cliff in Chu's wing.

Part of him suspected that he might have done a very rash thing indeed. All the stories he had heard about the Divide and the things that lived in it came back to him with unwanted vividness: creatures impersonating dead trees that impaled travellers on needle-sharp branches; caves that appeared to hold riches but closed shut like mouths when entered by the unwary; swarms of small, light-hating vampires that roamed freely at night but crowded fearfully together during the day, which meant that taking shelter in the wrong shadow could literally cost passersby their lives. Skender remembered the souls supposedly trapped in the stone cliff faces and was glad that Sal was with him. Although they didn't talk much at first, it was good to have company.

A constant, moaning wind swept along the floor of the Divide. It kicked up dust that made his eyes sting. The ground had a metallic tang that didn't smell quite natural. Skender's mouth filled with a strange taste that wouldn't go away.

"Over there," said Sal as the sun crept higher into the sky and there was still no sign of the Homunculus's wake. Skender turned to his left to see Sal nodding at a feature in the twisted landscape that he had missed from the air: a dry creek bed, three metres deep, that wriggled along roughly parallel to the ravine wall nearer the centre of the Divide. They headed for it and slid carefully to the bottom, where soft sand held the tracks of numerous feet, some of them human-sized.

Skender was instantly relieved at not having to walk in the open. The vastness of the Divide impressed itself upon him at ground level. He constantly felt as though he was being watched.

As they walked, they exchanged stories. Sal explained how he and Shilly had come to be with a party of Sky Wardens so close to the Interior. Skender listened with amazement as Sal recounted the creation of the Homunculus, Highson Sparre's pursuit of it across the Strand, the first meeting with Marmion and Kail, and the abortive ambush attempt on the edge of the Divide.

In return, he described how he had come to Laure and initially sought his mother in the tunnels beneath the city. It seemed weeks since Chu had rescued him and put him on the right path.

I'm sorry, Chu, he thought, favouring the aching muscles down his right side. He hoped she would understand. They both had priorities and his mother simply came first.

"So this licence thing," said Sal on a fleeting rest break. "The yadachi made it to help you see the wind. Is that right?"

Skender took the charm from within his torn robes and handed it to Sal, who turned the black sheet over in his hands, marvelling at it.

"Does it work on the ground?"

"It was working when we landed. I took it off so I could see more clearly."

Sal nodded, although it was obvious he thought Skender had made a mistake. "This could be just what we need to find the Homunculus. Remember when you crashed with Chu because you couldn't see the wind? You said it looked perfectly clear up there, above the Homunculus."

Skender nodded, then slapped his forehead. "Ach! If I put the licence back on, I can look for clear spaces ahead. They'll show me which way the Homunculus went."

Sal seemed more amused than irritated by Skender's oversight. "I knew if we banged our heads together long enough we'd think of something."

Skender averted his eyes as he took the licence back from Sal and placed it on his chest. Sal had changed since they'd last met, he mused, and it wasn't just the long hair and the stubble on his chin. He had become surer of himself, more confident. As a teenager, he had been stricken with guilt and conflicted at almost every turn. A smouldering, frustrated rage had seemed to fill him, keen for an outlet.

That rage appeared to have been tamed. Skender wondered how.

"Tell me about you and Shilly," he said as the black disorientation swept over him again. "It's good to see you guys together."

"We're good," Sal said. "Very good."

"Still living in that little town, in that old workshop?"

"Still there. Life has been quiet these last few years. It's made a nice change."

Skender could appreciate that. "At least you're not towing a couple of sprogs along behind you. That'd make things a little inconvenient."

Sal laughed. "Kids aren't an option for a while yet. We're still young. There's so much left to do."

"Like what?"

A shrug was his only answer.

"Fair enough. Rescuing your father and my mother is enough to start with." Skender stood up on aching legs and looked around. Sal's breath bloomed like smoke from his mouth. "Let's go topside and see what I can see."

They clambered up the dry riverbank and peered over the edge. The air currents on the ground looked very different to Skender. Flows coiled back on themselves in complicated ways as they hit stone; everywhere he looked he saw turbulence. It was like trying to pick out a clear patch on the far side of a wheat field without standing up.

He refused to be discouraged. "I think there might be something that way," he said, pointing in the rough direction they were headed.

"That's convenient."

"Wishful thinking, maybe."

They dropped down again and kept walking. Sal asked Skender about his father, and he explained that Skender Van Haasteren the Ninth hadn't changed at all since Sal and Shilly had visited the Keep. Tall and severe, his life consisted entirely of terrorising students—who seemed to idolise him—and occasionally arguing with bureaucrats from Ulum.

Even as he said the words, he remembered with a pang of homesickness the last time he had seen his father.

Go now. Forget about your homework. Some things are simply more important.

He shivered at the realisation that his father was a real person, with fears and desires the same as anyone.

They stopped an hour later, with the sun directly overhead. It seemed to be taking them forever to reach the Aad, and he wondered if it was all an illusion. Perhaps the crash-landing with Chu had been harder than he realised, and he was lying unconscious in the dirt, only dreaming that he had met old friends and was off on a new adventure. Dream or not, he sipped cautiously from the water bottle and handed it to Sal. His stomach was beginning to anticipate lunch.

On the far side of the Divide, miners swooped and circled in ever-expanding circles. Once in a while, one would fly over their position. Skender considered waving, but decided to keep walking. The flyers were searching for artefacts—not that Skender had seen anything in the way of treasure since landing—and weren't likely to help him in his quest.

Thus far, they hadn't seen anything truly weird, and that struck him as very weird indeed. His nervousness increased rather than decreased as time passed and nothing burst out of the ground to steal him away.

"What's that?" asked Sal, when next they climbed up for a look.

"I don't know." It was hard to see through the coiling winds. In the distance, clouds of brown air were rising from the valley floor. "Dust?"

"That'd be my bet. I wonder what's kicking it up."

"Doesn't look like a sandstorm." And it didn't. The air in that direction appeared no different to the air around them.

"Must be something on the ground then." Sal put the mystery aside for the moment. "Any sign of the Homunculus?"

Skender shook his head. He was beginning to regret landing so soon. If they had stayed aloft a little longer, maybe they could have caught sight of their quarry and saved themselves a long, possibly fruitless trek. Already he had become used to an aerial perspective. It was so hard to see anything from zero elevation.

But he didn't regret landing safely. That had been a major achievement. They could have broken their legs or skulls if he had waited and tried later, only to screw it up.

They picked up the wing and kept walking. There was nothing else to do.

Sal cocked his head, catching the faintest echo of a chimerical engine snarling behind him. It was hard to locate the source. He assumed it was Shilly and the wardens descending the southern wall of the Divide preparatory to crossing it. How they were doing it, precisely, he didn't know, but he wished them well.

There was another sound beneath it, one that had been growing steadily louder since their last rest stop. A faint rumble just under the edge of his hearing, he had at first thought he was imagining it. Now, however, the echo of Shilly and the others had allowed it to be separated out from other sounds, and it could no longer be ignored.

He stopped Skender. "Do you hear that?"

His friend cocked one ear and frowned. "No. What?"

Skender couldn't be deaf at such a young age, so Sal assumed that the licence was stealing from one sense in order to bolster another. "I think we need to take another look."

They inched over the top of the crumbling bank and gasped at what they saw.

An army was walking along the bottom of the Divide. That was Sal's first impression. The cloud he and Skender had glimpsed an hour earlier, now even larger and thicker, was being kicked up by hundreds of feet marching heavily on the dirt. The combined sound of so many footfalls caused the rumble he heard. He could make out few individuals in the crowd marching towards him, but he could tell one thing very clearly.

"They're man'kin," he breathed.

"Are you sure?" asked Skender.

He nodded, not quite daring to believe it himself. He had never seen this number of man'kin in one place before. He didn't know so many existed in the entire *world*. But he couldn't discount the evidence of his own eyes, and they told him that several hundred stone creatures were approaching the creek's winding path along the bottom of the Divide. If he and Skender didn't get out of the way, they were going to be in a lot of trouble.

The impression of an army quickly faded. The mass of man'kin weren't walking in ordered columns or in step. They weren't wearing uniforms, and weren't even of uniform size, shape, or colour. Some looked passably human, in the form of monarchs and soldiers, with only the cold granite of their flesh and raiment to reveal their extraordinary natures. Others had human bodies with grimacing animal faces or extra limbs, or were incomplete, being torsos or busts carried by their more mobile companions. This detail surprised Sal, as the man'kin called Mawson had once vehemently declared that "'*Kin never carries 'kin.*" To see them breaking that rule was an extraordinary thing.

Stone animals—horses, elephants, lions, and camels among them—travelled as equals alongside grotesque gargoyles and mythical creatures. Some of the stone shapes were enormous, giant lumbering forms that seemed fashioned to no plan at all.

Their heavy tread vibrated under Sal's fingertips where he clung to the side of the riverbank. Close up, the unruly march would sound like an avalanche.

"Where are they going?" Skender asked.

Sal didn't know, but it looked to him like they were following the Divide westwards, away from the Aad. They certainly didn't appear to be crossing the Divide, given that they were drawing closer, not heading to Sal's left, where distant Laure lay on the far side of the mighty canyon.

"Maybe this is normal," he said. "Maybe this happens all the time around here."

Skender looked doubtful. "What are we going to do?"

"I don't know. We can either lie low and hope they don't see us, or run and hide somewhere else." Even as he considered the second option, he remembered the wing they carried between them. It would be hard to make any sort of speed unless they left it behind.

Skender's charmed eyes scanned the landscape from their low-lying position, looking for an alternative place to shelter. There wasn't much that Sal could see: a few weatherworn rocks, some jagged splits in the baked topsoil, and the withered, twisted trunk of a long-dead tree. Perhaps, he thought desperately, the man'kin were too heavy to run quickly.

Skender's gaze caught on a detail to his right, then backtracked. "Look!"

"Where? At what?"

"Oh, I forgot. You won't be able to see it." His index finger indicated a patch of empty ground. "The Homunculus went that way. I can follow its wake in the air, just as you said!"

Any excitement Sal felt at having finally caught the trail of the Homunculus was quashed by the lack of cover in that particular area. If they stayed put, the trail might fade before the vast crowd of man'kin passed; if they ran for it, the man'kin would see them and . . .

Sal didn't know what would come after that. The decision came down to how much he was prepared to risk: losing the trail again or being attacked by hundreds of creatures made of animated but decidedly solid stone.

Then a point that should have been obvious occurred to him.

He dropped down from his perch and pulled Skender after him.

"This is what we're going to do," he said. "We're going to run for the wake as fast as we can, and we're going to do it now, before the man'kin get any closer."

Skender's face reflected his own previous uncertainties back at him. "But won't that get us killed?"

"Not if we run fast enough," he said, "and get to the wake before they do. The man'kin can't survive without the Change. If they try to cross the wake, they'll go back to being nothing but statues."

Skender nodded. "Nice one."

Together they hauled the wing to a section of the creek bed that would be easier to scale. They would have to move quickly once spotted to avoid being squashed, crushed, or any of the other gruesome fates Sal imagined would befall them if the man'kin caught up too soon.

"Ready?" he asked as they poised themselves to climb and then run.

Skender nodded, a nervous excitement in his eyes. Sal wondered if Skender's throat was as dry as his was.

"Okay. Let's do it."

They scrambled out of the dry creek, dragging the wing after them. The man'kin assembly looked much larger than it had before; a vast throng lay behind the foremost ranks that hadn't been visible from so low to the ground. Sal began to have second thoughts, even as Skender pointed to where he had seen the wake, but it was too late to turn back. Blank stone eyes were swivelling to focus on them. A cry went up. More giant heads swung around. The rumbling of stone feet became thunderously loud.

Sal ran, following Skender across the pebble-strewn ground, heading across the face of the man'kin horde towards the canyon wall. He couldn't see the wake so he didn't know how far away salvation lay. All he could do was try to keep as much distance as possible between himself and the monsters lumbering in their direction.

He risked a glance over his shoulder. A slender statue more than two metres tall, with skinny arms, tapering fingers, and slitted eyes, led a motley pack of nightmarish creatures that ran, rolled, leapt, and pounced towards the two fleeing humans. The crunching of stones under their heavy tread sounded like fire tearing through saltbush, and Sal knew that if they caught him the result would be just as deadly.

"Is it much further?" he yelled at Skender, feeling his breath beginning to burn in his lungs.

"Almost there! Run faster!"

"I'm running as fast as I can!" Sal put his head down and concentrated on moving his legs. If he didn't expend energy worrying about what was behind him, he told himself, then he would have more to spare getting away from it. The theory was flawed, but as long as it worked Sal could live with it.

He almost pulled it off.

Skender scrambled up a low rise and slipped on a bed of smoothly polished stones. The wing jutted into Sal's solar plexus, winding him. As he shifted it to a new position he felt a cold stone limb clutch at the back of his neck, and he ducked instinctively.

Ducking and running at the same time was too much for his balance to cope with. He, too, slipped on the pebbles and went down. A forest of heavy legs instantly surrounded him, stamping and kicking, and missing his soft flesh by bare centimetres. He curled into a ball and put his hands over his head.

"Sal!" Skender yelled at him from outside the granite forest.

"Don't stop!" he shouted back. "Keep running!"

"But I'm here! You can make it!"

Sal peered through his fingers at Skender, just visible beyond his assailants' legs. He was standing on a seemingly unremarkable patch of sand just metres away. The marks of the licence had completely faded. As hoped, the man'kin were leaving Skender completely alone.

"Quick!" Skender shouted. "Come on!"

But Skender couldn't see what Sal could. The man'kin were fighting among themselves, presumably for the right to squash him to

a pulp. Sand and fragments of stone covered him as the strange creatures collided mightily with each other, cracking and splintering with
every kick and punch. The air was thick with the Change.

"*The human enslaves us!*" roared one of them, its voice heard as much
through Sal's head as through his ears.

"*It freed Mawson*," said another, deflecting a blow that would have
pulverised his left leg. "*It does not need to die.*"

"*It does not need to live!*"

Sal rolled to one side. A broad foot cracked the ground where his
head had just been. The leg of one of his defenders brushed him by
accident, flinging him aside as easily as a rag doll.

"Why are you doing this?" he yelled, clutching his shoulder. "I
have nothing against you!"

"*Humans are our enemies.*"

"*They enslave us!*"

"Not me!" he protested.

"*What is that around your neck?*" A stone finger thrust towards him.
The face it belonged to—a hideous gargoyle visage—sneered con-
temptuously. "*You know it is one of us.*"

Sal clutched *yadeh-tash* to him. Yes, he did know that the pendant had
a similar charmed nature to the man'kin; but it wasn't mobile, and it had
once been Lodo's. He had never thought of releasing it, as he had Mawson.

"I'll free it," he said, "if it wants to be freed."

"*Its thoughts are small. It knows only rain.*"

"*It is one of us!*"

"*It is nothing. The Angel says that humans are nothing. They are not
worthy of our anger.*"

"*The Angel says run.*"

"*The Angel says we must be free!*" the gargoyle bellowed.

"*The Angel isn't here. We chart our own intersections.*"

As the man'kin argued, Sal spied a gap between their legs. He took
a deep breath, then lunged for Skender's furiously gesticulating arms.

He made it halfway through the forest of stone legs before the man'kin reacted. A roar of anger went up from half of them and he was suddenly crawling under several tons of angry rock.

Before he could be flattened, a broad hand reached down, grabbed the back of his tunic, and thrust him forward. He flew through the air with a wail and landed at Skender's feet.

"Quick!" Skender tugged him away from the man'kin scrum. "Back here!"

Sal scrabbled in the dirt, trying to increase the distance between himself and the menacing shapes. The gargoyle threw off the hands of those trying to hold it back, and thudded threateningly closer.

"That's far enough, buddy," said Skender, to both Sal and the gargoyle. He stopped Sal from going any further backwards, and stood firm in the face of the angry man'kin.

It halted dead in its tracks as though smacking into an invisible wall. As Sal had hoped, the man'kin were powerless to cross the wake.

"*What?*" it hissed. "*What is this . . . this lesion?*"

"It's not our doing," said Sal, lest the man'kin found more reason to despise them. "I'm tracking the creature that causes it. A Homunculus."

It was hard to tell, but Sal thought he saw fear pass across the gargoyle's hideous face.

"*The one from the Void,*" it said. Its voice actually shook. "*The Angel was right. The one from the Void is among us!*"

"The Void?" asked Skender. "We've both been there. So what?"

The gargoyle didn't answer. Its hostility had boiled away like water in a dry kettle. Turning its back on them, it ran towards the rest of its number, still flowing by like a wave of dusty lava, and most of the others followed it.

Two remained. One in the shape of a slender woman with a stone shawl and sad expression stepped closer. Several chips had been knocked out of its smooth lines during the fight. The loss didn't seem to bother it.

"Do you know Mawson?" Sal asked it. He was uncertain which one had mentioned his family's old man'kin. "Is that why you helped me?"

"*Mawson is free no longer,*" it said. "*Mawson is gone.*"

"Do you mean he's dead?" Sal asked, alarmed. "How?"

The man'kin didn't answer. It walked dolefully away, and the remaining one took its place. Sal, prior to that moment, would have doubted how seriously he could take a stone pig, but under the circumstances he felt no urge to laugh.

"*The one from the Void is among us,*" it said, as the gargoyle had. "*Do you not know what this means?*"

"It's obvious that we don't."

"*We must run.*"

"From what? One of us?"

The pig didn't answer. It, too, went to leave.

"Wait!" cried Skender, exasperated. "Where are you from? Where are you headed? What's this Angel thing you keep mentioning?"

The pig half-turned. "*You do not see time the same way we do. We see one event in its entirety while you follow it from beginning to end. We see the many ways future and past diverge from the present while you see only one path. You ask me to explain things you cannot understand.*"

Sal remembered Mawson saying as much, years ago. He gave in, knowing that arguing with man'kin rarely got him anywhere. "Thank you, anyway, for saving us." He assayed a clumsy bow towards the pig, and hoped he didn't look too stupid.

"*We are saving ourselves,*" said the man'kin. "*You are needed in this world. Anyone with eyes can see that.*"

The pig trotted heavily after its fellow, leaving Sal and Skender trapped in the Homunculus' wake, more puzzled than ever.

THE ROAD

**"Humans haven't conquered the Earth.
We merely inhabit it. That others share our illusion
of primacy only reinforces its falsehood."**
THE BOOK OF TOWERS, EXEGESIS 6:9

Shilly ate a quick meal while Chu explained the way across the Divide. The food Marmion's party had brought with them was simple and healthy: porridge and conkerberries, soaked in water, accompanied by acacia seeds. It didn't make much of a breakfast, but Shilly was grateful for it. Her whole body ached from lack of rest.

"There's a way down the Divide wall a couple of kilometres south-west of here," Chu said through a mouthful, wincing as the motion tugged at her injured scalp. The top half of her leather uniform was torn in several places, so she had removed it and now wore a white undershirt, trusting to a henna charm Shilly had drawn on her right shoulder to keep sunburn at bay. Her wound had been salved and bound; much of her head was covered with a cream-coloured bandage, like a Surveyor's turban. "I've seen it from the air but don't know how passable it is. If we can follow it down the cliff, there's a road that leads straight across to Laure. We call it the Fool's Run."

"For any particular reason?" asked Marmion.

"What? Oh, the obvious one." Chu was unfazed in the face of the warden's confrontational mood. "My advice would be to keep your foot to the floor and your fingers crossed."

"What's the main threat?" asked Kail pragmatically.

She shrugged. "I don't know. To be honest, I've never met anyone who tried the Run in either direction."

"So it could be all hearsay."

"Could be. We could stroll across at our leisure and encounter nothing more dangerous than a flat tire." Her dark, uniquely shaped eyes held a grim amusement. "Are you a dice-playing man, Habryn Kail?"

"No, I'm not."

"Good. This is one bet I'd leave for others to take."

"Any word from Sal?" asked Warden Banner, her round cheeks pink and eyes tired.

Shilly shook her head.

"We must act," declared Marmion, "on the assumption that his attempt will fail. If he succeeds, well and good, but I am not a dicing man, either. We'll take this Fool's Run to Laure and wait for the Homunculus there. Being on the wrong side of the Divide doesn't frighten me. We're not completely powerless. I trust, though, that there will be no more surprises in store for us," he added, looking pointedly at Shilly.

She bit her lip, tired of arguing with the man. When they were safely behind the charmed Wall of the distant city, she and Kail could work out what to do about getting to the Aad in time to help Sal, and Skender, with or without Marmion's assistance.

And anyway, she grudgingly acknowledged, a very small chance existed that she could be completely wrong about the Homunculus. If it *was* heading for Laure, as Marmion still believed, and she convinced him to concentrate on the Aad, thus allowing the Homunculus to slip past them, he would have good reason to be angry at her. Tackling the problem on two fronts did make more sense.

"I think," said Chu, "we'd be stupid not to expect a surprise or two. That's the one thing you can be sure of, so close to the Divide."

Once again, Shilly and Tom led the way in the buggy, with Banner and Chu as their passengers. The young flyer gave directions, pointing over Tom's shoulder at the terrain ahead. Shilly had little to do but watch

Tom drive, so her thoughts inevitably wandered to Sal. She had grilled Tom for more information about what had happened to Skender's mother, but his replies had been vague. Pigs and rabbits played a part, apparently. She could make no sense of it.

Highson Sparre lay on a makeshift stretcher in the back of one of the buses, tended by the same warden who had treated Chu's head wound. His name, she had remembered, was Rosevear and, although he looked young, Shilly had to admit that he knew what he was doing. Shilly hoped Highson would wake soon, and that she would be there when it happened.

They drove several kilometres along the southwestern leg of the Divide, away from Laure. The morning grew hotter and the far side of the canyon vanished into a shimmering curtain. If she squinted, Shilly could almost make out several black specks suspended against the blue sky. More flyers, she supposed. When she asked Chu what they were doing, she learned that the flyers—or "miners," as Chu called them—were actually scavengers picking at the past, taking what they could and turning a profit from it.

She marvelled at the revelation, but she didn't question it. There seemed to be little else around for the city to exploit: no fields, no rivers rich with fish, no nearby trade routes. It was either grave-rob or die.

"There," said Chu finally, pointing. "That's it." Ahead, a broad cleft had been taken out of the lip of the Divide. Tom brought the buggy to a halt. They jumped out to take a look.

Shilly regarded the weathered carriageway with suspicion. Rocky, and water-scarred, it snaked laboriously down the side of the canyon wall, switching back on itself to form a series of long, not-quite-parallel lines that led tortuously down to the bottom of the Divide. It seemed to be both intact and wide enough for the buses along its length, but Shilly didn't have an Engineer's eye. To her, the distance to fall if something went wrong seemed very, very great. There were no railings.

"The gradient is worrying in places," said Banner, pacing back and forth in order to view the road from a number of different perspectives. "There are protective charms to overcome. They've kept the road passable, but it's going to be tricky."

"It's either that or fly down," said Chu with a grimace. "And I don't think any amount of charms will make those wheels of yours airworthy."

Tom was so caught up in the problem that he missed her joke. "No, but we can make them *ground*worthy. Lower their centre of gravity; beef up the suspension; encourage the wheels to improve their traction. There are ways."

"I guess there'll have to be, but I still think I'll walk behind you. No offence."

"None taken," said Banner.

Shilly considered her options. She shared Chu's anxiety about the vehicles slipping, but the descent was awfully long for someone with a bad leg.

"I'm going to sit in the back with my eyes shut and fingers crossed," she said. "Don't expect me to take the wheel at any point."

"No worries," said Banner. "You won't have to."

Marmion's buses rolled up behind them and the discussion was repeated, with the same conclusion. Several of the wardens volunteered to walk with Chu—ostensibly to lighten the loads but perhaps out of shared nervousness.

"Just don't pull too far ahead," said one of them. "We don't want to be left behind."

"That," said Kail, his all-seeing gaze following the many switchbacks all the way to the bottom, "is unlikely to be a problem."

Banner took the wheel for the first leg, inching the buggy onto the incline with exaggerated caution. Shilly did exactly as she said she would, at first, lying on the back seat and keeping her eyes firmly closed. But she soon found that entirely too nerve racking. Each jerk and jolt sent her heart pounding, and it seemed to take forever to reach the first bend.

She ended up opening her eyes and fixing her gaze firmly on the far side. Laure itself wasn't visible, apart from the summit of a single tall tower, but she could see smoke rising in streams from behind its protective wall. The plumes flattened out as they hit fast-moving air at a higher altitude and were swept away to the east.

As her eye wandered in that direction, she caught sight of a cloud within the Divide. It hugged the southern wall near the Aad but its source was hidden to her eyes. She watched it, wondering if it had something to do with Sal, and noticed that it seemed to be drawing nearer. Whatever caused it was inching along the Divide.

Not "inching," she corrected herself. At that distance, the base of the cloud was probably a hundred metres across; it would be moving as fast as a person could walk. She resolved to keep an eye on it during the descent.

Her world soon became one of tense tedium. The buggies never moved much faster than a sluggish stroll, and the group of wardens bringing up the rear first caught up with then overtook the buggy. Shilly listened to their conversation with a feeling of jealousy but had no real urge to join in. She was content to listen to Chu describe life in Laure as she passed while Shilly rested her legs.

It didn't sound like much, if Chu's opinion was accurate. She described a town that had been isolated for too long; everyone knew everyone else; someone such as her, whose family had moved there three generations earlier, was still regarded as an outsider. Nothing changed; the rain rarely came; life was always on a knife edge; the young of each generation invariably hoped to get away but always ended up becoming as inward-looking as the parents they had rebelled against. To Shilly it sounded no different to Fundelry, only on a larger scale.

Not once did Chu mention the yadachi or the blood rituals that Banner had mentioned the previous night. Perhaps, Shilly thought, she was trying not to scare her new companions away. That would make sense, given that she had no other way of getting home. When she raised her arm to point at something down in the Divide, Shilly thought she glimpsed a line of old, small cuts up the girl's arm, but she didn't have the stomach to ask about them.

Somehow, after an hour of slow but steady descent, she managed to nod off. The gentle rocking of the buggy as it traversed the difficult road overcame her anxiety and lulled her into a shallow, dreamless sleep, with Sal's pack behind her head as a pillow.

When she stirred, the buggy was still and everyone had gathered at the nearest bend to look northeast at the same cloud of dust she had spotted earlier.

Shilly wiped grit from her eyes and took up her stick. The cloud was much closer. She could make out vague shapes at its base, but she couldn't tell what they were. Some of them looked like people.

"Man'kin," said Kail, lowering a brass telescope from his eye. "A thousand or more, travelling as one."

Even Chu seemed surprised by this declaration.

"This isn't a common occurrence, I take it," said Marmion.

"No," she said. "They often travel in pairs, and we occasionally see groups of a dozen or so, but never this many at once."

"Maybe they're lost," said Shilly.

"Wherever they're going," said Kail, "they're heading right for the Fool's Run."

"Of course they are." Marmion ran a hand through his thinning hair and turned to look downward. "No walking from here on. We'll have to step up the pace."

Shilly followed the direction of his gaze. They had stopped roughly halfway down the canyon wall. The Fool's Run was faintly visible below—a thread stretching across the floor of the Divide, deviating only to avoid the largest of obstacles. One stretch passed across the remains of a giant beast, slicing without pause right through a rib cage large enough to enclose a small town.

The gathering dispersed. Tom took the wheel of the buggy and gunned the motor. Chu slid into the rear seat with Shilly and couldn't hide her nervousness as they recommenced their descent.

This time, sleep wasn't an option. Tom rode the brake, accelerator, and steering wheel with furious intensity, incessantly adjusting their course along the weathered road. The constant change in momentum was as unsettling as their increased pace. Shilly tried her best not to look over the edge at the still substantial drop to the bottom of the Divide, but she found it impossible to avoid completely. There was something hypnotic about the drop and the way it decreased, metre by slow metre. She felt strangely as though they were tunnelling deep into the Earth. The rocky cliff oppressed her as much as the drop on the other side. She was being crushed between them, like a bug between two fingers.

"Goddess," she groaned at one point, "how much *longer?*"

"We're getting there," said Banner—giving her information she could see with her own eyes but couldn't truly accept.

Shilly sank back into her seat and quashed the thought that she would never reach the bottom, that they would go slower and slower the closer it came, leaving her stuck on the cliff face forever.

They surmounted one significant obstacle—a landslide that had blocked the last two legs of the road and needed to be cleared before any of the vehicles could pass—and then they were down. Not a moment too soon, Shilly thought. The man'kin were thundering closer with every second. It was clear that the wardens had been seen. Several of the ferocious-looking creatures had broken free from the leading edge of the horde and were running headlong towards them.

As soon as the second bus—the one carrying Highson Sparre—safely descended, Marmion urged them onto the Fool's Run.

"Go!" he shouted, waving. "Go!"

Tom put his foot down hard on the accelerator. The wheels threw up stones in their wake. Shilly held on as the buggy leapt forward like

a goat freed from its post. The road—mercifully level and straight—
swept by beneath them.

Tom whooped with excitement, but Shilly didn't share the sentiment. Three of the leading man'kin changed course to intercept them
further along the road. One had the shape of a bare-breasted woman running on all fours, with the hindquarters of a lion and a naked child riding
her back. The second possessed scales and a broad bearded mouth filled
with sharp teeth; two curving, spiked horns grew out of its head. The
third was only vaguely humanoid, its limbs jointless, flexing and whipping like snakes as it ran, its bullet-shaped head menacingly featureless.

The man'kin put on a surprising turn of speed. Shilly clutched the
buggy's metal frame. It was going to be close. The shouts of the
man'kin rose above the whine of the engine. This surprised her, as they
looked so feral as to be incapable of language. It was hard to make out
the words they called until the fastest was close enough to strike.

"*More humans!*" screeched the bestial woman. "*Why won't they leave
us alone?*"

It lunged at them. Tom jerked the buggy out of range. The
man'kin shrieked and fell back as they accelerated along the road. The
other two had already diverted their attentions to the bus behind
them. It dodged a clumsy attempt by the horned man'kin to spike its
metal side. Peering over the back of the buggy, Shilly saw wardens on
the back of the bus scrambling to get out of range of the snarling beast.
Kail wrenched the bus from side to side, slamming into the whip-crea-
ture and sending it flying. Then he, too, was past the main threat.

The second bus wasn't so lucky. The bestial woman had planted
itself in the centre of the road, head dipped low to ram. In a desperate
attempt to avoid the collision, the driver turned the wheel too far and
lost control. The bus skidded off the road in a cloud of dirt and threatened to tip. "Don't stop!" yelled Shilly, although the driver couldn't
possibly hear her. If the bus came to a halt it would bog for sure in the
powdery soil.

She could make out Marmion yelling instructions from the front passenger seat. Behind him, the wardens had linked hands and seemed to be shouting. As the bus stabilised, wheels spinning, slowly dragging itself back to the road, the horned man'kin tossed its head and charged.

Two things happened in quick succession. First, the wardens in the back of the bus raised their hands as one and brought them down again, hard. Shilly felt a ripple flow through the Change, although she couldn't see what had happened. Only as the horned creature's feet scrabbled for purchase on the suddenly slippery sand did she realise: the wardens had frozen the traces of moisture lying under the ground's topmost layers, rendering the creature unable to find its footing.

It tried nonetheless. Its legs kicked and its spine twisted. Instead of spearing the bus with its deadly horns, it merely broadsided it, sending it wobbling again.

Then the slender whiplike man'kin placed itself between the bus and the other man'kin. It flailed at the horned creature, and drove it off howling in pain and anger. Its blows drew bright sparks from the wide stone back.

The wheels of the second bus found purchase on the road at last and fishtailed out of reach of the bestial woman. The man'kin child on its rump shook its fist as the wardens sped away. Shilly could see its mouth opening and closing but couldn't hear the words. Its face was a mask of fury.

As the man'kin horde receded into the distance, Shilly felt more puzzled than relieved. Why had one of the man'kin defended the second bus against its fellows? What had the bestial woman meant by *more* humans?

"Sal!" she said. "It was talking about Sal! We have to go back!"

"No! Keep driving," said Chu, her eyes still fixed on the man'kin astride the road, her face pale with fear. "Keep driving!"

Banner reached back to grip the young woman's shoulder. "It's okay," she said. "We're not going to stop for a good while yet." When

Shilly went to protest, she added, "We can't go back. You know that. The road will be thick with man'kin by now. To turn would kill us all."

Shilly forced herself to see the sense in Banner's words. No word had come from Sal, but the certainty that he was alive burned in her. She clung to that knowledge like a life preserver.

Chu remained tense, but she, too, nodded and pretended to relax. Shilly could see her hands shaking where they rested in her lap. Only then did she realise something.

"That's the first time you've seen a man'kin up close, isn't it?"

Chu nodded. "They're not allowed in the city. They're dangerous."

"Not all of them are," said Shilly, thinking of Mawson. "They're like people. Some are good, some bad. Did you see the one that helped us out back there?"

"It was horrible," she said with a shudder.

"Looks can be deceiving."

"As long as there's a wall between me and them, I'm happy to be deceived."

Shilly dropped the subject, knowing it would take more than words to convince Chu. The young flyer turned her attention forward, closing herself off to further conversation.

Banner still twisted to the rear, and Shilly realised that she was looking at something behind the buggy. At the same time, Tom eased off on the accelerator. Shilly turned to look, too, fearing that a new man'kin threat had appeared. The truth was much less exotic. The first bus had fallen behind, allowing the second to overtake it. It was difficult to see what was going on through the dust the buggies kicked up, but she could make out Marmion waving impatiently for them to continue. Maybe, she thought, they had wanted Highson safe in the middle of the convoy rather than at the end. Or perhaps she was just being charitable, and Marmion was worried about no other skin than his own.

Banner nodded and Tom increased their speed. They continued on across the bottom of the Divide, leaving Sal and Skender far behind.

THE RUIN

**"Put behind you all thoughts of the outside world,
for such are distractions and dangerous.
The rules you knew are irrelevant. Those who enter a
Ruin should do so only in the clear and certain
knowledge that they may never return."**
THE SURVEYOR'S CODE

Skender stood facing the blank stone wall and resisted the urge to kick it. He and Sal had tracked the Change-dead spoor of the Homunculus across several kilometres to its terminus just short of the Aad. Instead of following a straight line—as Sal explained that it had from almost as far away as the Haunted City—it wound its way around and between obstacles, sticking close to the wall of the Divide where possible. Towards the end, for no apparent reason, it had kinked to the right and headed for the cliff. There, abruptly, it ended.

"I can't see a door," Skender said, tracing his hands over the rough sandstone. Layers of ancient sediment hung before him, preserved for eternity—or would have been but for the great rending that had separated the cliff face from its match on the far side of the Divide.

"And we can't find a hidden door by using the Change because the Homunculus has sucked it dry." Sal paced back and forth at the edge of the wake, testing for any sign of an opening: a sliding stone, a trapdoor, anything. "But there must be one!"

Skender succumbed to frustration and kicked the stone. That gave him a sore toe to match his headache, but it seemed appropriate. Their search had come to a dead end.

He turned away from the cliff and looked around. The sun was fading into the west, casting a shadow across the floor of the Divide. Soon, that shadow would hit their location and they would lose any chance of finding an entrance.

Look on the bright side, he told himself. The tide of man'kin had finally run out. A few last stragglers had eyed the humans hatefully as he and Sal had continued on their way, careful never to leave the safety of the wake. A couple had tried to engage them in conversation, but they rarely said anything of relevance. One declared that the mysterious Angel had told it about them, but nothing else had been forthcoming. Who the Angel was, how the Angel could possibly know about Sal and Skender, and why that detail was important, remained a mystery. After a while, Skender had stopped responding to calls for attention from the stony mass of man'kin.

As he stood gazing out across the Divide floor, he saw another cloud on the far side of the mighty canyon, along the eastern leg. At the rate it was moving, it would encounter the Wall protecting Laure before nightfall. Skender hoped the city's defences were ready for an onslaught.

"There *has* to be a way in," he muttered, turning back to the problem at hand. "We're just not seeing it."

"We could wait until the wake fades and try then."

"How long would that take?"

"A few hours, perhaps."

"The Homunculus could be anywhere by then. And if the wake has faded, how are we going to follow it?" Skender pointed at the second cloud on the far side of the Divide. "Anyway, I'm not sure I like the idea of being defenceless with so many of these things roaming around. I think we should just think harder."

Sal sighed and sank to a crouching position with his back against the stone. "I'm very nearly all thought out, I'm afraid."

Skender could see that his friend was exhausted. Sal had explained that few people in the wardens' search party had slept the night before;

the summoning of the storm had drained him further. There were heavy bags under Sal's eyes; his attention occasionally drifted.

Skender lifted the water bottle from around his neck and offered it to Sal. The container was more than half empty, but it was the only reward they had for pressing on. No plants grew on the bottom of the Divide, so they couldn't even chew leaves or twigs for moisture.

Ignoring his own thirst, he considered what they knew. The Homunculus had an agenda of its own, one which involved the Aad. Towards the end of its journey, it had obviously made a beeline for the Ruin. The wall couldn't be the dead end it appeared to be, otherwise what was the point of coming here? The Homunculus couldn't have doubled back on itself, since it would have encountered Sal and Skender along the way. So it had come to the wall for a reason. They just had to *find* that reason . . .

His gaze drifted upward to where the sunlight cast the top of the cliff in brilliant gold, and he wondered if he should step out of the wake and study the complex weave of air through the charm of the licence. He immediately knew he didn't need to.

He laughed, but the news wasn't all good. "I found it!" he told Sal, pointing up. "See?"

Right at the top of the cliff was a spur of rock from which projected a metal hook.

"A rope would have been tied to it." Sal climbed to his feet and put his hands on his hips. His head tilted back to study the new development. "Or a rope ladder. Either way, the Homunculus climbed up there and reeled the ladder in behind it."

"And here *we* are," said Skender, "stuck on the ground in its wake."

Sal nodded. He moved back several metres, trying to see what lay at the top. "There doesn't seem to be anything else up there."

"I think that's the idea. We wouldn't have noticed anything if the Homunculus hadn't led us here. It's the perfect place for a hideout, or the entrance to one." He looked to his left, at the pile of rubble that was the Aad's doorstep, half a kilometre away. "I can see only one way open to us at the moment, if we're going to go up there."

Sal sighed again. "I think you're right, my friend. We can always double back when we're at the top."

Skender put a hand on Sal's shoulder to stop him as he went to pick up the wing and head off on their new tangent. "There's something else we should think about. The ladder can't have been hanging around forever, waiting for the Homunculus to come along. The miners would have seen it. Who put it there, and why?"

Sal sighed wearily. "Yes, that did occur to me. There's no way we can know right now, unless you've had any other blinding revelations . . . ?"

Skender shook his head. "Alas."

"Then we'll just have to keep our eyes peeled." Sal handed him back the water bottle. "Let's get going before I fall asleep on my feet."

Skender agreed wholeheartedly. They had no idea what they were heading into, but the Divide *definitely* wasn't safe, and he had no desire to experience it after nightfall.

The wing slotted into well-worn grooves in his fingers. He hoped Chu would appreciate the effort they were making to look after it. That hadn't been the deal at all, he thought, as they raced the encroaching shadow for the entrance to the Aad.

Sal sighed with relief as they left the Homunculus's wake. The very moment they did so, the normal background potential returned and the familiar tingling of the Change hit him. He felt in tune with the world again and revitalised for it. The wing wasn't as heavy; his feet no longer dragged. He could think again.

There was likely more to come: significant Ruins were steeped in the Change. He automatically assumed that the Ruin Skender called the Aad would be like any other. But as they reached the tumble of masonry at the base of the city, there was no surge in the Change. It was, if anything, ebbing away. He stopped to see if the Homunculus was nearby, but he couldn't see or sense it anywhere, and Skender's wind-seeing charm, which had returned upon leaving the wake, discerned no distinctive spoor of the creature. This was something else.

As they climbed the rubble towards the ruined city proper, Skender's black markings faded, and Sal's connection to the world faded with it.

"It's a Change-sink," he said, feeling the weight of exhaustion settle over him again like a heavy blanket. "A natural blank spot."

Skender was nodding, touching the deadened stone of a tumbled column as though it might rear up and bite him. "No wonder no one comes here. The air feels smothered."

"Do you want to keep going?"

Skender didn't hesitate. "Of course. Don't you?"

Sal nodded, although he would have done anything rather than keep walking. Fatigue had taken root in his bones again. He had forgotten how it felt to be awake.

They climbed higher, to what might have once been street level. It was hard to tell exactly how the original city had stood because the ground had tilted under it and most of the buildings had collapsed as a result. Mounds of rubble lay between Sal and Skender and a relatively intact portion of the city. It was clear, though, that what Sal thought of as a city was really a slice chopped out of a larger metropolis. The Aad lay open to the Divide on three sides and had decayed heavily around those borders. Only the very heart of it retained any structural integrity at all.

Skender had described tunnels gaping open to the Divide near Laure. During their ascent, they had seen nothing of the sort. Sal suggested that they had been covered over by landslides and were now only accessible from within the ruins. Skender didn't have a better solution, but he did look disappointed. It would have been much easier for him, Sal supposed, if they'd found his mother on their own. They could have dispensed with tracking the Homunculus.

The Change-sink in the Aad wasn't as deep as the Homunculus's wake, but it nonetheless cut them off from everything outside the city.

"Where do you think the heart of it is?" Skender asked.

"The tower, perhaps."

"That would make sense, I guess. It's the only recognisable landmark."

"Does that make a difference?"

Skender shrugged. "Beats me. The study of Change-sinks is a forgotten art, even by me."

Sal didn't ask further questions. He was more interested in whether his father had woken and given an account of his reasons for summoning the Homunculus. He almost stopped and turned back, feeling a sudden and very strong concern for Shilly. He wanted to talk to her, to let her know he was all right.

One glance back at the Divide, which was filling with darkness as dusk's shadow swept across it, put paid to that idea. There was no going back, not through nightfall and man'kin and whatever else might be out there. He had to keep moving forward.

The last rays of sunlight rushed over the Aad, casting the tower in a blaze of golden fire. Sal stared at it, hypnotised by the strange beauty of the moment. The dead city surrounded them, its air filled with dust and decay. No animals disturbed the stillness; no plants invaded the tumbled masonry. He could have been standing at the end of history, surveying all that remained of humanity's works.

The thought was maudlin. Much of the world already looked like this. Wardens and Mages alike built homes among the ruins, constantly reminded that theirs was an echo of a bygone age, one that had been capable of works unequalled since. What had happened to those lost builders was for the most part unknown. The Cataclysm had wiped them out and left the Change in their wake. Their world was difficult to imagine.

The last light of sunset abandoned the ruins and continued its march up the side of the Divide. The city plunged into gloom.

"What do we do now?" whispered Skender. "It's going to be pitch black before long."

"We should have brought some matches and a candle."

"And food."

"Let's not be greedy," he said, refusing to regret their impulsiveness. He took in their surroundings while a dusky light lingered. "We should find somewhere to take shelter." His body ached; the thought of rest was overpowering. "Maybe we can explore when our eyes have adjusted."

They hurried through the ruined city. Most of the buildings had fallen in completely or were teetering on the verge of doing so. Their best hope lay south and uphill, at the furthest point from the Divide, where the ground beneath the Aad angled up to vertical. Gradually, the remaining walls became higher, their interiors less wasted. Finally, they managed to find a low building with all four walls standing and a relatively intact ceiling. There was no way of telling what it had once been, since no shapes of furniture or tools seemed evident. It had no doubt been stripped of anything useful long ago. Sal paced out the full extent of the small space and declared that it would do.

"Do you want to wait here while I look around?"

The darkness was absolute. Sal could barely make out Skender's silhouette against the open doorway.

The suggestion was irresistible. "Maybe just for a little bit," Sal said, sinking down into a corner next to where they had placed the wing. His feet and head throbbed; his throat was utterly parched. "You'll let me know if you find anything, won't you?"

"Of course. This place is far too creepy for heroics."

Sal smiled and closed his eyes.

"Don't go anywhere until I get back."

Skender waited for an answer, but none came. Sal's breathing became slower and more regular. He was already asleep.

"Right," Skender said to himself. "No point in sticking around, then."

Leaving the bottle of water by his friend's side, he steeled himself to explore the eerie and potentially Homunculus-infested Ruin. Outside, he took a moment to note every detail of the location of their hiding place; good as his memory was, he knew it would be difficult finding his way back in the dark. The cliff obscured a fair proportion of the night sky, including the moon. It was hard to see even the ground beneath his feet.

He set out slowly and cautiously, picking his way through the rubble with exaggerated care. It wouldn't do to trip and twist his ankle. He had no clear destination in mind, and gravitated to the central watchtower by default. As the largest extant structure, it was the obvious place for someone to hide, although being the obvious place rendered it the least likely to contain anything hidden. Still, Skender reasoned, he had to start somewhere. Who knew what he would stumble over along the way?

It seemed to take him forever to navigate the cramped, littered streets, even though they gradually became less buckled. The buildings around him stood taller and firmer. He tried to keep the sound of his footfalls to a minimum, but they echoed back at him with crystalline, startling clarity. He froze at the slightest noise, listening for footsteps other than his own. All he heard was the pounding of his heart and the faint whispering of wind across jagged stone.

As the tower grew taller over him, he imagined dark faces staring at him from its round windows, and the ghosts of the Haunted City came, unwelcome, to his mind. Those bodiless spirits were confined forever to their ancient towers, able to escape only with the assistance of people on the outside—people like Shilly, and Sal's mother, who invariably paid a terrible price for their effort.

He shuddered, remembering the Homunculus at its most horrific, its four arms extended to attack Marmion and its face a writhing mass of eyes, mouths, and noses. The image had been easy to keep at bay during daylight hours, but the darkness encouraged it. Every time he turned, he expected to see that hideous visage about to leap on him.

A disease; bad luck; inhabited by creatures of the Divide . . .

Finally he stood at the base of the tower. Ten storeys high and broad enough to park several buggies, it seemed much larger than the natural cliff behind it. A single rectangular entranceway, twice his height and width, gaped open to the night air. If there had ever been doors, they were long gone. Skender tracked delicate carvings along the lintel—vines, perhaps, or snakes—but couldn't see well enough to make them out.

He still possessed a very faint sense of the Change. The heart of the sink couldn't be the tower, for otherwise no potential would remain at all. With a feeling of invading a tomb, he walked nervously into the shadow of the tower's interior and looked around.

No lights burned within, and it took his eyes a long time to adjust. There was no sign of occupation by human or animal or anything else. A rotting spiral staircase led up to the next floor and down to a basement. Skender was unwilling to explore in either direction, for the moment. There were other places to look before he would be forced to such extremes of courage. There could be anything in the depths beneath the tower—a mausoleum, perhaps, lined with bodies he couldn't see, only touch—and the upper floors could be structurally unsound.

He ventured as far as he dared into the suffocating blackness, then hurried out into the cool night air and took several deep breaths.

From far across the black gulf of the Divide, the navigation light at the top of Observation Tower winked at him over Laure's protective Wall. The previous night, when he had soared over the city lights for the first time, seemed weeks ago. He longed to be in his bed in the hostel with the sheet over his head. His belly ached for a decent meal.

Stone clicked against stone in the darkness, away to his right. He held his breath and retreated into the doorway. It could have been perfectly innocent, but he intended to take no chances. The night was thickening around him. Anything could be stirring.

He saw nothing and the sound wasn't repeated. But his stomach rumbled again, drawing his attention to the fact that the night *smelled* different. The faintest hint of smoke tainted the crisp night air.

Where there was smoke, Skender told himself, there had to be something to burn. And he had seen barely a stick in his exploration of the Divide. Whatever was burning must have been brought into the Aad, and the thing that had brought it was probably nearby.

He followed his nose away from the tower. The source of the smell proved difficult to trace. Sometimes he felt he was getting closer only to lose the smell entirely down a side street. Other times, when it faded almost to vanishing and he was on the point of giving up, it came heavily on the breeze from another alley or archway.

His nose led him to the western edge of the city, on the far side from where he and Sal had arrived. The smell was definitely stronger, although its source remained hidden. It wasn't wood smoke, he thought, or tobacco; coal, perhaps, or another solid fuel. His gut tied itself in knots at a faint tang of frying that joined with the smoke in the air. Meat and toast! If the growling of his stomach didn't alert every Homunculus and man'kin for a dozen kilometres, he would be amazed.

Then, distantly, came the sound of voices. He slowed to a creeping pace as he approached the ruins of a building jutting from the base of the cliff. The door and windows were open to the night air, so he could tell that no one was inside, but his nose and ears insisted that both the fire and people lay within. Barely daring to breathe, he inched through the main door and tiptoed along the entranceway. Debris crunched under his feet, and he shushed it nervously. The voices grew louder as he explored deeper into the house where it bit into the cliff face. There, next to a room that must once have been a kitchen but was now stale and empty, he found an enormous ballroom. Or so it seemed to him, with little more than a glimmer of starlight and faint echoes to measure its extent by. Parts of the ceiling had fallen in; rubble lay everywhere. In the shadows on the far wall, he made out four wide fire-places, each as large as his bedroom in the Keep.

Three of them had collapsed. The fourth was the source of the smoke. The fire wasn't, however, burning on the cold grate. Both the voices and the smoke were coming from above him. Skender stood in the fireplace and looked up. Far over his head, the chimney kinked suddenly to the left. Yellow light flickered.

The lyrics to a bawdy song about a tavern girl called One-Legged Meg echoed incongruously down the chimney. The singer didn't sound like the Homunculus. Faint jeers accompanied the tune. Someone barked a command and the song ceased midchorus.

There were people in the Aad. Skender knew he should go back to Sal, but one last thing held him back. At the top, opposite the hole through which the light issued, he made out a hook similar to the one at the top of the cliff. That explained how people came and went through the fireplace—but, once again, any attempt by him to go up there was stymied. If he and Sal could find or make a rope of some kind, he thought, they might be able to throw a loop over the hook and haul themselves up.

He turned to go, and heard a noise echo through the empty ballroom. It sounded like a footstep.

Time to get out of here, he told himself, creeping from the fireplace with steps so soft he felt he was floating on air.

"You make noise enough to shift the bones of the dead!" boomed a voice out of the darkness.

His fright was so great he actually squeaked.

The voice laughed. "That's it, my lad. Hold perfectly still. You've seen enough of the city for one night, I think."

Skender smelled someone large and male coming out of the darkness, arms spread wide to capture him. His paralysis broke. He ducked and ran for the door, feet scrabbling on dirt. His would-be captor laughed again but made no move to follow. Only as Skender reached the door did he realise why.

A foot kicked out of the darkness and tripped him before he sensed a second person waiting for him. He fell heavily and skidded across the floor, into a wall. Stars exploded behind his eyes. He tried weakly to right himself and to run but was too slow and stunned. Strong hands went over his mouth and under his left armpit. With a grunt of effort, his captor lifted him up and carried him away.

THE LETTER

"In cultures where blood is valued, the dead are
frequently drained of fluids before interment.
The liquid remains are preserved in perpetuity by any
means available: in ornate vials, sacred ponds,
vaselike reliquaries, or even private lakes;
or, where water is not readily available,
the remains may be carefully dried and placed in urns,
for even dust retains a measure of potency."
THE BOOK OF TOWERS, EXEGESIS 28:9

"Flash your headlamps," said Chu, leaning over Banner's shoulder as they approached the city Wall. "That way they'll know we're not ghosts."

The vast expanse of stone threw the sound of snarling engines back at them as the convoy approached. Surrounded on three sides by steep cliffs and the Wall ahead, she was already feeling closed in. The renewed threat of the man'kin—a second wave coming in from the east—lent the situation an urgency that was alarmingly real. If the Laureans didn't let them through in time, they would be caught between sentient rocks and a very hard place.

The warden followed Chu's suggestion. The lower lines of giant charms reinforcing the Wall's mighty stone blocks stood out sharply when the light returned. Giant circles overlapped squares and triangles with bold, thick strokes in a variety of colours, combining to form a single, sprawling pattern. She could see where other, now faded, signs had once done the same job but been painted over down the years. Their intricacies appealed to her.

Far above her, at the summit of the enormous stone edifice, a light flashed back.

"Well, that's a start," Chu said. She didn't sound especially relieved. They had tried attracting the attention of flyers far above, but Shilly couldn't tell how successful they had been. The closer Chu got to the city, the more nervous she became. "Keep going, right up to the base of the Wall, and let's see what they do."

"Is there a chance they won't let us in at all?" asked Banner.

"A small one," Chu admitted. "It's not as if people come this way very often. At all, actually; the usual entrance is on the far side of the city. I don't know what they'll make of us."

"Great," said the warden. "You could've told us this before we left."

"It didn't seem relevant. Given time, I'm sure we can convince them."

Shilly glanced behind her, unable to make out the man'kin on their tail through the headlights of the buses. Time was something they definitely didn't have much of.

The buggy bounced over a series of deep ruts in the baked-hard earth then skidded to a halt in front of the Wall. A cloud of dust enveloped them as Banner swept the beams of the headlights across the impeccable stonework. Mighty grey slabs formed a vertical, mortarless barrier that curved for a hundred metres on either side. It seemed to bulge inward, but Chu assured her that it looked the same on the far side. The Wall was thickest, therefore, where it met the sides of the Divide, and thinner—relatively speaking—in the middle. She wondered if it was hollow. The top was too far away to make out in the darkness.

"Over there," said Tom, pointing, the first to notice the gate. Banner accelerated for it, jerking Shilly back into her seat. The gate was an unprepossessing metal hatch three metres square with hinges that looked strong enough to withstand the end of the world. A circle with an X through it stood out in faded red paint.

Red, thought Shilly: the colour of ancient deserts and Stone Mages. The colour of blood.

A shiver of apprehension went through her at the thought of the Blood Tithe.

Chu jumped out of the buggy as soon as it came to a halt. Tom and Banner weren't far behind. Shilly limped stiffly after them, squinting in the brightness of the headlights focused on the forbidding portal.

Chu banged on it. "Open up!" she cried. "Let us in!"

There was no immediate reply from within.

"Hello? I know you're listening. We haven't got all night!"

The two buses chugged to a halt behind them, adding yet more light and dust to the scene.

"What's going on?" asked Marmion, jogging up to them. "Why isn't the gate open?"

"Give them a moment," said Chu, shifting from foot to foot. "Someone must be on duty. They might have forgotten how to—"

"STATE YOUR NAME," boomed a voice from the hatch. Tom, who had been examining the hinges closely, jumped backwards into Shilly. She barely kept her balance.

"My name is Chu Milang," said Chu with a pained expression. The voice from the other side of the hatch was loud enough to physically hurt.

"WHO? SAY THAT AGAIN."

"Stop shouting! I'm Chu Milang and I'm a miner. Check with the Magister if you don't believe me."

"WHAT ARE YOU DOING OUT THERE?" asked the voice at a slightly reduced volume. It seemed to be coming from the hatch itself.

"Trying to get in. What do you *think* I'm doing? Open the door and let us through!"

"I DON'T HAVE THE AUTHORITY TO DO THAT."

"Who does?"

"MY SUPERVISOR'S ON HER WAY DOWN. YOU NEED TO TALK TO HER."

"Listen to me," growled Marmion, elbowing his way through the crush. "I'm not going to stand here arguing over who has the authority to do what and who doesn't. My name is Sky Warden Eisak Marmion and I am on the business of the Alcaide. If you don't open this door right now, there will be consequences. Do you understand?"

"I UNDERSTAND, SIR, BUT THERE WILL BE CONSE-QUENCES IF I *DO* OPEN IT."

"*You're* not likely to be flattened by several hundred tons of stone. Open this door immediately or you'll have our deaths on your conscience!"

Nothing happened for a moment. Shilly assumed that the gatekeeper had gone for advice. She could clearly picture him: a young, inexperienced functionary given a forgotten responsibility in order to keep him out of the way. He might have had his feet up on a desk somewhere, dreaming of promotion; he might even have been *literally* dreaming when their call came through. The promotion he desired probably hinged on what he did next, just as their lives did.

"I think I can open it," whispered Tom to Marmion.

"Give him a moment," said the warden in a loud voice. "I'm sure he'll see sense."

Ancient metal bolts clunked deep within the Wall. A faint layer of rust shook from the hatch. With a deep groaning sound, it swung open towards them. Shilly hopped out of the way as it picked up speed and slammed into the stone beside her. The crashing sound it made echoed for a full ten seconds.

"Right," said Marmion, his mood taking on a self-satisfied edge, "let's get out of harm's way."

The small crowd scattered. Rather than walk back to the buggy, Shilly stayed where she was, with Marmion. The open hatchway revealed a tunnel leading through the base of the mighty Wall. It was easily wide enough to accept the three vehicles, and they roared through without fanfare. Marmion waved Shilly ahead of him once the last bus was past, and then he followed.

The Divide looked very dark without headlights to illuminate it. Shilly, looking back the way they had come, could barely make out the man'kin and the cloud they were kicking up. But she could hear their cries of frustration and anger.

"Okay, you can close the hatch now," Marmion called to the gate-keeper.

"WHAT DID YOU SAY? IT'S HARD TO HEAR YOU FROM THE—"

"Just close it!" he yelled.

The heavy metal door creaked and swung solidly home. The boom seemed even louder in the close confines of the tunnel than it had outside.

"WAIT THERE," said the gatekeeper through the ringing in Shilly's ears. "DON'T GO ANY FURTHER."

The smell of burnt alcohol was thick in Shilly's nostrils. Marmion overtook her without a glance as she limped along the corridor. It led to a large antechamber lit by a faded orange glowstone anchored in the high ceiling. That more than anything reminded Shilly that she was no longer in the Strand. She had crossed the Divide and entered the Interior for the second time in her life.

Highson Sparre lay still and unresponsive in the back of the second bus. She wondered what he would think when he woke up and found himself on the other side of the world.

"Chu!" The young flyer's head snapped up at the whip of command in Marmion's voice. He pointed at the far side of the room. "This road must lead somewhere. Take us. We're in your hands."

Chu looked as though she would rather have anything in her hands than Marmion and his demands. "Aren't we supposed to wait here?"

A barrage of heavy blows rained on the hatch behind them. Marmion glanced at the tunnel, then turned back to Chu. "Do you know if that door can withstand the combined weight of a hundred man'kin or more?"

She shook her head.

"Well, neither do I," he said. "I'm not waiting here to find out."

"Hang on," said Shilly, looking around at the gathered wardens. "Where's Kail?"

"He stayed behind," said Marmion.

"*What?*" An image of Kail being squashed by the tide of man'kin flashed horribly through her mind.

"He got off when we stopped on the Fool's Run, after the first attack. I ordered him to track Sal and Skender while we went on ahead."

"He didn't mention that to me."

A suspicious look crossed Marmion's face. "Should he have?"

She turned away, face burning. Kail hadn't betrayed her, she told herself; he simply had to obey Marmion's orders.

"No," she said, already wondering what chance she had of convincing Marmion to go to the Aad without Kail to back her up.

"Good. Now, no more talking." His voice echoed dully in the large chamber as he addressed the group as a whole. "Let's be on our way. Chu, over to you."

He inclined his head to the young flyer and hurried back to his bus.

Shilly watched Chu closely as she directed them along a series of broad stone passageways that sloped upward at a steep angle. If the flyer were to make a bolt for it, it would be soon.

Four wardens dismounted to swing aside a heavy metal door and slam it shut behind the buses when they had passed. The air became stuffier and more full of fumes the further they went. Shilly imagined themselves burrowing out of the ground like worms. She had no idea what to expect of the surface. All she had seen of Laure from a distance was one towertop peeking over the vast stone Wall. Would its citizens be white like Skender and most other people in the Interior? Or would they have the same skin and eyes as Chu? Anything was possible so close to the Divide.

Another door, heavier than the others, required six wardens to push open. Banner almost ran over a skinny youth standing behind it, waving his arms.

"Stop!" he yelled. "You must stop!"

Banner obeyed. Shilly recognised the voice of the gatekeeper, even though it was much reedier than it had been when amplified by the metal of the hatch.

"You can't just drive away like this!" he protested, coming to stand over the buggy. His skin was a blotchy white and his blond hair stood in disarray. He wore a scruffy uniform of gold on black—with no robes, torcs, or tattoos visible—and looked about eighteen. His darting gaze took in the buggy and its passengers, and settled on Marmion as he approached from the rear.

"Why not?" Marmion asked.

"The Tithe . . . my supervisor . . ."

Marmion waved away the stammered protestations. "Chu. Who was that you mentioned before? A magistrate of some kind?"

"The Magister," she said.

"Take us to him."

"*She* doesn't take kindly to people just turning up on her doorstep."

"I'm sure this good fellow will give us an introduction."

The guard backed away, his hands waving in front of him and his eyes wide. "Oh, no. You wouldn't dare."

"I'm afraid we have no choice. We're on a mission from the Alcaide and nothing must stand in our way."

The guard's larynx bobbed. "I, er—"

"Come on. Misery loves company." Chu scrunched over to make room next to her in the back seat. "We need you to show us the way out of here, anyway. I'm only going to get us lost."

Moving slowly, as though unwilling to believe he was actually going along with it, the guard climbed aboard and sat down. His long-fingered hands gripped the metal frame tightly.

"Which way?" Banner asked, glancing over her shoulder at him as Marmion jogged back to his bus.

"Go—" His voice broke. He swallowed and tried again. "Go straight on. Turn right at the junction."

"Thank you," said Chu. "Do you have a name?"

"Gwil. Gwil Flintham."

"Thank you, Gwil. I'm sure the Magister will understand."

He couldn't possibly have gone any paler, Shilly thought, but he did.

Any hope that they might emerge into fresh air was soon quashed. The city stewed in a thousand odours, each stronger than the last. Many were completely unfamiliar, but some she recognised, buried deep in the mix: coffee, rich and warm at the back of her nostrils; camel and goat shit, and wet animal hair; incense and tobacco smoke; meat sizzling on a grill, making her mouth water; rot, and human *everywhere*.

The streets possessed no clear regularity, branching and re-branching without warning, and tending to tip from side to side as though the ground beneath had buckled and been paved without being graded flat. Every free space was used in one way or another, built upon or over to bewildering effect. Buildings teetered at odd angles, clumsier and shorter than the buildings of the Haunted City and made from plaster and brick, not glass. They had a lived-in, almost temporary air; she wouldn't have been surprised to come down the same street a week later and find half of them gone. Banners stretched across the streets between them, declaring street names, advertising products, warning of hazards. The brightly coloured fabric didn't move in the still, thick air. Their florid, hand-painted characters added to the garish nature of the streets, with their tiled walls and gilded window frames. Beads and bells hung from every doorframe. Chalk graffiti added embellishments to anything found lacking. The local alphabet was more angular and fragmented than the curling, spiralling script of the Strand, but Shilly didn't question the fact that she understood the signs as easily as the speech around her.

And the people! Shilly tried not to stare, but it was hard; the streets were crowded under warm, glowing lamps bright enough to dispel the stars above. Laure's citizens displayed a mix of all colours and shapes adorned in all manner of fashion. Some draped themselves in brightly dyed robes. Others adopted styles similar to Chu's, with women wearing pants and tight-fitting tops. Some men and women wore translucent veils across their faces; many sported tattoos and piercings of great diversity. Their voices blended in a rich mélange of accents, too complex and dissonant to disentangle as merchants argued with buyers, commuters squabbled over who had right of way, and uniformed guards did their best to keep order. Not since the underground metropolis of Ulum had Shilly seen such chaos.

Apart from pedestrians, there were bicyclists, carts pulled by animals and people alike, and the occasional engine-driven craft. The latter were noisy and battered, most likely traders from out of town, much the same as them. At least, she thought, they drove on the right side of the road, when the roads were wide enough for two-way traffic.

Gwil Flintham, their unwilling guide, called out directions to Banner as she negotiated the crush. No one paid them any mind, except to honk or yell when they got in the way. Only occasionally did Shilly catch a bystander staring quizzically at the blue robes and dark skins of her companions. When they saw her looking, they quickly turned away.

"Do you live near here?" she asked Chu, whose attention seemed to be elsewhere.

"Eh? I wish." The flyer returned to reality with a jolt.

"Is it far? We could drop you there, if you need a change of clothes or anything."

"Thanks, but I'll be fine."

"Are you sure? We can pick you up later."

"Really, it's okay."

"Suit yourself." Chu's voice had an edge that warned Shilly not to push any further. "What about Skender? Where's he staying?"

"I'll show you after we've seen the Magister. Old Urtagh'll probably throw out the regulars to make room for you lot, if you need it. Nothing brings in the business like a bit of novelty."

"We won't be here for long," said Shilly, "I hope."

"You might not last the night if your friend Marmion gets the Magister offside."

"He's not my friend. Far from it."

"That seems to be the effect he has on people."

"Take the next right," said Gwil into Banner's ear. "There's a checkpoint. Your papers will be examined. Without paying the Tithe, you'll never be allowed to enter the Old Sector."

"Really?" said Shilly, imagining Marmion's response to that news. "This should be interesting."

The argument was short but heated. Reluctantly, the guard backed down, but only with the assurance that the wardens would have a Tithe exemption form in their possession on the way back. Marmion didn't ask what would happen if they didn't comply, and Shilly couldn't help a feeling of relief at having avoided the issue one more time. She didn't know exactly how the Tithe was extracted, but the idea of it made her feel queasy.

With a brisk wave of one arm, Marmion ordered the convoy through. The closer they got to the Magister, the cleaner the air became and the sicker Gwil looked. Around them, the streets broadened and became more regular; walls were made from the same sturdy grey stone as the Wall; edges became clearer, lines better defined. Shilly could tell just by looking that the suburb they had entered was one of affluence and influence. It was still crowded with buildings and apartments, but it possessed none of the overt flourishes of the other areas she had seen; perhaps, she thought, the people who lived here didn't need to show off. There were only a few of them walking the streets, leading pet cats on leashes. In places, there were even trees— albeit strange ones with broad, floppy leaves and trunks that looked like they were wrapped in burlap.

"Is there any chance," Gwil asked, "of being let go any time soon?"

"You know that's not going to happen," said Chu. "We're both stuck, good and proper."

"What are *you* worried about?" he shot back. "You're a miner. Laure needs you. The Magister eats guys like me for breakfast."

Chu laughed low and humourlessly. "None of us are safe where the Magister is concerned. Believe me."

Shilly was starting to be alarmed now. "Who *is* this woman? She sounds absolutely awful."

"She is," said Chu.

"They say she's two hundred years old," said Gwil in a hollow voice. "She drinks a bowl of blood for breakfast and walks with a cane carved out of the Earth's black heart."

At that Chu laughed more naturally. "You listen to too many stories."

"There's nothing wrong with using a cane," said Shilly, rattling hers between her feet. "Or being old and a bit odd."

Gwil was not reassured. "I just wish I hadn't been on duty tonight. What have I done to deserve this?"

Shilly felt sorry for him, then, at being dragged into their misadventure.

"Stop here," he said with grim finality, indicating a building that was so squat and broad it looked like a miniature version of the Wall. A metal fence surrounded it, sporting a gate shaped like two big eyes. "This is it."

Banner pulled up at the curb outside and killed the engine. The two buses did the same. Barely had they pulled to a halt when two functionaries in yellow and black uniforms ran from the entrance to wave them on.

"You can't park here," said one. "This is for official vehicles only."

"We are *on* official business," said Marmion, striding confidently forward and smoothing down the sleeves of his robe. "If you would be so good as to announce us to the Magister, that will help facilitate our speedy departure."

"The Magister is in session," said the man. He stared at the arrivals as though they were likely to vanish if he willed it hard enough. "Unless you have an appointment—"

"I'm sure we can waive that formality, too." Marmion looked past the functionaries, at the gate and the building beyond. "Through here, was it? Shilly, Chu, Banner, and you, young fellow—" he clicked his fingers at Gwil, who jumped as if pricked from behind, "—come along. Let's see this done."

"I'm truly sorry, sir," said the functionary, barring Marmion's way. He didn't sound sorry at all. "I can't allow you through."

"Of course you can."

"No, sir. I cannot." The outstretched hands of the functionaries blocked the gate completely.

Shilly, limping around the buggy to join the group waiting to enter, wondered what Marmion would do now. Would he back down completely, or resort to using the Change on the wrong side of the Divide? Either way, it would be fascinating to see.

He simply reached into his robes and produced a small, crimson envelope.

"Be so good as to give this to the Magister," he said in a voice that was entirely too calm. "When she reads it, I'm sure she'll allow us through."

The functionary took it in one hand and turned it over to look at the back. Shilly saw the seal of the Alcaide imprinted on the flap: a curved sword crossed over a tall drum in purple wax. The functionary whistled piercingly, and a third appeared from within the building. She took the letter and disappeared inside.

A tense silence fell. Marmion waited patiently with his arms folded. Judging by the puzzled looks, Shilly gathered that this was the first the rest of the wardens knew of the letter.

"You," said a functionary to Chu. "Weren't you here the other night?"

"I was indeed," said the flyer with a resigned expression. "Enjoyed it so much I'm back for a repeat performance."

"You left your friend behind this time, I notice."

"How very observant of you."

"Stood you up, did he?" Chu turned away, and the functionary chuckled. "It didn't take him long to come to his senses. Stone Mages have got better things to do than hang around the likes of you."

"That's enough," said Marmion with an irritated look. "Are you employed to have fun at this girl's expense?"

"We see all sorts of people through here, sir," the functionary said, unrepentant. "There are only so many different types in the world, I figure. You get to know them after a while. I've seen *her* plenty of times." He indicated Chu with a disparaging nod. "She never comes just once. At first it's minor charges, small-time trouble. Then it's pleading for clemency from the Magister—and Her Nibs always gives them a second chance. Always regrets it, too. Before long they're back pleading for a third chance that never comes. And then . . ." The functionary shrugged. "We usually don't see them after that, unless it's on the gibbets outside Judgment Hall."

"Is that so?" Marmion regarded him through sharp eyes. "Your powers of observation must be particularly acute to have formed such an opinion from so few meetings."

"It comes with the job, sir. You learn to see patterns and—"

"Would you care to hazard a guess as to what sort of person *I* am?"

"You're a novelty, I'll admit."

"And her?" Marmion pointed at Shilly, then Tom. "And him?"

The functionary looked nonplussed. "It's too early to tell, sir."

"You mean you don't know?"

"I suppose so."

"Well, I hope you never will—and I hope in the future you'll keep your opinions to yourself. It serves only to make you look like a trumped-up fool who delights in picking on the weak. Do you want me to think that this is who *you* are?"

The functionary's face filled with blood and he took a step forward. "Now, listen—"

His companion took his arm.

"You're the one who should listen," said Marmion calmly. "Jumping to conclusions is dangerous. It's *always* too early to give up on someone. A chance remains that they'll surprise you, no matter how unlikely it seems."

Marmion looked up as the third functionary came out of the building. His calm smile returned. "Ah, here's your friend. With word to let us pass, I presume."

"You can go through," she did indeed say. "The Magister has granted you an audience."

"Thank you," said Marmion, sounding immensely satisfied. He bowed to the stunned functionaries. "It has been a pleasure. I'll see you again on the way out."

His robe billowed behind him as he strode between them and through the open door ahead.

"The audience is with all of you," said the third functionary. "Unless you're planning to wait here."

"No way," said Shilly, hobbling through the gate. "I'm dying to know what's in the letter."

"Me, too," said Chu, following her. Banner and Gwil brought up the rear, the young gatekeeper staring around him in startled wonder.

A similar feeling imbued Shilly. *It's always too early to give up on someone.* Marmion's words wouldn't leave her. She wondered if she was as guilty as the functionary of judging too hastily.

"Well, well." The Magister crouched on her seat like an overgrown praying mantis, her long fingernails clicking as they tapped the ball of her black cane. She hadn't said a word throughout the introductions and Marmion's brief precis of the situation, nor through the testimonies of Gwil and Banner. The red trimming of her black robe hung motionless, like rivulets of frozen blood. "This has been quite a week for visitors from afar. One cannot help but wonder what we have done to draw such uncommon attention from our neighbours. Can you explain this to me, Sky Warden Eisak Marmion?"

He bowed with unaffected deference to the forbidding woman on her black throne. Shilly couldn't take her eyes off her. She radiated such incredible potency and vigour that, despite her age, she filled the room with her presence. Every gesture and expression was magnified out of all proportion. Even the sound of her breathing seemed loud and full of meaning.

The crimson envelope lay open on her lap. She let it sit there and did not refer to its contents.

"It was not our wish to inconvenience you," Marmion said, "but circumstances have worked against us."

"In my experience," she said, "circumstances just happen. It's people who work against me."

"Very well, then. We are brought here by the misadventure of one of our colleagues, whose trail led us to the edge of the Divide. There we attempted to capture him and the creature he brought into the world: a Homunculus of unknown provenance. Our circumstances changed when this young woman—" Marmion indicated Chu "—interrupted our best chance to protect Laure from the threat approaching it. We had no choice but to repair to this position and try again. I ask only that you assist us to help you correct this unfortunate happpenstance."

The Magister regarded Chu closely. Shilly saw the young flyer's spine straighten as though bracing herself for punishment.

But the Magister's gaze shifted back to Marmion. "What do you want? Be more specific."

"A healer, first and foremost; accommodation, second. Freedom to move through the city, naturally."

"And what of this thing you seek? Do you expect us to help you catch it?"

"If you're offering us assistance, we will accept it—provided that I remain in complete charge of any operations."

The Magister's lips stretched like hide on a curing frame.

"Of course. You would expect nothing less."

"Excuse me," said Shilly, stepping forward. "There's something else we need, too."

"Oh?" Impenetrable green eyes swivelled to focus on her, and she forced herself to stand firm.

"Two of us are trapped in the Divide. Three, now. We need to help them."

"I am aware of their presence. Miners have brought back reports of people crossing the Divide on foot. I didn't believe them, at first. Few people would be so foolhardy. But with your arrival at our very gates, I had to give it some credence. Not to mention the storm-weaving that threw off a full day's work of atmospheric fine-tuning." Marmion went to say something, but a taloned hand waved him silent. "Does this have anything to do with your young friend, Chu Milang—the boy looking for his mother?"

"Yes, Magister Considine. He's one of the people Shilly's talking about."

"I see." The Magister's gaze hadn't shifted from Shilly. Her voice was as leaden as tombstones. "What do you expect me to do about this, Shilly of Gooron? If your friends are in the Divide, there's no succour I can send them. Their fate is sealed."

"I refuse to believe that. Sal is alive. I know that beyond doubt. And while he lives, I will fight to save him."

"With or without my help. Or my permission, no doubt."

"Yes."

"Intriguing." The Magister took a deep breath and set it free as a sigh. Her attention shifted to Marmion, and her eyes narrowed down to gleaming, hard points. "You may come and go as you wish. All of you may. A healer will be provided for your injured companion. Accommodation expenses I will meet, within reason. Members of my staff will contact you to discuss how best to deal with this—what did you call it—this Homunculus?"

"Yes, Magister Considine." Marmion bowed a second time. "Thank you."

"I'm not finished. I have no resources to offer you in your search for your friends outside the city. That will be entirely up to you. And there is a condition."

"Yes?"

"You will accept the Blood Tithe, Sky Warden. Without argument."

Shilly waited for Marmion to refuse, but she was surprised. "Of course, Magister. We will abide completely by the traditions of your city. At the conclusion of this meeting I will be happy to offer what is due."

The woman crooked an eyebrow at Marmion's obsequious tone. "Good. Now, tell me one thing, Eisak Marmion, before that is taken care of."

"Of course."

"My boundary riders send feverish reports of mass migrations from the east. Not only am I beset upon by foreigners with their begging bowls, but I have man'kin to contend with as well. The Wall has not seen such a concerted assault for many generations. Should I be preparing myself for invasion?"

"Alas," said Marmion, "of this I know nothing. We encountered two groups of man'kin in the Divide. Their loyalties were inconsistent, but they definitely travelled en masse. We were clearly not the first humans they have encountered in recent times."

The Magister nodded solemnly. "If the man'kin have united, for any reason, that is cause for grave concern. They are dangerous enough without organisation or strength of numbers behind them."

"I am convinced," Marmion added, "that it has nothing to do with our quest. The timing is simply unfortunate."

"I see." Her teeth flashed again. Shilly was put in mind of a waiting shark. "I have learned never to convince myself of anything. Time offers the best counsel. I shall await what it tells me."

"Indeed, Magister."

"Gwil Flintham."

The young guard straightened so quickly he almost lost his balance. "M-magister?"

"I assign you to the service of our guests, since you have proven so incompetent at gatekeeping."

Flintham looked like he was about to wet himself with relief. "Thank you, Magister," he said with a hasty bow. "It's more than I deserve."

"Indeed." Her dark gaze swept the room. "Now, you will all leave me so I can return to my evening's schedule. Do not attempt to barge in on me again, or my patience will be severely stretched."

"We understand." Marmion bowed a third and final time. "I will convey to the Alcaide that Laure's hospitality is undiminished."

"Just get out of my sight," she said crossly. "Your machinations weary me."

Marmion seemed startled by her sudden ill grace. He turned and hurried for the door, waving the others after him. As they left, Shilly was sure she heard the sound of crumpling paper.

A functionary showed them to a spare antechamber where the rest of the wardens waited in a nervous huddle, watched over by a dozen red-robed yadachi. A dish of razor-sharp knives and wicked-looking needles rested on a bench in one corner. Marmion reassured his charges that everything was in order, and presented himself first without the slightest visible qualm to the official who had come to take their Tithes.

Shilly watched anxiously as the robed woman nicked Marmion's skin just above the wrist and collected the blood in a slender glass tube. The tube was corked and handed to another yadachi, who affixed a label to it and put it on a table nearby.

"Where does it go from here?" asked one of the wardens as Marmion stepped back, pressing a clean white patch to the small wound.

"Into the Blood Library," said one of the attendants. "It's stored there until needed."

"For what?"

"That depends. If you should require a flying licence or medicine, it will be brought out of storage and the charm tailored to fit you exactly. Otherwise the Tithe will be employed in the usual way: to power the pumps that draw water up from the depths below us. The chimerical energy blood contains makes up for what we lack in stone or sea. All contribute annually to the Tithe; the Tithe in turn keeps us all alive."

The explanation sounded as though it had been learned by rote.

"Aren't we . . . ?" The warden who asked the question looked at the yadachi surrounding them, then lowered her voice. "Won't this give you power over us?"

"That's just a myth," said the yadachi with the knife, waving Shilly forward. "Bloodworkers only succeed with the consent of the donor. We can no more hex you than you us."

"Is that true?" Shilly asked Marmion, averting her eyes as the blade descended on her wrist.

"Yes," he said.

So why did you refuse the Tithe earlier? she wanted to ask, but the pain in her wrist distracted her. The blade was exceedingly sharp, and its sting brief. She didn't cry out as some of the wardens had, or feel faint. Apart from a slight lightheadedness, she felt no different afterwards. Her sample joined the others in a growing line. She hoped never to need to see it again.

Chu looked bored when the time finally came to leave. The two guards waiting at the gate looked up expectantly, but turned quickly away. Marmion's triumphant bearing left no room for ambiguity.

"Here are your temporary papers," said the functionary accompanying them. She pressed a thick wad of documents into his hands. "There are several forms you must complete and return here no later than tomorrow morning. We will require daily updates on your situation and plans, and prompt notification of any change of address or circumstance. Failure to honour these requests will incur immediate penalties. Do you understand?"

Marmion nodded. "Of course. I'll see to the details myself." He gave the papers to Banner, who pressed them onto another, younger warden. The functionary bowed and went back into the building.

The two on the gate watched stonily as Marmion prepared the convoy for departure.

"Accommodation first," he said, "then we'll meet to discuss our plans. Chu, do you have any suggestions?"

"Somewhere clean," put in Shilly, crinkling her nose. "We don't want to make Highson more sick than he already is."

"The Black Galah," she said. "That's where Skender was staying."

"Show us there, then. I trust your judgment," Marmion said.

"Why?"

"It's not as if I have much choice."

"But you *do* have a choice. You've got the run of the city, now. You can do whatever you want."

"It's not that simple."

"Isn't it? You waltz in here and order people around as you like. Even the Magister is doing what you tell her to. Why can't you just produce another letter and have things exactly the way you want?"

Marmion glanced over his shoulder, then walked Chu and Shilly away from the functionaries.

"You two must think me stupid," he said, sotto voce, "and so must the Magister. I know a bureaucratic stall when I see one."

"What?" Chu blinked, startled.

"I have no idea what's in the letter. The Alcaide simply told me to show it to the Magister if we needed her help."

"But you didn't—" Shilly stopped in midsentence, seeing Marmion's ignorance over whether the ruler of Laure was called a Magister or Magistrate in an entirely new light. "It was an act."

"Of course. A power play. Do you think we would've got this far if

Magistrate Considine hadn't wanted us to—if she thought us a threat? Right now, she believes I'm nothing but a fool and a nuisance. If I let her have her way, she'll bog me down in paperwork for days, and we'll lose any chance of catching the Homunculus. Obviously, I'm not going to allow that to happen."

"What *are* you going to do?" asked Chu, staring at him with new respect.

"Go about my duty, of course—and you will help me. As well as being a local, I want you with me because you've seen the Homunculus. The fewer people who know about it, the better. We don't want to cause a panic. Understood?"

Chu nodded.

Marmion clapped her on the shoulder and went off to organise the wardens.

"Is he for real?" Chu asked Shilly.

"It appears so." Shilly felt like she had been hit by a bus. Chu didn't look much better. The young flyer's face was pale and the bandage on her head was tinged with crimson.

"You don't really have to stick with us any longer, you know."

Chu looked at her in surprise. "What?"

"You got us across the Divide as you promised. No one would blame you if you went home now. Not even Marmion could force you to stay if you really didn't want to."

Something dark and complicated passed across the flyer's features. For a brief moment, Shilly thought she might cry again.

"My wing," she said. "I can't leave until I've got it back."

Shilly nodded, thinking: *Gotcha. That's as good an excuse as any.* Even when prompted, Chu had made no noises about family or home, and Shilly was certain now that she wasn't hiding anything on that score. There was nothing to hide at all.

"Why don't you crash in Skender's room?" Shilly said. "It's getting late, and it's not as if he'll need it for a while."

THE CAGE

"There is no depth that has not already been plumbed by Humanity."
THE BOOK OF TOWERS, FRAGMENT 358

Sal didn't know what woke him. One moment he was sound asleep, not even conscious of the hard stone floor on which he lay, the next his eyes were open, trying to glean a single detail from the absolute blackness around him. His confusion was complete, but his reflexes were keen. Even as he tried to work out where he was, he lay absolutely rigid, hardly daring even to breathe.

He was in a room. A stark rectangular doorway let in a faint glimmer of starlight. The smell of dust reminded him that he was in the Aad. His first thought was that Skender had woken him—but if that were so, why was Skender being so quiet?

The more Sal listened, the more certain he became that someone other than Skender was in the room with him. He didn't move lest he betray his presence. The night was utterly silent and still. He couldn't hold his breath forever. Something had to give, and soon.

The sound of footsteps came from outside the room, growing louder on the cobbles.

"Don't make a noise," whispered Habryn Kail from the darkness. "I know you're awake. Stay quiet and I'll explain when they've gone."

The tracker was invisible, one with the shadows. Sal had no idea who "they" were, where Skender was, or how Kail had got there. He felt utterly disoriented.

The footsteps came closer, slow and methodical, right up to the entrance to his hiding place. A faint silhouette appeared in the doorway, and held there for a heartbeat. Sal didn't move even his eyes. The pounding of his pulse seemed loud enough to give him away.

The figure moved off to check the building next door. Sal let out his held breath with a hiss. As the footsteps receded up the street, checking each doorway, one by one, he felt Kail approach. Sal went to sit up and found the water bottle propped beside him. He opened it and drank cautiously, even though his thirst was profound.

"I don't know who they are or what they're looking for," the tracker breathed, easing down to squat lightly beside him, exuding a smell of well-worn leather, "but they've been at it ever since I got here."

"When was that?"

"An hour ago. I followed your trail from where you landed. You weren't even trying to hide it."

"I didn't know we needed to."

"Well, I erased it as I went, so no harm done."

"Where's Skender?"

"I was hoping you could tell me that. His trail leads away from here, deeper into the city, but I didn't get a chance to follow it. If I had, that fellow just now might have found you. Instead I hid, ready to offer you my assistance should you need it."

Sal looked at the dark shape crouched next to him. The tall tracker radiated an unnerving intensity in the darkness.

"What are you doing here?"

"Marmion told me to find you. I don't think he much cares for the idea of you roaming around at will."

"And he'd like to know if we get lucky and find the Homunculus."

"I'm sure that possibility has occurred to him."

"Where did you last see Shilly?"

"In the Divide, on the way to Laure. They should be there by now, barring mishaps."

Sal absorbed all this news. Skender was missing; there were people in the Aad; Kail had been sent to help and keep an eye on them; Shilly was safe.

"Did you bring any food, by any chance?"

Kail rummaged in a pack and pressed something into his hand. Sal unwrapped the small bundle. The slightly bitter smell of dried blood-wood apple filled his nostrils. He concentrated on nothing but eating for several mouthfuls, the aching emptiness in his stomach demanding to be filled.

"We have to find Skender," he said when some of the urgency had passed.

"I agree," said Kail out of the darkness. "We will need to be very careful, though. If he's been caught by those people out there, we don't want to join him."

"They *are* people, then? They're not anything else?"

"No. They stink of sweat and hide, just like us. And alcohol fuel, too. Some of them have been driving recently."

Sal remembered Skender saying that before he and Chu had crashed on top of the Homunculus they had seen vehicles driving along the edge of the Divide. It hadn't sounded likely at the time, but here was evidence that it might be true.

Kail described what had happened after Sal and Skender disappeared: the group of wardens had been buzzed by three busloads of strangers who hadn't stopped to introduce themselves. Shilly had reasoned that there was a connection between these strangers and the Homunculus, and Kail was convinced, now, that she was right.

"The Homunculus missed them at the rendezvous," he said, "and it came here instead. How could that be a coincidence?"

"So if we find them, we find the Homunculus?" said Sal. "And maybe Skender, too?"

"Correct."

"Then that's what we'll do. They're all over the Aad, you said. They've found Skender, so they'll be checking to make sure there's no

one else here with him. They might search all night. All we have to do
is follow one of them back to their lair and we've got them."

"In a manner of speaking."

"Well, we'll know where they are, anyway. Once we know that, we
can get away, call for Marmion and the others, and it's all over."

"You make it sound simple," rumbled Kail. "I can think of a
number of things that might go wrong."

"Sure, but do you have a better plan in mind?"

"No. I just wanted to make certain that you're going into this with
your eyes open. A single slip could give us away."

"I know. Don't worry. I'm very good at keeping my head down.
I've had to be, to keep out of the Syndic's hands all these years."

"Indeed." Kail emitted a single exhalation that might have been a
laugh. "As one of the people who tried to find you and your parents all
those years ago, I can fully attest to that."

Sal wished he could see the tracker's face. Kail's words could be
taken many ways. Knowing how they were intended might make a
great deal of difference one day—when their quest was over and they
returned to their normal lives. Sal had no intention of being taken into
custody again, even by people who had, for a time, been his allies.

He moved across the room to tuck Chu's wing behind the door, so
that a casual glance during the day wouldn't see it. If he'd managed to
sleep half the night without disturbance, he felt confident that it
would be safe for the time being.

"Let's just do it," he said. "Let's find Skender and the Homunculus
and get out of here. This place gives me the creeps."

"I think," said Kail, coming to stand beside him, "that's the point."

Skender sat in a cage and stared at his mother. She lay on her side in
another cage on the far side of the room. Her braids had been cut off,
exposing grey roots; one eye was blackened and swollen; bruises ran up
her jawline to her left ear, where a trickle of blood had left splatters down

her neck. The arms of her rust-red travelling robe had been torn away, exposing thick lines of tattooed symbols and more bruises. Skender couldn't see her hands; they had been tied behind her back. Her knees and feet were drawn up, like a child sleeping. She looked very thin and frail.

"She's going to be pissed when she sees you," said the large albino occupying the next cage along. "You idiot."

"It's good to see you, too, Kemp."

"What are you doing here? Haven't you ever heard of the Surveyor's Code?"

"Are you saying you don't want to be rescued?"

"I'm not saying that at all." Kemp thrust an arm through the metal grid separating them. "I just don't think you're in much of a position to make it happen."

Skender rose unsteadily to return Kemp's clasp. Kemp's hand was broad and very strong. Skender could see scrapes and cuts where he must have tried to free himself, to no avail. No amount of rough bluster could hide the intense worry in the albino's pale-as-glass eyes.

After dumping him, dazed, in the dungeon with their other prisoners, Skender's captors had left him alone. It was easy to see why they wouldn't worry about him escaping. The dungeon had only one exit and no vents, the latter explaining its powerful smell. Two flickering gas lamps cast shadows that danced and writhed across the walls. There were ten cages, each secure enough to hold a full-sized man'kin, but only five were definitely occupied. The metal bars surrounding Skender on three sides were crosshatched and thick. The fourth side was a wall of solid stone, as were the floor and ceiling. The other cages currently contained Skender's mother, Kemp, and one other of her companions—the disgraced Sky Warden Shom Behenna, also unconscious. A stone bust that might have been Mawson leaned against the bars next to his mother, but the Change-sink enfolding the town had turned him back into dead stone. The rear of one of the corner cages was shrouded in darkness. Skender couldn't tell if it was empty or not.

His mother hadn't moved since his arrival.

"Is she all right?"

Kemp's worried look deepened. "At first they thought Behenna was in charge, but she owned up after the first beating they gave him. The bastards. They're going easier on her, but it's all relative. I don't know how much more of this she can take."

Skender couldn't believe what he was hearing. *Beatings?*

"Do you mean she might . . . ?" He couldn't finish the sentence.

"Either that," Kemp said, "or she'll just tell them what they want to hear and take what comes next. They won't believe we're ordinary Surveyors. They think we're here to steal something from them."

Skender thought of his mother's mysterious mission. "*Are* you?"

"Of course not. We didn't even know they existed until they ambushed us a week ago." Kemp looked defeated and haggard. His pale skin was dirty and his colourless hair lank. He slumped heavily against the stone wall of the cell and sank down into a sitting position. "The leader is a prick called Pirelius. You don't want to get on his bad side. When Behenna tried to stand up for your mother, four days ago, they stopped feeding him. They smack him around occasionally, for the fun of it."

Skender looked at where the ex-Warden lay in his cage, two along from his. Shom Behenna had shaved his head and begun tattooing it in the style of a Surveyor. He, too, wasn't moving.

"I do what I can to distract them," said Kemp, "but they're not falling for it. They know that making me watch is just as bad as an actual beating. Worse, even. They probably know your mum won't talk but are hoping I might. If that doesn't work, they might try the other way around, with someone else. They're certain to, once they work out who *you* are."

A river of ice-cold water flooded through Skender's gut at the thought that he might be tortured to make his mother confess to something she wasn't guilty of.

"We have to get out of here," he hissed.

"Tell me something I don't know." Kemp rolled his eyes and nodded at the cage in shadow. "If the thing in there can't escape, I don't know how *we* can."

Skender turned to stare at the corner cage. The chill in his veins only intensified as he realised what it contained.

"They brought it in a few hours before you," Kemp explained. "Strangest thing I've ever seen."

"Was it awake?"

"If it was, it wasn't moving. Not at first. It crawled into the shadows an hour or so ago."

"Have you tried talking to it?"

"I don't know if it *can* talk."

Skender thought of Tom's warning. *Find the Homunculus, and you'll find your mother. If you don't, you'll never see her again.* Tom had been right on that score. Unfortunately, he hadn't said anything about being unable to escape afterwards.

"It was talking just fine the last time I saw it."

He stuck one arm through the bars toward the corner cage, and waved it.

"Hey," he called. "Hey, you! You said you've met me before. Come out and talk to me, since we're such good buddies. We've got to get out of here!"

Kemp shushed him. "Keep it down. They don't like it if we make too much noise."

"Don't they? Well, let's see them do something about it. Hey!" He whistled piercingly through two fingers. "Come out where I can see you and tell me who you are!"

Something stirred at the very rear of the cage. *That's it*, thought Skender, as if he was talking to a nervous dog. *There's a good boy. I won't hurt you.*

"What's all this racket?" snarled a rough voice from the doorway. Skender withdrew his arm as a surprisingly small man in leather pants strode into view. His moustaches hung in thin rattails, as did the fringe of hair above his neck and ears. His skin was a piebald mix of colours under a dense desert tan. Instead of tattoos, a mess of scars stretched up each arm and down his chest.

"Eh?" Bulging eyes took in Skender as the man bent to pick up a long, wooden stick from the centre of the room. "The new pet raising a ruckus, is it?"

Skender backed away as the stick came up and pointed at him through the crosshatched bars. It was easily three metres long with a split and splintered tip. He didn't want to think about the stains.

"Leave him alone, you freak," said Kemp.

"That's fine coming from you, whiteskin," Rattails jeered. "Shut up while I teach this young rabbit to behave."

"If you hit him, you'll regret it!"

"Don't worry. You'll get yours, if you keep that up."

Rattails slipped the business end of the stick through the bars and rammed it forward, catching Skender hard on the shoulder. The blow was surprisingly powerful and painful. It knocked him spinning off his feet.

"Are you going to be a good rabbit?" Rattails withdrew the stick and leered through the bars. "Or do I have to poke you again?"

Skender blinked back tears of pain and humiliation. Rattails was just dying for him to talk back. Given the slightest excuse, he would beat Skender to a bloody pulp.

"Pick on someone your own size," said Kemp from the cage next door.

"That's not the way it works, whiteskin." Rattails raised the stick. "You should know that by now."

Skender thought of Chu saying: *I can fight my own battles.*

He clambered to his feet, wincing as he moved his shoulder.

"Ah, good. I like a moving target."

"That must be something of a novelty," said Skender, "given your breath. Most of your prisoners must keel over as soon as you come into the room."

Rattails shifted his grip on the stick. His nostrils flared. Skender flinched as the stick jabbed at him again, aimed this time for his unprotected abdomen.

The blow never fell. Kemp lunged through the bars of his cell and caught the stick in one hand. With a defiant roar, he used his superior weight and the bars between them as a fulcrum to lever the other end out of Rattails's hands. Before their jailer could snatch it back, he slid it out of reach and snapped it clean in two.

"Hey!" Rattails glared at them both as Kemp slipped Skender half of the broken stick through the bars joining their cages. The albino hefted it like a spear and tested its jagged end.

"Want to try to take it from me?"

Rattails shook his head. "Rabbit thinks it's clever. Thinks it's got spirit." A slow, cruel sneer spread across the face of their jailer. "I'll leave you two for Pirelius. I'm sure he'll have something to say about this, when he gets back."

Rattails ran out of the dungeon with a sadistic leer. The scars down his back flexed like molten wax.

"Well, that showed *him*." Kemp threw the stick to the ground and sagged back against the wall. His words were brave, but his body language couldn't lie. Skender took no comfort at all from the heavy shaft of wood in his hands. As good as the defiant gesture had felt, they were still on the wrong side of the bars.

"Now what?" he asked.

Kemp shrugged. "Now's the time to tell me you didn't come here alone, that there's an army of Mages out there just waiting to attack."

Skender thought of Sal sleeping off his exhaustion in an empty building in the Aad. "Not exactly." And if his mother couldn't find a way to penetrate the Change-sink shrouding the Aad, he had little chance of succeeding. "I think we'll have to see what happens."

Skender glanced at the corner cell, but the Homunculus had gone back to hiding in the shadows.

THE CONFESSION

"As relics of the past go, belief in god and the afterlife is perhaps the most quaint. They serve merely as distractions from the truth we all must accept: that this world and this life is all we have. Calling vinegar wine does not make it taste any better; such lies alter nothing and benefit no one at all."
THE BOOK OF TOWERS, EXEGESIS 28:22

Barely had Shilly fallen asleep, it seemed, when she was being shaken awake by a hand at her shoulder. She sat up, startled, unsure for a moment where she was.

"Shilly," said a voice she recognised as belonging to Warden Banner. "It's Sal's father. He's conscious."

It all came back to her then. She was in the hostel room she shared with two female wardens. They had checked into the Black Galah not long after meeting with the Magister. Instead of discussing their plans then and there, Marmion had ordered them all to bed. No one had argued. The drive to Laure had been long and exhausting and it didn't seem like anything else would happen that night.

She hurriedly dressed. "Did Marmion call for me?"

"No, but I knew you'd want to be there." The dumpy warden put a finger to her lips and handed Shilly her walking stick. "Third door on the right. I wouldn't bother knocking."

Shilly hurried out of the room. The Black Galah wasn't a classy establishment by any stretch of the imagination, but it was sufficient to the wardens' needs. The landlord, a swarthy, bottom-heavy man called Urtagh, had cleared the building to make room for the expedition and found parking spaces for the buggy and two buses. Skender's room was a tiny attic space at the end of one of the halls; Chu had said goodnight and disappeared into it immediately. Shilly was on the other side of the building, near the two communal bathrooms. The sound of pipes chugging through the night might ordinarily have kept her awake—after the endless quiet of the underground workshop in Fundelry—but exhaustion had quickly won out.

She reached the door Banner had indicated. It wasn't locked. She could hear voices on the other side: Marmion's, insistent and demanding, and another that sounded exactly like Sal's. Her heart leapt to her throat.

This was her chance to find out what manner of creature Highson had brought into the world. Ghost, golem, or something even worse?

After a single deep breath, she lifted the latch and plunged inside.

"What is the meaning—?" Marmion sank back into his seat on seeing who it was. "Of course. Wild camels couldn't keep you away."

She ignored him. "Hello, Highson," she said to the man on the bed in the centre of the tiny room.

Highson Sparre lifted his head. He wasn't a tall man, but he had a powerful presence. Even in a weakened state, wearing nothing but a soiled vest that was unlaced to his midsection and a sheet to cover his legs, he dominated the room. He had honey-coloured skin and hair that had once been pure black but was now mostly grey. Time had left his face lined with grief and determination. On seeing her, he reached out with one hand.

"Shilly." His voice was ragged but there was no denying the welcome in it.

She took his hand and clutched it to her chest. Tears surprised her, and she held them back with difficulty. He looked so *old*.

"Sal, too?" he asked.

"He's off with Skender, otherwise he'd have been here now."

"You shouldn't have come," he said, shaking his head. "You're putting yourselves in danger."

"You can talk," she said, ignoring Marmion's mute frostiness. The warden sat on the far side of the bed, torcless and dishevelled. The wisps of his hair hung askew over one ear. Like Shilly, he had obviously been woken from a deep sleep.

"You *will* talk, Warden Sparre," he said, indicating that Shilly should pull up the remaining chair. "Do you see what your actions have done? This isn't just about you. One person is already dead. The next one might be a great deal more important to you than some Gunidan lowlife. Understand?"

Highson put a hand over his eyes. Not to shade them, Shilly realised; the lantern flame on his bedside table was barely bright enough to cast a shadow. He was hiding tears of his own. A wave of grief radiated from him so powerfully that Shilly felt the strength give out in her bad leg. She sat down, feeling breathless and abruptly unsure that she wanted to know what had reduced Sal's father to such a state.

"I'm not going to pretend," he said with wavering voice, "that I can justify my actions. I know what I've done, who I've hurt. That's exactly why I'm here. In my own way, I'm trying to undo the hurt I've caused in the past. I was trying to make things better."

Marmion made an unsympathetic noise but didn't interrupt. Shilly held her walking stick tightly between her knees as Highson Sparre unburdened himself.

"It started five years ago, when you were tricked by the ghost in the Haunted City." Highson addressed Shilly, not Marmion. His eyes were sunken. "That was the first time we ever suspected that Sal's mother didn't die of natural causes. Seirian was a determined woman and she was trying to escape. A ghost tricked her into thinking it could help her. When she realised that she had been deceived and tried to stop the ghost from breaking free, the effort drained her dry. Her mind was lost into the Void Beneath, and her body slowly wasted away."

Shilly listened with her heart pounding hard. She remembered the ghastly visage of her own ghost as it had burst out of a silver mirror, embodied thanks to her ignorant efforts. It would have killed her as casually as squashing a bug once it had no need of her; but for Sal's cousin Aron she would be dead now, and many others with her.

"What does this have to do with the Homunculus?" Marmion asked.

"Patience." Highson raised a hand. "I'll get there. First I need to tell you how it felt to know that the woman I loved had been murdered. If I had seen it coming and taken the appropriate steps, her death might have been avoided. I know she didn't love me the way she loved Dafis, but that wasn't the point. Her life had been ruined and her last hope of happiness snatched from her. That was worse, in a way, than losing her in the first place.

"And there was more to come. Skender, Sal, and Kemp were trapped in the Void Beneath. Skender returned with stories about minds surviving in the Void. *Lost* Minds. People who end up in the Void don't die right away, it seems; they linger as long as their memories last. Only when they've forgotten who they are do they fade away forever. This was radical stuff. No one had caught a glimpse of the Lost Minds before. But it had the ring of truth—and Skender is a Van Haasteren, after all. If anyone was going to remember the truth, it would be him."

Minds surviving in the Void, Shilly echoed to herself. She had never heard anything about this before.

"You believe the word of a troublemaking child," said Marmion, "when it flies in the face of everything we know?"

"What *do* we know, Eisak? Precious little."

"We call it a Void for a reason."

"Perhaps the wrong reason: there's an emptiness where knowledge remains to be found. If you don't believe me, follow it up with Master Warden Atilde or the Surveyor Iniga, who also heard Skender's story. Or you can allow me to continue and let events speak for themselves."

Marmion didn't back down from the challenge, but he did indicate that Highson should go on.

"The most important thing Skender told me was that someone helped them escape from the other Lost Minds. That person had forgotten her name, but she remembered losing a son. Skender thought it was Sal's mother. He told me, in effect, that Seirian might still be alive in the Void."

Shilly stared at him. Hearing a river of grief underlying his words, she began to see, then, where the story was going.

"You tried to bring her back," she said.

"For five years—five awful years spent noting every reference to the Void I could find and hoping she wouldn't fade away before I came to her. There are dozens of ways into the Void, but no reliable ways out. Obviously there was no point me being trapped in there as well, although in the end I had to balance risk against effectiveness. Each time I tried to find her, I took a chance I might not come back."

"Each time?" asked Marmion. "How many times did you perform this dreadful experiment?"

"Nine: five trial runs to make sure I was doing it right; four for real on the night itself. I returned intact each time, but with no memory of what had happened within the Void; every last trace had been naturally erased. I might have found Seirian, or nothing at all. There was only one way to tell."

"And that was to bring her out with you," said Shilly, marvelling at the audacity and obsession that had led Highson to such extremes. Trawling the Void for a lost love—especially one who didn't reciprocate that love—was an unbearable kind of torture, and a work of magnificent madness, both. If it had worked, it would have offered hope for anyone who had lost friends or relatives in Change-related accidents. That it obviously hadn't worked only made it more tragic.

"Her body was long dead," Highson explained. "Her mind would need a vessel if it was to survive in this world. Some Stone Mages use the empty-minded as shells to save them travelling across the Interior, but there was no way that I could morally or logistically pursue that course. Seirian didn't have the training required; I couldn't very well steal a body and force her to take it; and who was I to put an innocent, if absent, person through such straits? I had to find another way around the problem.

"I chose to make a Homunculus—and that was, strangely, the easiest part. Look hard enough and you'll find detailed procedures in several old texts. People have made Homunculi for many reasons, seeking everything from immortality to slave labour. Such bodies are stronger than ours and designed to take the shape of the mind within them, so the final results are completely lifelike. Or so the theory goes.

"Obtaining the ingredients required was more complicated, as was getting everything into one place at the right time without anyone noticing. I hired Larson Maiz to help with the grunt-work, but he was supposed to leave once the apparatus was in place. He shouldn't have been there when the Homunculus quickened, as I hoped it would, with the mind of Seirian."

Marmion made an exasperated noise. "This story grows more outlandish by the second."

"You don't have to believe it," said Highson with a flash of anger. "You're the one who wanted me to tell it to you. Remember?"

"You said you went into the Void four times, that night," Shilly said to forestall an argument.

Highson nodded, and dropped his gaze to his hands. "That's right. The first three times, I came back with nothing. A Homunculus initially has no shape of its own, but possesses the *potential* for shape. Like clay that hasn't been fired, it needs a mind to press form upon it. So each time I opened my eyes and saw that formless stuff, I knew that I had failed. I didn't need to remember what had happened in the Void: the proof was right there in front of me. I needed to go again, to try harder, to reach deeper."

"Wasn't it dangerous?" Shilly asked.

"Very, but what happened to me didn't matter. Seirian was the most important thing. Finding her and bringing her back with me." He took a deep, shuddering breath. Shilly expected Marmion to hurry him along. But the warden was silent for once.

"When I woke up on the cold ground after my last attempt and saw the stars, I was utterly drained by my many voyages to and from the Void Beneath. I stood up in the centre of the charm I had designed for the attempt. The Homunculus, for a second, looked as inanimate as ever, but then the process began. The lifeless flesh stirred; a blue flame danced across its skin; its eyes opened. It became—*something*.

"At that moment, I knew that my failure ran deeper than simply not finding Seirian. The creature before me was not of our world and its form was not one the Homunculus could easily contain. I stood, stunned, as a war between mind and body ensued. The night around me bent and twisted; flames spread, forcing me back. I wished in vain that I had prepared some means of stopping the Homunculus should something go wrong—but why would I ever have imagined the need for it? The only thing I had anticipated bringing into the world was the woman I loved, not the creature that writhed in hideous birth-throes on the ground before me.

"There was an explosion of chimerical energy. I was flung into the bushes and momentarily stunned. When I came to, the fire had died down. Only an unearthly glow remained in its wake. The earth itself seemed to burn, perhaps in outrage at the thing that stood upon it, a dreadful mess of limbs and features, as agonised by its emergence into our world as I was confused by its presence. What had gone wrong? What had I *done*?

"Then Maiz appeared. The fool had been lurking in the bushes, perhaps out of curiosity, perhaps awaiting an opportunity to steal some of the more valuable-looking items I had brought with me. The fire flushed him out. He sank to his knees before the newly formed Homunculus and begged for his life.

"The creature didn't seem to hear him. It was disoriented. It tried to talk and failed. Maiz couldn't understand it, and neither could I. Somehow its words were obscured. Maiz shook his head, too frightened to speak, and the creature became frustrated. Its form shifted, threatened to dissolve. That only made Maiz more frightened. He thought it was attacking him. He screamed. With the last of my strength, I ran forward to separate them—too late. Maiz fell to the ground at the Homunculus's feet, dead, and the Homunculus turned on me next.

"I thought I, too, was about to die."

"Why didn't you?" asked Marmion.

"That's the wrong question, Eisak. The right one is: why did *Maiz* die?"

"He died of fright," put in Shilly, remembering all too clearly what Tom had told her, back in Fundelry.

Highson nodded. "I agree. Maiz wasn't young, and his health was far from perfect. You've seen what the Homunculus looks like. It's not implausible."

"So it didn't mean to kill Maiz," said Marmion with scepticism written broadly across his face, "and it didn't try to kill you, either."

"Exactly. I was utterly vulnerable. I barely had the strength to stand. Indeed, as it confronted me, I fell down before it, certain my time had come. I fainted, exhausted. When I came to, I was unharmed and it was gone."

"Did you set off after it immediately, or did you consider telling someone else what had happened first?" The warden's question had a sharp edge, and Shilly could understand why. If Highson had explained the details of his disappearance earlier, much inconvenience might have been avoided.

"I tried to send a message to Risa Atilde, who would have disapproved but at least understood. I wasn't successful. Assuming that I was still drained by the exertion of the summoning, I decided that I should get moving as quickly as possible, before the Homunculus gained too much of a lead. There was nothing I could do for Maiz, after all, and I had enough supplies to last a day. I didn't think I would need any more than that. Not until much later did I learn that my inability to call for help stemmed not from me, but from the Homunculus itself. Something about it and its wake cancelled out every charm I tried to cast.

"I ran and walked to the limits of my endurance. When my food and water ran out, I kept walking. I didn't stop for any reason, even to sleep. Whatever the Homunculus was, I was responsible for it. I certainly wasn't going to turn back, even if it killed me."

Shilly remembered the way she had first seen the creature: striding out of the desert with Highson Sparre slumped lifelessly in its arms. The pursuit had ended in a way Highson couldn't possibly have foreseen.

"If it hadn't brought you to us," she said, "you probably *would* have died."

Highson nodded and rested his head back on his pillows. "I know. Don't think I haven't wondered about that. When I finally caught up with it, I was barely conscious. I had lost sight of why I was there, what the Homunculus was for—who, even, I was supposed to be. I had become a creature that walked, nothing more. I was delirious and dehydrated. I don't remember what happened between us." A confused frown flickered across his face. "The next thing I knew, you had found me and it was about to kill you. I've been lying here thinking about everything that's happened, but I still don't understand why it would do that."

Marmion raised a hand to cut off that particular avenue of inquiry. "Shilly says it spoke to her and Sal when it gave you to them." The warden turned to her. "Tell Highson what it told you. Perhaps that'll jog his memory."

"It knew Skender's heart-name." She found Highson's puzzled, hurt-filled gaze hard to meet. "It said that your summoning hadn't been successful, and that you couldn't keep up with it. It asked us to look after you. When you told it not to hurt Marmion, it said that there had been enough death, and it let him live."

"Ring any bells?" Marmion asked Highson.

"Nothing," he said. "I don't know Skender's heart-name, so I couldn't have told it to the Homunculus, consciously or otherwise."

"It said," Shilly explained, "that Skender had met it before."

"Could it be a golem? A ghost?" Marmion asked. "They both have affinities for heart-names."

"It also said something about the two of them not being part of the world, when they met."

"Where else *is* there, except the world?"

"Only the Void." Highson's brows knotted in puzzlement then rose in alarm. "No, it couldn't be. Surely not!"

"What?" asked Marmion, leaning forward.

"There was another thing Skender spoke of after he and Sal emerged from the Void. He mentioned meeting someone there, someone apart from Seirian."

"Another Lost Mind?"

"Yes, or something much more than that—perhaps the very first of the Lost. The Oldest One, it called itself. It claimed responsibility for the Cataclysm."

Marmion glanced at Shilly, checking her reaction, before asking, "And you think this may be the being inside the Homunculus, instead of Seirian?"

"I don't know. Skender had no reason to lie, but there's no record in the *Book of Towers* supporting the story he told us, and there were so many other things to worry about at the time. There was no way to follow it up."

Marmion nodded, still looking at Shilly. She wondered if he thought she was hiding information from him. He probably wouldn't believe her if she told him the truth. Sal had never mentioned meeting anything in the Void Beneath, and he had been there with Skender. So had Kemp. Their memories had probably been erased, as Highson's had been, and Skender had kept his to himself. After all, what importance would such information have beyond the circles of historians and scholars of the *Book of Towers*?

It claimed responsibility for the Cataclysm.

Even if the creature *was* the Oldest One, they still knew next to nothing about its motives or capabilities.

"Where is it now?" asked Highson, shifting under the covers as though trying to get up. "We need to find it, talk to it—"

"Don't worry about that." The warden stood and walked around the bed. "It's out of your hands, now. I want you rested and recovered and ready to move."

Marmion tried to usher Shilly out of the room, but she stayed firmly put. "Have you seen a healer?" she asked Highson, putting a hand on his arm to calm him down.

"Someone was here earlier, when I awoke."

"He's being looked after," Marmion reassured her. "Come on, Shilly. Let the man sleep."

She would have given in out of tiredness but for Highson's hand suddenly gripping hers. "Let her stay a little longer," he said. "It's good to see a familiar face."

Marmion reluctantly acquiesced. "I'll be back shortly. We all need rest."

The door shut behind him, and locked with a solid clunk.

Shilly turned back to Highson to find him staring at her. His intensity was startling and made her feel suddenly uncomfortable. The hand on her arm gripped just a little too tightly.

"Where's Sal?" he asked. "What are he and Skender up to?"

"Didn't Marmion tell you? I assumed you knew."

Highson shook his head. "The man is a fool. He won't tell me anything."

"Sal and Skender are chasing the Homunculus and Skender's mother. Tom thinks they're linked somehow. Habryn Kail, a tracker, has gone after them."

"I know Kail," said Highson a little too sharply. "Is there more I should know?"

"That's it, really. Marmion thinks the Homunculus is headed here, to Laure, but I think it's actually meeting up with people in the Aad. We haven't heard otherwise from Sal, so that's where I'm going next."

"All right." He nodded and lay back on the pillow. "Tell me something else, then: why did the Homunculus try to kill Marmion?"

"Because Marmion tried to kill it first."

"I thought your answer might be along those lines. Why does Marmion want it dead? What's he so afraid of?"

"I don't know." Marmion, *afraid?* She hadn't quite looked at it that way. "The thing inside the Homunculus, I guess. What it could be."

"Why? It helped me. It means us no harm."

"We don't know that, Highson—"

"But we do. The last time I tried to find Seirian in the Void, I decided that I didn't want to come back without her. I was committed to finding her or dying. Since I obviously didn't find her, I shouldn't be here now. I should be one of the Lost Minds. I only live now because something brought me out—and what else could that have been but the Homunculus?"

"Wait," he said when she tried to interrupt. "You already know there's more. When I was following it in the desert, what hope had I left? I knew it wasn't Seirian ahead of me. I wasn't trying to kill myself, this time. In a sense, I was already dead. I had surrendered everything the last time I dived into the Void, and emerged empty-handed. I was nothing. *Nothing.*"

The despair in Highson's voice was awful to hear. Tears came to Shilly's eyes again, and she gripped his hand even tighter.

"It brought me back, Shilly. Twice. It wouldn't let me die. What sort of monster would go to such lengths?"

The lock clicked and the door opened. Shilly pulled away from Highson as Marmion opened the door. She stood, hoping the turmoil of her thoughts didn't show.

"Are you done here?" the warden asked.

"Yes. I should really hit the sack. We've got a lot to do in the morning."

"It does sound that way," Highson said, his own distress carefully hidden. "Thank you. Come again soon."

"I will." She bent over to kiss his cheek, and didn't quite manage to avoid the cloying despair in his eyes. "It's good to see you."

He nodded as she left the room.

Instead of trading places with her, Marmion closed the door behind both of them and took her arm before she could move away.

"Keep this to yourself," he whispered into her ear. "Until we know exactly what we're dealing with, I don't want any unhelpful or unnecessary speculation."

Unnecessary speculation? She almost laughed out loud. Minds surviving in the Void Beneath, Sal's mother one of them; an ancient being claiming responsibility for the Cataclysm, possibly abroad in the body that should have been Seirian's; the Homunculus's mysterious journey, stopping to save Highson Sparre twice along the way.

A wry waspishness nearly overwhelmed her. "I think it's a little late for that, don't you?"

She pulled free and walked back to her room, feeling Marmion's stare between her shoulder blades all the way. Only when she heard Highson's door open then close did she breathe normally again.

The mysteries were multiplying, not shrinking. She lay in bed, thinking about everything she'd learned, as the early hours of the morning lay heavy as mortuary slabs. She came no closer to an explanation.

THE CADUCEUS

**"and in the ruin a wondrous relic
bone-thing broken ancient old-thing
dug up deep from times forgotten
hungry mindless Change-dead lost"**
THE BOOK OF TOWERS, FRAGMENT 49

Sal watched as the last of the men and women vanished into the old house. "Do we follow them now?" he asked Kail in a soft voice.

The tracker shook his head. They had been peering through a chink in an upper-storey wall two streets along for almost an hour. Sal was getting bored, but he saw the need to be cautious. The search party was returning empty-handed from their combing of the ruins. People were going into the house and not coming out.

But they weren't inside the house itself. That he could tell. The windows were dark and the stone walls silent. The house was obviously an entrance to somewhere else. The tunnels under the ruins, he assumed.

"We need to find another way in," Kail breathed back. "There will be lookouts or traps this way, for certain. We'd never make it, not without the Change on our side."

"How else are we going to get in, then?"

"These people are obviously concerned about security. They wouldn't let themselves be cornered if someone found them. There has to be another entrance."

"It could be anywhere."

"I know. That's why we're going to ask for directions." Kail looked sideways at Sal. "I've been counting heads as they come back in. There are only a couple left out here now. We're going to introduce ourselves to one of them."

Sal shifted uncomfortably, remembering darker, more desperate times. "I'm not fond of violence."

"Who said anything about violence? I just intend to apply a little pressure." Kail looked up at the sky. "It'll be dawn soon. If we're going to do it, we do it now. Coming?"

He moved away from their viewpoint in a crouch. Sal hesitated, then followed, fervently wishing he knew what he was getting himself into.

"Another visitor? How interesting."

Skender stood at the back of the cage as the man Rattails and Kemp called Pirelius approached the bars between them. He was broad-shoul-dered and filthy, with a shaved head and dense beard. Thick notches had been cut into his ears, leaving them ragged and scarred. He wore layers of leather and cotton that hadn't been removed for years. They certainly smelled that way to Skender in the still, lifeless air.

"Got a name, boy?

"Of course I have," he replied.

"And a stick, too. A fancy lad, you are." Thick fingers of one hand laced themselves around the bars of his cage while the other hand produced an iron key. It worked inside a lock set in the wall above the cage until it clicked. Bolts retracted into deep holes in the ceiling and floor. The door swung open until there was nothing between Skender and Pirelius but air.

"How safe are you feeling now?"

Skender gripped the stick in both hands and tried not to look as worried as he felt. Pirelius's eyes were empty and cold. Behind Pirelius were seven equally hideous men and one woman. Rattails watched with gloating from the dungeon's doorway. Pirelius grinned hungrily, revealing gaps where two lower teeth should have been.

Skender hadn't been afraid until Rattails poked him with the stick. He was terrified now, more so than he had been when stuck in the caves under Laure. If he had any doubts about what Pirelius was capable of, all he had to do was look at his mother, battered and bruised on the other side of the room.

"It wasn't him," said Kemp from the cage next door. "It's not his fault. It was me."

"Shut up, whiteskin. I'm not talking to you." Pirelius didn't even glance at the albino.

"Hop on out, little rabbit," jeered Rattails. "Don't make him come in after you."

"What do you want?" Skender asked. "Why are you doing this to us?"

"Why? Because we can." Pirelius stepped into the cage entrance. "We're a law unto ourselves, here. Locals don't come to the Aad because they think it's haunted—and I suppose it is, in a manner of speaking. Haunted by us. The flyers say the air is bad, so even they stay away. What do you think, boy?" He sniffed. "Fresh enough for you in here?"

"We're not doing anything to hurt you."

"Oh, no? Just by being here you hurt us. You'll betray our little secret—if it hasn't already been given away. That's what I want you to tell me, boy. Who sent you here, and why? Tell me, and I might forgive you for breaking Izzi's stick."

Pirelius took another step towards him and unwound a leather cord from his waist. Skender looked at Kemp, but there was nothing his old friend could do. Pirelius made sure to stay well out of range of the albino and his half of the stick.

"I'm not bluffing, boy." Pirelius's voice was low and dangerous. "Don't think I am. Your whiteskin neighbour is untouched only because I don't trust him. He's the biggest, and I don't intend to give him an opportunity to turn the tables. He's made it pretty clear what he'll do if he ever gets the chance. So he's going to stay nice and tight in that little box until someone else breaks and tells me the truth. It might as well be you, don't you think? Because if it's not, tonight's not going to end very well for you."

"I don't know what you're talking about," Skender said. "There's no secret. There's nothing to tell."

"No?"

The leather thong lashed out and caught Skender across the face. It happened almost too quickly for him to see it, much too fast for him to raise the stick in self-defence. The pain was so startling and so sudden that his hands flew to the spot and the stick dropped to the ground, forgotten.

"You—" Skender flinched, and turned away to hide the tears. Pirelius didn't laugh, but the others did. Kemp was calling him, but all he could hear were the jeers and the cries to hit him again.

Pirelius did, and this time the blow fell across his shoulders. It stung like acid and pushed him forward, into the bars separating him from the empty cage next door. He clutched at it and wished with all his heart that Tom had warned him not to go wandering off in the dark on his own. If he'd just stayed with Sal and waited for daylight—

"What's it going to take?" Pirelius bent over him, his voice an outraged roar. "A broken arm? An eye poked out? I'll make sure you get it. And I will get what I want. I'm not an idiot, you know—although *she* might treat me like one. You're muscling in on my territory. Maybe you think my cut is too high. Maybe you think I'm greedy, getting fat down here on the front line. Well, look at me. Do I look fat to you? There are other ways to pay. You can tell *her* I said so—and if I have to kill a couple of you to deliver the message, I'll do it!"

The lash struck in time with his words, beating the point home. Skender didn't try to defend himself, physically or verbally. It was clear that Pirelius had passed the point beyond which he could be turned back. There was nothing Skender could do but ride it out.

While his body fell under the blows and curled into a ball in the corner of the cage, his mind did the same, in its own way. He huddled around himself and let the pain grow distant. Someone was crying; it might have been him, but he couldn't tell. The voices were as faint as starlight. He faded out completely for a moment.

When he came to, the blows had stopped falling. He heard a banging of bars, a strange voice calling, and much milling about and confusion.

"Keep away from it!" Pirelius cried to his underlings. "It's dangerous. You saw what it did to the man'kin!"

"Yeah, but it can't hurt *us*, can it?"

"We don't know that yet. We don't know what it'll do when it's not taken by surprise. Who knows what it's thought of for you poor fools!"

Skender heard a general shuffling of feet as people backed away from whatever was making the commotion.

"Put *him* in the cage next to it," Pirelius ordered. "Unlock the door between them. Maybe that way we'll find out what else it can do."

Skender kicked out as a shadow fell across him. Strong hands gripped his arms and legs, hauled him out of the cage and across the room. The bruises on his back and shoulders burned like fire. The world spun dizzily around him.

He fell to the ground again and a door clanged behind him.

"Throw him the stick." Pirelius laughed. "Fat lot of good it'll do him. Maybe he'll change his mind about talking when he sees what sort of company he'll have to keep in here."

Pirelius's mocking laugh echoed as he left the dungeon, followed by his cronies. Kemp called Skender's name over and over, but Skender didn't know how to answer. The banging gradually subsided. He heard the shuffling of feet nearby, the grate of metal against metal.

He clutched at the ground beside him and found his half of the stick. He pulled it to his chest.

"Who is wrong here, Galeus?" asked a very strange voice. "Have you done something to deserve this?"

Skender's eyes opened and focused with difficulty on the Homunculus's face, just centimetres from his own.

ᕽ   ᕽ   ᕽ

"I'll never tell you anything," spat the wriggling, whippet-thin lookout in Kail's arms. "You're wasting your time!"

Kail didn't say anything. He just shifted his grip on his captive's wrist and eased his weight forward to apply leverage to an already over-stretched joint.

The lookout gasped with pain and shook his head in defiance.

Sal watched from the sidelines, unsure what to do. Kail had led him unerringly to where the scruffy lookout had been searching through a series of stablelike structures in a distant sector of the ruins. How the tracker had known he was there, Sal didn't know, and there hadn't been time to ask questions. The lookout didn't stand a chance; on top of possessing the advantage of surprise, Kail was his superior in every respect—height, weight, reach, and skill. The lookout had gone down without a sound.

"Which way?" Kail repeated into the man's ear. The man's skull-hugging cap fell away, exposing a scalp covered in ugly scars. "Tell me or I'll wrench your arm off at the elbow."

The look of pain on the lookout's face was unbearable. Kail sounded absolutely willing to make good his threat, and there was no doubting his capability.

"No—let go!" the lookout gasped. "I'll tell you!"

"Smart fellow." Kail eased off the pressure, but only barely. "Be quick about it."

The lookout sketched a route through the outer edges of the ruins to a natural crack in the stone wall of the Divide. At the bottom of the crack, four metres down, was a concealed entrance that led into the tunnel system belonging to the ancient city. There the inhabitants of the Aad lived, if the one Kail had captured was to be believed.

"Who do you work for?" Kail pressed him.

"Pirelius."

"Who does *he* work for?"

"No one. Ah!" The lookout squirmed helplessly as Kail reapplied the pressure. "We trade!"

"And rob as well, I presume." The lookout winced, but nodded. "Some people came through here not long ago. Friends of ours. What happened to them? If they're dead, you're going to wish you were, too." A frantic headshake. "Where are they? Be precise."

More instructions followed. Sal wished Skender was with them to remember the details. Their route would take them to a dungeon along various natural corridors and through a chamber the lookout called "the sink room."

"What's that?"

But the lookout seemed to have crossed some sort of threshold where the fear of getting into trouble with Pirelius was worse than any threat Kail could make. He shook his head and wouldn't elaborate.

"Doesn't matter," said Kail. "We've got all we need to know." He changed his grip to apply pressure to the lookout's throat, and squeezed.

"Wait," said Sal.

Kail's hard violet eyes looked up at him. So did the lookout's, wide and desperate.

"We can't leave him here," said the tracker, as though talking to a child. "He'll give us away at the first opportunity."

"But we can't just kill him!"

"Why not? I'm sure the courtesy wouldn't be returned."

"I don't care about that. We're not like him—at least we're not supposed to be."

Kail squeezed tighter. His grin was feral. The lookout began to turn purple. Dirt-blackened fingers scrabbled for leverage, without success.

"I mean it," said Sal.

"I know you do." Kail winked. The lookout sagged, and he let go. "That'll slow him down for a while. And when he wakes up, he'll be glad to be alive. That's exactly how I want him to feel."

The tracker produced a length of twine from his pack and proceeded to tie the lookout's wrists and legs together, and gagged him so he couldn't call out.

Sal watched impotently, feeling like the butt of a joke he didn't want to understand.

Kail stood up and wiped his hands on his pants. "Now, I suggest we get going before he's missed. Any objections?"

Sal shook his head. After briefly checking to make certain that the lookout's nose was unobstructed, he followed Kail into the first glimmer of dawn light.

Skender's eyes were crossing and uncrossing, or so they felt. The Homunculus's face was in a state of constant flux. Its skull shrank and expanded like a blacksmith's bellows. Two eyes became four became three. He didn't know where to look.

Who is wrong here, Galeus?

He scrabbled shakily backwards, away from the strange creature. Had it been an ordinary person, it would have been crouched on all fours, bending over him. As it was, it appeared to have four legs and three arms. One hand reached out to him, then retracted.

"What are you?" he asked it. "How—how do you know my heart-name?"

"That's not important. Why were they beating you? Who are these people? What is this place?"

Skender struggled to think. Only five people in the world knew that his true name was Galeus: his father, his mother, Sal and Shilly, and a girl he'd had a crush on two years earlier. The golem in the Haunted City had used it, but a golem wasn't human so it didn't count. There was only one other, and Skender wasn't sure if that counted as human or not.

Your name is Galeus. We weren't part of this world, then.

Through the chaos of the Homunculus's face, Skender made out confusion and indecision—and something else. The Homunculus radiated a sense of weariness so powerful that for a moment Skender forgot the throbbing bruises on his back, shoulders, and face.

Certainty filled him, then. As crazy as it seemed, he *had* met this creature before.

The one from the Void, the man'kin had told him, in the Divide.

"You're the Oldest One," he breathed. "I met you in the Void Beneath. What are you doing *here?*"

The Homunculus shook its head in a blur of motion. Features smeared and overlapped with frightening rapidity. "The Void wipes everything clean. You can't possibly remember."

"I remember everything! You told me about the Cataclysm and the twins who caused it. One of them died, you said, and something happened. The world fell apart—or came back together—but you didn't remember which one of the twins you were. You—" He stopped, then. "Goddess. You're *both* of them!"

"I—" The Homunculus quivered like someone having a fit. "We— we are lost. So much time has passed. Nothing is the same. What *is* this place? Who are these people?"

Skender stared at it, finally seeing past the monstrosity to the strange truth beneath. The Homunculus was two people at once—two bodies in one, blending and merging in a constant flow of limbs and features. Sometimes the two bodies acted in accord, giving the appearance of just one person, albeit slightly blurry. Other times, there was no common ground, and they devolved into chaos.

It—*they*—were trapped in the Homunculus.

"Why are you here?" he asked. "Does this mean we're about to have another Cataclysm?"

The Homunculus reared away, at war with itself, and fell, unable to coordinate all its limbs at once.

As it thrashed on its back like a bug trying to turn over, Kemp called to Skender, his voice thick with worry. "What's happening in there? Are you hurt?"

Skender managed to stand, although his back screamed with the effort. His cheek was swollen and dead to the touch. A mental numbness threatened to creep over him, as it had after the crash with Chu. He fought it with all his strength.

"I don't know what's happening, Kemp. I don't know what to do."

"Just stay away from it. Keep out of reach and maybe it won't hurt you."

"I'm not worried about that." He passed a hand across his face. "Something odd's going on, but I don't know what it is."

A low groan came from one of the other cages. Skender ran to the bars and peered through at his mother, who was stirring. He went to call to her, but stopped his tongue. Pirelius was bound to have someone listening in to see what happened with the Homunculus. The last thing Skender wanted to do was to give the bandit leader any extra information.

I'm not an idiot, you know, Pirelius had said, *although* she *might treat me like one.*

His mother went still again. He turned away. The distraction had given him an idea.

Kemp didn't seem to know what the Homunculus was, but what if he really *did?* He would feign ignorance, just as Skender would try to keep secret from Pirelius that his mother was also one of the captive. If Kemp *did* know, then it was possible that the people the Homunculus had intended to rendezvous with were Skender's mother and her expedition, not Pirelius and his gang. That would solve several mysteries quite neatly, since Pirelius appeared to have captured the Homunculus, not conspired with it, and the Homunculus didn't even know who Pirelius was.

When we come back, his mother had said, *we'll have found something wonderful . . .*

For the life of him, though, Skender couldn't work out how to use the information to his advantage.

The Homunculus stood quivering in the shadows, watching him silently. Its combined form had stabilised. Now Skender merely felt as if his eyeballs were vibrating every time he looked at it.

"Why are you here?" he asked the twins. "What do you want?"

"There's something we have to do," the Homunculus said—and now that he was listening properly, Skender could hear that the odd discordant tone to the voice came from two voices speaking not quite at the same time. "But it's been so long. Our memories are only slowly returning." One hand touched its chest, where Skender could faintly make out a strange mark. "We were protected. The Ogdoad marked us. The devachan couldn't erase us completely. We made it this far. Now it's all going to start again."

"What's going to start?"

"Our life," said the Homunculus. "Our lives, and perhaps our deaths. The future is flexible. This world-line is diverging even as we speak, so we have to hurry. We have to get out of here. Now!"

The Homunculus took a step forward. Skender raised his hands in a placating gesture as the form before him began to disintegrate again.

"Believe me," he said, "I want to get out of here as badly as you do. But yelling's not going to help anyone. We have to *think*."

"I've had nothing to do *but* think," said Kemp from his cage on the far side of the room, "and a fat lot of good that's done anyone."

"Yes, but you didn't have me with you, then." Skender pushed the pain and exhaustion to one side and forced himself to concentrate. There had to be something they could do from within the cages, instead of wait—perhaps hopelessly—for rescue. The stick at his feet was patently useless against Pirelius, but that might not be his only weapon.

He looked at the Homunculus. "You have no reason to trust me," he whispered, "but I think we can work together to get us all out of here. Are you willing to give it a try?"

The Homunculus nodded. "We don't have much choice."

"That's the way I see it." Skender held out a hand. "Let's shake on it. No, just one of you," he said when both right hands came up in rough synchrony.

The arm split into two. "It won't work," the twins protested. "We've tried."

Skender went to take the proffered hand. His fingers slid through the shadowy limb as though it wasn't even there.

"Yes." Skender felt relief as his hand retreated. "I was hoping that might happen."

Sal and Kail hurried through cramped tunnels, taking great care to pause at each intersection lest they stumble across someone who would sound the alarm. Thus far they hadn't seen a soul.

Kail went first, lighting the way with a small pocket-mirror and directing Sal with hand signals. The tunnels were ancient and dirty: many of them had flexed and split with the shifting stone around them, forming odd intersections and dead ends where none had obviously been intended. Sal saw evidence that people had been using the tunnels for a long time in the form of dark patches on the walls where hands had pressed for balance, graffiti both proud and profane, and rubbish. The stink of human occupation became steadily stronger, until Sal quite lost the musky scent of the tracker ahead of him.

Twice Kail ducked his head too late to avoid banging it on collapsed ceilings and unexpected lintels. His step was surprisingly light, given his size. He cursed just once, when a stone slipped under his foot and his knee caught a sharp outcrop. Sal, the smaller and clumsier of the two, had to frequently swallow gasps of pain. He could see why the tortuous route was kept only for emergency exits, not everyday traffic.

As they wound deeper into the bedrock, Sal noticed that his sense of the Change was becoming increasingly distant. The last shreds of his connection to the living flows of the world were being muffled.

"Can you feel it?" he asked Kail.

The tracker nodded. "We're coming closer to the heart of the Change-sink."

"The mysterious 'sink room,' perhaps."

"Let's find out."

Their pace slowed to a bare creep. Kail extinguished the pocket-mirror. A faint pinkish glow came from the end of the tunnel. Sal paid close attention to his physical senses. If there was someone waiting for them, they were silent, and much cleaner than the lookout.

Kail paused at the entrance for several breaths, watching and listening closely, then waved Sal forward.

"What do you make of this?"

Sal edged over the threshold by degrees. The room consisted of little more than a cave with rough floor, ceiling, and walls. The air hung thick and heavily within it, despite two other entrances that opened from the far side. The pink glow came from a fat stalagmite that crouched to one side, its flanks creamy and smooth, and perfectly dry. The source of the light wasn't the stone, but many knuckle-shaped objects embedded in the stone, like fragments of glass stuck in a slumped candle. They came in several sizes, from a baby's fist up to a melon. Sal circled the stalagmite to get a better look. In the utter heart of the Change-sink, his eyes strained to make out any detail at all.

"What is this made of?" he asked. "Bone?"

"They're glowing," stated Kail unnecessarily. The pink light was actually many different shades mixed together, including blues, greens, and purples.

"It looks like opal." Sal reached out a finger to touch one of the objects, but pulled back with a hiss. The tip of his finger had gone numb.

"I've seen fossils made of opal before." Kail's eyes traced out the curve made by the objects in the stone. "This could have been the spine of a snake, perhaps. A sea-snake."

"Maybe. What it is *now* concerns me more."

"Definitely the heart of the sink."

"I think so, too."

"Perhaps we should break it." Kail reached into his pack and pulled out a knife. "We need an advantage, and this might just provide us with one."

He worried at one of the smaller fragments at the base of the stalagmite, forcing the blade into the soft limestone and wriggling it back and forth. The blade bent, but nothing gave.

"Try that one," said Sal, pointing. "There's a crack. See it?"

Kail shifted his attention to the fragment Sal suggested. The blade slipped into the crack and immediately popped out a section of stone. Progress was swift from there. With a grunt of satisfaction, Kail scooped out a thumb-sized opalescent jewel into one hand and held it up to his eye.

"Still glowing."

And the sink was undiminished. "Oh, well. Worth a try."

"Maybe if we give it some distance—"

The sound of footsteps came from one of the other entrances, quickly followed by voices. Kail grabbed Sal's arm and hurried him into the smallest of the tunnel mouths. The finger he held to his lips was lit by the fragment still in his hand. The light then disappeared into one of his pockets. Kail shook his fingers to bring the circulation back.

"—should have been watching the east side," the louder of the two voices was saying as it grew nearer. "Find him and tell him I said to get his act together. We haven't got time to fuck around."

"And if I don't find him?"

"Then you make sure whatever happened to him doesn't happen to you as well. Is that clear enough for you?"

"Yes, Pirelius."

Two men entered the sink room. There they split up. One, the smaller of the two, took the corridor Sal and Kail had come down. The other brushed past the entrance in which Sal and Kail were hiding and took the remaining way. Two sets of heavy footsteps receded in different directions.

"The enterprising Pirelius." Kail's voice was little more than an exhalation. "According to the directions our friend gave us, he's heading for the dungeon."

"We'd better follow, then."

"Keep an eye on our tail. I don't want that other guy doubling back and catching us."

Sal nodded. They trailed Pirelius to the place where the lookout had said the others were being kept. Their progress was rapid. Sal was acutely conscious of how visible they were from either end of the long, straight tunnel. Voices came from ahead. Kail slowed as they approached it.

"Planning something?" Pirelius bellowed at some hapless lackey. "Of course they'll *try*, but what do you think they're going to do, exactly? They don't have the Change; they don't have any weapons; two of them can barely even stand. The most they can hope for is that you'll do something else stupid and give them a chance. Now get in there and find out what's happened to the boy!"

Sal heard a shove and the scuffle of feet on dirt. He and Kail reached the entranceway in time to see Pirelius following a pigtailed man out of a small antechamber into what was obviously the dungeon proper. The air was thick with smoke, but that couldn't hide the odour of human degradation. The antechamber contained several tables and cabinets. Items scattered on the tables had a horrible look about them: leather stained with brown splatters; corroded metal tools ending in sharp hooks and points.

A conversation ensued in the dungeon. Sal couldn't make out the barked orders, but he did recognise a voice speaking in response.

"Skender's in there," Sal hissed. "We have to get him out."

Kail nodded. "We can either pull back and plan something for later, or jump them now. There are only two of them, after all."

"That we know of."

"And they might be armed." The tracker's expression was torn. "I don't like this situation one bit. We're exposed here and at a disadvantage. We can't take too long to decide."

Something niggled at Sal, but he couldn't put his finger on it. "I think we should have a plan before barging in. We don't want to get ourselves trapped."

Kail nodded again. "Right. Timing is the better part of triumph."

They retreated up the tunnel, Sal forcing himself not to think that he was abandoning his friend. They would return for Skender just as soon as it was safe to do so. "Safe" being a highly relative term, of course. He and Kail had infiltrated right into the heart of enemy territory. They were significantly outnumbered, and only Kail had anything like the experience required. If only, Sal thought, they could call for help.

The wish brought to the foreground that which had only nagged at him before. His senses tingled as they reconnected to the world around him. The Change was returning!

Before he could tell Kail, the tracker froze. Ahead of them, a silhouette had appeared at the end of the tunnel.

"Someone's coming!" Kail hissed, turning. "Get back!"

Before either of them could move, a blood-curdling scream from the dungeon froze Sal's feet to the floor.

Skender heard voices outside the dungeon. The Homunculus stepped away from him, its form shifting fluidly as two people inside one artificial body moved in slightly different ways. It reminded him of a shadow with a solid, well-defined central core and a nebulous penumbra. The penumbra seemed to interact perfectly normally with the inanimate world—the ground, Kail's bola, the bars of the cage—but when it came to people, something else entirely happened.

"It's will," one of the twins had said, half of the Homunculus's double mouth moving at odds with the other half. "You possess will, so we have to work together to touch you."

"We've been together for so long," said the other half, "it sometimes takes more effort *not* to work together."

They explained that they had first noticed the effect with Highson Sparre. Skender hadn't entirely understood the explanation but he was prepared to accept it for now. As long as it worked as he hoped it might. Sometimes intuition was enough.

Pirelius swaggered into the room, followed closely by Rattails.

"What? Not dead yet?" The bandit leader sauntered casually up to Skender's cage. "Looks like you and the monster have become entirely too chummy. Get him out of there."

Pirelius turned away, leaving Rattails to look uncertainly from him to the cage and back again.

"How?"

"Go in there and drag him out, of course."

"That won't be necessary," said Skender. "I'll cooperate." He walked through the open bars to the neighbouring cage, the one the twins had previously occupied, and closed the gate between them.

"Good rabbit," said Rattails with undisguised relief.

"You don't get off so easily, you idiot." Pirelius cuffed the jailer across the head. "The door between them is still unlocked. You're going to lock it."

"Why?"

"Because I want you to. And because I don't trust them. They're definitely up to something, as you said. Let's not give them a chance to show us what it is."

Rattails gulped, considering his options. The locking mechanism for the cell Skender had just vacated was above the connecting door. Rattails would have to get into the cell with the twins to seal Skender in.

The Homunculus watched from the back of its cell, eyes coming and going as the twins' postures shifted.

"Not a terribly sensible design," said Skender. "Did you build them yourself?"

"Found them here when we moved in. They were animal cages, appropriately enough." Pirelius's stare was decidedly unfriendly. "Swap cells."

"Or else?"

"Or I'll kill your friend over here." Pirelius indicated Kemp, watching silently with a worried look on his face.

"I thought you said he was dangerous."

"That's not the same thing as valuable. We have too many mouths to feed around here as it is."

Skender shrugged and did as he was told. When he was done, the twins went through the door in the opposite direction.

"Now we're getting somewhere. In you go," Pirelius said to Rattails, shoving him. "Keep the cage between you and it and you'll be safe enough."

Rattails reluctantly approached the entrance to Skender's cage, the key in his hand. "Put the stick on the floor, rabbit. Now get back and stay back."

Skender did as he was told, pressing himself against the cold stone at the back of the cell.

Rattails reached above his head and unlocked the door. Swinging it open, he stepped inside. Just two paces separated him and the adjoining door, but there would be a moment when his back was turned. Rattails obviously couldn't decide who was the greater threat: Skender in the cage with him or the Homunculus just a short distance away through the bars. His eyes flicked rapidly between them. With a nervous, mincing step, he hurried across the gap and raised his hand to put the key in the lock.

"Now!" Skender lunged forward and stooped as though to pick up the stick. Rattails jumped and turned to defend himself. Skender ignored the stick and rammed headlong into the jailer's midriff. Rattails fell backwards, taken off-guard, and slammed against the bars.

For the moment, Skender had the upper hand. Rattails was winded and unclear what had happened. But his cunning was still intact. He hadn't dropped the key. His lips peeled back in a snarl and his fists bunched.

Then he stiffened and went pale. The key dropped unnoticed to the floor and his hands flew up in claws to the back of his neck.

Behind him, the twins had both pairs of arms stretched through the gaps between the bars. One of the twins reached for Rattails's neck, while the other clutched at the small of his back. All of their individual hands passed unimpeded through Rattails's body. Where their hands met inside the jailer's flesh, however, they became very substantial.

Rattails opened his mouth and shrieked with pain. His eyes rolled up into his skull and his legs kicked out. Both arms flailed uselessly and another shriek ripped from his throat.

It was the most awful sound Skender had ever heard. He staggered away, as surprised as anyone by the sudden transformation. He hadn't intended it to work *so* well.

Movement out of the corner of his eye prompted him to stop gawping and think fast. He scooped up the key Rattails had dropped. "Keep back!" he warned Pirelius, who had lunged forward to shut the cell's outer door. "One more step and we'll rip out his spine!"

"Have it," Pirelius snarled. "I don't need it!"

"No—no—no!" Rattails's scream ended on a rising, wordless note as Skender threw his weight at the cell door before it closed on them. Pirelius growled and pushed back. The bandit's superior weight was too much for Skender. His feet began to slip in the dirt floor.

"Kemp! Quick!" Skender tossed the key past Pirelius, across the room. It skittered on the ground and landed just outside Kemp's cage. The albino snatched it up and reached through the bars for the lock.

Pirelius roared in anger. "I'll kill you! I'll kill you all!"

Then a very strange thing happened. A wall of fog billowed into the dungeon from the chamber outside. Thick and heavy, it was soon dense enough to hide the far side of the room from view. Everything stopped as the weirdness of the phenomenon hit home.

Skender remembered a charm Master Warden Atilde had shown him and his friends in the Haunted City—a charm that turned dust into fog. There was plenty of dust in the Aad, but there was a profound absence of the Change. Or should have been.

The fog roiled and thickened, bringing the muffled sounds of a commotion from the antechamber.

Pirelius stepped away from the door. Surprised, Skender stumbled out of the cage. Thick-fingered hands went around his throat and tugged him upright. The stink of Pirelius enfolded him.

"Skender! Can you hear me?"

Sal's voice came out of the fog like something from a dream, but Skender could manage only a squawk in reply. He was too busy being strangled.

"We're in here!" Kemp yelled back. "So's the Homunculus!"

"Don't come any closer," Pirelius shouted, "or I'll break your friend's neck!"

"Skender?" Sal's voice grew louder. Skender dimly perceived a shadowy figure in the entranceway to the dungeon. "Skender!"

Pirelius's fingers closed tight over his windpipe and Skender felt the world begin to grow black.

THE HANGAR

"When you look anywhere using the Change—be it into the past or the future, or into someone's mind, or just into another place—you send part of yourself in the process. If the connection is severed, you may never get that part back. When that happens, it falls into the Void Beneath and cannot be recovered."

THE BOOK OF TOWERS, FRAGMENT 243

Shilly snapped out of a daydream in the middle of the Sky Wardens' meeting at the sound of Sal's voice in her mind: *"Carah—we're in the Aad and we've found the Homunculus. We need your help!"*

She bolted upright, knocking over a glass of water. "Tom! Give me your hand!"

The Engineer looked as startled as everyone else, but didn't hesitate. He reached over the table, ignoring the puddle spreading across maps and notes. She gripped his hand tight and Took what she needed. The mnemonic required to communicate with Sal long-distance formed instantly in her mind.

"Sal! I hear you! What's happening? Are you all right?"

She didn't breathe as she waited for a reply.

"Sal?"

Nothing. The mental contact had been fleeting and was now utterly gone. She released Tom and he sank back into his seat, looking dazed.

"What is it?" asked Marmion. "Was that Sal and Skender?"

Shilly opened her mouth to confirm his guess, then hesitated. There were two options open to her. She could tell Marmion everything and hope that he didn't dismiss it as misdirection on her part. He still talked as though the Homunculus was coming for Laure and made preparations to capture it. The morning's planning session had consisted entirely of ways to structure an ambush outside the city Wall, assuming the swarm of man'kin had moved on. Marmion hadn't once mentioned the story Highson Sparre had told them in the dead of the previous night, so the question of what the warden wanted with the Homunculus remained: she didn't want to hand it to him on a plate if all he planned was its casual destruction.

The alternative was to keep the news to herself and make her own plans, perhaps with Chu's help. The flyer watched keenly from where she sat on a low cupboard in one corner of the room, eager for news of her wing. But what chance did the two of them have in the face of the Divide? Just getting across it on their own would be difficult, let alone dealing with whatever Sal had encountered in the Aad.

The warden was staring fixedly at her, waiting.

Blast it. As much as she hated throwing herself upon Marmion's mercy, she didn't see that she had much choice.

She nodded in response to his question, and sat down.

He turned away. "Gwil, I have a job for you."

The Magister's lackey jumped. "But I—"

"Take these forms. I believe Magister Considine is waiting for them." Marmion handed him a sheaf of papers. "I'll have a list of requirements for you when you return, so be quick about it."

"Yes, sir." The thin young man glanced around the room, then hurried from it.

"Right," said Marmion when the door had shut behind him. "What do you know?"

She repeated what Sal had told her. "They're in the Aad, and they've found the Homunculus. I think they're in some kind of trouble."

"The Aad? You're certain of that?"

"That's what he said."

"I'd like some more information. Make contact with him again and—"

"I tried. Something's cut him off." Worry gripped her heart. "He asked for help. I think we need to act quickly."

Marmion ran a hand across his scalp. What few hairs remained stood up for a moment then sank back down flat. Shilly could see the conflict naked on his face. He was facing a decision similar to hers: trust her and commit all his resources to a move that might be unsuccessful or stick to his guns and maybe miss a crucial opportunity.

"Very well," he said, sounding resigned. "We'll go to the Aad and help Sal and the others. Any thoughts on how to get there?"

"We could use a buggy," said Tom, looking drawn.

"It'll take too long," said Banner. "All the way across the Fool's Run, then up the side of the cliff, then along the edge—"

"We could cut along the bottom of the Divide," said another warden, "once we reached the far side."

"Or go straight across."

"The ground's too rough." Chu spoke up. "And that's not even mentioning the man'kin. Would you want to break an axle with those guys bearing down on you?"

Marmion shook his head. "Obviously not, but it's either that or turn up too late. Do you have an alternative?"

The flyer looked down at the floor. Her dark hair covered her bandaged temple and obscured her face.

"Only one," she said. "Skender and I talked about it, but it was way out of his league."

"Let's hear it."

"We charter a heavy lifter and fly over."

"How difficult would that be?"

Chu looked up, obviously surprised that Marmion hadn't immediately dismissed the suggestion. "Well, it's not cheap."

"Money won't be a problem. How many people can one of these dirigibles bear?"

"Up to twenty, as long you don't want to carry any freight."

"So we shouldn't all go, given there might be Skender's mother and party to rescue as well." Marmion nodded. "Will we need to hire a pilot, or can you fly it for us?"

"I could probably manage it."

"Can you or can't you? We need more certainty than that."

Chu's chin lifted. "My father was a lifter pilot. He let me use the controls sometimes. I may not have Skender's memory, but it isn't something I'd forget in a hurry."

"Good," Marmion said. Shilly wondered if he noticed the emotional undercurrent to her voice, or cared if he had. "I want this organised immediately. Take Banner and get things moving. If anyone asks difficult questions, refer them to me."

Chu slid off the bench and Banner stood. "What about Magister Considine?"

"I'll let her know in due course." Marmion looked around innocently. "You'll notice that her envoy is currently absent. When he returns, I'll be sure to forward the appropriate paperwork through the appropriate channels. How long it takes to process is out of my hands."

Banner nodded her understanding.

"I want us airborne in two hours. We'll rendezvous in one." Marmion's decisiveness swept the table, setting the wardens abuzz with new energy. "Where, Chu?"

"Ahmadi Hangar," she said. "That's where the lifters are kept. I'll be waiting for you."

"Good." Marmion smiled thinly in thanks. "Now off you go while we work out who stays here to take the heat."

Chu and Banner left the room. Shilly gripped her stick with both hands. This was one argument she was determined not to lose.

A short time later, she knocked on Highson's door. A voice called softly for her to enter. Sal's father was asleep. The healer attending him, a woman with ash-grey hair and jet-black eyebrows, let Shilly sit by the bed while she finished a routine check on his condition.

"His heart is strong," she said. "Once his tissues are rejuvenated, he'll be as hale as ever."

"What will that take?"

The healer's teeth were broad and very white. "Lots of water and a few good meals. That's all."

Shilly noticed the bowl of soup barely touched on the bedside table. Highson looked even older than he had the night before. She didn't think his recovery was going to be that simple.

While the healer fussed over him—with more concern than her words seemed to warrant—Shilly took his hand and took from him the strength she knew he possessed.

"*You're not sleeping so deeply that you won't hear me,*" she said through the Change.

He became conscious with a strange flurry of nonsensical thoughts, the winding sheets of dreams in which he had become entangled.

"*The Void. There's a face—*"

"*There's not. Wake up, Highson.*" She waited patiently as he got himself together.

"*Shilly? Why—what are you doing here?*"

"*I came to tell you that we're going to get Sal. He's found the Homunculus, in the Aad like I thought it would be.*"

"*Is Marmion going with you?*"

"*Yes, and he hasn't mentioned what he intends to do with it when we've caught it. He's keeping very quiet on that score.*"

"*You'll be careful, won't you?*" His face showed no sign of animation, but his hand gently squeezed hers.

She remembered something Tom had said while approaching the Divide just a day earlier. He recognised the landscape, but not from ground level: he had dreamed it from above, suggesting that at least he would make it that far.

"*I want you to do something for me, while we're gone,*" she said, dodging the question. "*I want you to listen to the healer and get better. We didn't come this far to bring back a corpse—which is what you might as well be if you're not careful.*"

"*What do you mean?*"

"*I mean you need to let your guilt go. None of this is your fault, and neither was what happened to Seirian. It wasn't your responsibility to bring her back. Who knows what that thing Skender saw in the Void was? It could have been the palest shade of who she was, or it could have been something masquerading as her in order to win his sympathy. Either way, bringing her back could have been an even bigger disaster than it has been.*" She allowed a faint note of humour to enter her mental tone. "*I mean that in the nicest possible way, Highson. The other side of the argument is that you built the Homunculus; we're going to need you to help us deal with it. Don't fade away because you think you deserve to be punished.*"

"*I—*" His eyelids fluttered. "*I know what you're saying, Shilly, and I appreciate it, but—*"

"*I'm not doing this for you. I'm doing it for Sal. You're the only person close to his mother that he's ever likely to talk to again. And he's the closest thing you've got to her, too. So you both need each other, whether you'll admit it or not. Concentrate on what's in the world before looking for redemption elsewhere.*"

"*You've obviously been thinking about this.*"

"*All bloody night, and I tell you, I'm knackered. I don't understand either of you, and the last thing I want to do is go off on some balloon ride across the Divide. But I'm going. And you're going to be here when we get back. Sal will want to see you when he arrives. You'll be sitting up for him, won't you?*"

His lips twitched. "*You're nothing like Seirian, you know,*" he said, "*but you remind me of her. I don't know why.*"

"*Well, for starters,*" she said, "*we both love your son.*"

"Go on," he croaked, with the faintest of smiles. "You have a balloon to catch."

The healer straightened from her ministrations with a cluck of tongue against teeth. "He must be dreaming," she said. "That's a positive sign."

"I think you're right," Shilly said, letting go of Highson's hand, and hauling herself upright. "If he doesn't start showing immediate signs of improvement, I'll boil my cane and eat it."

"That won't be necessary, dear." Again, the bright, white smile.

"It'd better not be."

The morning seemed to fly by and drag at the same time. Although Shilly had won a berth on the heavy lifter—as the person Sal was most likely to contact—Marmion hadn't actually given her anything to do. Unwilling to sit on her hands, she volunteered to help the wardens in their preparations, but she found them in much the same state. They couldn't use the Change on the Interior side of the Divide. Kail's bolas were suddenly the most effective weapon available, and he was missing somewhere in the Divide. An air of nervous expectation dominated the assembly.

In the end, Shilly opted to leave them to it and headed for Ahmadi Hangar ahead of them. She needed to keep moving—and the chances were that Marmion would call for departure at the last possible moment, leaving her hurrying to keep up. If she was there first, she couldn't be left behind.

A street sweeper gave her directions and she followed them as quickly as she could. The city was as restless as she felt, full of arguments and irritations. A display of fruit tumbled, sending dried figs in a spray across the sidewalk. Two women picked up the pieces of a jar, disagreeing over who had broken it. Far above, sitting on thin poles and dressed in long red robes that waved like flags, the local weather workers uttered wailing cries that went on much longer than she thought was humanly possible. They didn't seem to take breath. If the wind heard their calls, there was no sign of rain in the sky. As it had been since Shilly approached the Divide, the blue infinity stretching beyond the tip of the highest towers was unbroken and absolute. Her skin felt dry and itchy.

She recognised Ahmadi Hangar as soon as she saw it. The building was broad, long, and tall like a brick grain store. It had many windows and two massive doors in its roof, both open. As she watched, a heavy lifter rose gracefully through them and into the sky over the city. The balloon was shaped like a giant seed with a long, deep basket suspended beneath. A stream of mottled brown charms swept down the outside, their purpose not immediately obvious. Two propellers hummed at the rear, glowing brightly with the Change. She could hear the raucous buzzing of an alcohol engine, its chimerical output channelled into the propeller's mechanism. The charms reacted to the wind, shying away from it or drawing closer depending on its direction and strength. When a particularly strong gust swept down the street past her and lifted a wave of sand into the sky, the underside of the heavy lifter turned a deep black, just for an instant, and it bobbed in the air like a boat on the sea.

She watched in wonder as the lifter rose clear of the hangar and glided ponderously away. Its shadow swept over her, giving her a momentary chill.

Someone whistled at her. She lowered her gaze. Chu was waving from a window in the side of the hangar. Shilly waved back and crossed the street, dodging a camel and its rider who flicked a gaudy fan at her with a look of exasperation. As she did so, she noticed a handsome, bearded man watching her from the corner of the hangar. He turned away when she looked at him, and ducked down a side street. Shilly might have wondered if she had imagined it, had not years of hiding in Fundelry honed her instincts. She hadn't been followed, but someone had definitely noted her arrival.

The entrance wasn't visibly guarded, so she strolled unhindered into the vast space. The giant chamber had room for six heavy lifters. Two enormous dirigibles hung suspended at the rear of the hangar, with walkways leading from the gondolas to laddered gantries. A wire fence separated the viewing area she occupied from the working space. There she saw large barrels of oil and machine parts in various stages of repair. The air smelled of grease and fire. Voices called from one side of the hangar to the other; tools clanged against metal. Over it all hung the twinkling of the Change, like frost caught by sunlight.

"You're early," said Chu, appearing at the entrance to a stairwell.

"Thought I'd see how things stood down here."

"Oh, it's coming together. There's a lifter free, but the paperwork is daunting." The flyer stepped closer to whisper. "We're being stalled."

"Why?"

"The Magister, I guess. She probably wants us to stay put, where she can keep an eye on us." Chu looked frustrated and wary. "Why anyone would keep us from paying to go to the Aad is beyond me. There's nothing there but a big dangerous Ruin."

"So you're told." Shilly nodded slowly, pondering Chu's comment about the Magister keeping an eye on them. "Someone was watching me as I came here. Have you noticed anything else odd?"

"No."

"Is Banner around?"

"Inspecting the works of the lifter we've been allocated." Chu pointed at the dirigible in the right rear corner of the hangar. "We got that far, at least. Come on through."

Shilly happily obeyed. She remembered seeing a pod of whales once, in the sea to the south of Fundelry. The dirigibles looked even larger than the whales, although the fact that they were hanging in the air above her, not swimming heavily through water, might have had something to do with that.

Chu opened a gate in the wire fence and waved her by. A man in overalls walked past and saluted them with a wink.

"I haven't been here for a while," Chu said in explanation, "but people still know me. My mother died when I was born, so I grew up on the hangar floor. It's where I took my first steps, learned my first words—mostly from the mechanics. Dad wasn't too happy about that last part. He used to say that I could swear before I talked and fly before I walked. It might well have been true."

The memories were obviously good ones, but Shilly sensed sadness, too. "What happened to him?"

"An accident. One of the old lifters was in for a refit. The bladder needed a thorough patching all around the lower aft area. Someone sold Dad a dodgy batch of cloth and it burst during a test run. It happened right over the city. Could have been a total disaster, but Dad managed to steer it as it fell. Took it into the Wall, shedding most of its momentum before it hit. The impact killed him in the process."

Shilly saw tears in the flyer's eyes and a simmering resentment in the cut of her jaw.

"The inquest ruled that he should have been more careful with the repairs. So much for gratitude. The guy who sold him the cloth is still trading, although no one here will do business with him. And, well, life goes on. I'm not good enough with my hands to follow in his footsteps, so I just fly. When I can."

"It doesn't sound like it's been easy."

"There's no reason why it should be." Chu's response was sharp. "The world owes me no favours. I take what comes my way and try not to think too much about it."

Shilly recognised that feeling. Life was tough for someone on their own, and it fostered toughness in return. Shilly wondered if Chu's father had left much in the way of money. Perhaps that and the recent loss of her licence explained the lack of accommodation. She could have been roughing it on the street for weeks. In Laure or any other city, that wasn't a pretty thought.

Whatever she's been doing, Shilly concluded, *she must be pretty desperate to hang around the likes of us . . .*

They walked in silence under one of the giant docks. It was the biggest thing Shilly had ever seen—easily bigger than *Os*, the Sky

Wardens' ship of bone. This seemed large enough to hold all of Fundelry, with room to spare.

"How did you hurt your leg?"

Shilly was craning her neck upwards like a tourist and didn't quite catch what the flyer had said. "What?"

"Your leg. If you don't mind me asking."

Shilly hid a slight smile. *Tit for tat*, she thought. *I poke your weak spot and you poke mine.*

"I'd rather talk about Skender. How long have you known him?"

Chu looked disconcerted. "Only a few days."

"How are you finding him?"

"You know." The flyer looked anywhere but at her. "He's smart, obviously—but he's kind of dumb, too. He doesn't see what's right in front of him half the time, he's so wrapped up in his thoughts."

That sounded familiar. "He's not like us. You know about his memories, don't you? He sees something once and it's always in his head. The backlog swamps him if he doesn't keep it in check."

Chu stared up at the heavy lifter, and nodded. "Everyone has baggage."

"He has enough baggage for everyone."

They had reached the base of one of several scaffolds leading, via various ladders and ramps, up to the gangplank.

"Can you climb up there?" asked Chu. "If not, I can arrange a freight elevator for you."

"No, thanks," she said with a tart smile. Anything rather than be considered *freight*. "I'll just be a little slow."

"Well, we're not in any great hurry at the moment. Why don't you go on ahead while I—?"

Chu stopped at a commotion from the hangar entrance. Voices echoed in the vast space, overlapping too much for Shilly to disentangle. A group of more than a dozen people had formed near the gate through the fence. She couldn't make out their identities against the bright background of the day. They seemed to be arguing.

Then a group of eight broke away and marched steadily towards her location. Robed in blue, they were obviously wardens. The rest followed, shouting and waving.

"That looks like your friend Marmion," said Chu, her eyes sharper than Shilly's. "And Tom. There's stationmaster Shusti—the guy who was stalling me earlier. Looks like he's called the guards. And—oh, great."

"What?" Shilly asked, more concerned by the dread in Chu's voice than her misidentification of Marmion as a friend. "Who is it?"

"Only some of that baggage we were talking about. Hold on; here they come."

The babble of voices resolved into a full-scale argument.

"I will *not* take no for an answer," Marmion was insisting. "My credentials are sound, and so is my credit. I act with the full authority of the Alcaide. You've seen the letter from Magister Considine. I can't understand why you persist in obstructing me—except out of deliberate, unwarranted malice."

Stationmaster Shusti was an overweight man with an elaborate coif and a sweeping, silken robe. His ample cheeks boiled red with anger. "This is outrageous! You cannot walk in here and expect me to ignore basic safety regulations. We have standards to conform to, and procedures to follow—"

"Who cares about procedures? This is an emergency! Three of my people are in grave danger and I need to help them. Don't blame me if I walk all over you on the way. Either help me or stand aside."

Shusti spluttered. Shilly had to admire Marmion's gall. He certainly was a dab hand at facing up to bureaucrats and functionaries, a skill no doubt learned from his years in the Haunted City.

Three guards in black and gold who had been bringing up the rear hurried forward to block the ladder Shilly and Chu were standing next to. There the rolling argument came to a temporary halt.

"I'm sorry, sir," said one, "but we cannot let you pass."

"This again?" Marmion opened his arms in a long-suffering gesture and rolled his eyes. "People might die because of your incompetence. I bet our treatment wouldn't be so shabby if we were Stone Mages. This is outright discrimination, and I will not tolerate it!"

Chu came forward. "One of the people we're going to rescue *is* a Stone Mage," she told the guard. "Do you really want the Synod breathing down our neck for not helping?"

"A Stone Mage, huh?" scoffed a voice from the back of the huddle. The handsome young man Shilly had seen watching her pressed forward. His uniform presented a bold red square on each shoulder. "He's no more a Stone Mage than I am."

"Shut up, Kazzo," said Chu. "You don't know what you're talking about."

"No? How many Skender Van Haasteren the Tenths are there? I did some research into your little friend. He's just a student, not a Mage. You lied about him, so who's to say this lot isn't lying, too? Whatever you're up to, you need to be stopped."

There was an arrogant, malicious gleam in Kazzo's eye. He was enjoying hurting Chu, that was for certain. Shilly instantly felt bad for baiting her.

"We are taking this lifter," said Marmion to the guards, his voice low and dangerous. "Stand aside."

"No, sir. Not until I have proper authorisation."

"You're outnumbered eight to three."

"Not for much longer, sir."

The sound of footsteps drew Shilly's gaze to the entrance. More guards had arrived, and it didn't look like they were going to give Marmion what he needed.

"Excuse me," she said, forcing her way past the nearest guard. He reached out to stop her and she swung her walking stick at his legs. The stout wood cracked hard against his shins. He gasped and hopped away.

She raised her stick like a sword as a second guard approached. "What sort of men are you, to attack a poor crippled girl?" She indicated that Chu should start climbing. Marmion and the other wardens came around behind her. The guards drew nightsticks but didn't wield them.

"This is outrageous," spluttered Shusti. "How you of all people came to be involved in something like this, Chu Milang, I don't know. Your father would be appalled."

"Don't you give me that," the flyer said as she scurried up the metal rungs, "you puffed-up, self-important fool. You're the only person here who'd try to use Dad against me."

"You'll never get clear of the gantry!"

"No? Looks to me like someone's been sloppy with the stays. I don't know how that could have come about. It wouldn't have happened in Dad's day."

Shilly glanced up at the lifter and noted that all bar two of the ropes securing it hung loose. She glimpsed Banner's face peering over the side of the gondola, followed shortly by the sound of an engine turning over. The propellers at the rear of the dirigible glowed brightly and began to rotate.

"Stop them!" yelled Shusti as the last of the wardens climbed up the ladder and Shilly prepared to follow. The three guards had moved off to another ladder, not waiting to deal with her. She only hoped for enough time to get up top before reinforcements arrived.

She climbed as fast as her gammy leg would allow. Holding onto her stick also slowed her down, so the gap between her and the last warden grew steadily greater. The pounding of feet on the ramps above vibrated through the ladder, becoming louder the higher she climbed.

She reached the first series of ramps and hurried along them. The next wave of guards was already climbing the ladder behind her. She cursed under her breath and stepped up the pace. They could, if they moved fast enough, cut ahead and catch her.

And then what? Would Marmion halt the mission on her behalf? Or would he keep going and leave her behind?

She gritted her teeth against a growing ache in her thigh and swore to save him from having to choose. She had two more ladders to climb before she reached the gangplank level. Already wardens were swarming across it to the gondola.

"Hurry, Shilly!"

She didn't need Chu's shout of warning, and she didn't waste breath replying. She reached the next ladder and heaved herself upwards. It was shorter than the last, but still looked daunting. The entire length of her leg was aflame by the time she hauled her leg over the top of the ladder.

The shouts of the guards followed her along the walkways. They were converging on her rapidly, from behind and along the second route. To her dismay, she realised that the group coming up the other ladders was going to arrive before her. Marmion would have to cast off or be boarded.

The gangplank swayed as someone ran across it from the direction of the gondola. She heard banging as she started to climb the last ladder. A nut pinged from the scaffolding before her, then bounced off metal stanchions and tumbled through space to the ground far below. The guards' ladder wobbled precariously and their yells turned from anger to alarm.

"Another step," yelled Tom, "and I'll let you fall!"

The guards cursed him and began to retreat.

Shilly gratefully crawled over the top of the ladder, onto the gangplank level. Tom was instantly beside her, pocketing a large wrench and taking some of her weight with a hand under her shoulder. Shilly forced herself to concentrate on her footing and not think about the distance to the ground as she limped across the swaying gangplank. The moment they were aboard, the two remaining ties fell away.

"Stand back!" Chu's voice echoed through the hangar as the guards on Shilly's heels reached the edge of the gantry. The lifter rocked and began to rise. The sound of its engines grew to a roar. The propellers disappeared into a glowing blur. Shilly let herself be pressed into a seat, her weight suddenly seeming greater than normal. Sunlight fell across her face, momentarily blinding her.

Then they were away. With the grace of a sailing ship, the heavy lifter surged upwards, clearing the sides of the hangar's hatch and ascending into the open sky.

Literally breathless, Shilly marvelled at the city laid out around and below her. It seemed to get darker the further inward she looked, going from a faded brown at the edges to a gleaming tower at the very centre. Beyond its walls, natural and human-made, she saw wrinkled brown land and the vast scar of the Divide to the south. Grey mountains to the northeast were wreathed in white. A strong wind blew across her face, stealing her words.

"Well, we're committed now."

Tom had moved off, not waiting to be thanked for his assistance. The gondola's passenger area was smaller than it had looked from the ground, barely wide enough for two people to stand together; long curving benches hugged its interior walls and took up valuable floor space. Chu had said it would seat twenty but half that number seemed to completely fill it. Panelling carved from a warm red wood covered the metal frame connecting the gondola to the dirigible overhead. Its sides were open to the air from waist-height upwards, apart from at the very front where curved sheets of clear glass protected the pilot. There Chu sat, frantically pulling at the controls. At the opposite end of the gondola, Banner and Tom crouched head to head, talking loudly over the throbbing of the engine. A rolling, driving vibration shook the entire frame.

"Are you unharmed?" Marmion stopped to check on her as he moved forward to consult with Chu. Shilly nodded, although her leg ached and her hip was on fire.

"What happened back there?" she asked. "Did you tread on someone's toes?"

"We bucked the system. That never goes down well with people who care about such things."

"Could it really be as simple as that?"

He shrugged. "Maybe. We'll find out when we get back, I suppose."

Shilly was reluctant to think that far ahead. As Marmion went aft to talk to Banner, she moved forward to watch Chu. The flyer was working up a sweat at the controls, moving levers and adjusting dials at a furious rate. Shilly didn't know what any of them did, but they looked fiendishly complex.

"Can I help?" she asked.

"You can watch out for company," Chu told her. "Let me know if anyone gets too close."

Shilly scanned the sky. Several flyers were visible, circling through the morning air over the city. "What will we do about them if they do?"

"Gesture rudely. There's not else much we *can* do in this thing. I left my slingshot at home. But it's not as if they're going to shoot us down or anything. The lifter is too valuable."

"How long until we reach the Aad?"

"An hour or so. I'll push it as fast as I can."

Hearing defensiveness in Chu's tone, Shilly stopped talking. She divided her time between keeping an eye on the sky and watching the city creep by beneath them. She tried to find the Black Galah as the city streets rolled past, but she missed it. The dirigible sailed clear over the Wall, and then there was nothing but the Divide and its strange geography below them. She saw the hair-thin line of the Fool's Run angle away to the west and fade into the distance. Dry creek beds and sandy plains reminded her of home, but there was no sea nearby. Water hadn't visited the canyon for years, by the look of it. It was as parched as the deepest desert.

She spotted four low brown clouds: more man'kin were on the move. Grateful she wasn't down among them, she performed a rough mental tally of how much time had passed since Sal had called her. It had been an hour at least, and another hour would pass before they reached the Aad. From there they had to find him and Skender.

She only hoped Sal could hang on that long. It was the best she had to offer.

THE LIBERATORS

"Animals have minds that exist entirely in the present, with little or no thought of tomorrow or yesterday. Humans travel from past to future in a dynamic tension between the two extremes. Man'kin exist in all times at once, hence their ability to foretell or reveal things that are not known to us."
MASTER WARDEN RISA ATILDE:
NOTES TOWARD A UNIFIED CURRICULUM

"Don't come any closer," shouted Pirelius, "or I'll break your friend's neck!"

"Skender?" Sal froze at the entrance to the dungeon. He could feel his fragile grip on the Change slipping, which meant that either the Homunculus was close or the sink was reasserting itself. He squeezed every last drop out of the charm Master Warden Atilde had taught him, making the fog as thick as any he had ever seen. That was more important than trying to call Shilly again—and for once he didn't care if the charm went out of control completely.

"Skender!"

Through the dense, echoless air, he heard a strange choking noise, then a gruesome thud. The fog billowed in the lamplight, and he rushed forward, unable to stand impotently by while Skender was being hurt.

What he found was Skender sitting up on the rough floor, rubbing his throat. A familiar face hovered at his side. Sal hadn't seen Kemp for five years but he had changed only in details. Apart from thick jet-black tattoos on his wrists and forearms, his skin was still utterly white and he still looked utterly intimidating.

"Glad you could make it," Kemp said, helping Skender upright with a tight, almost pained expression. His colourless eyes took in the fog. "This is your doing, I presume?"

"The best I could manage under the circumstances."

"Well, it helped. Got me close enough to clock the guy trying to tie Skender's neck in a knot."

"I hope," gasped Skender, "you gave him a thump from me."

"Don't worry. He won't be getting up for a week."

The fog thinned further. Sal looked down at the ground, but could see no fallen man. "Are you sure about that?"

Before Kemp could answer, an indistinct figure approached. Sal stiffened, bracing himself for Pirelius, then recognised the fluid outlines of the Homunculus. The last dregs of the Change drained out of him like water from a leaky tank.

Creation of my father, he thought. *Does that make you my brother?*

"It's okay," said Skender, taking his arm. "They're on our side."

"'They'?"

"It's a long story. Let's just get out of here."

Sal was shocked to see a massive bruise forming on Skender's cheek. Other marks discoloured his arms and throat. "Are you sure you're all right?"

"I have to be." He turned to Kemp. "Open the other cages. If we can wake up Mum and Behenna, we can be on our way."

"Don't forget Mawson," said Kemp, hurrying off through the last wisps of fog.

"Shit." Skender wobbled unsteadily. "We can't carry everyone—and Chu's wing, too. You did bring it, didn't you?"

"It's where we left it, safe and sound."

"I hope so, for your sake. She'll be very unhappy if it's damaged."

A mewling sound drew Sal's attention to an open cell where the pigtailed bandit he had seen earlier lay writhing on the floor. "What happened to him?"

"He got in our way." Skender didn't waste time explaining. Kemp had opened three cage doors and was bent over the inert body of Shom Behenna. Skender hurried to another cage.

"Mum! Wake up!"

Abi Van Haasteren moaned and raised her head. Sal winced at the sight of her bloodied features. She looked as though she had been used as a punching bag. "Skender? Is that you?"

He knelt next to her and helped her sit up. "Yes, it's me."

"What are you doing here?"

"I came to find you. Dad sent me."

"You—" She put her tied hands to her temples. "Your father shouldn't have done that." Her eyes clearly weren't focusing properly, but they tried to look at him anyway. "I'm glad you're here, though."

"Can you stand? We need to get moving."

"Sal. You, too?" Abi Van Haasteren's gaze fixed briefly on him as she clambered feebly to her feet. Sal cut the bindings on her legs and ankles with two swift cuts. "Thank you."

"You're welcome."

"What's *that*?" she asked, looking behind them both, to the Homunculus.

"When I was in the Haunted City," Skender said, "I told your friend Iniga about meeting someone in the Void Beneath. Don't pretend you didn't hear about that."

His mother looked uncertain for a moment, then nodded. "I remember something. It was a long time ago, though."

"Sure. Well, this is that person—actually two people in one. They helped us escape."

"Thank you, too, then," she told the ghostly figure. The Homunculus's form shivered, then firmed.

Sal, his mind reeling, hurried off to help Kemp. The albino was still trying to rouse Behenna.

"I can't wake him," said Kemp, smacking the ex-warden's cheek hard enough to leave a mark on the man's dark skin. "I'd offer to carry him, but there's Mawson as well. I don't think you're strong enough for either of them."

"That's okay. Kail can help."

"Who?"

Sal could have kicked himself. There had been no sign of the tracker since they had separated in the corridor outside the antechamber. Kail had said that he would hold off the bandits bringing up the rear while Sal looked after Skender. Now everything outside the dungeon was very quiet.

"Goddess." Sal stood and ran out of the cage. The antechamber was empty. Two unconscious bandits lay face-down in the corridor outside. Sal followed the tunnel back to the room with the stalagmite. The glowing fragments had faded in brightness. Sal briefly acknowledged Kail's guess that the sink might stop working if the piece he had taken was far enough away from the rest. Breaking the natural charm had effectively returned the Change to the Aad, allowing him to call Shilly and summon the fog.

The tracker's pack lay abandoned near the stalagmite. Kail himself was nowhere to be seen. Neither was Pirelius. Both absences worried him. If the bandits regrouped and tried to take Skender and the rest captive again, Sal wasn't sure any of them had the skills to mount much resistance.

He felt the Change returning now he was away from the Homunculus. He considered calling Shilly again, but precious time was passing. Reluctantly, Sal picked up the pack and hurried back to the dungeon, hoping that everyone was ready to move.

To his relief, they were. Kemp had Mawson—a granite bust that definitely weighed far too much for Sal to lift—cradled in his arms, while Skender helped his mother stay upright. Shom Behenna, still unconscious, hung like a child in the arms of the Homunculus, much as Sal's father had a day earlier.

"Are you okay with him?" Sal asked the Homunculus. He sounded as uncertain as he felt. He wasn't quite ready to accept the idea of the creature being an ally, although he had never been entirely convinced that it was an enemy, either.

"This body isn't natural," it/they responded with familiar discordant tones. "It doesn't need food or water, and it doesn't tire or sleep. Everybody should have one."

Was that a joke? Sal couldn't tell. "Well, let us know if you need a hand. I'm happy to help."

"After you, Sal," Skender said. "You do know where you're going, don't you?"

"I think so." Sal took one last look over the ragtag group he would be leading out of the dungeon, and caught sight of the injured man on the floor of the cell behind him. The agonised squirming had ceased, but one hand still scrabbled spastically at the dirt. Sal didn't know what had happened to the man, or what he wanted to do about it, but the fact that the others had paid him no mind at all told him that perhaps he shouldn't worry.

"This way," he said, and they were moving at last.

Skender followed Sal up the tunnel with his mother leaning heavily on his arm. Abi Van Haasteren was taller than him by a good thumb's length, but she was so stooped and weakened by her tribulations that she seemed much smaller. Skender could feel her wincing every time she put her right foot down. He could smell her blood.

"You shouldn't have come, Skender," she said again. "You broke the Code."

"I know, but I didn't swear to uphold it. You did."

"Indeed. Stop here for a second."

They had reached a rough-hewn chamber with a squat stalagmite in the centre. She leaned away from him and studied something sticking out of its smooth, water-polished side. It looked like part of a fossilised spine. Her eyes were wide and voice hushed.

"Yes, I thought so."

"You know what this is?" asked Sal.

"It's the Caduceus. I glimpsed it as Pirelius brought us to the cells."

"It's the source of the sink, right?"

"Yes, only it doesn't seem to be working now." Her broken-nailed hand stroked a hole in the side of the stalagmite. "Part of it's missing."

"Kail has it."

"What's *he* doing here?" asked Skender.

"Marmion sent him to keep an eye on us."

"Well, he's not doing a very good job."

"I don't know where he is, but I'm sure he'll catch up eventually. He can handle himself." Sal looked uncertain for a moment. "Come on. Through here."

Skender's mother pulled herself away from the stalagmite with obvious difficulty, her need to study the artefact stronger than her fear of being recaptured. Skender took her full weight again as they resumed their hurried exit.

"Dad always said that your curiosity would get you into trouble one day."

"And I've always known he was right." She laughed softly. "But it worked out in the end, didn't it? We found what we were looking for. Our understanding of the world will increase accordingly."

Skender glanced behind him at the twins toiling steadily under the weight of Shom Behenna. He was keen to find out how she had known about their return to the world and what she had hoped to learn from them. But just then wasn't the time for an interrogation. She obviously wasn't keen to talk about it with everyone around.

"I hope it was worth it," he said.

"Absolutely." She squeezed his arm. "You'll have to tell me later how you got past Pirelius and his thugs. When they ambushed us, we didn't stand a chance."

Skender was about to say that he hadn't, in fact, got past her captors at all, and that he had the bruises to show for it, but Sal made shushing noises from the head of the party and he took the hint. They were still in enemy territory and could easily be captured again if they weren't careful.

The route they followed led along exactly the sort of tunnels Skender had been looking for under Laure. He was gratified to that extent, but he still felt slightly stupid for searching the wrong side of the Divide. If he'd had Tom with him from the start—or just Tom's ability to glimpse the future—things might have gone very differently.

He idly wondered what it would be like to go through life experiencing occasional flashes of one's fate. He had once read in a biography of a seer that prophecy was like having memories of the future, and that these future memories were no different from having memories of the past. Ordinary people lived with vast amounts of information from their younger days, but not all of them remembered it correctly or used it when they should. People forgot things and disagreed with other people about what had "really" happened. Skender could see how having some knowledge of the future could be problematic under those circumstances. If people couldn't always agree on what had happened in the past, how could one person be certain all the time about what would happen in the future?

Skender came from a long line of Skender Van Haasterens, all of whom possessed perfect memory, all of whom had taught at the Keep. He knew exactly where he had come from, and he had a pretty good idea where he was going. Once that had seemed stifling; now he considered it a blessing. Unless something utterly unexpected came along and threw his life completely off-track, he would soon be back where he belonged.

Something utterly unexpected like Pirelius, he thought; or Lost Minds from the Void Beneath, back in the world for unknown reasons; or Chu, if she would ever talk to him again after he stole her wing, crashed it, and possibly lost it forever . . .

The exit from the tunnels glowed with daylight. This threw Skender for a moment: the last thing he remembered of the outside world was utter darkness, when he had been following a faint thread of smoke to the entrance of the bandits' hiding place. Now the sun had risen and he could smell hot dust in the air. He could also hear shouting and the sound of stone breaking.

Sal stopped at the base of a crack leading upwards through raw, unfinished rock. A series of natural steps led to fresh air and clear sky. It looked dauntingly blue. Sal hurried up the steps to check the lie of the land.

"Well," he said, "this complicates things."

Skender eased his mother into a sitting position and edged his way past Kemp and Mawson. "What? What can you see?"

"Man'kin."

"In the Aad?"

Sal nodded grimly, and Skender climbed to see for himself.

The sun-baked ruins, visible from his elevated position, were spread out before him. The crack partly severed a retaining wall on the edge of the city, where it abutted the sheer cliff face. Below was a series of low buildings that might once have been barracks or stables. Their roofs had collapsed long ago, leaving just stubs of walls pointing at the sky. Through these stubs walked a stone creature fully three metres high. Vaguely insectile, with a huge, tilted head and long, bladelike arms, it didn't seem to notice the bricks it sent tumbling. Cutting a swathe through the ruins to Skender's right, it angled up and back into the ruins proper.

There, Skender caught sight of people running. These were the source of the shouts. Now that they had lost the cover of the Change-sink, Pirelius's goons were coming face to face with the inhabitants of the Divide.

So would the escapees from the dungeon, Skender thought, if they emerged at the wrong time.

"We need to get Mawson up here," said Sal, "away from the Homunculus and its wake. We might be able to talk to the man'kin through him—at least find out what they want."

Skender scurried down the stairs to convey the request to Kemp. The albino, who had just put the bust down so he could rest, feigned irritation. He hefted Mawson into the crook of one arm and slowly eased himself up the crack. Skender, determined not to miss out on anything, followed.

"There are plenty of hiding spots," Kemp said, leaning Mawson on the lip of the crack and peering out at the ancient walls. "I can make a dash for one while you keep an eye out."

Sal nodded. "Take Skender with you. He can watch for my signal and act as a runner."

Skender nodded, although the thought of breaking cover amongst the man'kin made his bowels turn to water. The ruins looked awfully open under the bright light of the sun.

Kemp levered himself up onto the edge of the wall and jumped down. Skender helped Sal slide Mawson into Kemp's waiting hands, then jumped down after him. The sudden exposure was alarming. He could hear the man'kin crashing through walls and buildings all around him. The sound of their destructive vigour echoed off the cliff face and surrounded him with the clamour of breaking stone. He could almost feel the gleeful violence the man'kin wrought through the ground under his feet.

Kemp scrambled twenty metres to a relatively sheltered corner and managed to put Mawson down without dropping him. Then he fell back against the wall and wiped sweat from his brow. His barrel chest rose and fell.

Skender sank down next to him and looked behind them. He could see Sal peering out of the crack in the wall, and waved. Sal raised a hand just enough to show that he had seen them. Then Skender turned to Mawson, remembering how the man'kin in the Divide had told him that Mawson was "gone." It hadn't meant that Mawson was dead, just that he was temporarily out of action, thanks to the Change-sink and the Homunculus.

"How long do you think it'll take for him to recover?" he asked Kemp.

"How should I know?"

"*Use your ears,*" said the man'kin, "*and your eyes. The evidence of both senses will give you the answer you seek.*"

Skender jumped as Mawson's stone form shook, raising a small shower of dust that had settled into his angular lines. His face moved like an elaborate clockwork machine, jumping by increments from expression to expression. His mouth didn't open when he spoke, but his stone eyes tracked.

"Listen to me, Mawson," said Kemp. "I need you to talk to the man'kin around us. What do they want? Why are they destroying everything?"

"*They are not destructive. They are freeing the stones from captivity.*"

"What stones?"

"*The ones bound into walls and roads and other human artefacts.*"

"Is that all they want?"

"*For now.*"

"Will they attack us?"

"*I cannot say. Their natures are imprecise.*"

"What do you mean by that?"

"*Their meanings are clouded. They are . . . frightened, you might say.*"

Skender caught the slight hesitation. Fear wasn't something he normally associated with man'kin.

Kemp, obviously used to deciphering the confusing speech of Mawson, didn't pause.

"Frightened of what?"

"*The one from the Void.*"

Skender sat up straighter at the familiar phrase. "The Homunculus! What do you know about it?"

"*We know that its existence is inimical to us.*"

"Why?"

"*Because that is its nature.*"

"What if I told you there was nothing to be frightened of? Could you reassure the man'kin out there, tell them not to be afraid?"

"*There is reason to be afraid.*"

"But it's just two people—twins, in one body."

"*They do not belong in this world.*"

Skender gave up. This wasn't the time for a philosophical discussion about the nature of the twins. "Can you at least tell the other man'kin that *we* aren't their enemies? All we want to do is go home."

"*They know what I know: that you intend us no harm. Beyond that, I cannot speak for them. These are untamed 'kin. They are not as civilised as I am.*"

"Well, thanks for trying. At least they won't be able to hurt us if we stick with the Homunculus."

"Unless one of them falls on us," said Kemp.

Skender looked up to see Sal waving frantically at him. "Wait here. I'll see what he wants."

He checked that the space between their shelter and the crack was clear, then dashed across. The sound of the man'kin at work was no less disturbing for knowing that they were intent on liberation—in their own way—not wanton destruction. He vividly remembered the fury of the man'kin he and Sal had encountered in the Divide: Mawson's use of the word "untamed" was odd but completely appropriate. A misunderstanding could have serious consequences.

He scrambled into the crack. The first thing he noticed was the body of an unconscious bandit lying face-down further up the corridor.

"What happened?"

"We're blocking their emergency exit," Sal said. "We can expect more of them as the man'kin work their way closer to their front door. What's the situation out there?"

Skender explained the little he and Kemp had learned from Mawson. "We should be safe enough," he concluded, "but there are no guarantees."

"We'll just have to hope for the best, then. It's not as if we have much choice."

Sal clambered down to help Skender's mother up the rough stairs. She assisted as best she could, but her grip was dismayingly weak. Skender tried not to think about the journey that lay ahead of them— not just through the ruins, but across the entire Divide as well. He didn't know what Sal had in the pack slung across his shoulders, but he doubted it contained enough food and water for all of them.

When Skender had eased his mother to the ground on the far side of the crack in the wall, watching warily as he did for man'kin, he climbed back up to help with Behenna's dead weight. The Homunculus pushed with Sal from below, then clambered up and over to help Skender on the other side. The artificial body looked even more unusual in the light of day. When the twins' limbs didn't exactly overlap, Skender half expected to be able to see through them. That wasn't the case at all. They were blurry around the edges but not translucent.

Working together, they managed to get Behenna out of the crack. Sal scrambled down after him.

"Now," he said, "all we have to do is get Kemp, and—"

He stopped, looking across the empty space to where the albino and Mawson were hiding. Skender followed his gaze. Every muscle in his body stiffened at what he saw.

Kemp was on his knees, facing them. Pirelius, as shaggy and dangerous as a giant mad dog, stood behind him. One hand gripped a bunch of Kemp's hair, forcing his head back; the other hand pressed a large knife to his throat. The bandit leader's glare was malignant and full of loathing.

Pirelius cocked his chin. The message was clear. *Over here. Now.*

Sal pointed at his chest. *Just me?*

Pirelius shook his head. *All of you.* The blade bit into Kemp's skin, sending a tiny rivulet of crimson down his throat. *Don't push your luck.*

"I guess we do as he says," Sal said.

Skender couldn't take his eyes off the gleam of the blade. "What does he want?"

"Let's ask him." Sal straightened and stepped out of cover.

The flyer swooped precipitously close to the heavy lifter, and Shilly did exactly as Chu had suggested she do: gesture rudely at it. The wing's pilot—the same handsome, arrogant man who had accused Chu of being a fraud—returned the compliment and glided away.

"Ignore him," said Chu. "There's nothing he can do. If they were going to pop our bubble, they would've done so ages ago."

"What are they doing here, then?"

"I guess they want to find out what *we're* doing. Miners are always looking for new leads. And who knows what the man'kin will leave behind in their wake?"

Shilly peered over the side of the gondola at the migration below. She could make out the individual frontrunners, but the full extent of their numbers was hidden from her view by dust. And more were coming around the bend of the Divide. It looked as though every man'kin for a thousand kilometres was uprooting and moving on.

Their intentions were unknown. And when she looked ahead to the Aad, at the clouds rising from the ruins, her uncertainty took on an urgent note.

Marmion came forward, holding onto stanchions to keep his balance as the lifter swayed beneath him.

"Any word from Sal?"

"Nothing." The continuing silence was yet another cause for concern. "Is there anything you can do to hurry things along? We're almost on your territory again."

"We're flying, Shilly, not sailing. I'm sure the last thing Chu wants is us blowing her off course."

"Couldn't have said it more politely myself," said the flyer, "but we're not far off now, anyway. If you guys want to start talking about somewhere to touch down, that would be good. I'd argue against using the anchors, just in case we need to get away quickly. When we find Skender and the others, we can use the ladders and ropes to haul them up and get them away."

Shilly glanced at Marmion to see how he would react to the idea of rescuing the Homunculus, but his face didn't change.

"What about the tower?" he asked, pointing at the ruins. "Could we attach the heavy lifter to that and climb down from there?"

"It's a possibility," Chu said. "I'll aim for it and we'll see what the air is like."

"Well, that's something we *can* help you with. Every warden is taught to see the wind."

"Really?" Chu looked deeply envious for a moment. "Then I guess you'll come in useful after all. Tell me when you're ready and you can start giving me directions. That'll make my life a lot easier."

Shilly edged away as Marmion closed his eyes and concentrated. The small amount of the Change Marmion called on didn't add much to that already buzzing in and around the structure of the heavy lifter. But she felt the shift in the world as his mind interacted with it in much the same way as a musician might shift key in the middle of a song.

Chu watched the warden with all the attention she could spare. Her desire seemed as keen as Shilly's. Both of them lacked the innate potential for the Change that made Sky Wardens, Stone Mages, yadachi blood-workers, and the occasional wild talent like Sal the envy of everyone—although Shilly had long ago gotten over her resentment of that fact.

When one of the bubbles in Marmion's torc began to glow like a miniature star caught in perfectly clear amber, Chu gasped. His eyes opened. They had turned a clear, translucent blue, the same colour as the sky.

"We're cutting across a dense current," he said, leaning forward to peer out of the gondola. "I can see it running like a river from the southeast."

Chu nodded. "That's what's making us rock. There should be another one ahead, tending south. It's usually there this time of day."

Marmion's charmed gaze sought details where Shilly could see none. "Yes," he said. "You're taking us a little high. Bring us down and you'll catch it. There'll be some turbulence, but it won't last. It's just the boundary where the two flows brush by each other."

Chu nodded and obeyed his instructions without hesitating. The lifter's nose dipped and a shudder ran along its length. Shilly held on tight as the turbulence worsened.

A hand tapped her shoulder. She turned around to see Tom looking at her, slightly green around the ears.

"Is everything okay?" she asked.

He sat down next to her. "You haven't called Sal since we left."

"I know. I figured you'd be tired from what I'd already taken."

"I am, but you're worried. You can try again if you want to."

She was more grateful than she could say for the offer, even if she wouldn't let herself accept it. "He'll call me if he can. I'd rather you conserved your strength for when I really need it."

Tom nodded quite seriously.

Shilly had been half-joking, but his lack of amusement gave her reason to be seriously concerned.

"Unless you're trying to tell me that I *should* call him now? That you've dreamed me doing it?"

"No."

"Okay. We'll just have to wait and see what happens, then." *Like always*, she thought, telling herself to emulate his insouciance.

The heavy lifter shuddered and dipped again. When she checked their progress, she saw the Aad much closer than it had been before.

Chu and Marmion were still discussing possible landing sites.

"That rules the tower out," said the flyer, pointing.

Shilly craned her neck to see. Smoky brown haze hid the details, but a small group of people appeared to be waving at them from the summit of the ruined city's watchtower.

"Are they—?"

"I hope not," said Chu. "Look at the base of the tower."

She squinted to make out the details. The figures she saw were the same colour as the background stone, making their nature immediately obvious: they were man'kin. But what they were doing was less clear. They appeared to be circling the tower's ground level, stopping occasionally to strike the stone walls as though it was a giant drum.

Not strike, Shilly corrected herself after a longer look. They were taking stones from the wall and flinging them away. *Dismantle.*

"Can we get down there to help them?" she asked Chu, filled with horror at the thought of what it must be like on top of the tower while monsters did their best to collapse it.

"I don't know." Power surged through the propellers with a deep thrum. The dirigible's angle of descent steepened. Instead of travelling in a straight line, Chu guided them around a sweeping curve, with Marmion calling directions along the way. The gondola tipped and swayed like a ride in a fair. Tom's face turned greener than ever.

Behind her, the wardens tied ropes to eyelets along the gondola's edges. Banner walked from knot to knot, testing them for strength.

"I don't think it's them," said Marmion as the tower came closer.

"That doesn't matter," said Shilly. "We can't just watch them die!"

"Too late," said Chu as part of the tower's wall collapsed. The structure tipped like a drunken sailor. The people on the top ran hopelessly back and forth. One fell off.

Shilly couldn't watch any longer. Marmion was right. None of them looked like Sal, Skender, or Kail, but that was irrelevant. They were still people, and no one deserved to die in terror and agony.

When she steeled herself to turn back, the tower was gone. Only a rising cloud of stone and mortar dust remained.

"Now we know why Sal sent for us," said Marmion. "The man'kin have gone on the rampage."

"Is there anything we can do to stop them?" Shilly asked, hoping it wasn't too late already. The thought of Sal on top of a tower like that, screaming, made her feel sick.

"They are creatures of the Change," Marmion said. "To kill them, you have to kill the Change itself, and that is obviously impossible."

"Not for the Homunculus." A tiny candle of hope still burned in her chest for Sal; her sense of *him* remained undimmed. "Where it is, they'll be safe."

"And unable to call us," said Tom, his face a mask of concern.

"Yes, there's that." Shilly craned as far as she dared over the edge of the gondola. The heavy lifter hovered directly over the city. She could see several man'kin wreaking desolation through the already ruined streets. Rubble lay everywhere she looked. It was hard in places to tell what damage was new and what the result of time and the weather.

Twice more she saw people, none of them the ones she sought. Three ran out of a structure attached to the Divide wall and made a beeline for the edge of the city. A giant, lion-shaped man'kin chased them for a block, snapping at their heels. Its heavy tread brought down the remains of a nearby building. It stopped to perform an odd dance among the shattered stonemasonry while its victims took the opportunity to flee. Shilly shuddered to think what the man'kin might have done had it caught them.

"Do you see anything?" asked Marmion.

She shook her head. A half-dozen flyers had kept pace with them from Laure. They circled warily around the heavy lifter, distracting Chu. The one with an attitude problem had drifted away, possibly as struck as she was by the devastation below.

"If we've come all this way for nothing—" Marmion started to say.

"Wait." Shilly took his arm. "Look!"

One of the flyers on the edge of the ruin had suddenly dipped. It began to tumble, then just as suddenly recovered—as though it had left a bubble in which its charms had stopped working.

Shilly knew only one thing that could have that effect.

"The Homunculus! It's over there!"

Chu looked to see where Shilly was pointing, then wrenched the controls of the heavy lifter. Ponderously it began to turn.

"Be careful," Marmion warned her. "Don't get too close. The wake extends further through air than it does across the ground."

"I know," she said. "I haven't forgotten what happened the last time I flew over it."

The edge of the ruins came nearer. Shilly made out a long wall carved from the side of the Divide. It had cracked in several places, like a gap-toothed lower jaw. At first she couldn't see anyone, but then a huddle of people came into view, tucked inside the remains of a series of small buildings.

She instantly recognised Sal by the colour and cut of his hair.

"There they are!"

"What do I do now?" asked Chu. "I can't get too close or we'll lose the rudder charms and the props."

Shilly scanned the area around the group. One solitary person crouched off to one side, perfectly still, but she couldn't tell who it was. A large man'kin was heading towards them, crashing through ruined walls like she would through stalks of wheat.

"Let me think," she said. "There has to be a way."

"You've ruined everything!" Pirelius snarled. The knife bit deeper into Kemp's neck, and the albino squirmed. "I should kill you all right now for what you've done!"

"Calm down." Sal held out his hands in a gesture of conciliation. "We didn't come here to ruin you. We just wanted our friends back."

"Liar!" Pirelius spat in the dirt between them. One eye was bruised and swelling. "*She* sent you. No one else knew I was here. No one else knew about the sink. No one else had a fucking *motive*. So don't feed me that crap, or I'll kill the freak!"

"Got it." Sal clenched his fists in frustration. The desperate fury in the bandit's eyes convinced him that the threat wasn't empty. Kemp's tunic was already dark with blood. A millimetre deeper and his life would be spilling onto the dirt. "What do you want?"

"I want to make her pay." Pirelius's crooked teeth flashed malignantly through the rankness of his beard. "You're going to help me."

"I don't even know who *she*—" He bit off the rest as the knife shifted again. "How are we going to help you?"

"The man'kin are everywhere. They're bringing the whole place down." The whiteness of Pirelius's eyes betrayed a hint of fear. "I don't know how she called them, but there's no way to fight them. I'm not going to die here. That *thing* is going to get me out of here."

Sal turned to the Homunculus, which was still effortlessly holding Shom Behenna in its arms. Its features shivered under the bright sun.

"I may have lost the sink," Pirelius went on, "but I'll have the next best thing. Your ugly friend here stops the man'kin cold in their tracks. With it I can get clean away, and *she* can't do a thing about it."

"We don't want to help you," said the Homunculus.

"You will if you don't want to see your friend here dead."

"He's not our friend. We don't know him."

"That's your answer, then?" Pirelius's nostrils flared. "If I kill him, it's on your conscience."

The Homunculus put Behenna down on the ground. "We have our own destination. You can travel with us, if you wish."

"Not good enough. I want revenge, and I know how to get it." Pirelius dug the point of the blade into the muscle under Kemp's jaw. "I'm losing patience!"

Heavy stone footprints thudded towards them from the other side of the wall. Sal backed away as a mighty stone man appeared, trailing a cloud of dust. For a moment he was sure that it would step right through them, but it hit the boundary of the Homunculus's influence and instantly stopped.

Beyond its noble brow, he saw something even stranger: a blimp descending over the Aad with light flashing from its prow. Someone was holding a mirror up to the morning sun and using it to catch their eye.

Pirelius hadn't spotted it. His attention was firmly fixed on the Homunculus.

"All right," it said, "we'll go with you. Set him free and we'll leave this place together."

"Oh, no," said Pirelius. "It's not that simple. I saw what you did to Izzi in the cell. It's not going to happen to me. You." He nodded at Skender. "Tie all its hands together and its feet in pairs. When that's done, and not before, I'll let the big freak go."

"I can't," said Skender. "They helped us!"

"You'll do it or I'll take you instead," Pirelius snarled.

Sal leaned in close to Skender and hissed in his ear, covering his words by rummaging in Kail's pack. He produced several lengths of slender, soft twine. Skender nodded, tight-lipped, and didn't argue.

The Homunculus, whether it had heard or not, cooperated as they lashed its limbs together. Its flesh was cool and waxy to the touch, with no visible markings like tattoos or scars. Sal's hands moved quickly, conscious of the dirigible growing nearer over Pirelius's shoulder.

He and Skender stepped back when the job was done. The Homunculus was as human as it had ever looked, although it still seemed to have too many eyes and mouths.

"Right," said Pirelius. "Come here."

The Homunculus obeyed. When it was within arm's reach, Pirelius put his foot in the small of Kemp's back and pushed him face-forward into the dirt at Sal's feet. The knife jabbed into the Homunculus's side as Pirelius tested the knots. Sal didn't know how much damage an ordinary blade could do to the artificial body, but it was clear the Homunculus wasn't prepared to take a chance. It was frozen—with fear or hopelessness, Sal couldn't tell. Perhaps both.

He wanted to say that he was sorry, but there wasn't time.

"Get ready to run," he whispered to Skender as he helped Kemp to his feet. "We have to get out of the wake so the dirigible can come in closer, and I don't think our friend there is as dead as he looks." The frozen man'kin swayed on the very edge of the Homunculus's sphere of influence, its eyes watching them unblinkingly.

"How are we going to carry everyone?" Skender whispered back. Rope ladders dangled over the side of the gondola as it grew nearer.

"We'll have to leave Mawson behind for the time being."

"It's been a pleasure doing business," sneered Pirelius, shoving the Homunculus ahead of him. "Don't try to follow or I'll stick you like pigs."

Sal ignored Pirelius as he hurried away towards the Divide. The drone of propellers rose up out of the sound of stone smashing. He couldn't see the edge of the Homunculus's wake as Skender had in the Divide, but he could take a rough guess as to where it was. Kemp wordlessly wiped the blood from his throat and picked up Behenna. Skender put an arm around his mother and helped her stand straighter.

"I'll go first." Sal waved both arms over his head, away from the man'kin, hoping the pilot of the dirigible would understand. Seconds later, it did shift course, coming in lower over the ruins in the direction he had indicated. He tensed to run.

Then, with a subtle grinding noise, the man'kin turned and took a step. Sal backed away automatically, even though he knew he was safe in the wake. He expected it to come between him and the dirigible, but instead it walked around the wake and followed Pirelius down the slope towards the Divide. Its step became thunderous. The bandit looked over his shoulder in alarm, and picked up the pace.

"Maybe we're not tasty enough," said Skender.

"I don't care what it's doing. I'm just glad I'm not about to be squashed."

Sal helped Skender and his mother to the first of the ladders. Abi Van Haasteren was too weak to climb on her own, but allowed herself to be hauled up by the blue-robed wardens into the dirigible. Sal could see Shilly now, leaning out of the front of the gondola. He waved as Kemp and Behenna went up in the care of the Wardens, then he went back with the albino for Mawson.

Later, he had told Skender. *We'll come back for the Homunculus later.*

He was the last to leave the ground.

Þ

We don't want to help you.

You will if you don't want to see your friend here dead.

He's not our friend. We don't know him.

That's your answer, then? If I kill him, it's on your conscience.

And the knife had dug into an innocent throat, drawing blood in a steady trickle.

The Homunculus—

—the Oldest One—

—the Mirror Twins—

—watched in despair as, yet again, they were entangled in another petty plot. One life was nothing when compared to the fate of a world. But who were they to claim the high moral ground if they failed to intervene when an innocent was threatened? They had seen in their own lives what one life might mean in the balance of things.

We have our own destination. You can travel with us, if you wish.

Not good enough. I want revenge, and I know how to get it. I'm losing patience!

Death and torture. The new world was no different to the old one. They were part of it now, and innocence was purely relative.

All right. We'll go with you. Set him free and we'll leave this place together.

The decision was made. Only the details remained. They went passively along with what they were told to do, holding out their hands to be tied as though offering themselves for sacrifice. So long as the innocents went free, the rest could be worked out later.

A giant stone form loomed over them as the knife blade transferred to their back. Its point brought back memories of winter in another world, of roaring metal engines and blood pouring in a stream to the ground. Images of death overwhelmed them.

Paralysed by the past and trapped in the present, they let themselves be pushed into an uncertain future.

*This world-line is diverging even as we speak, so we have to hurry. We have to
get out of here. Now!*

The words they had spoken to the shadow called Galeus remained
as true as ever. Nothing was going remotely as planned. They had
thought their troubles over when they escaped death on the top of the
giant ravine, but the fallacy of that assumption had soon revealed
itself. The bottom of the ravine was rugged and desolate. Strange creatures traversed it, creatures whose substance ranged from the nebu-
losity of air to the concreteness of stone. They felt themselves being
watched from all angles. The ravine's inhabitants were drawn to and
repelled by them at the same time. When the twins tried to approach,
they shied away and vanished.

Whispers taunted them from the edge of the lighted area surrounding them. The darkness ahead remained absolute. They felt more
exposed than ever, and lonely. The latter surprised them. Was that all
it took, one brief contact with the shadows, to make the twins miss
something they had not experienced for eons?

Friendship, companions, support . . . ?

We have each other, they reminded themselves.

It wasn't the same.

Then—disaster. Strangers leapt out of the jumbled ravine floor and
surrounded them. A net swept over them, too strong to break, and tangled them in its cords. Voices snarled and blows fell. They were taken
captive and locked in a cell.

Brutality and ignorance. The politics of fear. The twins didn't
know who was fighting whom, but they recognised victimisation when
they saw it. The language of abuse was universal. They tried hard not
to care. A higher purpose drove them. They couldn't afford to become
mired in power plays. But they were human, despite everything. Deep

down, they didn't want to stand apart from the world they were trying to save.

Hey, you! You said you've met me before. Come out and talk to me, since we're such good buddies.

Who is wrong here, Galeus?

The question came from the twins almost unwillingly. And even as they asked it, they knew they were committed. But with commitment came confusion. Their thoughts fragmented. If one person, undecided, could be said to be in two minds, did that mean that they were in *four*?

Their new body strained to contain them.

The world convulsed. For a moment, it seemed that all would come undone.

When they returned, the world had indeed changed. They had allies, now. They weren't alone.

The knife in their back prodded the twins forward. They stumbled, finding it hard to balance with their legs tied in pairs and all their wrists bound. What would their allies do now? Would they stage a daring rescue attempt? Would they trade someone else's life for theirs? Would the ones with knowledge of the Change exert their will over the world to save them?

The twins tried not to feel resentment as Galeus and the others fled in a small blimp and sailed off over the ruined city, out of their sight. The twins had volunteered for this duty, after all. And they had lived longer than all of the others put together, even if most of that time had been spent outside the world. It was better than idly watching as blood spilled at the hands of a psychopath.

The twins didn't know if their new body *had* blood, but they weren't prepared to find out the hard way. The distant past held memories of knife wounds for both of them. Blood and horror. Death and despair. Back when they had had names.

You don't know what you're doing, they told the man at their back.

Shut up or I'll put a hole in you.

But we have somewhere to be. Somewhere important.

So do I, and you're going to take me there. Get moving!

The shadow pushed the twins forward, and they let momentum carry them, stumbling, along the streets of the city. They could hear the sounds of the ravine's inhabitants as they reclaimed the ruins. The shadows had called them by an unusual name. *Mannequins*, perhaps. They looked like nothing so much as statues come to life. The shadow with the knife seemed afraid of the ones in the city, although Galeus and his friends treated the one called Mawson with respect. It was difficult to understand the allegiances of those around him. The rules had changed.

Names . . . Galeus's mother was among those the twins had helped to rescue. She was safe now, flying away in a blimp to somewhere called Laure. Laure was the city on the other side of the ravine. And Galeus's friends called him Skender for some reason. Names were slowly sinking in. The twins needed names if they were to get a handle on the new world, and on the doom that threatened it.

Their destination—the wrongness—hung over them like a storm front, deep and dark and growing larger every day. Even when they stood still it seemed to grow, responding to their presence. The air was thick with hunger. It made their head hang.

Don't slow down! The shadow at their back shoved them again. *Keep moving!*

More words fell into place. *Your name is Pirelius.*

So what if it is?

You remind us of someone. A wolf. What was the name of the man we hurt in the cage?

Forget him. He's irrelevant.

The twins remembered the feel of bone and gristle under their joined fingers. It had sickened them, even though they understood the necessity for it. *We could have killed him.*

And I could kill you. Remember that.

It's wrong to kill.

Goddess! Am I going to have to gag you?

The twins fell silent, not because of Pirelius's threat, but because the man had triggered another memory. Pirelius wasn't the first to mention a Goddess, but it hadn't seemed especially significant before.

Peace, Seth, someone had told them, once. *This is neither our first meeting nor our last. In your future, the Goddess awaits.*

They didn't know who had said the words, although an image of a woman, glowing, green, came with an exhortation to remember. Remember what? The details didn't stir.

Who is the Goddess? they asked Pirelius.

All they received in reply was a snarl and another poke with the knife. Their captor picked up the pace and began to sing words the twins hadn't heard since the misty days of their former life. The bizarre juxtaposition of the exotic and the familiar made their minds spin.

Half a league, half a league,

Half a league onward—

Far overhead, the blimp ploughed silently through the air, visible as a faint smudge against a midnight sky. Terror and loathing brought a kind of connection to the world, the same as anger, but it was fading. Resignation took its place, and the world was grey by that light.

THE FUGITIVE

"Body, mind, will: on these three pillars rests all life on this Earth. The Change works through them in an act of glorious, ongoing combustion that casts light on dead matter and drives the shadows back into the night."
THE BOOK OF TOWERS, FRAGMENT 252

Climbing a rope ladder was a lot harder than Skender expected. He swung crazily beneath the heavy lifter, wishing there weren't so many wardens watching him, making encouraging noises and reaching to help him when he came in range. He felt dizzy and winded when he finally hauled himself over the edge of the gondola and collapsed with no grace at all onto the wooden floor. There were so many legs. He worried about the ability of the dirigible to keep its numerous passengers in the air.

"Here." A young warden offered him a hand and helped him to his feet. "You're safe now. Let me take a look at your face. That's a nasty bruise you've got."

Skender fended off the warden's ministrations. He could feel the dirigible turning under him, heading back for Laure, no doubt.

"Wait!" He pushed through the crowd to the front. "We can't leave yet."

"Grown attached to the place, have we?" asked a familiar voice from the pilot's position.

"Chu!" She looked exhausted, and the bandage on her head was brown with dirt and dried blood. They eyed each other warily. "I didn't expect to see you here."

"Why not?"

"You're already in enough trouble, aren't you?"

"I guess this rescuing thing is becoming a habit. You can pay me double."

The dirigible was turning.

"Wait. Don't take us to Laure just yet. We have to head up into the ruins, towards the tower."

"There's no tower any more, stone-boy. The man'kin brought it down."

"But you know the direction, right? We just need to go back for a second."

"Go *back?*" The officious, balding warden who led the expedition from the Haunted City squeezed into the front of the gondola. *Eisak Marmion*, Skender remembered. His eyes were a startling cerulean in colour. "Under no circumstances are we going back. We have to follow the Homunculus!"

"I know, but not yet," Skender insisted. "Chu, your wing is hidden in a safe place. I can find it for you."

"My wing?" She looked up at him with her eyebrows raised. Behind the expression he glimpsed disbelief, relief, caution—a welter of complex emotions. "I'd assumed you'd mangled it and left it in a ditch somewhere."

"Why would I do that? Sal and I have been lugging it all over the Divide. I knew you'd kill me if I didn't bring it back in one piece."

"I've trained you better than I thought, clearly."

"I'm sorry," said Marmion, "but the wing is irrelevant. We have to keep on this heading. We can't take any more risks."

"Who's flying this thing?" Chu asked him. "If I say we're going to get my wing, that's exactly what we're doing."

"Then you'll be doing it without my help. I will refuse to give you the directions you need to fly."

"That doesn't matter. Skender, do you still have that licence of yours?"

He felt under his robes. The bandits had paid no attention to mere paper when they had searched him. "Indeed I do."

"Good. Put it on and do your stuff. If the man'kin have stomped on my wing, your luck is going to change fast."

Skender plastered the licence to his chest while the warden went off smouldering. The tattoos spread across his skin and vision, bringing the winds over the ruins to vivid life. Despite his many aches and pains, he felt good. His mother was safe; Chu was safe; and so was he. He felt bad about Rattails and what they had had to do to escape, but all they needed to do now was get back to Laure, and everything would be fine.

"Take us up the ridge and you'll catch a current right across the city." She made room for him on the seat next to her, and he squeezed in. "Then it's clean flying all the way."

Shilly didn't want to let go of Sal's hands, but she had to so he could be checked over. He seemed fine to her, despite the dried blood covering him: a little rough around the edges, and he definitely needed a wash, but they all needed one, she supposed. His long dark hair was full of dust, and he was sunburned even through the charms. He would have freckles when the redness faded. She would like them, even if he didn't.

His blue eyes didn't leave hers. They warmed her.

"I missed you," he said.

"I worried about you."

"You shouldn't have. I always knew you'd rescue us in time."

She feigned puzzlement. "Really? That wasn't the deal, as I remember it. You were supposed to meet us in Laure."

He waved away the point. "Details, details."

The warden declared him fit and gave him a bottle of water. He swigged, and managed to spill most of it when Marmion jogged his shoulder from behind.

"Where to now?" Shilly asked the balding warden. "Ready to face the music in Laure?"

"Don't even ask," Marmion muttered as the heavy lifter swung around.

"We should look for Kail and the Homunculus," said Sal. "They're both still down there somewhere."

"I know exactly where Kail is, thank you very much. He's doing his job, as we should be."

A small piece of the puzzle fell into place. Shilly remembered the lone figure she had seen watching Sal and the others from a distance. "Kail is still tracking the Homunculus, isn't he? He was keeping back in case it made a break for it. When it did, he followed."

"No," said Sal. "That's not how things went. The Homunculus isn't running away at all. It's been taken hostage by Pirelius—the man who kidnapped Skender's mother and the others. It's his prisoner."

"No honour among thieves, huh?" she asked.

"I don't think they knew about each other," Sal said. "In fact I'm certain of it."

"The Homunculus wasn't coming to the Aad after all?" Shilly abandoned her previous theory with a slight feeling of foolishness. "I was so certain of it."

"Laure it is and always has been," said Marmion. "And here we are chasing after some fool girl's lost property!" He stormed off to bother someone else. Shilly was glad to see him go. The blue of his eyes had faded along with the mote of light in his torc, leaving both dark and glowering.

"Listen," Shilly said to Sal in a low voice, with her mouth right against his ear. "Your father woke last night. He told us what the Homunculus is."

"It's from the Void," he said, nodding. "Skender says it's actually two people in one body—twins from before the Cataclysm."

"Twins?" She knew she shouldn't be surprised that he knew as much as her, and more besides. He had been with the Homunculus on the ground, whereas she had been hearing about it secondhand. "There's so much to catch up on," she said.

Sal nodded distractedly. He had her stick in his hands again, and he stared at it, not her, as he asked, "How is Highson? Is he well?"

"He'll be okay."

"You don't sound certain of that."

She took Sal's hands off the stick and put them back in hers. "He's had a tough time of it. You'll have to be patient with him."

"We could take him back to Fundelry with us. That's the perfect place to recuperate."

Shilly thought of Tom and his prophecy regarding the ice cave. She knew better than to relax just yet, or even to think about home. Although she missed the workshop and the friends she had left behind, they still had to get back to Laure—and only the Goddess knew what sort of reception awaited them there.

"I'd rather just be here and now for a bit," she said, "if that's okay with you."

Sal smiled, and kissed her.

The heavy lifter headed deeper into the Aad, then dipped over streets Sal thought he recognised. It took him a moment to realise what was going on. When ropes went over the side, followed by Skender and two wardens, he understood.

The propellers thrummed as Chu held the dirigible in position, defying the prevailing winds. Sal kept an eye out with the others for man'kin or bandits, but apart from some rogue statues disassembling walls several blocks away, the ruined streets were clear. The bandits appeared to have completely vanished. They were either dead, Sal thought, or had gone to ground.

Although he knew he was safe in the air, he was still relieved when Skender and the wardens returned, carefully suspending Chu's wing on a rope between them. He couldn't see the flyer's reaction, but he could tell that Skender was pleased with himself.

"If we're finally done here," shouted Marmion from the rear of the gondola, "perhaps we can get moving!"

Chu tilted the dirigible into the wind and gave it its head. They were soon rising high above the Aad and picking up speed.

Sal stretched his legs out as far as he dared. Compared to his one brief jump with Skender, this was a much better way to fly. But he didn't feel relaxed. They had forgotten something important; he was sure of it. And not just the Homunculus, temporarily abandoned to its fate . . .

"You can see the damage so much better from up here," Shilly said, her chin propped up on the edge. "The man'kin could flatten a city in days, easy. No wonder people in Laure are so scared of them."

Sal picked out the spoor of several mass-migrations hanging in plumes over the mighty canyon. He wondered what held such allure for them in the west, and how it related to the enigmatic Angel.

He told Shilly about the artefact they had found in the bandits' lair. It seemed reasonable to assume that it had been there ever since the Divide's formation, since without it the man'kin would have destroyed the ruined city years ago.

"So this Polonius guy—"

"Pirelius."

"Whatever. He was just taking advantage of something he found? It wasn't part of a big plan or anything?"

"He didn't strike me as much of an original thinker."

"I'll bet it was him and his gang who buzzed us after you and Skender went after the Homunculus. They were probably coming to warn us away, not to meet anyone."

"What happened? Did he attack you, like he did Abi Van Haasteren?"

"No. You scared him off with your little storm trick. Otherwise we might have ended up down there, too."

Sal didn't know exactly what had happened to Skender and the others in the cells, but the thought of Shilly in the hands of the bandits made his stomach turn. Kemp had a thick bandage around his throat and seemed to be sleeping with his head lolling half out of the gondola. Skender's mother was still being cleaned and treated; Sal heard grim mentions of broken ribs and stitches were being sewn by the wardens looking after her. Shom Behenna's eyes were open, but he wasn't looking at anyone in particular. His fists were tightly clenched, constraining a powerful rage.

Sal caught Tom's eye, and nodded. The young Engineer pointed at the view over the side of the gondola.

"Ah," said Shilly, noticing. "His dream."

They were above the edge of the Divide, flying much higher than Sal and Skender had the previous day. Sal could see where they had laid the ambush for the Homunculus and where they had jumped off the edge. The creek they had followed to the Aad was a tiny track barely visible from the air.

His eyes drifted southward, to the plain rent in two by the mighty canyon. Parched landscape stretched forever to the south. Somewhere out there, at the end of a very long journey, was Fundelry and their home. If he let his eyes unfocus, he could almost see waves in the shimmering mirage that lay at the limits of his vision. He wished he could step through a Way and breathe deep of the salty air, just for a moment. It would steel his nerves for what lay in store for them.

Chu turned the gondola so it was heading north, to Laure.

"Why wasn't Marmion surprised about Kail?" Shilly asked him.

"I guess Kail talked to him when the Caduceus broke, just like I talked to you," he said. "Now Kail isn't affected by the wake because he isn't in it. He could've been keeping Marmion up to date the whole time you were coming."

"That would explain why Marmion agreed to leave so readily. I *thought* he caved a little too easily." She looked annoyed at herself. "He could've said something, especially if he knew you were alive. That selfish bastard was just covering his hide. If things went wrong, he could always blame me."

"Unfortunately," Sal said, "that does sound true to character."

She shook her head. "Just when I think he might have a little bit of Lodo in him, somewhere—"

"Don't, Shilly. He's not Lodo, and he never will be. The fact they're related doesn't mean they're at all alike. Look at *my* relatives, for instance."

She smiled wanly. "True. But I can't help wishing, you know? He's the closest thing I've got to family, apart from you. It'd be nice if blood did run true, just this once. Is that too much to ask?"

"Maybe." Sal's experience with family had been universally bad: not just the Syndic wanting to control him, but a grandmother deep in the Interior who had tried to do the same. He felt no kinship with these people, whom he hadn't known existed until five years earlier. He owed them nothing.

His real father, however, was a more complex issue.

A small commotion drew their attention back to the distant ground below. Skender had spotted the wake of the Homunculus. Several brass telescopes—standard equipment on the heavy lifter—were being passed among the wardens. Sal heard references to Kail and man'kin, and he eagerly took his chance to look when his turn came.

He saw three people on the rugged, red-earthed ground, not far from the Aad. Two walked ahead of the third: Pirelius and the Homunculus, followed by Kail. Even the tracker looked tiny from that height. All headed towards Laure. Behind them were several man'kin. More converged on the three travellers like feral dogs to unattended cattle.

Sal passed the telescope to Shilly, who confirmed his impression.

"We have to rescue it," he said. "*Them.* Whatever."

"How?" she responded. "If we come within a hundred metres Pirelius will cut its throat. And even if he doesn't, how would we get away? It would kill the charms as soon as we brought it aboard."

A ludicrous image of the Homunculus dangling from a rope ladder all the way back to Laure occurred to him. He quashed it. "We have to do *something*."

"And we will, but not now. In a strange way, it's probably safer down there than it is up here."

"How do you figure that? If Marmion wants the Homunculus

dead, all Kail has to do is attack Pirelius. Either he beats Pirelius to it and kills the Homunculus himself, or Pirelius holds good to his threat and kills the Homunculus for him. It's a win-win situation."

"Not for Kail," she said. "Killing the Homunculus makes them all vulnerable. You said it yourself: the only thing keeping the man'kin at bay is the wake, so neither of them will want to get rid of it."

The thought reassured him somewhat. Brother or half brother or whatever, he still felt guilty at abandoning the Homunculus. *Later*, he promised again. *Later.*

"I talked to Kail after you left," she went on, "and he seemed reasonable enough, within reason. He's Marmion's man through and through. He'll obey orders even if he doesn't want to."

"He probably saved our lives back there."

"Maybe because Marmion hadn't ordered him not to. He didn't step in when Kemp was under the knife, remember."

"I assumed that was because there was nothing Kail could do about it. If Pirelius had so much as jumped, he'd have cut Kemp's head half off."

"He would have done it," said the albino from the far side of the gondola. "He would've done it just to hurt you. Pirelius is crazy. I'm surprised he didn't do it anyway."

Sal sensed that the wound to Kemp's dignity ran deeper than the shallow cut to his throat. Beside the albino, Mawson sat squarely upright, watching the world with the patience of stone.

"It's good to see you again, Mawson," Sal said to break the tension. "You've obviously been keeping busy."

The bust didn't look especially pleased to see him. "*You gave me the freedom to pursue my own interests. I do so to the fullest extent of my abilities.*"

"Why the Surveyors? I didn't know you were the curious type."

"*This world has many secrets. Some have dwelt long enough in the dirt. Some must never be uncovered.*"

"I'm sure the Surveyors don't see eye to eye with you on that last point," Shilly said.

"That is correct."

"Was it you who brought Skender's mother here, then?" Skender had looked around, twisting in his seat to overhear the conversation. "Did you tell her there was something to find?"

"I did not."

Abi Van Haasteren stirred. "We came here for the Caduceus," she said, her left eye fluttering open. The right was swollen shut. "There are references to it in several very old texts, but only one talks about its final resting place. I deciphered it two months ago. As soon as I could put an expedition together, we came to claim it. I didn't know it had already been found."

Skender peered askance at her. "The Caduceus? But I thought you came here to meet the Homunculus."

"Why would you think that?"

"Well, it was coming to the Aad, and so were you."

"That's the extent of your reasoning?" An affectionate smile took the edge off her rebuke. "No wonder you're not a Surveyor."

Skender's ears went bright pink. "I should have guessed there was more to it when Pirelius got so angry at you for trying to steal from him."

"We weren't stealing from him. Not knowingly, anyway. And it wasn't me he was angry at. It was the Magister."

"Why?"

She shrugged. "He wasn't one to talk much about his reasons."

"At least you know the Caduceus is there for certain, now," said Shilly. "You can go back to get it once things settle down."

Abi Van Haasteren nodded. "Believe me, I'd like to."

Skender was still frowning. "So the twins are going to Laure, as everyone first thought. What could they possibly want there? They've been in the Void Beneath since the Cataclysm. The city didn't even exist when they were born."

There was no sound apart from the droning of the engines. Sal hadn't absorbed all the facts that had been thrust upon him in the previous hours. They were slippery, and didn't quite fit together. Shilly had explained that his father had been trying to rescue his mother from the Void. The twins Highson had summoned by mistake originated in a time before his world had even existed. This was worse than ghosts and golems. This just didn't make any *sense*.

"Maybe Highson isn't telling us everything."

"I don't know about that," said Abi Van Haasteren, "but I know what's waiting for us in Laure. The Magister has placed the people we left behind under house arrest and impounded our vehicles."

"All of them?" asked Skender.

Shilly nodded.

"Great. Now we're really stuck here."

"How do you know this?" Marmion asked.

"The quartermaster is an old friend. I called ahead to let him know that we were safe, and he gave me the news."

"I didn't know he was a Stone Mage," said Skender.

"He isn't. He studied at the Keep for a while when I was a student, then followed his own calling. The yadachi don't encourage other forms of Change-working in their city, but he always had a penchant for things that fly. They welcome his skills and tolerate his methods."

Sal didn't know who they were talking about, but put that mystery away with all the others. Someone would fill him in while they travelled.

"I guess we know what we're getting into, now," Shilly said. "The question is: what are we going to do about it?"

"We'll think of something," Marmion said, his expression dark and determined. "Just take us back to Laure as fast as possible, Chu. That's where the Homunculus is headed. The sooner we get there, the sooner we can sort this mess out, once and for all."

THE TRAP

> "The Change can be used for evil,
> but it is in itself neither good nor evil.
> Would one fault the morals of a stone, or
> cast blame upon the actions of the wind?"
> *THE BOOK OF TOWERS*, FRAGMENT 256

The return trip took much longer than when Skender and Chu had flown over with the wing. The heavy lifter was slower and loaded down to boot, so they barely outran Pirelius and the twins below. Skender found himself missing the forced intimacy of that first flight. Chu was kept busy constantly adjusting the trim of the heavy lifter. It took much more than just a raised arm or outstretched leg to bring it back on course. How she kept track of the many levers and handles he didn't know.

Noon came and went. When not attending to the winds ahead, he watched the ground creep by beneath them. Having been down there, he could better comprehend the scale of the wrinkles and cracks that seemed so minuscule from the air. He could also appreciate the mass and momentum of the man'kin migrations as they crawled like ant swarms along the Divide floor. He was heartily glad to be no longer within their reach.

From his elevated position, he could see that the migrations' dust trails were bending north, also heading for Laure. When he swivelled to quiz Mawson about it, he found the man'kin being interrogated by one of the wardens, who was frowning as most people did after talking to Mawson for too long.

"What do the man'kin want?" Skender asked into a break in the conversation.

"*We want the same thing you do*," said Mawson. "*To survive.*"

"But what can kill you, apart from a sledgehammer? You don't need to eat, drink, or breathe. You don't die of natural causes. The only disease I've ever known you to suffer from is mould."

"*We are mortal. We begin and therefore we must end.*"

"Is that why the untamed man'kin are afraid of the Homunculus?"

"*Yes.*"

"Could it kill *you?*"

"*It does, every time we fall under its shadow.*"

Skender nodded, wondering if he was beginning to appreciate the problem. When a man'kin became tangled in the wake of the twins, it ceased to be. That the man'kin returned to life when the twins moved on was irrelevant. For an awful time, a living mind was reduced to nothing. That would be worse than sleeping, worse even than the Void Beneath. Who wouldn't be afraid?

"What about the Angel?" he asked. "Can you tell me more about that?"

"*The Angel is necessary*," said Mawson, his heavy stone features wrinkling into a frown. "*It is the gathering point, the focus.*"

"Of what?"

"*Of us.*"

"Do you mean the man'kin, or humans, too?"

"*The Angel draws many kinds towards it. We will not all survive without it.*"

"Why not?"

"*Because the Angel is essential to our survival.*"

"Why?" he asked, even though he knew he would probably regret it.

"*Because without it we will not all survive.*"

He shook his head. Man'kin didn't see the world the way ordinary people did. Their sense of logic and causality wasn't so much circular as bound up in loops. They saw the future, past, and present all at once, but not just *one* discrete version of the future or the past. It depended, apparently, on which way they were looking—when "which way" had less to do with the orientation of their gaze than with what they were trying to see.

"Can you be any clearer than that?" he tried.

"*To me it is perfectly clear,*" said the stone bust with eyebrows raised. "*Your questions are as obtuse as ever.*"

"Skender!" called Chu. "Stop chatting and get those eyes of yours pointing forward."

Skender did as he was told. "What?"

"See anything unusual?"

He looked around, studying the flow of the wind. The heavy lifter was nearing the Wall. The currents were chaotic there, but for the moment the dirigible was in no danger.

He looked behind them and saw nothing out of the ordinary there, either. Pirelius and the twins had taken to a creek bed, as he and Sal had. That he couldn't see them was no cause for alarm; at least one warden watched them at all times, tracing their every movement via a telescope focused on the Divide floor. He was sure he would've heard if something had gone astray.

"No, why?"

Her stare challenged him to try again. "What about the other flyers?"

"What about them? They're—" He stopped in midsentence, realising then what she was hinting at. "They're gone! What happened to them? Where did they go?"

"They flew away."

"Why?"

"I don't know, and I don't like it." Chu gripped a lever tightly in both hands. "Keep an eye out. I think something's up."

He agreed. Without the mocking calls of Kazzo and his buddies, the sky had fallen eerily silent. Chu seemed apprehensive as she worked the controls, which he could understand. Casting her lot with the Sky Wardens had seen her wing returned, but now she was tangled up in their messy quest. She had helped them cross the Divide and steal the heavy lifter; if they were in trouble with the Magister, so was she.

Her nervousness was infectious. Skender kept his gaze moving, looking everywhere for anything out of the ordinary as the charm-painted Wall grew steadily larger ahead.

"I wish we could just fly away," he told her, feeling a sudden and almost overpowering urge to be reckless. "Leave everything behind and keep on going."

"Why don't we?" she responded, adjusting the heavy lifter's trim with a deft tug on the controls before her.

"Marmion would freak, for a start, and Dad would be unhappy if I left the buggy behind. How much fuel does this thing have, anyway? My home is a long way away from here."

"Let's go to the Hanging Mountains instead," she said. "To hell with Marmion. We could just dump him and run."

Chu's grin told him she didn't expect him to take her seriously. He didn't doubt, though, that the sentiment was an honest one, and he was genuinely tempted by it. He had rescued his mother; the twins were irrelevant. What else did he have to hang around for?

The suggestion drew his gaze to the northeast, where the grey wall of mountains seemed to hang on the edge of visibility. A shelf of white cloud obscured the largest peak, like a single blossom on a stunted branch. He wondered what the fog forests and the balloon cities really looked like.

Reality intruded in the form of turbulence as they entered the complicated airspace over the city. He laughed at himself and his notions. First a date, then an adventure that practically amounted to elopement? Yeah, right. If the Magister kicked Chu out of the city or made life too uncomfortable for her to stay, *then* maybe she'd leave, but not before. While she had a shot at getting a licence, she would stay exactly where she was.

Thinking of the licence reminded him that he had a job to do. The heavy lifter rocked as the winds around them surged and roiled. Skender gave Chu an update on the currents ahead, and she adjusted course, aiming roughly for Observatory Tower, where she had unsuccessfully tried to steal eagle eggs. When he next looked at her, her grin had faded.

The gondola shuddered more strongly than before. A puff of cold brushed Skender's cheek.

"This feels wrong," said Chu.

"Your bones again?"

"Yes. Are you *sure* you can't see anything?"

He couldn't honestly be sure. The wind tumbled around them, looking much the same as before, but he wasn't as familiar with the ways of the city as she was. He could be missing the obvious.

A splash of red caught his eye in the city below. He looked down, through the wind. One of the city's weather-workers, the yadachi, stood on a pole, arms outstretched and mouth open. The crimson-robed figure appeared to be staring right at them.

The sight accompanied another gust of wind. Skender shivered. A second yadachi became visible to his left, also with arms outstretched. The weather-worker's mouth hung open, wailing an endless prayer to the sky for clemency.

Or for something else entirely, Skender thought. The heavy lifter rocked violently as a new force struck it from the side. Skender hung on tight. The gondola swayed violently, prompting cries of alarm.

"What was that?" Chu yelled, wrestling with the controls.

"The yadachi! They're doing something to us!" That he couldn't see it didn't prove him wrong. The yadachi had made his licence using the sample of blood he had given them, so presumably they knew how to interfere with it from a distance. Again the gondola bounced. "We have to land!"

Marmion came forward through the crowded gondola, steadying himself against the increasing turbulence with every step. "Your mother reports that the hangar is guarded," he said. "If we try to land there, we'll be arrested immediately."

"On what grounds?"

"We've been charged with trying to bring a man'kin into the city without permission. And we're guilty as charged."

Skender thought of Mawson. "Sure, but—how did they know about him?"

Chu scowled. "Kazzo must have told them, the little shit."

"However they knew," said Marmion, "it presents us with a problem. Is there somewhere else we can put down?"

The dirigible shook. The sky quaked. "Under this kind of attack? No. It's too risky. We could blow sideways and tear the bladder."

"What about Slaughter Square?" asked Skender.

"Not enough clear space there, either."

"So we just turn around and go back? Or give in?" Marmion's expression was grim. "I don't think so."

Chu thought for a moment as the many spires and towers of the city drifted by below. They looked very sharp.

"I suppose we don't need to land *as such*," she said. "Tell the quartermaster that if he doesn't want to see the heavy lifter damaged, he should meet us at the top of the armoury. We'll be there shortly."

"What does this mean?" asked Marmion.

"No backing out now," she said, so softly only Skender could hear her, then, more loudly: "Have the ropes ready. We'll be getting off soon."

Shilly hung on tightly as the gondola rattled around them. The sound of creaking wood and flapping canvas made it hard to talk, so she didn't quite know what was going on. The spars and stays of the dirigible were sparkling as though wet with dew. *That* she understood. Someone was using the Change against them. By the way Sal's hand tightened around hers, she could tell that he had noticed, too.

Sal's lips moved, and she leaned in closer to hear what he had said.

"Welcome to Laure," he repeated into her ear. "Are they always this friendly?"

"Wait until they come for the Blood Tithe," she said, showing him the small cut on her wrist. "They really know how to lay it on."

The heavy lifter descended in fits and starts, approaching the hangar it had departed from. The attack eased off as they grew nearer. The meaning was obvious: *do as we want and we'll give you less grief.*

Marmion took a message to Abi van Haasteren then relayed a reply back to Chu, but Shilly couldn't hear what was said. He also spoke to Banner, who began issuing orders among the other wardens.

"Get ready," Banner said to Shilly and Sal. "We're going to be using the rope ladders."

"Great." Her leg was still painful from the overexertion prior to their departure. The thought of having to go through all that again was an unhappy one. "This should be fun."

Her jaw clicked painfully shut when the heavy lifter lurched upwards and to the right, sending wardens staggering and clutching for handholds. The gondola tilted at a sharp angle for at least ten seconds before levelling out. The glimmer of the Change immediately brightened and a renewed battering hit the hull.

"Sorry about that!" called Chu from the front, barely audible over the dirigible's many complaints. "Just wanted to throw them off for a second. Now, get ready to move when I say so. We might not have long. And be careful! It's a long way to fall."

Shilly searched the buildings around them, wondering where they were headed. One stood out from the rest: a tall, blocky structure with what looked like ramps protruding from its summit. Several flyers swooping around it scattered as the heavy lifter approached.

"Oh, no," she breathed, realising what Chu had in mind. The heavy lifter couldn't land up there, but it could come close enough to allow people to disembark. Unless the turbulence kept up and Chu was unable to hold it completely steady . . .

A shadow fell over them. The light turned brown. She had barely enough time to recognise the signs and cover her face before the sandstorm hit. The city's weather-workers clearly had more in their arsenal than just air.

A barrage of choking and cursing filled the gondola. Shilly tried to peer out between slitted eyelids, but the onslaught was too intense. Stinging grains peppered her forehead and cheeks, reminding her of her dream of the buried shape in the dunes. She didn't know how Chu was supposed to see, let alone pilot the heavy lifter in to dock.

"Right!" shouted Sal, standing. "This is something I can help with!"

"Not too much," said Shilly, clutching his hand and keeping her face covered. "If we can't see out, that means they can't see in."

He squeezed back to show that he understood. Through their touching skins, she felt him gather his concentration to form an image in his mind. It was a simple one, based on a charm every weather-worker knew: two pairs of parallel lines crossing to make an X. But he had altered it to suit their needs. The end of its delicate lines curved inward around the central area like the fingers of a clutching hand.

"*Better this way,*" she said through the Change, showing him a subtle variation that would work even more effectively. "*Are you feeling up to it?*"

Instead of answering, he reached out to touch the world, and it instantly responded.

She felt a bubble open up around her. The sand and noise fell away, allowing her to breathe properly. Wiping grit from her eyelids, she blinked and looked around. She was standing in a sphere of clear air with Sal and Abi Van Haasteren's left leg. Sal flexed again, and the bubble expanded. She saw its edges sweep outwards into the swirling sand. Where the bubble reached, the storm instantly dissipated.

A third push saw the bubble encompass the entire heavy lifter. With one last shower of sand, the air was clear. Cries of relief and confusion rose up out of the storm's roar.

Shilly stood up to check the extent of the charm. Sal hadn't killed the storm completely; he had simply formed a quiet patch at its heart.

The wind still swirled around them, just outside the gondola. The sand hissed like a snake trying to get in, reminding her of something she had recently dreamed.

"Let's not sit here gawping!" she shouted, feeling the effort it was taking to maintain the charm against the combined will of all the yadachi. Sal's eyes were closed as he concentrated on maintaining the image in his mind. "We haven't got all day!"

The wardens kicked into action, rolling up ropes and readying themselves for the next step. Everything was covered with sand, prompting more than a few sneezes. Shilly's eyelids felt rough and raw.

Skender and Chu called for help with directions. The way ahead was completely obscured by the storm. Abi Van Haasteren moved painfully forward to lend her assistance: with Sal otherwise engaged and the heavy lifter back in Stone Mage territory, she and Skender were the only active Change-users in the gondola. Shilly could feel their wills probing through the storm like insect antennae, searching for their destination. It wasn't long before a shadow slid over the heavy lifter. They had reached the tower, safe and sound.

That wasn't the end of their trials, though. A giant, hairless man with ornate tattoos all over his scalp and upper body—the quartermaster, Shilly assumed—waved at them from the uppermost ramp. Chu guided the dirigible as close as she dared, and the wardens tossed out their ropes. The man caught them and tied them to rings at the edge of the platform. The heavy lifter strained against the ties as the sandstorm raged around it, but the knots held.

Shilly shook her head in denial as rope ladders followed the ties. The gap between gondola and platform might be only a few metres but there was no way she was going to be able to cross the distance, not with her leg still sore from the chase that morning.

The first warden went across as soon as a ladder was in place, stretched horizontally through empty air. She crabbed from rung to rung to the far side, swinging like a child on play equipment, apparently paying no mind at all to the drop beneath her. Another rope ladder followed, allowing wardens to disembark two at a time. The gondola rocked as the weight it bore steadily lessened. Tom clambered over with his eyes tightly shut, followed by Kemp. All too soon there was only Sal, Shilly, Marmion, Skender, and Chu left. Mawson had been bundled up in a rope sling and swung over like a side of beef. Chu's wing had gone the same way. Shilly would be cursed rather than suffer the same indignity. She shook her head violently when Marmion suggested it.

"We don't have time to argue, girl," he said, a gust of wind making his thin hair wave like seaweed.

"The rest of you go," she said, looking over the edge of the gondola. The storm hid any view of the ground, but she knew it was horribly far down. "I'll stay here with Chu."

"I'm going, too," the flyer called back. "The quartermaster will take the lifter away and put it down in the hangar to distract the yadachi. They're tracking Skender's licence, so the quartermaster will take that with him as well. If we stay here too long, they might figure out what we're up to."

Shilly felt a mixture of shame and anger, the latter directed firmly at herself. The plan made perfect sense. She was the one thing holding it up.

Because she couldn't bear the thought of being separated from Sal for another moment, she finally agreed. Skender and Marmion lashed a rope seat around her waist and thighs and gave her another rope to hold onto. Then she was being hauled across the gap with all the grace of a reluctant cow herded onto a cart. She hoped her eyes weren't as wide with fear as they felt.

Hands caught her on the far side and helped her to her feet. Skender followed with her walking stick, and he handed it to her as the last of the ropes around her fell away. Marmion came next. The quartermaster went to relieve Chu, allowing her to cross while he kept the dirigible stable. Then it was Sal's turn.

Shilly watched with concern as he climbed over the edge of the gondola and took hold of the ropes. His movements were slow and deliberate, so as not to break his concentration. Even so, the need to balance took its toll on the charm. Thick tendrils of sand curled around the dirigible with the sound of a brush fire, making him blink. He stopped halfway across, swaying, and it seemed for a moment as if distraction might get the better of him. Shilly put a hand over her mouth, wishing she could do something to help.

When he started moving again, it was all she could do not to cry out with relief and encouragement. One step, two steps, three—then finally he was within reach of the wardens. They hauled him to safety just as the bubble collapsed and the storm returned in full force.

"Cut it free!" The wardens took up Marmion's cry as Shilly gripped Sal's arm and hurried him away. She could feel the platform bucking under her as the weight of the dirigible pulled at it. "Cut it free!" Ropes snapped with twanging sounds. The heavy lifter's engine throbbed. She felt rather than saw it pull away. The last thing she saw were the propellers glowing like eyes, fading into the swirling sand.

They hurried off the platform before the sheltering storm dissipated. "This way!" Chu led them to a wide, wooden cage suspended over a steep drop by thick chains. When they were all inside, she pulled a lever and it began to descend. The sound of the wind and the stink of sand faded.

"What are we going to do next?" asked Skender. "The quartermaster won't fool them for long."

"When we reach the Black Galah, we'll split up," said Marmion. "Half of us will get the vehicles. The rest will break the others out of house arrest."

Shilly wasn't thinking that far ahead. "I'll just be glad when I have solid ground back under my feet." The cage was moving too slowly for her liking. She imagined them sinking into a ring of city guards like turkeys in a cage, ready for the chop.

The fear proved to be groundless. The base of the tower was deserted, the only sound the eerie, distant wail of the yadachi.

"The atmospherics have scared everyone off," said Chu. "No one in their right mind would come anywhere near here right now."

They bundled from the cage and out into the street. Shilly shook gritty sand from her robes and hair. The heart of the storm was swinging away, following the heavy lifter. Echoes of the yadachi's wailing song shifted and faded around them, a constant, ululating background. The confines of the city seemed especially close after the endless vistas of the sky.

"I'll just slow you all down," she said as Marmion gathered the wardens together. "You go ahead. I'll catch up."

"I'm not leaving you here alone," said Sal.

"I didn't mean *you*." She took his arm. "You're staying to keep me company."

"Me, too," said Skender. "You'll need me to show you the way."

"Then I'll have to stay, too," said Chu, hefting her end of the wing.

"No," said Marmion. "I need someone to give us directions, too, and we have plenty of spare hands. Tom can help you carry the wing."

"But—"

"Chu, please. The fewer stragglers, the better. We may have to leave in a hurry."

Skender's mother looked like she might argue as well, but Marmion was making sense. Even Shilly had to admit it.

There was no time for farewells as the wardens hurried off, furrow-browed Shom Behenna bringing up the rear. The odd bunch moved as one, driven by grim determination. So much was left undone: the Caduceus, Pirelius, the Homunculus, Highson Sparre. A handful of outsiders versus an entire city. If Marmion thought it was hopeless, he didn't let it show.

Chu looked over her shoulder at Skender, her expression unreadable, then she rounded a corner and was gone.

THE ALARUM

**"In the flickering flame and the crumbling stone,
in the stagnant water and air turned stale,
we perceive the end that awaits us all."**
THE BOOK OF TOWERS, FRAGMENT 110

The three of them stood for a moment in the streets of Laure. It occurred to Sal that it was the first time they had been alone in one place since the Haunted City. He felt fourteen again, just for a moment. They looked awkwardly at each other, waiting for someone to take the lead.

The sound of booted feet approaching snapped him out of it.

"I think that's our cue."

"Right behind you, Skender," said Shilly.

"Okay. Along here should do for a start."

They hurried across the street and ducked down an alley lined with vases full of dead plants and painted-over windows. Sand pooled in the corners and drains. Sal called up a mnemonic he hadn't used since leaving Fundelry, one designed to divert attention from them, if they didn't move quickly enough.

"You came this way before?" Shilly asked, the two-step rhythm of her gait echoing off the brick walls.

"Not exactly, but don't worry. I've seen the city from the air. It's all in my head now. And this way we avoid the yadachi."

Sal allowed Skender's point. The longer they could keep the red-robed bloodworkers off their back, the better.

They took a left at the end of the alley and then an immediate right. The clouds parted and the sun appeared. Shadows lengthened as the day aged and the yadachi's song eased. The sky to the east remained brown. Sal could hear the storm howling in the distance. He was glad to be out of it, and even gladder to be no longer fighting it. Breaking was easier than creating—undoing the work of the yadachi took a lighter toll on him than had whipping up the brief flurry in the Divide that had saved him and Skender from falling to their deaths—but he still felt the cost of it. Something at the core of him was drained, as though his bones had gone soft. Maintaining the small concealment charm took an effort.

They hurried through the streets. Citizens gradually reappeared, people coming out to sweep off steps or wipe dust from windows. They gave the strangers in their midst no more than a quick glance. A chained guard dog barked at them from a fenced-off yard, making Skender jump. Two dark-skinned children with hair in plaits waved at them from an open doorway, and Shilly waved back.

Skender had taken off the licence in the heavy lifter. The tattoos on his arms and face had dwindled back to nothing. His eyes had returned to their normal colour. His ochre robes remained ragged and his face bruised, but the lack of obvious Change-working made him slightly less conspicuous.

"So, tell us about your girlfriend," Shilly said to him, prompting a look of panic.

"Girlfriend? What? Did Chu say something to you about that?"

"No."

"Oh." A flurry of conflicting emotions passed over his features. "Right."

Shilly couldn't hide her enjoyment at his reaction. "How did you meet?"

Skender told her the story Sal was already familiar with: that he had been rescued by Chu from the tunnels under Laure and agreed to help her get her licence back. Sal listened with amusement. Just like Skender of old, always getting into tight spots and requiring help to get out of them. It didn't sound like he was having much luck with his side of the deal.

"Did your father really send you here?" Shilly asked. "I can't imagine him letting you out of his sight again."

Skender shrugged. "He's the same as ever. A bit older, and grey around the edges with it. But he's stuck in the Keep; the only way we'll get him out is on a bier. Someone had to come help Mum, so it had to be me."

There was an undercurrent of uncertainty. The decision had obviously been harder than he made out.

"You know," he said to Sal, "I didn't tell you this earlier, but I brought that old buggy of yours. Do you remember it?"

Remember it? thought Sal. He had spent half his life in it. "Sure. How's it running?"

"Like a dream. It's in the garage of the Black Galah. You can take it for a drive, if you like, later."

Sal feigned enthusiasm, although the thought of the old buggy brought back memories of the death of his adopted father, and of Shilly's accident. And he wasn't cheered by the news that it was in the Galah's garage—it had probably been impounded along with the Wardens' vehicles.

A quartet of guards came towards them up the street. Shilly waved the three of them into an alcove, where Sal tightened the weave of the charm around them.

The guards ran on by without a glance, the sound of their boots fading into the background wailing of the yadachi.

"They were definitely looking for someone," whispered Sal.

"How do you think the others are doing?" Shilly responded.

"Fine, as long as Marmion hasn't started shooting his mouth off."

"So they're screwed," said Skender, pulling them out from cover. "Come on. We're not even halfway."

They hurried along the street. Sal was acutely conscious of the day passing. What with the slow crossing of the Divide and the time it was taking to rejoin Marmion, anything could be happening to the Homunculus. The longer it took them to work out how to rescue it, the guiltier he felt.

"Whatever happened to Lodo?" asked Skender. "I haven't heard anything since we closed the Way to Fundelry on you."

There was a long silence. Sal didn't know whether to answer for Shilly or to let her say it.

"He died," she said, examining the cobblestones passing beneath her feet.

"I'm sorry." Skender looked uncomfortable.

"It's not your fault. You couldn't have known."

That was the truth. There had been many times Sal would have liked to contact Skender, but the distance between them had been a considerable obstacle, and security was an ongoing concern. Although mail did travel from the Strand to the Interior, there was no guarantee that letters wouldn't be opened or their origins traced. A similar risk applied to calling through the Change; crossing such a large distance would take enormous energy, and such efforts were not easily hidden.

"It's hard to believe it's been so long," Skender said. And there it was, the *other* hard truth. He wasn't fourteen any more. Time had passed, and all three of them had changed with it. Waiting for things to be the same as last time was inviting disappointment.

"Lots of things have happened," said Sal. "We've put a lot of stuff behind us."

"But not everything. I mean, you two are looking so good. I always hoped it would work out for you, and it obviously has."

"How's that?" asked Shilly. "We're in the same mess as you, remember."

"But you're together. That's the way it's supposed to be. You were *destined*."

Shilly made the same noise she had five years earlier, whenever that notion had been raised. "That doesn't make it any easier, believe me. We may look good now, but it hasn't always been like this. We've argued and broken up and sworn we'd never talk to each other again, just like any other couple."

Skender looked incredulous. "Really?"

"Of course. Wait until you've been with someone as long as us. Then you'll know what it's like to have scars no one else can see."

Sal could tell that Skender was disappointed. He understood that. Love wasn't supposed to be painful, and in the stories Sal had been told as a kid it didn't seem to be. Yet there were times he'd thought that, if he'd known just how vulnerable it would make him, he might have stayed in the Haunted City with Highson and devoted himself to a life of celibacy.

He was glad he hadn't.

"It's worth it," he said, clapping a hand on Skender's shoulder. "Believe me. Shilly's just trying to give you a scare. Don't let anyone talk you out of something like this—least of all yourself."

"Thanks." Skender looked equal parts relieved and terrified.

"I agree," said Shilly, "and maybe it'll be Chu—even though that'd mean you're *really* following in your father's footsteps."

"What?"

"Oh, you know. He's not exactly the adventurous type, is he—and who did he marry? A Surveyor. I bet they see each other, what, once or twice a year? Now you're flirting with a flyer from the other side of the Interior. It's a recipe for exactly the same disaster."

Skender looked aghast. "I didn't . . ." he stammered. "I mean, that is—"

"Wait." Sal held up his hand. Behind their conversation, the song of the yadachi had changed. Instead of the usual wailing tune, the weather-workers had adopted a newer, more complex tonality that called and echoed across the rooftops. Rhythms developed in one place then faded, only to spring up again in another, far removed from the first. Intricate counterpoints wove through the towers like tangled threads. "Listen."

"I hear it," said Skender, his head cocked. "It sounds like they're talking."

"Maybe they are," said Sal, scanning the sky visible from street level. Nowhere did he see the blood-red robes of the city's weather-workers. "Are you sure they couldn't have seen us?"

"No," said Shilly. "This has nothing to do with us."

As she said the words, a strange new noise rose up over the city. It sounded like a giant cow lowing, but its pitch was much too deep to come from a living throat. Its volume increased until Sal could practically feel the air vibrating.

"What is it?" asked Skender, his hands over his ears.

Shilly shook her head in confusion as more tones joined the cacophony. Sal realised then that it was giant horns blowing, sounding powerful calls over the city. There was no melody or beat, just one growing chord containing notes high and low, as dissonant as a hundred voices yelling at once.

People ran by with looks of fright on their faces. Skender grabbed one and repeated his question.

"What is it?"

"The alarum," came the reply from a thick-moustached man with flour on his hands. "It only sounds when the city is in danger!"

"From what?"

"The man'kin are attacking!" The baker hurried off and ran into a house on the next corner. The sound of his door slamming was audible along the street.

"Man'kin attacking?" Skender looked puzzled. "The Magister wouldn't raise such a panic over Mawson, would she?"

"I very much doubt it." Sal thought of the man'kin migrations in the Divide and the way the Aad had been taken apart, and he shivered.

Shilly looked up the street then back the way they had come. Her expression was one of deep concern. "I think we need to find out what's going on outside."

"When we catch up with the others—"

"We'll probably be arrested." She studied Skender a moment. "You've got the city map in your head, right?" He nodded. "There must be a way onto the Wall. I bet we can see everything from up there."

Skender looked uncertain. "I don't know, Shilly. If the man'kin are really attacking, then the Wall is the *last* place we want to be."

"That depends on how you look at it." She glanced at Sal, who nodded. "Standing here all day isn't going to help anyone, that's for sure."

"All right." Skender thought for a moment, rubbing a hand through his thick brown hair. His fingers left brown smudges on pale skin. "Yes. Let's keep going the way we were for a bit, and then take a right instead of a left. That should put us on the right road."

"How far?" she asked.

"A fair hike. Half an hour's walk at least."

Shilly irritably tapped the ground with the tip of her cane. "Too long."

"We could hail a lift," Sal suggested. "Do you have any local money, Skender?"

Skender turned out his pockets, resulting in barely enough spare change for a game of two-up.

"It's okay," he said in the face of their disappointment. There was more than a hint of resignation in his voice. "I know what to do."

"A Stone Mage?" Shilly said in disbelief as the cab rattled its way through the streets of Laure. "They'll believe anything here, obviously."

"Well, I *am* a Mage," said Skender defensively. "Almost."

"And I'm *almost* sure that charm you performed was just an illusion. What happens when our driver realises you've cheated him?"

Skender shushed her in case the man steering the cab heard her over the combined racket of the alarum and the engine. "Yes, that's all true. But he wanted proof, and it was the best I could think of. Hopefully he'll be well away from us when it wears off."

Skender avoided Sal's speculative gaze and tried to get comfortable on the worn leather seat. In lieu of a fare, the driver had wanted a charm to fix a spreading bald spot. Lacking time for the usual restorative tattoos—which rarely worked anyway—Skender had simply fooled him into feeling hair where there wasn't any. It wouldn't be long before his fingertips revealed the trick.

And now, somehow, Shilly had made him feel *guilty* about it.

He forced himself to concentrate on their travel instead. The cab was rattling through side streets toward the outskirts of the city, where it had been built up along the sides of the Divide. The Wall itself was sacrosanct, as far as development was concerned; no one built there. Every other surface around it was encrusted with housing blocks and apartments, all craning for a better view over the city. Remains of the original settlement, the Old City that had subsided after the coming of the Divide, were visible among the newer buildings: stubby, round-edged structures with slits for windows and low roofs. From a distance, a strange mould seemed to have covered the ochre stone from top to bottom in squiggly patterns.

Skender was glad they hadn't walked. The roads were increasingly winding and steep—a fact he hadn't truly appreciated from the air. They hung on to straps and each other as the cab's spluttering alcohol engine strained to maintain walking pace up the steepest stretches. Skender stuck his head out at one point to look back the way they had come. The expanse of the city lay below them, smudged brown in the wake of the sandstorm. The heavy lifter was nowhere to be seen. Only a couple of flyers circled over the towers, braving the aftershocks of the unnatural weather. Skender didn't envy them.

"Any word from Marmion?" Shilly asked.

Sal shook his head. He had tried to contact the warden through the Change to let him know what they were doing, but Marmion either couldn't or wouldn't reply. When they tried Skender's mother, her response had been curt.

"Can't talk. Yadachi waiting for us at the hostel. Keep your eyes open, and don't worry."

They were on their own. Skender's doubts rose sharply. Obeying his mother's request was going to be difficult, if not impossible. What those bloodsuckers were doing with her and Chu and the rest of the wardens just didn't bear thinking about.

The cab squeaked to a halt three-quarters of the way along a service road leading to the top of the Wall, the driver protesting that he dared go no further while the alarum was sounding. Skender thanked him as they got out and stretched their legs. His tailbone was numb from the constant bouncing. Shilly mimed brushing, as of an errant fringe, and the driver gratefully mimicked her actions, thinking he was adjusting his new locks. She gave him a thumbs-up, then turned and shot daggers at Skender.

"I give in," he said as the cab spluttered back down the hill. "I'll send him the proper fee later."

"How?"

"His registration number was on the dash. There'll be records somewhere."

"Good enough." She pointed up the road with her cane. "Let's keep moving."

They hurried up the steep slope, the powerful lowing of the alarum goading them on. "I don't know what you think we're going to do up here," he said, daunted by the height. It felt like weeks since he and Chu had retrieved the wing from storage at the very base of the Wall. "Dropping rocks on their heads isn't going to bother man'kin terribly much."

"It might make them think twice."

"It might just make them angrier."

"If you're not careful, I'll drop *you* on them instead." She tugged at the curls of her short hair, taking her frustration out on herself. "Honestly, Skender, I don't know what else to do. But I know I'm not going to just sit around and wait for someone else to fix the problem. It's not that I don't trust the Magister to do it right—it's just that I don't trust her to do it *well*. If you know what I mean."

Skender thought he did. The sharp-taloned woman occupying the throne of Laure was bound to have numerous tricks up her black sleeve. That only made him more nervous. He was certain she wouldn't lose any sleep if a couple of out-of-towners got caught in the crossfire.

"Hold up," said Sal as they rounded a corner. The way ahead was blocked by a heavy gate and several Laurean guards looking menacing in their uniforms.

"A welcoming committee," said Skender.

"I think not." Shilly barely broke step. The guards arranged themselves in a line across the gate as the trio approached, their expressions a mixture of cautiousness and forbidding determination.

"Stop right there," said the leader, a broad-shouldered woman with a red fringe poking out from under her close-fitting helmet.

"It's okay," said Shilly, coming to a halt in front of her. "We're only here to observe."

"No one's allowed through. It could be dangerous."

"We can look after ourselves."

"Spare me the arguments. I've heard them all before."

"This happens every day, does it?" Shilly didn't back down from the guard's unblinking regard. "We might be able to help."

"How?"

"I'm not going to lie and tell you we're something we're not," she said with a glance at Skender, "but we're more capable than we look."

"You'd have to be."

"And someone we know is out there, in the Divide. Don't we at least have the right to find out if he's okay? You can come with us if you want to make sure we're not up to no good. Give us a break, will you?"

Behind the guard's bluff demeanour, Skender thought he detected a hint of uncertainty. But orders were orders, and she clearly intended to follow them.

"Sorry. You'll have to leave. Come back after the emergency is over and you can have a look around."

"Listen," said Shilly, taking a step forward and poking at the woman's breastplate with her right index finger, "if you think we're just a bunch of stupid tourists with nothing better to do than—"

Strident honking and the chugging of an engine behind them interrupted her. Skender turned to see a battered two-seater cab approaching along the road. A blond youth hung out of the passenger side, waving a flat leather case in one hand. The driver stopped honking when it was clear he had gained the guards' attention, and slid to a gravelly halt in front of them.

The youth hopped out of the vehicle and hurried to where the guards stood in his path.

"Make way, make way!" he yelled, producing a piece of paper from the case and thrusting it into the face of the woman confronting Shilly—the guard blinked, startled, and took it from him. "My name is Gwil Flintham and I come with the authority of the Magister! These people are to have the run of the Wall. They are not to be interfered with. Is that understood?"

"Uh—" The guard frowned at the form, with the regal seal of Laure prominent at top and centre. Skender didn't have time to read what it said—it was snatched back too quickly—but it had the desired effect. "I guess you'd better go through, then."

She gestured and her contingent of guards fell back. The gate swung open with a deep groan.

"Thank you," said the mysterious Gwil Flintham with a short nod. "Wait here. We'll call if we need anything."

Skender kept his lips carefully buttoned as they bustled through the checkpoint. He could feel the eyes of the guards on them. Only when the gate clanged shut and he was certain they were out of earshot did he dare whisper to Shilly, "Who is this guy? Do you know him?"

She made introductions with an amused gleam in her eye. Gwil Flintham, former gatekeeper and recently assigned to keep an eye on Marmion and his gang, looked as though he couldn't decide whether to faint or crow with delight.

"When we received word from you," he explained as they walked the last hundred metres to the top of the Wall, "Marmion didn't know what to do. Yadachi were waiting for him and everyone at the Galah. The Magister herself was on her way to deal with them; it looked pretty bad. Still did, when I last saw. But we couldn't leave you out here on your own. You wouldn't get very far without the right kind of authorisation, and I was the only one who could leave the hostel. So I faked the paperwork and came after you."

"Thank you," said Sal.

"My pleasure." The gatekeeper's eyes were wide and his cheeks were bright pink splotches in otherwise pale skin.

"We'd better move quickly. If the guards back there check on us, we'll be in big trouble."

"We're going as fast as we can," said Sal.

"I know. But still . . ."

They came to a series of broad stone steps that wound backwards and forwards up to the top of the Wall. Natural rock blended by degrees into massive, granite slabs that could well have outlasted the Cataclysm. By the time Skender reached the summit of the stairs, he was in awe of the masons responsible. Each corner was carved with a delicacy that belied the weight of the slabs; the seams were almost invisible, such was the perfection of every edge. Tiny, ornate seals no larger than his thumbprint had been carved into the centre of each block. Time hadn't worn them away, but the meaning of the complex figures eluded him.

The view from the top was spectacular. The Wall curved ahead of

him, a graceful arc isolating that corner of the Divide from the rest as
effectively as a dam. To his left were the towers of the city, reaching
upward for the sky, and to the right was a red and gold wasteland. Two
parallel handrails ran along the top of the Wall, protecting pedestrians
from a fatal misstep. Gwil unhesitatingly led the visitors between
them. A fitful wind snatched at Skender's robe, making him acutely
conscious of where he put his feet.

This is stupid, he told himself. *I've climbed cliffs higher than this in the
middle of the night. There's nothing to be afraid of.*

But there was, and he knew it. Back home, the cliffs were natural,
not built; there were plenty of handholds; and falling was the only
thing to worry about. In Laure, there were hordes of man'kin at the
bottom making angry sounds that vibrated through the stone and up
his calves.

He hugged the right-hand rail and peered as far over the edge as
he dared. The air below was hazy with dust and difficult to see
through, but he glimpsed enough to be certain. The stony mass that
milled at the base of the Wall was larger than all the previous migrations put together, and more were on their way. The crowd stretched
as far as he could see, and in it he saw no sign of Pirelius and the twins.

"Why?" he asked, wondering if the vibration he felt beneath his
feet really came from the horde below. "What are they doing here?"

"They don't like us," said Gwil. "They never have."

"But why *now*?"

"I don't know."

Skender remembered what Mawson had said about the man'kin in
the ruins. "Maybe their success in the Aad has gone to their heads.
They've come to free the stones they think you're imprisoning in Laure
and the Wall."

"How? The charms painted on the Wall aren't the only defences we
have. The stones themselves are charmed, just like the gate some of you
came through yesterday."

Shilly stopped to examine a tiny sigil carved into one of the giant slabs. Her fingers softly caressed the ancient grey stone. "You're right," she said, "but why would the builders do that?"

She reached out a hand to steady herself as the Wall jolted beneath her. Skender staggered and grabbed the nearest handrail for balance. The hollering of the man'kin rose up over the howling of the alarum.

"What's going on?" asked Gwil.

"I think," Shilly said, "that coming up here might have been a very bad idea."

"What?" Skender couldn't hide the panic in his voice. "It was your idea in the first place."

"Well, I've changed my mind."

"Why?"

"The man'kin are talking—talking to the stones."

Sal knelt next to Shilly. Instead of helping her to her feet, he put one hand flat against the stone, as she had.

Skender gripped the rail tighter as another rolling wave spread through the Wall. His palms tingled where they touched the rail. He felt disoriented, confused. His voice seemed to come from a very long way away, swallowed up in the roar of the man'kin like a bush in a landslide. "What are they saying?"

"I don't know yet," said Shilly, "but whatever it is, the stones are listening."

THE WALL

"Only the very brave and the very mad
find no fault in their actions."
THE BOOK OF TOWERS, EXEGESIS 4:11

Shilly saw it perfectly in her mind. She didn't need the Change to enhance her natural vision; the Wall was crawling with it. All she had to do was touch the stone and reality came crashing in on her.

People didn't build doors out of glass because it was brittle and would shatter at a solid blow. Doors were made of wood, which was flexible and able to absorb an impact.

It was the same with the Wall. Stone was strong and heavy but not terribly flexible. If struck hard enough, it, too, would shatter. For a wall on the scale of the one protecting Laure, built to resist an enemy more powerful than the average battering ram, shattering was a real risk. If all the stones were bound together as one, joined into a single, rigid shield, there was a small—but not zero—risk of someone striking it just the right way to bring it down. Even the repeated cycle of night and day could cause it to crack and split.

The solution lay in the sigil beneath her hand. She could read the truth of it in the way the stones nestled against each other, even if she couldn't decipher the signs themselves. They were bound together, linked by the charms, but not permanently. There was some give in the joins. They could flex and shift as necessary. The determining of that necessity was not left up to the architects, who knew that time might allow such knowledge to fall into disuse and disappear. That ability was imparted to the stones themselves.

Shilly understood this in a flash. It made sense, and it matched what she felt beneath her fingertips, and through the Change.

The stones were alive, and they could move.

The voices of the man'kin had a strident, hypnotic rhythm.

A shudder knocked her feet out from under her, sending her sprawling onto her backside. Sal fared no better. Gwil yelped like a puppy as he danced to keep his balance. Skender clung to the handrail for grim life.

It was too late for them to run. They could only hang on and hope. The clamour of the man'kin and the wailing of the alarum were lost under the grind and groan of shifting rock. Shilly squeezed her eyes shut. She tried not to wonder what it would be like to fall to her death or to die in an avalanche—or both at once, as was likely when the Wall collapsed. Each time the stone beneath her lurched, she expected the world to drop out from beneath her and the end to begin.

Sal's hand found hers and gripped tight. She heard a keening sound and realised that it came from her own throat.

Not long enough, she wanted to shout. The unfairness of death gripped her. *I'm too young to die!*

Then the turbulence began to ease. The rocking and swaying settled down to a trembling vibration, as though the Wall was quivering with exhaustion. The sound of stone sliding against stone ceased.

She dared to open her eyes.

The first thing she saw was a heavy lifter riding the wind high above her, its polished wood catching the bright sunlight. A crimson standard hung from the front of the gondola, and she knew that the Magister was aboard.

Reconnoitring, she wondered, *or fleeing?* There was no way to tell.

The second thing she saw was Sal's face leaning over her. His lips moved, but her ears were so numbed by the clamour of moving stone that it took them a moment to hear what he was saying.

"Are you hurt? Can you stand up?"

She didn't know, but she tried. The surface of the Wall was still shaking, but not so much that she couldn't keep her balance. Sal's hand stayed in hers. When she was upright she embraced him tightly, feeling shocked and overwhelmed that they were still alive. The Wall *should* have come down. There was no knowing why it had not.

"What happened?" she asked, putting a hand to her temple. "Did the man'kin stop?"

Sal edged closer to the outer edge of the Wall, where Skender stood, peering carefully over.

"They're doing something down there, that's for sure." Skender's expression was as disbelieving as her own. The bruise on his cheek stood out starkly against deathly pale skin. "And look—there's someone we know."

He pointed down into the vast crowd of stony shapes. A clear patch stood out right on its edge, a space in which the man'kin refused to tread. It took Shilly a moment to understand what she was seeing.

"The Homunculus!"

"And Pirelius," Sal added, identifying the second person in the bubble. The Homunculus's wake stretched behind it like a ribbon, winding across creek beds and craterous holes in the Divide floor. There was no sign of Kail.

Before she could ask where the tracker might be, the sound of running feet rose up over the alarum. Shilly looked back the way they had come and saw at least thirty armed guards sprinting towards them.

There was nowhere to hide and no point trying to run. Shilly straightened, forming a tripod out of her legs and her stick to maintain balance on the trembling stone. She had no intention of moving just because someone told her to.

"What in the Goddess's name are you four doing up here?" shouted the leader, a different one to the woman they had deceived at the gate.

"We're acting under the authority of the Magister," Gwil began, raising his briefcase.

"That doesn't matter. You have to get out of here. It's not safe."

"Why not? The Wall hasn't come down. The man'kin have been repelled. Haven't they?"

The guard didn't waste time replying. A suspicion that Gwil's supposition—and Shilly's own—might be deeply flawed began to dawn on her. The guards hadn't come to arrest them. Most of them ran right past them to take up stations along the Wall's northern edge, not facing out to where the man'kin waited, but inward, towards the city. They looked down.

Only then did she realise that the calling of the man'kin was coming from *both* sides of the Wall, not just the outside.

"Oh, no," she said, limping across the top of the Wall and looking down. Rooftops and spires clustered around the Wall for much of its length. The base was almost invisible.

"There!" cried one of the guards, pointing down. A cloud was rising from under a ramp leading to a warehouse that had seen better days. Through a gap in the woodwork, she glimpsed a stream of dark shapes moving into the city.

The guards ran to join the one who had shouted. From packs slung over their shoulders they produced golden, glassy spheres, which they lobbed down on the man'kin. Flashes of light blossomed where they struck. The stone creatures roared.

Shilly's knuckles turned white as they gripped the rail. The spheres operated on the same principle as the trap she and Sal had planted outside the workshop in the dunes. Light, stored and amplified in the crystalline lattice of the glass, found explosive release when that glass was shattered. Man'kin weren't flesh and blood, but they weren't invulnerable, either. Stone bodies blew apart in the brilliant explosions; others lost limbs or faces.

And they weren't the only casualties. Each flash of light brought down walls and sent bricks flying. The area appeared to have been evacuated—sensible, she supposed, given the Wall was under attack—but she still worried that someone would get hurt. Anyone still down there was likely to be blown to bits if the man'kin didn't pulverise them first.

From her elevated viewpoint, she could see more guards converging through the city streets. Some leapt across the rooftops to attack from higher ground. They fired golden globes with slingshots, sending them arcing high overhead to fall in the midst of the man'kin. More stone flew. More buildings collapsed. The air was full of the sound of devastation.

"They tunnelled!" said Skender over the racket. Shilly couldn't blame him for not grasping the situation straightaway. The man'kin didn't need to bring down the Wall to get into the city. All they had to do was rearrange the stone blocks comprising the Wall so they could walk right through it. She kicked herself for not seeing it earlier.

"We have to stop them," she said, crossing back to the far side to look down at where the man'kin were swarming into the tunnel mouth. She could see it clearly, now she knew it was there. It looked like little more than a shadow on the base of the Wall, but stone figures were going into it and not coming out again.

"Hey, you!" she yelled at the guards. "Try on this side! You'll have better luck hitting them, and do less damage to the city."

The leader of the guards saw the sense of that, and ordered his troops to do as she said. Soon the golden globes were falling in graceful arcs through clear air straight into the swarming masses of man'kin. It didn't seem to deter them. They clawed their way forward. Nothing was going to turn them back.

"This is useless," Shilly said, turning to Sal. "We have to close the tunnel somehow."

"There's only one way," he said, nodding further out into the Divide. "The Homunculus won't be able to close the hole, but it could plug it well enough."

"Yes!" She gripped his arm with excitement. His plan would work if only they could put the Homunculus in position quickly enough. But how to get word to Pirelius?

Someone else was obviously thinking along the same lines. The heavy lifter she had noticed before was moving across the sea of man'kin towards the clear spot Pirelius occupied. A blue-robed figure leaned over the side, waving.

Shilly squinted. "Who does that look like to you?" she asked Sal. He didn't reply.

"Sal?" She turned to look at him. His eyes were hollow. He didn't see her. "Sal, are you all right?"

Sal was elsewhere.

"*I know you're out there,*" he sent through the Change. With senses other than the usual five, he probed the complicated topography of the Divide and felt a flicker of the mind he was looking for. "*If you're out there, you can hear me.*"

"*Loud and clear,*" Kail responded. The tracker's mental voice was weary but firm. "*Is that you on top of the Wall?*"

"*Yes. Where are you? I can't see you. You're not in the wake, otherwise we wouldn't be able to talk.*"

"*Where I am isn't important. What's happening is . . .*"

Sal's extra senses shifted, and suddenly he was experiencing the Divide through Kail's eyes and ears. The vision was a pale echo of reality, one painted on top of the view he was actually seeing, but clear.

Pirelius was stumbling over the rough ground, his eyes darting at the man'kin all around him. He drove the Homunculus on with the knife pressed firmly in its back. The Homunculus walked with both heads down, letting itself be shoved, edges blurry and indistinct. The man'kin throng snarled and badgered them from outside their protective bubble. Pirelius ignored them. Bizarrely, he seemed to be singing.

"Cannon to the right of them,
cannon to the left of them,
cannon in front of them—"

"Pirelius!" called a voice from above. "You have to listen to us!"

Pirelius waved a beefy fist at the sky and kept lurching onward. Heavy stone feet had thoroughly churned the ground they walked upon. Ahead, Laure loomed. Sal could see himself at the top of the Wall, near the guards dropping globes down on the man'kin. An artificial storm raged at the bottom of the Wall. Light flashed and thunder rolled. Clouds of dust rose up, dark and ominous. The beginnings of night spread across the floor of the Divide as the sun faded into the west.

"Boldly they rode and well,
Into the jaws of Death,
Into the mouth of Hell—"

"Pirelius! We need your help!"

Kail's eyes lifted, giving Sal a glimpse of the heavy lifter descending over the fugitive and his hostage, testing the edges of the wake. Sal was surprised to recognise Marmion hanging over the edge of the gondola.

"She says you'll be well paid!"

Pirelius barked a vinegary laugh and kept singing.

From outside the vision Sal felt a hand tugging at his arm. It was Shilly, trying to attract his attention.

"Are you all right? What's going on?"

He did his best to focus on her. "I've found Kail. He's showing me what's going on down there."

"Is that Marmion with the Magister?"

"Yes."

"What's *he* doing there?"

"She must have brought him when the lifter came for her, since he knows more about the Homunculus than anyone. Or thinks he does."

"But—"

He waved her silent. Something was happening on the Divide floor.

A guard in black and gold leather armour had swung by rope from the heavy lifter into Pirelius's bubble of safety. Pirelius taunted him loudly and brutally, while keeping the Homunculus carefully in the way. The guard circled both of them, trying to find an opening, but Pirelius was too canny. Feinting to his right, he kicked out with his left leg and caught the guard by surprise. He staggered back a step and was caught up in the relentless crush of man'kin. With a scream, he was swept away.

"You morons," yelled Pirelius up at the dirigible. "You won't get rid of me that easily!"

"What do you want?" yelled Marmion.

"She took what was rightfully mine, and I want her to pay!"

"Who?"

"The Magister, you idiot. Tell her to talk to me herself, not cower behind some spineless lackey!"

Marmion's head withdrew, then returned a moment later. "She has nothing to say to you."

"Really? We'll see about that when I reach the bottom of the Wall. How are you going to keep the man'kin out when the charms stop working?"

"What do you mean?"

"You know what this creature can do. You've seen it with your own eyes." Pirelius gave the Homunculus a push, sending it staggering forward. "It kills the Change, so it can kill the Wall. That's all that keeps the man'kin outside the city. When I get close enough—"

"You're an idiot, Pirelius!" hollered a new voice. The Magister's face peered over the edge of the gondola.

"Ha!" crowed the bandit. "You appear at last, you old witch! Now you realise the threat I am, you deign to speak. Well, I'm not listening. Nothing you can say will deter me!"

"How about this? The Wall has already been breached; the man'kin are already inside the city. You're wasting your time on a fool's errand. You've failed!"

The sound of the Magister's laugh was chilling over the crashing of the man'kin.

Pirelius wrenched the Homunculus to a halt. He craned his neck to see. The tunnel mouth leading through the Wall was obscured, but the number of man'kin milling outside it had obviously shrunk. They had to be going somewhere.

Although the city was under attack and its last defence had failed, just as Pirelius had hoped it would, the bandit seemed almost bereft. He looked from the Wall to the Magister and back again, a man who had lost everything, even one shot at retribution.

"Let's leave," said the Homunculus, speaking for the first time. "We'll take you to safety. You can put all this behind you and make a new life elsewhere."

"Don't listen to it!" shouted the Magister. "You can have a life right here, right now. I'm prepared to make a new deal with you."

Pirelius looked up at her with hatred in every line of his face. If he had his way, the heavy lifter would be struck from the sky and crumpled like paper, killing everyone aboard. Sal could feel his loathing even through Kail's mind. The time for songs and bravura had passed. His grim determination to hurt the Magister consumed him.

Gradually, a smile formed on his face.

"You want me to help you," he said as the dirigible drifted lower over him.

"Yes."

"How have they got in? A tunnel?"

"We need you to close it, stop them coming through." The Magister's eyes glittered. Her expression was haughty, even when asking for aid. "Do it, and you walk away free. Both of you."

"No!" said Marmion, lunging forward to take the Magister's arm. Guards pushed him back.

"You have my word on this," the Magister said to Pirelius, ignoring the Sky Warden.

Pirelius's laugh was no less chilling than hers. He raised the knife so it pressed against the Homunculus's neck. "Your word is worth less to me than the life of this monster. I should kill it now and rid the world of both of you."

"And die yourself, without its protection? Your posturing doesn't impress me, Pirelius." The Magister's voice betrayed not the slightest fear that he might do as he said. "I'm a businesswoman. Let's talk business or the next thing I drop on you won't be a guard."

Pirelius spat in the dirt. "Hag."

"I have no idea what you think I did to you, but calling each other names solves nothing."

The bandit pushed the Homunculus into motion. It staggered forward like a sleepwalker. "This isn't over," Pirelius said. "We will have a reckoning."

This the Magister didn't grace with a reply. Her head retreated and the heavy lifter surged smoothly forward.

Sal dropped out of the vision. Someone was shaking his shoulder again. He blinked and focused on the real world.

"What is it?"

Shilly pointed over the interior side of the Wall, a worried look on her face. He was startled by the transformation in the city. Fires were burning where the man'kin had broken through the Wall. Thick smoke belched along the city streets. The city guards had fallen back several blocks as a heavy tide of man'kin filled the streets. Creatures of all sizes and shapes swarmed over the cobbles of Laure, an irresistible mass of living stone.

The press was formidable. Those man'kin that could escape the crush, did. Some climbed up onto roofs and took station on the eaves, roosting like gargoyles. Others weren't content to sit only a floor or two up. They leapt from building to building, seeking ever-higher vantage points. At least two were scaling towers just a handful of metres away from the Wall itself.

That was a concern. Sal backed away as a large, fat man'kin with a cherubic face climbed hand over hand to the top of a nearby tower, the ease of its movement belying its sheer mass. From that vantage point, it turned to look at them with dead, stone eyes.

"Oh, shit," said Shilly, gripping Sal's upper arm painfully tight. "I think it's about to—"

She didn't finish as, with a crunch of stone and a roar of effort, the man'kin leapt across the gap between them and onto the Wall.

THE MAN'KIN

"Earthquakes, bushfires, flash floods, hurricanes: we
ignore these signs at our own peril."

THE BOOK OF TOWERS, EXEGESIS 10:24

"Run!"

The command came from the leader of the guards, and Skender
didn't hesitate to obey. The sight of the giant man'kin—at least four
metres high and weighing several tons—launching itself from the tower
was enough to make him move. The force of its leap was sufficient to
topple the tip of the minarette it had been standing on, sending bricks
and tiles crashing down onto the streets below. With a deafening crunch,
the broad chest of the man'kin struck the edge of the Wall not metres
from where he stood. Its fat fingers scrabbled for purchase and caught
the guardrail. Metal twisted with a painful squeal but held. Stone
ground against stone, and the man'kin hauled itself up onto the roof.

Skender, running almost backwards, hypnotised by the creature's
massive strength, tripped over the ragged hem of his robe and fell awkwardly onto his side. Shilly shouted something but he couldn't hear
her over the heavy thudding of man'kin feet. A guard threw one of the
light-globes into its back. Bright energy flashed, followed by a surge
of heat so powerful Skender averted his eyes.

"Hold!" shouted the leader of the guards. Skender blinked and
looked up into the giant statue's face. It stood over him, so close he
could reach out and touch its leg. A globe thrown now was just as
likely to kill him, and the first didn't seem to have done any damage
at all.

"*MAWSON*," the man'kin said in a voice like mountains falling.

"Sal set him free," Skender protested, scrabbling backwards on his hands and feet.

The man'kin followed as though tied to him with string. Its expression was blankly intimidating. "*MAWSON FRIEND.*"

"He's our friend, too. He wouldn't want you to hurt us."

The man'kin shook its head and reached down with one bulbous hand. Skender tried to run but barely made it upright before massive stone fingers wrapped around his torso and pulled him into the air.

"No!" Its grip was tight. He could hardly draw breath enough to shout, "Don't!"

"*MAWSON FRIEND MUST.*"

Skender felt himself raised up high. He closed his eyes, nerving himself for being dashed to the stone. He thought of Chu and was glad she wasn't there to see this.

"*MAWSON FRIEND MUST LOOK.*"

The moment of his death didn't come. He remained suspended in the air, firmly contained by the creature's stone fist. His many bruises complained, and for once he was grateful for it. While he hurt, he remained alive.

The man'kin shook him.

"*MAWSON FRIEND MUST LOOK NOW!*"

The creature's leaden words finally sunk in. Skender opened his eyes. The man'kin held him disconcertingly high above the top of the Wall. The view was almost as impressive as it had been from under Chu's wing. The spreading stain of the man'kin horde darkened the streets below, while the mass of living stone outside had shrunk to less than a quarter its original size. The twins and their captor cut a straight line through them, with the Magister's heavy lifter following discreetly above.

The man'kin shook him so hard his teeth rattled in his head. The world swung jarringly around him. When it settled down, he was staring to the east, at the Hanging Mountains. The sun was fading into

the west, wreathing them in shadow. The ridge of clouds he had seen
from the heavy lifter was still banked hard against the distant peaks—
a permanent fixture, perhaps—but now something else was visible. A
tendril of white led down from the mountains. It looked like the mountains had grown a tail. The tail wound through the foothills and out
into the plains, following a zigzag course that reminded him of something he had seen before. It took him a moment to remember where.

The white tendril was following the path of the Divide, as he had
seen it from the wing. It wasn't actually white, but dirty brown with
a foaming edge. The foam reflected the sky back at him, making it
appear bright against the surrounding plain. The leading edge was
growing visibly nearer.

"Oh, shit," he said, the enormity of what he was seeing momentarily freezing his capacity for thought.

"Skender?" called Shilly from far below. "Answer me!"

"You can put me down now," he told the man'kin.

"*LOOK?*"

Skender took in the face of the giant creature as it deposited him
gently back on the Wall. Its face wasn't built for expressiveness, but
now he could see that it was worried, not angry.

"Yes," he said. "I looked, and I saw." He recalled the man'kin shouting among themselves as they argued over whether or not to kill Sal. *The
Angel says we must keep moving*, one had said. And the stone pig that had
spoken to him afterwards had tried to explain: *We are saving ourselves.*

"That's what you're doing in the Divide, isn't it?"

"*ANGEL.*"

It could take a while for the creature to build up the verbal
momentum to complete a sentence. Skender turned instead to Sal and
Shilly, who had left the guards standing at a cautious distance and
pressed forward to help him. Gwil Flintham was a dot in the distance,
still running.

"I'm okay," he told them. "I think this big lug was sent up here by

Mawson. There's something coming down the Divide, out of the mountains. It's huge, and it's frightened the man'kin."

"*Frightened* them?" echoed Shilly disbelievingly.

"*ANGEL SAYS.*"

"Remember that the man'kin don't see time the way we do. They see it all at once, in a big tangle, and it's hard for them to tease out individual threads. Before we left the Aad, Mawson told me that he and the other man'kin were afraid of the one from the Void, the Homunculus. That's what I *thought* he meant, but I was wrong. They know that when the twins come, something else, something terrible, is going to happen. And it's on its way right now."

"*ANGEL SAYS RUN.*"

"What is it?" asked Shilly, glancing at the man'kin then back at Skender. "Can we stop it?"

"I think it's a flash flood—and a big one. We need to let the Magister know. If it comes this far and hits while the Wall is breached . . ."

It wasn't a thought he wanted to complete aloud. He wasn't familiar with rivers that flowed the year round, but had seen sudden surges tear down a watercourse that had been dry for months, tossing boulders as though they were pebbles and ripping trees right out of the ground. The tiniest chink in a bank or dam could be widened in an instant under the force of such a deluge. Nothing could withstand it.

In his mind, he pictured the city flooded as a wall of water burst through the hole made by the man'kin. He felt ill. Chu and his mother were down there, along with thousands of other people. He couldn't stand by and let them die.

"That's what we missed," said Sal, looking annoyed at himself. "Down in the Divide, the man'kin told us they were running. I thought they were running *to* something, not *from* something. We have to help them."

"How far away is it?" Shilly asked. "How much time do we have?"

"I don't know exactly, but it was moving fast. Minutes, not hours."

"Would the Wall withstand it, even intact?"

"I suspect there's only one way to find out."

"The man'kin sure picked a shitty time to attack," fumed the leader of the guards, who had come up behind them and overheard the conversation. "If it wasn't for them, we'd be perfectly safe."

"And what about *them?*" Shilly snapped at him. "They're living things, too. I bet the Magister wouldn't have willingly given them refuge, not in a million years."

"Well, they've killed *all* of us now, haven't they?"

Skender shook his head and held up one hand.

"Listen," he said. "Can you hear it?"

Both Sal and Shilly looked along the Divide to the east, straining to hear what was coming.

"Wrong direction," he said, pointing the other way. "Listen closely—and if you don't hear it, that's a good thing."

"You're starting to sound a lot like Mawson yourself," Shilly said in brittle tones. "Want to explain what you're talking about?"

"The fighting's stopped," he said, pulling them closer to the twisted rail. "I'm starting to think that it never really started."

Shilly felt hundreds of pairs of eyes turn to look at her as she peered over the edge of the Wall. The man'kin horde had overrun a large swathe of the city's slums, filling every niche and nook with their presence. They sat on roofs, windowsills, and doorsteps, and straddled the meandering roads. None of them moved, except those at the very edge of the slum area, where city guards still objected to their presence. Their territory was no longer expanding, however. For the moment, they seemed content to simply occupy what they had taken.

All of them were looking up at her and the man'kin who had climbed high to deliver its message.

ANGEL SAYS RUN.

They weren't running now, and that could only mean one thing: it was too late to run any further.

"We have to close the Wall, and fast," she said, feeling the certainty of it right down in her bones.

"There are still more coming through," Skender objected, pointing.

"I don't care. If they don't shut it soon, everyone will die." *Goddess,* she thought, *if the* man'kin *are scared, then we don't stand a chance!* "We have to get word to the Magister."

"And tell her what?" asked Skender.

"To stop Pirelius!" said Sal suddenly, squeezing her arm painfully tight.

"Why?"

"The Magister has sent him and the Homunculus to block the tunnel so the man'kin can't get into the city."

Skender's eyes widened. "If the twins are in there, the man'kin won't be able to fix the breach. The stones won't move."

"Exactly." Sal thought for a second. "I'll call Kail and see what he can do. You two think of a way to stop the Homunculus in case he fails."

"There's one easy way," said the guard, hefting one of the globes.

"What's wrong with you?" Anger flared deep in Shilly's gut. "The Homunculus and the man'kin both deserve to live as much as you do. Try dropping anything else from up here and you'll follow, okay?"

"It might come to that," said Skender. "Killing the twins, I mean, if we can't think of anything else."

"Then we'd better make sure we do." She put a hand over her eyes, wishing the sound of the alarum would let up just for a moment. The pieces of a plan rattled around in her head but weren't falling into place as fast as she would have liked. A lot depended on how much time they had left.

Sal was communing with Kail again and his absence unbalanced her. She wanted to talk to him, ask him if her ideas might work. But she didn't dare break his concentration until she had something definite to give him.

Vacillation wasn't an option.

She took her hand away from her face. "Right. We talk to Mawson and the other man'kin through our friend, here." The giant man'kin towered over them, as immobile as a rock but watching them closely through deep-set eyes. "We need to tell them that the flood is on its way. They have to start closing the tunnel, if they aren't already."

"I think we'd feel it if they were," Skender said.

"True. So they aren't. You pass on the message while I think."

Skender turned away to talk to the man'kin. Shilly put her hands on the guardrail and leaned out over the Divide side of the Wall. The scene below was one of chaos and broken earth. Man'kin still pressed against the opening to the tunnel, although the mad crush had faded. A dense pall of dust hung over them. She could see Pirelius coughing as he manhandled his prisoner towards the entrance to the city Wall. His pace was slow but steady. He was only a couple of hundred metres away.

As she watched, the heavy lifter monitoring the scene tilted upwards and gained altitude in a hasty spiral. The Magister and her crew were checking the news themselves, she assumed.

There had to be a way . . .

"Tell me something," she said to the guard she had snapped at earlier. He was still holding a globe in his hand, and was probably just as willing to lob it down on the Homunculus as he had been before. "How are the charms on the Wall maintained?"

The guard looked over the edge. The giant signs were extremely foreshortened from their point of view. "We send crews down once a month. Are you thinking of changing them, to resist the flood?"

She shook her head, although she had briefly considered it. She doubted anyone could repaint the charms in time, even with all the resources of the city behind them.

"You said you send them down, not up. So there must be ropes around here, somewhere."

He nodded, pointing at a hut near the far side of the Wall.

"Get them for me. We're going to need them, and soon."

"But—"

"Quickly!"

Shilly thought for a second that the guard might actually salute as he turned on his heel and hurried away, calling for his fellows to help him. Any amusement she felt was almost instantly crushed by the knowledge of what she had to do next.

"It's confirmed," said Kail. *"They see it, too."*

"Of course they do. Why would we lie?" Sal didn't try to hide his irritation, although he could understand both Marmion and the Magister being cautious before accepting such drastic news on his word alone. *"The next step is to ask Pirelius to turn back."*

"The Magister doesn't want to do that. She thinks Pirelius is lying—letting her believe that he's helping her, when in fact he intends to hold her to ransom at the very last."

"So she's going to do nothing, and assume he'll do the right thing without realising it?"

"That's her plan."

Sal couldn't tell through the Change whether Kail approved or disapproved. The plan did make a kind of sense, though. From Pirelius's point of view, the only threat to the city was the man'kin. He didn't realise that, in fact, it was he who might be critical in the crisis. If he was to find that out, he really could hold the city to ransom.

"I don't like the idea of risking everything on Pirelius unintentionally doing what we need him to do."

Kail didn't respond. When Sal sought the tracker out again, a stream of images and sensory impressions was all he received.

The Wall—so close now that it and the sides of the Divide blocked out most of the sky. This was the first time Sal had seen the city from that perspective, and he was startled by how forbidding it looked. From above, its architecture had seemed sweeping and bold. From below it was simply brutally functional.

Sal still couldn't see Kail, although he had to be well within eyeshot.

It occurred to him that the tracker must be using a charm to hide from sight. Glamours weren't complicated, but they could be draining. Kail was also relaying information to him, and probably hadn't slept for almost two whole days. Sal felt new respect for the man.

Pirelius looked around as though sensing he was being followed. The bandit was in a bad way, wearied and battered by his long trek through the man'kin horde. Sunburn on his scalp pulsed red and a streak of dried blood stretched from the corner of one eye into his beard. But his pace was unchecked, as was the ferocity with which he forced the Homunculus ahead of him. A steady stream of invective, punctuated by the occasional blow, rewarded the twins for their compliance.

Occasionally Pirelius looked up at the heavy lifter, still cruising weightlessly overhead. He did so with a naked shrewdness that told Sal that the Magister was almost certainly right. Pirelius was the very picture of obedience. It was too much to believe.

He became aware of movement beside him. Dropping out of the vision, he turned to see three guards hastily affixing a complicated series of grapnels and pulleys to the guardrail in front of them. Shilly oversaw their efforts closely, although it was clear they knew what they were doing.

"What's going on?" Sal asked, noticing a large coil of finely spun rope lying to one side, next to a pair of leather harnesses.

"I don't trust Marmion any further than I can throw him," Shilly said. "He'll pick up Kail, yes, but I'm sure he'd rather watch the Homunculus drown."

"Who's going to make him do the right thing?"

She squared her shoulders. "Me."

"What?" Skender, who had been eyeing the harnesses with some reservation, looked up in surprise. "Don't be ridiculous. It'll be me if it's anyone."

"Why?" she asked, ears reddening. "Because I'm a girl and a cripple?"

"No! Because I'm a climber and you're not."

"But it was my idea."

"So? You're needed up here. You're in charge. And Sal has to convey messages to Kail. It makes sense that I go. Doesn't it?"

Shilly's lips tightened, and Sal knew from long experience that she wasn't arguing because she thought she was right.

"I'm not afraid of going."

"Who said you were?" Skender rolled his eyes. "This is no time for pride, Shilly. Just let me do it."

"All right, all right," she said, and Sal could see the relief her back-down brought. "But you've got to be careful. How could I face your mother if anything happened to you?"

"Don't worry about her," Skender said, "because nothing's going to happen to me." He turned to the guards. "Are you ready yet?"

"Almost." The leader tossed him a harness. "Put this on and we'll hitch you up."

Sal and Shilly helped Skender thread the leather straps around his waist, thighs, and shoulders. They were designed for someone about his size—the smaller the better for such labour—and all the clasps looked well maintained. A complicated series of brass loops and stays connected it to the rope.

"Take this," said the guard as he attached Skender to the assembly. He clipped a pouch containing three flags to the harness. "Red for up, green for down, white to stop. Got that?"

Skender repeated it word for word. "What if I drop the flags?"

"You can't. They're all connected."

"But if—"

"Don't worry. You get into a scrape, kick out from the Wall and that'll be our signal to haul you up."

"I'll be keeping an eye on you," said Sal, "through Kail."

"Couldn't *he* do this?" asked Skender, a flash of nervousness showing.

Shilly shook her head. "I don't entirely trust him, either."

Skender resigned himself to his fate. "Right, then. I'm ready."

"Wait," said Sal as Skender walked, jingling, closer to the edge of the Wall. "You might need this, too."

"Hey!" Shilly exclaimed as Sal took her walking stick from her and handed it to Skender.

"I'll make you a new one," he said to her. To Skender, he explained: "It's a reservoir of the Change. I've been stocking it up for ages. I doubt you'll need it, but just in case . . ."

Skender's gaze danced between him and Shilly. "Thanks. I promise I'll bring it back."

There was no more time for talking as Skender put himself into the hands of the guards. They gave him gloves and showed him how to grip the rope. He adopted a wide-legged stance and backed up to the edge. When the last of his guiding hands fell away, he leaned out and down, while two of the guards operated a mechanical winch to gradually pay out the rope.

"A reservoir?" said Shilly to Sal as their friend disappeared out of sight. "You never told me that."

"I never needed to. And that's a good thing, right?"

She punched his arm. "Let's get back from the edge. Things could start shaking again any time soon, and you're going to have to keep me upright now."

He did as he was told, while at the same time dipping back into Kail's senses.

The Wall was a vast, solid mass. He could barely make out Skender against its sheer enormity. The sky at the top seemed impossibly far away. The heavy lifter had fallen back, cautious of coming too close lest a stray gust of wind sent it crashing into the stone. Pirelius picked his way over ground heavily scarred by the passage of the man'kin. Ahead, the tunnel gaped like a mouthful of jagged teeth.

Sal felt a vibration through his fingertips that he at first assumed was the stone of the Wall moving again. But it lacked any of the grinding, scraping sounds that had accompanied it before. Only gradually did he work out that its source wasn't his fingers at all, but Kail's.

The flood was coming.

THE FLOOD

"There are many ways of existing. Some creatures have no minds at all, or none that we would recognise as such; others are *just* minds, cunning intelligences hovering on the edge of the world.
The rule common to all is: like devours like."
MASTER WARDEN RISA ATILDE: NOTES TOWARD A UNIFIED CURRICULUM

Skender clung tightly to the rope and tried not to look down. This wasn't remotely like climbing. He was utterly at the mercy of the thin strand linking him to the apparatus at the top of the Wall. The guards turning the winch far above maintained his rate of descent. If the rope snapped, he would plummet instantly to his death. There was nothing he could do but dangle and hope for the best.

His descent was not so rapid that he risked skinning himself on the stone as it went past and he used his legs to keep at a distance from the Wall, kicking gently to maintain a rhythmic bounce. He felt like a bug on the vast expanse of the Wall. It seemed to stretch to infinity in all directions. The only details marring its smooth curvature were the giant charms reinforcing the sigils on each block of stone.

A cool breeze caressed his neck. He relished the touch of it on his raw skin and bruises until he realised its probable source. A wall of water was rushing down the Divide pushing all the air ahead of it. A breeze was probably the best he could hope for, suspended as he was on a string right in its path.

He made sure the flags were secure against his waist. *Red for up*, the guard had said. It was imprinted in his memory forever. He just hoped the guards operating the winch were conserving their strength for a late charge.

Shilly tore her eyes away from Skender as he receded down the Wall. Pirelius and the Homunculus were almost at the tunnel mouth. Movement out of the corner of her eye distracted her from the downward view, and she looked up.

The heavy lifter rocked from side to side, at eye level, painted pink by the falling dusk. The pilot turned it so it lay lengthways, parallel to the Wall, but its instability only seemed to worsen. Its fiery propellers spun furiously in an attempt to hold it in position.

Wind, she thought, glancing upwards. There were no clouds, but the sky to the east was growing darker.

Wind and spray. Time was running out.

"Faster!" she shouted at the guards turning the winch. "We don't have long!"

They pulled their handles with increased energy. One, red in the face, muttered to the other, "Who *is* she, anyway?"

Shilly ignored him. "What's happening down there?" she asked Sal, wishing she had her stick. She felt unsteady without it.

"Pirelius has stopped," he said, his gaze focused on infinity. "He's calling for the Magister."

Shilly nodded. "Looking for a rematch." Thus far, Pirelius was behaving exactly as expected. "Is she coming?"

"She's sent Marmion again."

"Good. Don't want to make it look too easy."

"*TUNNEL*," rumbled the giant man'kin, startling her. She jumped and turned to face it.

"What?"

"*TUNNEL CLOSING.*"

The Wall began to shake. Obviously this man'kin had got word to Mawson about the flood and told the other man'kin to start closing the tunnel. "Good. While that's happening, why don't you help those two with the winch? Can you do that?"

The round face of the man'kin swivelled to take in the guards and the winch. It took two ponderous steps forward and crouched down. The guards backed away, terrified as a giant stone hand grabbed the handle.

"*TURN*," it boomed, and did just that. The winch spun much faster than it had before. Rope vanished over the edge at a furious rate. "*TURN*."

"Excellent," she said, hoping against hope that she hadn't given Skender the fright of his life. "Make sure you stop when we tell you to, okay?"

It nodded. "*TURN!*"

The Wall quaked beneath them, and she clung to Sal for support.

"For the last time—"

At the sound of grinding stone, Pirelius stopped in midsentence and looked around.

"What?" He grabbed the Homunculus tight around the throat and pulled it closer to him, suspecting a trap. The blade at its throat gleamed. "Magister! What are you playing at?"

"Nothing, Pirelius," said Marmion, bellowing to be heard from the shaking canopy above. "Stay calm! The man'kin can't hurt you!"

Pirelius backed away from the tunnel entrance. The crush of man'kin around him hadn't thinned, and that surprised Sal. He would have expected them to make for other refuges once word spread of the tunnel's imminent closure, but they stayed tight around the man and his captive, and continued to ignore the invisible Kail.

It took a good while for the truth—that things weren't going the way Pirelius expected—to sink in. In fact, it took the solid chest of a man'kin to drive the point home.

"Wh—?" Pirelius recoiled from the frozen statue with a look of utter con-

fusion on his face. The man'kin consistently flinched from the Homunculus when it approached. This one—a three-metre-high bearded man in white stone with a beatific expression and outstretched arms—had not.

He backed away, and the frozen man'kin fell out of range. It shook its head, uncannily as though waking.

"The one from the Void is here," *the man'kin said.* "Tiden har kommit."

Pirelius just frowned at that, but the effect on the Homunculus was startling. It straightened with a jerk.

"What could you know about that?" *it asked the man'kin, its superimposition of faces twisted in anguish.*

"The time has come," *the man'kin stated matter-of-factly.* "It has always been. You are there. We are there with you."

"You weren't there! You couldn't possibly know!" *The Homunculus wriggled in Pirelius's grip, but the bandit clung tight. The blade bit deep into its throat, drawing not blood but a strange silver mist that bubbled and ran down its chest.* "We are alone!"

The sound of propellers whining drew Kail's eyes upwards. The heavy lifter was swooping lower in defiance of the rising wind. Sal couldn't have been more surprised to see Marmion dangling from a rope ladder if the Sky Warden had been stark naked and clutching a flower between his teeth.

"I'll kill it!" *screamed Pirelius as Marmion dropped to the dirt in the safety zone.* "I'll kill it!"

"I know," *said Marmion coolly, making reassuring motions with both hands.* "That's exactly what I want. And if you'll just stay calm, both our chances of making it out of this alive will significantly improve."

Skender was having trouble keeping up. One moment he had been descending at a steady pace, the next the world had dropped out from under him and the Wall was streaming by. He had cried out, fearing for a moment that the rope had snapped and he was falling to his death. But the harness still had a tight grip on his backside; he wasn't in free fall and hadn't skinned himself too badly against the store. Somehow the crew up above had found a way to accelerate his descent without dropping him.

Then, with the ground finally coming appreciably closer, the heavy lifter had lunged for him—or so it had felt—and he had covered his face with his hands, fearing a new catastrophe.

Death spared him again. When he dared part his fingers, the dirigible was heading for the sky.

Skender looked down. Someone else had joined the party below. A Sky Warden, judging by the colour of the robe. He groaned, recognising Marmion's bald spot. What was *he* doing there?

The ground was coming up awfully fast. He fumbled at the pouch, thinking, *Red for up, green for down, white to stop.* He produced the white flag and waved it. Nothing happened.

"Pay attention, you idiots!" he cried uselessly, flailing the flag in desperation as the ground swelled beneath him. "White to stop! White to stop! White to—"

With a throat-closing jerk, the winch suddenly slowed, forcing his chin down on his chest and the flag out of his hand. It flapped around his legs on the end of its string as he came to an abrupt halt a metre from the ground. He heard a "glurk" and realised that it had come from him.

The rope jerked again and he dropped the rest of the distance. His feet hit the ground and his legs promptly gave way. He landed face first, staring at Shilly's stick. He didn't even know he'd dropped it.

A stone snout poked him, hard.

"Ow!" Skender sat up and backed against the Wall with the stick in his hands. The reservoir of the Change in the carved wood trembled against his fingertips, aching to be let out. He stood and confronted his attacker.

It was the man'kin pig he had spoken to the previous day.

"*You are needed in this world,*" it said again, and trotted away.

Skender let out a panicky breath and looked around. The ground was as broken as a freshly turned field. Further along the Wall was a metal door, glowing red. The man'kin stayed carefully away from it. Several dozen man'kin congregated outside the tunnel mouth, to his left. He could feel the stone slabs shaking behind him as they closed ranks, gradually shutting the makeshift entrance to the city. A pang of compassion for the stone pig struck him: it would be stuck outside when the flood came. The water would dash it to pieces.

But what was death to something that saw all its life at once? He didn't know. He was, mainly, just glad that the other man'kin were ignoring him.

They stared, instead, at a confrontation taking place a dozen metres away. In the centre of a clearing, Pirelius and the twins had squared off against Marmion. Their voices were buried under the sound of the Wall rearranging itself, and another sound—a growing rumble the origin of which Skender tried not to think about. No one appeared to have noticed his arrival apart from the pig.

He went to move closer and was hauled up by the rope. He tugged on it, hoping the winch operators would take the hint. They did. Rope hissed to the ground, giving him much-needed slack. He followed the pig through a petrified forest of man'kin, none of whom paid him any attention. He was ready with the red flag and Shilly's stick if they did.

Words gradually coalesced out of the noise.

"—really think she's coming back for you?"

"Of course she is. We have a deal."

"*We* had a deal, too, and look where I ended up!"

"I don't know anything about that—but I *do* know that the Magister is afraid at the moment. You can use that to your advantage."

"Why should I believe you?"

"Because I'm down here with you." Skender was close enough to see Marmion's expression. It was one of determination and fear. "Would I take a risk like this if I didn't think it worthwhile?"

"Pah!" Pirelius spat into the dirt. "I don't trust anyone without knowing what they have to lose."

Skender peered from behind a statue of a horse as Pirelius dragged the twins away from Marmion. Pirelius came up sharp against a frozen man'kin, and flinched away from it into another.

"Get out of my way!" he bellowed, flailing with his free hand for the thong he had used to whip Skender into submission.

"They're afraid of the Homunculus," said Marmion, following him, "and with good reason. You have to listen to me."

"I don't *have* to do anything."

"Kill it or we'll all die!"

"No!" The twins' mingled voices rose up over the argument between the two men. "You must let us go! We still have work to do!"

Pirelius shifted his grip on the knife and plunged it deep into the Homunculus's shoulder. The twins howled and fell to their knees. Pirelius removed the blade and wiped it on his leather pants.

"I'm tired of this game," he said to Marmion. "Tell the Magister that if she's serious, she needs to come down here now and talk face to face, or—"

Pirelius stopped. It looked to Skender as though he had finally noticed that his main bargaining chip was worthless. The man'kin weren't attacking the city. They were standing around him and his captive, waiting for something.

His gaze took in the tunnel mouth for the first time. His eyes widened, then narrowed as he turned to Marmion.

"You lied to me, you dirt-faced, blue-coat bastard."

"I told you the truth, every word. The Magister is afraid because you can hurt her. You can use that to your advantage, if you're quick."

Pirelius stiffened as he looked over Marmion's shoulder, along the Divide. His mouth opened in shock, but no words came out.

Skender followed the direction of his stare. Over the heads of the man'kin, a foaming, dirty-white wall had appeared.

"Goddess," he breathed. The rising wind took the word from his lips and swept it away.

Shilly stared at the approaching flood, not quite able to comprehend the scale of it. She had happened to be staring up the Divide as it came into view, rounding the bend to the east. It looked like a giant wave rushing in from the sea, but there was no chance of it slowing and retreating, as normal waves did. This was growing nearer with the speed and power of a tsunami, sweeping up everything in its path.

"What's going on down there?" she asked Sal, barely able to tear her eyes away from the sight. "Why are they taking so long?" The view over the edge wasn't encouraging. No one had moved, and every second was precious.

"Pirelius has just worked it out," came her lover's distant reply. Sal's fingers clenched the rail as the Wall shook and rumbled beneath them. "I don't know what he's going to do."

"How long until the tunnel is closed?" she asked the giant man'kin. "Are we still in danger?"

The man'kin nodded.

A prolonged shudder forced them to their knees. Shilly resisted the urge to instruct the man'kin to haul Skender up to safety. Wishing with every breath Skender would hurry up, she peered over the edge and waited for the red flag.

Kail was as still as one of the man'kin caught in the wake. He hadn't moved throughout the entire confrontation. Sal could feel the ache in the tracker's legs and back and the patience with which he endured it. The older man was exhausted but his poise was perfectly intact. Waiting was an integral part of being a hunter. It was all about seizing the right moment to strike, no matter how long it took to come.

It was strange, Sal thought. The longer he dipped into the tracker's thoughts, the more he picked up. Not just fatigue and philosophy, either. There were glimpses of people and places he'd never been—from Kail's memories, he assumed—and emotions that triggered faint echoes in him. The most surprising was a surge of affection for someone he recognised instantly: Shilly, as she had looked on the edge of the Divide, shortly after he and Skender had flown away. Her expression was concerned and determined at once. He felt Kail looking at her with pride and sadness.

The mixed emotion was snatched away as Kail focused on events in front of him. Pirelius was a man who had never been particularly stable. Kail had watched him long enough to know that for certain now. Pirelius was backed into a corner, feeling betrayed and operating on the very limits of his resources, but he was far from stupid.

Kail could practically see Pirelius's mind working: in a moment the tunnel into the city would be closed, while something vast and terrible bore down on them from the east—a flash flood of stupendous proportions—that he would be caught up in if he didn't act soon.

The bandit was desperate and had never been more dangerous.

"The time for thinking is over," declared Marmion in exasperation. "If you won't kill it, I will."

The Sky Warden produced a slender blade from beneath his robes. It gleamed like ice in his hand. He lunged forward, and the deadly tip stabbed squarely at the Homunculus's chest. The Homunculus looked up from its daze and swayed away, too slowly. Its many eyes triangulated on death's bright, metallic sting, hypnotised by its inevitability.

Light flashed from Kail's left. Something bright and fierce left a sharp blue trail across his vision. It looked like a tiny ball of lightning, and discharged into the knife Marmion held. With a thunderclap the blade exploded, sending the warden flying backwards in a spray of metal and blood.

Pirelius staggered and fell to one knee. The look of surprise on his face was almost comical, but it didn't last long. He moved more quickly than Sal could credit, shoving the Homunculus with a roar, his sights set on the tunnel.

"He's worked it out!" said Sal, teasing his mind from Kail's with difficulty. "We can't let him use the Homunculus to stop the tunnel closing!"

"*I know*," said the tracker calmly.

Kail was already moving, coming out from cover and reaching with practised hands for the weighted cord dangling at his waist.

Pirelius travelled no more than three steps before coming face to face with a frozen man'kin. He sidestepped to his right and found another in his path.

"*Get out of my way!*"

The roar of water was almost so loud as to drown out his words completely. Kail caught sight of Skender struggling through the forest of living statues with rope and harness trailing from him. The stick in his hand was expended, useless, shrivelled, and black like charcoal. Kail waved him away.

Pirelius wrenched the Homunculus from side to side, finding man'kin frozen before him every way he tried to run. Kail felt the man's desperation rising in time with the roar of the flood. The leather thong dangling from his left hand cracked to no avail.

"*You!*" *he roared.* "*You have destroyed me!*"

The words were directed upwards, to where the heavy lifter had been. The sky was greying over; the dirigible had fled the gale preceding the flood.

The bola in Kail's hand spun as Pirelius backed away from a snarling stone visage with wide, despairing eyes. He had no hope left for himself. That much was clear. All he wanted to do was hurt the Magister before he died—and the Homunculus would be the instrument of his vengeance.

"No!" Sal heard himself cry aloud as Kail let the bola fly.

He could feel Kail's determination to do the right thing. Kail had made a promise—but Sal had promised, too, to rescue the Homunculus, to come back for it later. What could he possibly do now to stop the inevitable? Killing the Homunculus would solve everything: the city would be safe if the tunnel was allowed to close, and the world would be saved from the threat it presaged. That was what Marmion wanted.

The bola flew with deadly force and aim. With a sickening sound, it wrapped itself around Pirelius's neck and snapped it in two. The bandit dropped like a sack of stones, and the Homunculus fell free.

❦ ❦ ❦

The roar of the stones and the water was deafening. Skender, caught between the two, felt squeezed and shaken by two competing sonic shock waves. He gaped as Pirelius fell and blood sprayed from his mouth. The bola had seemed to come from nowhere.

"*Quickly!*" shouted a voice over the double roar. The man'kin were moving again, running to add their weight to the gradually closing gap in the Wall. It didn't sound like one of their voices.

A blur passed in front of his face and resolved into a giant man with a long, gaunt face and violet eyes. Skender jumped, then recognised him as Habryn Kail.

"*You are needed,*" said the tracker through the Change. "*Isn't that what the man'kin said?*"

Skender spurred himself forward to help the twins. A strong-fingered hand grabbed his arm.

"*No. You get Marmion. He needs you most.*"

Skender looked at where the Sky Warden lay in a pool of bright red blood on the ground. He hadn't spared a thought for Marmion since loosing the energy in Shilly's walking stick at him, halting the unjustified slaughter of the twins. But there was no denying that Marmion was helpless in the face of the flood. If he was still alive, Skender couldn't in good conscience leave him to die.

Why not? part of him asked. *That's exactly what you did to Rattails!*

There wasn't time to argue about ethics. He was already moving. Kail and the twins had at least a chance to save themselves, even if the Homunculus was wounded and Kail was hunched over like a man with no reserves left at all. His face was haggard. His chest rose and fell in rapid gasps.

Skender crouched by Marmion and felt for a pulse. Weak but present. He rolled the Sky Warden over onto his back and flinched at the ruin of his hand.

Deal with that later, he scolded himself. *Get out of this alive first.*

He pulled at the rope so he could reach the second harness. Putting it onto an unconscious person proved to be more difficult than he had expected. Marmion was a dead weight wrapped in robes slick with blood. While Skender worked, Kail and the twins exchanged words, heads pressed close so they could hear each other over the booming roar. The tracker appeared to be cutting its bonds.

Skender's heart raced as he fastened the last tie on the harness. He reached for the red flag, and hesitated.

A strange stillness fell. The air was shocked, compressed beyond wind into a solid thing. It caught the moment and held it. Through a thickening haze, the light turned yellow-brown—a herald of destruction, not night. The man'kin stood splayed against the Wall as though holding it upright. Kail and the Homunculus faced each other like wrestlers about to engage. Even the blood pulsing from Marmion's ragged wrist appeared to have ceased.

Kail looked at him, and his lips moved. "Go!" he seemed to yell, although Skender couldn't hear a sound. "Get out of here!"

The flag came up and waved without his volition. The twins looked around them, dazed.

Kail's lips moved soundlessly again. Skender thought he recognised Shilly's name on the tracker's lips—

Tell her what? he wanted to ask.

—then the rope wrenched him upwards so hard his head snapped back and the world went dark. He didn't feel the spray of water that soaked him to the skin, but he did retain enough partial awareness to wonder how it had come to be raining.

Shilly caught a flash of red at the bottom of the Wall. This wasn't blood, as it had been during the false alarm a moment ago. It was moving, *waving.*

"Turn the winch!" she shouted at the man'kin, not daring to take her eyes from the speck that was Skender far below. The wall of water rushing towards them was unbelievably high and moving at a speed that seemed impossible for something so *big*. "Reel in the rope!"

"*TURN!*" The big man'kin wrenched the winch's handle so hard sparks flew. "*TURN BACK!*"

"Dear Goddess," she breathed, backing away from the edge of the Wall with her hands clenched before her. The stones shook beneath her. "Are we in time? Will he make it?"

None of the guards answered, if they even heard her. Their attention was fixed on the flood. She gave in to the urge to look and the sickening reality of it struck her full in the face. Wind howled past her, flattening her hair and stinging her eyes. It brought with it a smell of wet dirt—and lots of it. The flood was a roiling, tumbling mass of mud and stone. Boulders rolled in and out of sight like grains of sand during a heavy swell. She wondered if any of them were man'kin or people from further up the Divide, and she fought the desire to throw up.

The Wall shook as the vanguard of the flood struck. The sound it made was a physical blow, and she staggered backwards into Sal, who was himself having trouble standing. She could hear nothing but the roar of water and stone. It overwhelmed her, and for a moment she could think of nothing else. She forgot the Wall, the city, the man'kin, herself. Her world was washed away as surely as if the flood had literally struck her.

A vertical wall of water shot up in front of her. The winch jerked, and would have been snatched away in the upside-down waterfall had not the giant man'kin grabbed it and yanked it down. The rope came with it, pulling Skender and a second person out of the torrent. The three of them fell in a tangle on the top of the Wall. Dirty water doused them all. Dozens of tiny fists seemed to be pummelling her as she clutched at Sal and the guardrail, terrified she might be swept away.

Then the deluge ebbed and she let herself fall. The roar of the flood hadn't subsided, but the front had passed them. The top of the Wall was several metres above the roiling currents filling the Divide from side to side. She sat up and stared in shock at a muddy deluge where the canyon had once been. The Wall shook at its passage. The stones flexed and didn't part.

Over the thundering current she heard voices and turned to see the guards cutting Skender and the person he had rescued from the rope. She hurried to join them and was surprised to see a blood-spattered Eisak Marmion next to her friend from the north, not the Homunculus. Both of them were dripping wet. Skender was out cold but seemed otherwise unharmed. His hands were empty. One of the guards tore Marmion's robe into strips; another tied the strips around the grisly stump where Marmion's right hand had once been. Scorch marks along his wrist and arm and the ragged edge of the wound told her some of the story.

Marmion would have a great deal to say about this, if he survived. She was already dreading the accusations. He had lost a great deal of blood and his face was deathly pale. For all her dislike of him, and her regret over a bond that would never exist between them—and her disappointment that he had been saved, not the Homunculus—she couldn't bring herself to hope he wouldn't recover.

Sal bent over him and the Change flexed. He reached out for her guidance, and she concentrated on the task at hand. The bleeding had to be stopped. The two of them descended with one will into the torn tissues and encouraged them to heal. Blood vessels sealed with sudden sparkles; skin tied itself in knots. They were small charms, something any village healer could have attempted, but they did the job.

A shadow passed over her, and she glanced upwards to see the heavy lifter sailing cautiously across the Wall, inspecting the waters before the daylight completely faded. She thought of Kail and the Homunculus and an unknown number of man'kin who had been caught in the deluge. She didn't know if the flood was a natural accident or part of some macabre design, but she was certain she wouldn't be the only one looking to apportion blame. Somehow, she swore, the dead would be honoured.

Her attention returned to Marmion's wrist and the small work that would save his life.

THE BROTHER

"A thousand years ago, when the Goddess trod this Earth, the Change was stronger than it is today. All were rich in it, but few possessed mastery over it. From the chaos emerged two heroes, wise and true, who led their people to victory over madness and misrule. Between them they sundered the Change, so all would possess some and none possess all. The Mage claimed the red earth and fiery sun while the Warden took dominion over the deep ocean and stirring breeze. Since that day peace has reigned. The Goddess help us should they ever be reunited."

THE BOOK OF TOWERS, FRAGMENT 141

Dawn painted warm colours over a tense and exhausted city. After a night of plugging leaks and shoring up foundations that had taken the brunt of the flood, the worst was finally over. Water surged along long-forgotten and poorly sealed tunnels; the yadachi turned their song onto the Wall and the foundations of the city, fine-tuning its natural resilience. Streets filled with water, but the stone barriers held. The torrent remained at bay. Thousands of people who never thought they would be troubled by too *much* water breathed easier.

Sal wasn't one of them. His problems hadn't ended with the safeguarding of the city—and his contribution to that had been minimal, once the flood had arrived. Barely had he finished healing Marmion when a new set of guards had arrived with instructions direct from the Magister herself. They had taken him, Shilly, and Skender into custody. Where Gwil Flintham had got to, he didn't know, but there had been no one to bail them out that time. As unimaginable forces assailed the Wall, they were frogmarched back to the Black Galah and placed in custody with the others. Only Marmion escaped that fate, and then only temporarily. Taken away by the yadachi for emergency medical treatment to his injured arm, enabled by the Blood Tithe he had given, he had returned six hours later, unconscious and bound heavily in bandages from the elbow down. Nothing remained of his right hand but a padded stump that stank of antibiotic salves.

Sal sighed, feeling responsible for the grievous injury. Yes, Marmion had tried to murder the Homunculus—and yes, Sal had done his level best to save Marmion's life, despite their differences—but no one deserved mutilation. That in the end it had been Skender who had blown someone up, not Sal, didn't assuage his nagging guilt.

Get over it, he told himself. *You didn't drag Marmion down there. You didn't place his hand on the chopping block. Even if he tries to blame you, you know he's as responsible for what happened as you are. Telling yourself otherwise is just a twisted sort of hubris you should have grown out of years ago . . .*

The wind carried with it a plethora of new smells, fair and foul. He had come out onto the roof of the hostel to watch the coming of day, unable to sleep and needing space to be on his own. The guard standing outside the room he shared with Shilly had been reluctant to let him go, until Sal explained that he had nowhere to run to and no reason to run without Shilly. That much was the truth.

Getting onto the roof couldn't have been easier. A steep flight of stairs terminated in an access hatch and a short ladder. The roof itself was mostly flat and tiled in red. He picked a place at random and watched the light of the sun creep across the sky, turning the water in the streets yellow. The view was impressive. He could see man'kin on rooftops closer to the Wall, doing much the same as him. Their stone eyes stared blankly at him. The city's population had accepted the stony refugees as a necessary evil, just so long as they abstained from demolishing the buildings around them. An uneasy truce remained between the two very different populations.

"The weather-workers are quiet," said a voice from behind him. "What do they call them here? Yadachi?"

Sal turned to see Highson Sparre easing himself slowly out of the hatch. He got up to help and was surprised at the lack of flesh on his real father's arms.

"What are you doing up here? It's cold, and I thought—"

"I'm not dead yet, Sal; I've just been sleeping too long. The guard told me where you were. I'm sorry I wasn't awake to meet you when you arrived."

"That's okay. I completely understand." Sal helped Highson down onto the tiles, then sat next to him. His father had been out cold when he and the others had returned to the hostel. Shilly had seemed disappointed by that, but wouldn't let him be disturbed. Sal hadn't pressed the point.

They enjoyed the view for a moment. Immediately after the deluge, Sal had seen people filling reservoirs while they had the chance. Now, however, a century's worth of refuse had burst out of the city's underground places, disturbed from desiccated graves. He didn't want to think about what such filth might contain, and hoped the city had sanitation measures sufficient to deal with it. Somehow, he doubted it.

"Yadachi, yes," he said, belatedly remembering Highson's question. "They've been singing all night. I guess their job is done for the moment."

Highson nodded distantly. His eyes gleamed in the light. The beginnings of a peppery beard spread like a stain over his brown-skinned features.

"I want to tell you," Sal's real father said, "that I'm sorry."

"For what?"

"For dragging you all the way out here."

"Don't be ridiculous. You were in trouble. We had to come." It was easier to parrot Shilly's logic than confront his own conflicted feelings.

"But it shouldn't have happened that way. You were safe in Fundelry. I've jeopardised everything we worked for. If you're caught now, it's my fault."

"First we've got to *be* caught. Then let's worry about who's to blame."

Highson nodded, grief writ deeply in the lines around his eyes. A squad of guards on cleanup duty splashed by below, sending ripples along the street. The fingertips of Highson's left hand rubbed the rough edge of a cracked roof tile as though trying to get rid of a stain.

"Did Shilly tell you what I did? Why I called the Homunculus?"

"She told me."

Highson nodded again. He seemed relieved.

"Sal, I want you to know——"

"Don't say it. Don't tell me you're sorry again, or that you loved my mother. I already know that. And don't tell me that you were just trying to put things right, because it's too late for that. Bringing my mother back wouldn't have fixed anything. I didn't know her, and she didn't love you. The man she loved is dead, and nothing you can do will bring *him* back, ever." He irritably blinked back the beginning of tears. "I don't think she would've thanked you."

"No," said Highson, "but I don't regret trying. And that's what I was going to say. I had to make the attempt. To let the opportunity go would have been too much for me to bear. Her death was so pointless. She deserved better. I needed to *try* to make it better, before I could truly let her go."

Sal studied his father for a moment. Highson wasn't meeting his gaze. The muscles of his jaw and throat were tight, making talking an effort.

"You said you'd redeemed yourself last time," Sal challenged him. "How long will this go on?"

That earned him a flash of irritation. "What do you mean?"

"You saved me from the Syndic five years ago. You said that was to make up for what happened to my mother. And now here we are one more time, except this time you're guilty of theft and at least one man has died. What's to stop you doing something stupid like this again? The Goddess only knows what you might bring out of the Void, given another chance. Or what Marmion might do to stop you trying."

Highson's face set. "I don't care about Marmion."

"You should. He's come to arrest you. I hope you realise that much."

"He can try."

"He might succeed, given your present condition."

"You wouldn't help me?"

Sal glanced down at his hands. There was a long silence.

"I'm not going home, Sal. Not yet, anyway."

Sal looked up to find his father staring at him. He remembered his naive hope that Highson might come to Fundelry to recuperate.

"You're going to try to escape."

"It's not escape I want. I want to see this thing finished."

"*What* thing?"

"The Homunculus. Whatever it—*they*—are."

"When you say *finished*—"

"I mean resolved. Not dead."

That was good. Sal didn't want another Marmion on his hands. "The twins were down in the Divide when the flood hit. The chances are they're already dead."

"I doubt it. If the desert couldn't kill them, why would a little water?"

"Are you sure about that?"

"As sure as I can be. I made the body they're in, after all."

Sal nodded, imagining the Homunculus tumbling and tossing in the giant surge of water as it raged through the Divide, battered by detritus caught up in the flood's path. He couldn't conceive of the violence it must have endured—but if it *did* endure, he could see it striving for the Divide walls, reaching for handholds on the raw rock, and clinging there until the initial fury subsided. Then crawling its way out of the water like some supernatural cockroach, and from there resuming its implacable journey.

His *brother* . . . ?

And suddenly he was wrenched back to the last time he and his father had spoken in private, as they walked down into the caverns beneath the Haunted City, where the Way would take them back to Fundelry.

"There's one other thing you should know," Highson had said to him. The memory was as fresh as yesterday. "I knew you were there, Sal. I knew I had a child growing inside the woman I loved. I gave you away, for her sake—and yours, too."

"Was it hard?"

"Unbelievably. Even then I think I had an idea of what you could be, given the chance. But I wouldn't be there to find out. Your mother was never supposed to be found; no one was ever supposed to know you existed. That was supposed to be the end of it."

"But it wasn't."

"No. And that still feels strange to me. All my life I've put thoughts of you from my mind. I couldn't let myself wonder where you were, what you were doing, what you were like. I couldn't hope that I might meet you one day and tell you the truth. I certainly never thought I'd be in this position."

"What position?"

"Helping you escape from my family, and Seirian's. It's like the past is repeating itself. I'm letting you go again. Only now I've seen you, come to know you—my child, Seirian's son—it's so much harder to let you go."

Sal had never known how to feel about that. Somehow Highson *had* found the strength or courage, or whatever it had taken, to let Sal go a second time. He hadn't pursued him across the Strand, for fear of the Syndic following; he had never been in touch. Highson Sparre had vanished out of Sal's life as though he had never existed at all. Was that really the only way it could have gone?

For the Homunculus, everything was different.

"Before I heard about your situation," Sal said slowly, "I felt something. A tear in the world. It nagged at me, made me nervous. I didn't know what it was at first, but then Tom came and told us what he knew. You brought something out of the Void Beneath, and it seemed logical to assume that *this* was the tear I had been feeling. The hole you opened to let the Homunculus into the world."

Highson went to say something, but Sal waved him silent.

"That's what I thought. I know now that I was wrong. The tear wasn't how the Homunculus came into this world. If it was, I would have stopped feeling it ages ago, when it healed over. So the hole has to be the Homunculus itself. It's a rip in the fabric of things—a rip that's getting bigger, the longer it's here. I can still feel it, out there, somewhere."

Highson nodded. "I don't know anything about rips or tears, but I know we have to work out why it's here and what it wants. It saved me—once in the Void and then again in the desert. I'm bonded to it now. It owes me an *explanation*." He took a deep breath. "I can't go anywhere until I've got it."

Sal felt incredibly weary. "Then I guess I'll have to help you."

"No, Sal. You've done too much already."

"I can hardly leave you here at Marmion's mercy, can I? And I'm not letting you go off on another mad march across the country. Not on your own. There might be no one to rescue you at the end of that journey."

"Marmion thinks we're already there—that the Homunculus is going to come back to Laure, where it's been heading all this time. Don't you agree?"

Sal thought of what he had seen in the last moments before his connection with Kail had snapped, and shook his head. It wasn't the time to tell anyone about that. "I think," he said, "that if the Magister decides to formally charge us with something, the point will be completely moot."

Highson nodded, looking puzzled at first, then letting the subject go. His gaze drifted back out to the city's drowned carriageways and paths. A handful of miners were circling in the quiet morning air, examining the damage. The eagles hadn't returned to the top of Observatory Tower.

Sal felt bruised and empty inside, as though part of himself had been forcibly ripped from him. What that part was, he didn't know for certain: the memory of rejection; or perhaps the wounded pride that had clung to that memory for five years; or something else entirely. But its absence ached in him. He felt hunched over, persistently askew although he tried to sit straight.

"It's going to take them a while to work out whether to be happy or not," Highson said.

"Who?"

"The people who live here. They wanted water, and now they've got it. But at what cost? How will they make their living with the Divide flooded? I don't envy them the next few months."

Neither did Sal. But, looking at his father rather than the view, he understood that Highson was lying.

Word came at lunchtime that the Magister would conduct a hearing the next morning in order to decide the fate of the visitors to the city. Sal, already chafing at having been cooped up for so long, didn't know how to take the news. On the one hand, he was glad that the wheels of Laure's bureaucracy were turning quickly. On the other, he was nervous of what the Magister's decision would be. If it went well for them, they could be freed by noon. If it went badly, they might never see the sun again. Or worse.

In order to keep himself occupied, he sought out the hostel owner and asked for a favour.

"What do you people want now?" Urtagh exclaimed, hands raised in a dramatic gesture, the veins in his ruddy jowls primed to pop. "More food? My best wine? My daughter? And why not? You've cast my business into disrepute. The guards have sealed the doors so paying customers can't get in. Take what's left, why don't you? I'm already ruined!"

Sal soothed him. "You'll be compensated. Don't worry. The Alcaide's pockets are deep."

"You say that *now*. How are you going to pay your bill if you're locked in a dungeon?"

"Is that all you can think of? What about the extra business that's going to come through here with the Divide flooded? People will be able to cross anywhere now, not just at Tintenbar and the Lookout. There'll be a fishing industry, tourism, and trade. You'll make up your losses in a week!"

Urtagh was only slightly mollified. "Okay, okay. How can I help you? I'm all out of playing cards."

"I want a stick. A straight one, tall enough to walk with."

Urtagh eyed him grumpily. "What for?"

"Just put it on the bill. I'll charm that smoky fireplace of yours if it comes within the hour."

It came in half that time, not the best piece of silky oak he could have hoped for but perfectly straight and just the right height. When he had finished with the fireplace, Sal unfolded the pocketknife he kept under the false bottom of his pack and began to carve.

"Don't act so disappointed," said Marmion in a peevish voice. "I may not look like much, but it's going to take a lot more than this to put me out of action. Stubbornness runs in my mother's side of the family."

Marmion glanced down at where his right hand used to be, then back up again. His eyes were red-rimmed but determined. Only the greyness of his skin indicated that he had been on the threshold of death at least twice in the previous day, according to his healers.

Sal was watching Shilly, who had opened her mouth to say something, perhaps about Marmion's mother's family. She held the pose for a heartbeat, then pursed her lips and leaned with both hands on her new walking stick.

Just moments earlier, word had come that Marmion was awake and working on their appeal to the Magister. They had hurried to the communal dining area to find him propped up with cushions and his arm in a sling, still dressed in a nightgown. His mood was one of defensive dignity. Every now and again he went to use his right hand, and through that tiny chink in his armour Sal glimpsed a world of hurt.

"I'm sorry," said Skender.

"So am I," Marmion said without looking at him, "but there's no point dwelling on trivialities when we've lost the Homunculus, a far more important thing than one hand. How are we going to ensure that we remain free to find it?"

Almost everyone was present to work on that question, seated on chairs, benches, and tabletops around the makeshift stretcher Marmion occupied. There had, apparently, been a huge row with the guards over Mawson. During the attack of the man'kin, they had insisted on taking the bust into captivity. Fearing that he would end up smashed to pieces by some disgruntled captain, Abi Van Haasteren had pointed out that a creature with neither arms nor legs was unlikely to do any damage to anyone. The guards had reluctantly acquiesced and let him stay.

The only person missing was Chu. As a Laurean citizen, she required different treatment from the visitors—and nothing Skender could say made a difference. In her absence, he was like an overwound spring, too full of energy to relax but with no way of letting off steam. Sal still didn't know exactly what was going on between the two, and he suspected Skender didn't, either. That ambiguity only contributed to the awfulness of waiting.

Censers burned incense in all four corners of the room, filling it with the smoky scent of desert plum.

"Unfortunately," said Marmion, "the Magister is well within her rights to press charges. We did subvert her authority and break the laws of this city. The Alcaide can apply pressure for clemency, later, but that doesn't help us right now. We don't know how much time we have. Even a single night might cost us dearly."

"You're still going to go through with it?" asked Shilly. "After all we've learned?"

"What we have learned only increases my certainty that the Homunculus is dangerous. It must be stopped."

"And how exactly do you think you're going to accomplish that without Kail?"

"It must be coming to Laure. Its path led right here, and the flood will only have delayed it. We have to be ready for it when it arrives." Marmion's stare dared her to defy him. "I can assure you that we are perfectly capable, even without Kail."

With his left index finger, he drew a shape on the table in front of him: a D lying on its back, as large as a small book. Sal heard a faint buzzing and knew instantly what Marmion was doing. Before the warden had completed the sign, his finger was tracing it through a faint layer of dew.

Marmion was using the Change.

A gasp went up from the other wardens. Abi Van Haasteren raised an eyebrow. Shom Behenna's scowl deepened. Breaking the oaths of the Novitiate was a serious matter. For that alone, Behenna had been stripped of his rank and sent into exile. Sal couldn't tell exactly how he was doing it, but whether Marmion was using the power of the deeper desert or the bloodwork of the yadachi, it ran against everything the man had been taught: that in the Interior, a Sky Warden was too far from the sea to use the Change.

"The Divide is flooded," Marmion explained. "Water has returned to the Interior. Nothing will be the same again."

Sal stood.

"I'm afraid it's not going to be that simple."

Every eye in the room swivelled to focus on him. He didn't flinch from their scrutiny. The time had come to unburden himself, and to make sure the conversation wasn't diverted too far from what mattered.

"What do you mean?" asked Marmion.

"You're so certain that the twins are headed for Laure. Why? Yes, the city lies right in their path, and once we ruled out the Aad, this seemed like the only alternative. But Pirelius had to drag them here by force. They pressed constantly to be allowed to go elsewhere."

"How do you know this?"

"You're not the only one who talked to Kail."

Marmion nodded. "I wondered about that. Go on."

"Just before the flood hit, Kail spoke to the Homunculus. You were injured, so you couldn't have heard what the twins said, and Skender was busy saving you." Sal and Skender had agreed to keep the details of how Pirelius had died a secret, out of respect for the missing tracker. "I'm the only one who heard."

"Heard what?"

"Kail asked the twins what they wanted at Laure. They said: *nothing*. He didn't believe them, so he asked again. Why would they have travelled all that distance with nothing at the end of it? It didn't make sense.

"The twins replied that their journey wasn't over yet. The thing they were looking for was still ahead of them. They didn't know how far away it was. They didn't know how long it would take them to get there. All they had was a direction."

"Did they say what the direction was?" asked Shilly, looking at him in surprise. Sal hadn't told anyone about what he had overheard Kail say, not even—especially—her.

"Did they say what they were looking for?" added Highson.

"No. They just pointed northeast."

Marmion exhaled noisily. Sal could understand what he was feeling. Frustration that, if what Sal said was true, his mission might not be nearly over yet; anger that his plans had been trumped yet again; uncertainty over whether this new intelligence was trustworthy or not.

"It changes nothing," Marmion said. "We still have to convince the Magister that we should be freed—and quickly. Let's concentrate on tomorrow for now, and work out what to do the day after that another time."

"Just don't assume," said Sal, "that it'll be easy."

"Believe me," said Marmion, "I won't."

Sal nodded and sat down. That was enough for now.

After nightfall, in their room, Shilly asked Sal why he hadn't told her about Kail's conversation with the Homunculus. She had spent the night reading a book from the hostel's meagre library while Skender and Sal challenged two of the guards to a prolonged game of Double Advance—anything to distract themselves from the uncertainty of their fate. Despite the day's preparations, everyone was nervous about the following morning. Marmion had endured long enough to eat a small evening meal, then had retired to his room to recuperate.

"I didn't tell you," Sal said sombrely, "because we were never alone. There was always someone listening in, watching us."

She nodded and pulled him closer. Her eyes hung heavily. The mattress beneath them was softer than they were used to in Fundelry, and he could tell by the way she moved that her leg still bothered her. That always made her tired.

"Do you think he's dead?" she asked, running a cool hand across his sunburn.

"Kail?" He thought for a moment. "Maybe. He was thoroughly drained at the end. I don't know if he had the strength to swim a stroke. You can bet that Marmion's looked for him, and if he hasn't found anything then I don't think we should hold out much hope."

Shilly didn't respond. Her breathing became deeper and slower, and the muscles of her face relaxed.

Sal relaxed, too, glad that he had avoided the issue of Kail's final words for one more night. He didn't completely understand why keeping them from her was so important to him. Part of it was obvious: he had seen the way she looked at Marmion, how his very existence confused and hurt her. *He's the closest thing I've got to family,* she had said to Sal the previous day, *apart from you.*

Sal didn't want to put her through anything like that all over again.

But that couldn't be all of it. He wondered if he was jealous, or afraid that he might lose a part of her that had always been his. That was irrational and demeaning of him, he knew, but he had to admit it, if it was true.

Tell Shilly, Kail had shouted to Skender, just moments before the link between him and Sal had slammed shut. Kail the pragmatist, for whom the ends justified the means. *Tell her I'm sorry.*

Sal just needed some time to work everything out.

With that thought echoing in his mind, he fell asleep.

THE NEPHEW

"There is no greater mystery than one's own family . . ."
THE BOOK OF TOWERS, EXEGESIS 4:18

The sand swirled in a whirlpool like water going down a drain. Instead of lessening, it only seemed to become thicker, denser, and more choking by the second. It stung Shilly's face and got in her hair. Her mouth was full of it. When she tried to breathe, all she did was suffocate faster.

Finally, stillness enfolded her. The sand had stopped moving because it was packed in tight around her. Its weight was constricting, immovable. Her body stood trapped from the tips of her toes to the top her head. She was buried alive.

She couldn't even scream.

After an unknowable time, she felt something change. The sand encasing her head shifted. The pressure fell away. Fingers scrabbled at her hair and light fell on her clenched eyelids. She strained for the air, yearning for freedom.

Released from its dry tomb, her head tilted back and her eyes opened. She saw a young, dark-skinned woman bending over her, looking down in horror at what she had uncovered. Shilly tried to tell her, *No, don't be afraid. It's only me!* But the words wouldn't come.

As the sand poured in, sealing her back in her terrible grave, she screamed with despair as well as dread. The face bending over her was one she knew well. The woman responsible for trapping her again was none other than herself.

᠌ ᠌ ᠌

There were better ways to wake up. Echoes of the dream haunted Shilly all morning as she queued to bathe and relieve herself, then queued again for the breakfast Urtagh laid on for his guests. The service was resentful—and would remain that way, she figured, until he could be certain of being paid—but the fare was good. She ate heartily, not knowing when she'd get the chance to do so again. If she was about to be condemned, at least it would be on a full stomach.

Not long after, a series of motorised vehicles arrived to take them to the hearing. One by one, groups of four were escorted out of the hostel by the guards and whisked off to Judgment Hall, where the Magister would see them. Shilly recognised the feeling in her gut as she waited for her and Sal's turn to come. It was one that had become awfully familiar to her, years ago.

The taste and smell of sand seemed to follow her everywhere she went. At any moment she expected her mouth and nostrils to seize up, just like in her dream. Her palms were too sweaty to hold hands with Sal.

When finally their turn came, they were parcelled off with wardens Eitzen and Rosevear and shown outside. The sun seemed bright through a smattering of low cloud. The streets were less waterlogged than they had been the day before, but the stench was becoming worse in the humid air. She lifted the hem of her cotton skirt as she crossed puddles, trying not to think about what sort of disease-carrying dirt might be getting through her sandals and onto her toes.

The vehicle waiting for them was black and official. Guards bundled them into the back and locked the doors behind them. Two benches and just one small window greeted them. Sal helped Shilly to a seat and sat down next to her.

He took her new walking stick from her when she was settled and ran his fingers along the charms he had carved down its length.

"Not so much, this time," she said. "We don't want it to go off by accident."

He nodded, looking sheepish but unrepentant.

The trip wasn't a long one, but her stomach had settled into a continuous flutter by the time they arrived. The big breakfast no longer seemed like a good idea. A new set of guards opened the doors and let them out. She hopped out first, not waiting for her stick. Even the stench of stagnant water was better than being in that tightly enclosed space.

Think of flowers, she told herself. *Think of ringing bells and glass jars full of pebbles. Think of kittens and birds in flight. Anything but sand and suffocation . . .*

Judgment Hall was an imposing structure, blunt and square like an ancient fortress. Gargoyles crouched high on its eaves—*just* gargoyles, not man'kin—and the shrivelled bodies of convicted criminals, drained of blood, hung in rows down one side. She blanched on seeing them, feeling more nervous and sick than ever. A number of people had gathered to watch the procession of outsiders coming to be judged. They didn't cheer or jeer, but Shilly felt the weight of their scrutiny keenly. What did they make of her, this scraggly-haired young woman from the south with walking stick and muddy feet? At least on the last point they had no grounds to think her odd.

Inside, the hall was all right angles and circles, with ceilings stretching up to milky-coloured skylights and cobwebs too high for cleaners to reach. Porters led her and Sal through a relatively small antechamber to the room in which the hearing would take place. Circular, with a raised dais in the centre, it reminded her of the public hall in the Haunted City in which she and Sal had been sentenced years earlier. Her anxiety peaked at the sight. *I thought we'd put all that behind us*, she wanted to cry out. *How did it come back to this?*

She told herself to take deep, even breaths and calm down. *Sometimes,* Tom had said, *a dream is just a dream.* She was taken to a seat at the front of the hall, settled down, and counted Sal's freckles to pass the time.

"It seems clear to me," said the Magister, perched on her throne in the centre of the hall like some twisted, arthritic crow, "that the failure here is yours, Warden Marmion. Failure to meet your Alcaide's expectations; failure to understand the nature of the thing you were sent to find; failure to safeguard your own people; failure even to keep yourself from harm. . . . The list is long. I open myself up to accusations of pettiness by focusing on the ways you failed to comply with the laws of this city, but it would be a failure on *my* part to do otherwise."

Her glittering green eyes scanned the accused, assembled before her. Chu, Gwil Flintham, and quartermaster had been frogmarched into the hall once the visitors took their seats. Skender's relief was palpable on seeing his friend. Shilly had waited for an audience to be led in after them, but the hearing was to be conducted entirely in private. She was glad of that, if little else.

"No one would deny my dedication, Magister Considine," Marmion said in reply. "Nor my determination." His skin was like tallow, and Shilly feared he might collapse at any moment. Yet he persevered, sitting through the many witness statements and questions as though nothing could move him. "My record is not untarnished, but that can be said of many here. If I have failed, I have paid the price for it." He raised his bandaged arm, then lowered it back into its sling. "We each have our path to follow. I ask only that you let me follow mine."

Shilly felt a new appreciation for the man at those words. He knew exactly what had happened to him at the base of the Wall. Skender, Shilly, and Sal had come directly between him and the objective of his mission—to destroy the Homunculus. In doing so, they had crippled him for life, yet not once had he accused them of malice or carelessness. He had simply, and silently, pushed through his irritation to some deep reserve of character she hadn't seen before.

She, crippled in a simple car accident, had blamed Sal for weeks.

"Do what you want to yourself," the Magister asked. "That is your prerogative. Can I, however, in good conscience set you free to wreak havoc upon those who will next cross your path?"

"With respect, Magister, the man'kin would have breached the

Wall whether we were here or not. The flood would have come irrespective of our actions. It is not, therefore, *I* who brought havoc to your city. One could even argue that the greatest threat to Laure came about because of *your* actions, not mine."

The Magister's expression didn't change, but Shilly felt the air in the hall become distinctly frosty.

"How so?"

Marmion sighed, his weariness showing. "This charade pains me. Must I remind you of the contents of the letter I gave you, the first time we met?"

"Of course not. I am far from senile. It contained an unsubtly worded warning from your Alcaide that trade between my city and the Strand depended entirely on his goodwill. Were he to remove it because I failed to treat his emissary with respect, we would suffer." The Magister's fingers stroked the head of her black cane. "I endured this blackmail with more dignity than it deserved. Its efficacy has expired."

"Indeed." Marmion's expression betrayed no suggestion that his bluff had been successful. The contents of the letter had truly been unknown to him, prior to that moment. "I therefore propose that we reach a new agreement. I won't tell the Alcaide—or the citizens of your city—where the goods he purchased *actually* came from, and you will let us leave unhindered."

The Magister laughed. "Let's not tangle our tongues around the truth. Pirelius was a fool, but a convenient one. You're a fool, too, if you think you can use him against me."

"Why not? Your puppet in the Aad, who kept you supplied with artefacts too dangerous for your own miners to retrieve or steal, was a brutal, sadistic monster. There are several people in this room who can and will testify to that effect, on both sides of the Divide." Marmion indicated Skender's mother and her crutches, Kemp with a bandage around his throat, Skender's many bruises, and the smouldering trauma of Shom Behenna.

"We make what alliances we can, Marmion. Laure hovers on the threshold of viability. We do not have the choices or resources you do, in more prosperous lands."

"That I can understand. But to abandon this ally of yours the moment he comes under threat—how does *that* look? You may not have caused the circumstances by which his miniature empire crumbled, but you certainly didn't help him out of them. You threw him to the flood with casual contempt."

"That was all he deserved. He was a monster, as you say."

"It's the principle that counts, Magister."

For the first time, the Magister's confident mien seemed to crack. She shifted awkwardly on her throne and tapped her cane on the granite at her feet. All traces of her half-smile vanished.

"I rule by virtue of my ability," she said, "not my popularity."

"Both are being tested, Magister Considine. There's no denying that the yadachi saved Laure when the aquifer beneath it drained dry. No one would gainsay you that. But you've been isolated too long, and become too comfortable apart from the world. Now, with water flowing in the Divide, Laure may no longer be so marginal. New leaders will arise with new skills. Will the city remember the one who saw it through the long drought? Or will its citizens remember only the mistakes she made as the old world transformed into the new? Will they come to view her bloodworkers as saviours, or as leeches sucking the life out of their new prosperity?"

"Empty rhetoric, Marmion. Get to the point, if you have one."

"It all contributes, Magister. The world is coming to Laure, whether you want it to or not. Events here have overtaken your regime. Your substantive crime, as I see it, is to have ignored the plight of an expedition of Surveyors from Ulum. You knew Abi Van Haasteren was in trouble, and you must have suspected that your ally Pirelius was responsible. You could have intervened at any time to have her released, but you did not. You put her life and the lives of those with her in jeopardy. You even blocked me when I tried to mount a rescue expedition, for fear of your petty deal being exposed. You hid behind the Surveyor's Code like the coward you are. This is a charge that will stick when it comes before the Stone Mage Synod—which tolerates the existence of your yadachi in its territory, but does not love it. Could your authority survive such an affront? Who would trade with you then, when you treat your allies with utter disregard—even contempt? When you allow your greed to overpower all notions of decent humanity?"

The Magister's lips had become thin white lines. "You dare," she hissed with all the venom of a desert snake striking soft flesh. "You dare to threaten me!"

"I do," said Marmion, "and you know it's more than just a threat. I will accept nothing less than an immediate release from custody. In return, we will forget what's been said here and move on. You won't hear from us again. Your dirty secret will remain just that."

The Magister took in those seated before her. Shilly could tell what she was thinking—or imagined that she could. The Magister could silence Marmion, but there was nothing she could do about everyone else. They were too many to get rid of entirely, not without bringing down further accusations upon her. She was trapped like a scorpion in a corner. And she knew it.

Somehow, against all the odds, Marmion had turned the tables on her.

"Get out of my sight," she said. "All of you."

"Does this mean—?" Marmion started to ask.

"It means that I have heard everything I need to hear. Now I must deliberate. You will be advised of my judgment in due course."

The Magister descended from the podium and walked haughtily from the hall. The tapping of her cane was inaudible over the voices rising up from the gathering. Shilly watched her go, thinking that, for all her stubborn dignity, she looked like nothing so much as an old, tired woman. Mortality hung heavy around her, thicker than her black and red ceremonial robes. No stick could support her under such a weight.

Shilly almost felt sorry for the Magister, then. *Almost*. She saw in the old woman a glimpse of her own future: isolated, outcast, forced to extreme lengths to survive in an obscure borderland few people acknowledged. She couldn't forgive the Magister, though, for keeping them waiting for her decision. It was one final, feeble arrow fired from battlements that had already fallen. It wouldn't change a thing in the end. Shilly would bet her good leg on it.

Porters steered the accused outside, to the waiting vehicles. The Laureans found themselves released into house arrest along with the visitors. Chu, Gwil Flintham, and the quartermaster settled into the hostel with relish. Their previous habitation had been less than comfortable. Too close to something called the boneyard, apparently.

The group split into subsections as soon as they arrived. The quartermaster and Abi Van Haasteren sequestered themselves in a booth under the stairs to catch up on old times. Tom and Banner pored over Engineering diagrams in the first-floor sunroom. Sal and Highson talked soberly over coffee in a quiet corner while Chu and Skender chatted with Kemp in the bar, even though Urtagh wouldn't serve them drinks until their financial status was confirmed. Shilly noted the way Skender's attention kept coming back to Chu, whether she was talking or not.

Shilly found herself watching the disgraced Sky Warden Shom Behenna playing a dice game with Mawson. Torchlight flickered off his black, partially tattooed scalp as he rolled and counted. The tallies grew quickly, with Behenna casting the dice for Mawson since the man'kin had no hands or arms to do it himself. It quickly became apparent that Behenna stood no chance of winning at all.

"What are you?" she asked him. "A glutton for punishment?"

He glanced at her, and seemed to seriously consider ignoring her. In the end, good manners or something else won the day.

"It's always like this," he said. They were the first words Behenna had said to her—perhaps anyone—since his rescue from the Aad. "Man'kin are unbeatable at games of chance. They have some means of influencing the dice that I can't detect."

"*This is untrue,*" the man'kin defended himself. "*A dice may roll many ways, but it stops just once. I cannot change the way it stops. All I can do is* choose *which way it stops.*"

"That's the same thing, isn't it?" Shilly asked.

"*I assure you it is not.*"

Behenna watched her, not Mawson, and didn't take any joy at her confusion. "I've been studying this for years, now. Man'kin see a very different picture of the world from us. In some ways it's bigger, broader; in others it's frighteningly constricted. Their lives are fixed in ways we can't imagine, with life and death set for them, and every point in between, too. But they can choose among a variety of lives at any moment. That, I think, is how they can make the dice fall the way they want them to."

"*I am not making the dice do anything they haven't already done,*" Mawson insisted.

"It just looks that way to us."

Shilly thought hard to get around the concept. "Like a fork in the road. Each path is a different number on the dice. The man'kin go along them all at once, and we go along just one of them. Mawson can choose which one he's on *now*, with *us*, so it looks like he's made us take that path, somehow."

Behenna nodded. "Maybe."

"Can Mawson make other things happen, then? Could he have picked a world where the flood didn't occur?" She hesitated before adding, "Where you and Abi Van Haasteren weren't captured?"

His wince was fleeting, but there. "No. They can only manipulate small, happenstance things, as far as I've seen. It's an interesting thought, though."

That was an understatement. The possibility that man'kin were pulling the strings of fate to make the world go the way they wanted it to was frightening. Just because Behenna couldn't see them doing it didn't mean that he wasn't being shown only what they wanted him to see . . .

No. The idea was ridiculous, she told herself. If man'kin could choose the future, why would so many have died in the flood?

"Roll me a six," she told Mawson, shaking the dice in her hand and setting it free.

It came down on four.

"What went wrong?" she asked.

"*Nothing,*" Mawson said with a bored tilt to his head. "*I grow weary of your attempts to explain the perfectly obvious.*"

She patted him on the stony shoulder. "Good for you. You're not a toy, and I shouldn't treat you as one. I apologise."

Mawson nodded. "*Thank you. And now, you see, I am exactly where I want to be.*"

Shilly laughed for the first time in what felt like days.

Word came from the Magister as the sun was setting. Delivered through an official spokesperson, it was brief and to the point.

"Magister Considine has considered your position and made her decision. Your liberty has been restored to you. All charges are dismissed and all privileges restored. You are free to do as you will in the city of Laure."

Applause greeted the announcement. Chu whooped in delight. Shilly turned to Sal, unable to believe it had all gone so smoothly. They embraced.

There was a sting in the tail, of course. "You will be presented with a bill for damages and services accrued during your stay. The Magister insists that this be paid before your departure. Noncompliance will incur the most serious of consequences."

"I understand," said Marmion from his makeshift bed in the common area. He looked weak and very tired, but his mind was alert.

There was no mistaking his satisfaction with the outcome. "Please convey my—*our*—gratitude to the Magister. We'll be out of here as soon as is humanly possible."

The spokesperson bowed and left.

"What now?" asked Skender, addressing the room in general.

"We celebrate, of course!" Chu snapped her fingers at Urtagh. "A round of araq, double time. Our credit's good. Hurrah!"

Marmion looked for a moment as though he might veto the order, but stayed his hand. Immediately unctuous, Urtagh passed small shot glasses around the room, and followed with a bottle of milky, foul-smelling liquid. The bar soon filled with the sound of coughing and expletives.

Shilly put her glass aside, untouched, as Marmion called Gwil Flintham and Warden Banner to him. They helped him stand and led him from the room. Following an instinct, Shilly slipped her hand from Sal's and trailed Marmion up the stairs.

"Can I talk with you?"

The injured warden didn't turn to look at her. He just kept climbing slowly and painfully, one step at a time. "About what?"

"About us."

"Can it wait until morning?"

"I'd rather clear the air now," she said. "It won't take long."

He acquiesced, and wearily waved her into his room after him. The low-ceilinged chamber smelled of herbs and buzzed with the Change. The proximity of water made possible many advanced healing techniques used by the Sky Wardens. Young Rosevear couldn't grow back Marmion's hand, but he could keep the wound from infection and encourage it to heal more quickly than it would otherwise.

Marmion lay down on the bed and dismissed Banner and Gwil. The round-faced Engineer squeezed Shilly's hand briefly as she went by, perhaps in encouragement.

"We'll be outside the door if you need us," said Gwil to Marmion. The former city gatekeeper looked uncertain about her being there.

"Are you *his* keeper now?" she asked him.

"I'm still responsible for him," Gwil said. "I don't want the Magister or the Alcaide accusing me of shirking my duty."

She raised her new stick. "You can't possibly think I'm here to finish him off. Can you?"

Gwil reddened and backed out of the room, his lank blond hair shaking as he went.

"That was in poor taste, Shilly." Marmion waved with his good hand at a selection of chairs along the Wall. "Sit. Talk."

She sat, nervous now the moment she had been half-dreading, half-hoping for had arrived. It wasn't just that Marmion looked so sick, although there was no denying that. His head eased back onto a pillow as soon as he lay down; his eyes closed. His skin still had a waxy sheen to it. She didn't want to add to his burdens.

But she could still hear Skender saying, *You're in charge*, on top of the Wall during the man'kin "invasion." Maybe he had been joking; maybe he had said it just to stop her from getting into the harness. Either way, it had rung true. Was being *in charge* really what she wanted? Making decisions was easy when the right one was obvious. But what about when those decisions might cost the lives of people around her? What if her judgment was wrong? What if the Wall *had* come down, and they had all died?

She certainly didn't feel *in charge* at that moment, of herself let alone anything or anyone else.

"I can't work you out, Eisak Marmion," she said. "You can be such a bastard at times, and it would be easiest to accept you as just that. But I keep glimpsing something else behind that front, and I'm beginning to realise what it might be."

"Oh, really? Do tell."

"It's fear." She hesitated. "I didn't see it at first. Highson spotted it before I did."

"So Highson put this in your head? And you believed him, naturally, after all the nonsense he told us."

"It's not nonsense. You know that as well as I do. He told us the truth—*and* he saved your life when he could just as easily have let the Homunculus kill you. A little faith isn't too much to ask, I think."

"I place my faith in what I can see and touch. The story Skender brought back from the Void is nonsense. That wasn't the first time I'd heard it, and I believed it as little from Highson's lips as anyone else. So-called Lost Minds, survivors from before the Cataclysm, some sort of bizarre *after*life—it's ridiculous! *This* is the only world there is, the one before us, which we touch with our hands and experience through the Change. There is no other."

"There's the Void Beneath."

"An emptiness for fools to get lost in. I am not a fool."

"Then why are you so afraid?"

"Of what? Of you?"

"No. The twins, of course."

Marmion sighed deeply. "I told you once that I don't have to justify my decisions to you. The same goes for me as a whole. You have no right to question my integrity. I can only forgive so much."

"I'm not asking for forgiveness, and I'm not questioning your integrity. There's nothing wrong with fear; sometimes it even makes sense. I just want to understand. When I have that understanding, maybe it'll make things easier. Next time we disagree over something like this, one of us might be killed." *And it won't be me*, she added silently to herself.

"I think," he started, and then seemed to reconsider. He began again: "I think you already know the truth."

"That you are trying to kill the twins because you're afraid of them." He didn't deny it, so she ploughed on. "But why do they terrify you? They haven't threatened you or harmed you in any way. They aren't evil."

"They threaten *everything*." Marmion's head lifted; his eyes blazed. "The world breaks down around them. You can see it happening in the man'kin, in the Change, the flood. Things are only going to get worse. The longer they're here the more tenuous our future becomes. *That's what I'm afraid of.*"

She was startled by his answer. "How do you know this?"

"You listen to Tom about his dreams. He's not the only seer in the Alcaide's service. Some foresee a time beyond which they cannot see, when the world as we know it ends. That time is coming soon—and the Homunculus is at the centre of it. That's why it must die."

Her first instinct was to disbelieve him. "Kail didn't say anything about this."

"Why would he? It's not his place to—and besides, he doesn't know."

"All right then, but it still doesn't make any sense. Why destroy the twins without finding out what they want or where they're going? At least hear what they have to say first. Maybe they have the answer for us, and killing them will seal our fate forever."

"Would you do nothing as the end of the world approaches, Shilly? I wouldn't." He sighed again, and his head fell back onto the pillow. "Neither would the Alcaide."

"So you have your orders, and that's enough for you. Is that all you want to be? The Alcaide's lackey?"

"All I want," he breathed, "is for this to be over."

Shilly looked down at her hands. If the seers were right, then things were more serious than she had realised, but there had to be a better means of saving the world than by taking innocent lives. She couldn't accept that plan, if it was all he had to offer.

It's always *too early to give up on someone,* Marmion had said. *A chance remains that they'll surprise you, no matter how minuscule it seems.*

She cleared her throat.

"Lodo used to say: trust is cheap; respect is priceless. No matter what you think of him, he was absolutely right on that score. We may never be friends, we disagree on lots of points, and I'm pretty sure I'll never trust you completely—but I do respect your conviction, and your determination to follow through. I wanted you to know that."

That was as far as she could go. The issue of how their differences could be resolved was better put aside for the moment. Until the Homunculus was next in their grasp, there was precious little they could do about it.

As to the rest, he obviously didn't want to take it any further, and she didn't have the energy to force him. The connection they had with Lodo and to each other was less important than the other issues surrounding them. Hard though it was, she knew she had to let it go or go crazy.

She stood, intending to leave before she changed her mind.

"Shilly, wait." His voice was soft, but there was a new tone to it that stopped her in her tracks. "I don't feel that I've done anything to earn your respect, but I am—grateful, I guess, that you think me worth the effort to understand. We're both trying to do what's right, and it's not simple for either of us." He took a deep breath. "I'll try harder. I know better, now, than to dismiss you, or to cross you."

Shilly nodded, wishing with all her heart that she could give him his hand back. She knew what it felt like to lose something fundamental in an instant—like the ability to walk properly or to grasp one hand in another.

"I also want to say," he went on, "that I'd like you to come with us when we go looking for the source of the flood and the Homunculus. Tom seems to think they're all connected—and that we'll need you along the way."

She thought of home and the people she'd left behind. "I'll consider it," she said, heading for the door. Her courage was spent. Now she just wanted to get out before he asked her for anything else she couldn't refuse.

"One last thing."

She froze, hearing nothing but the sound of her breathing.

"I'm sorry that Kail is gone," he said softly. "He and I weren't close, but I knew his background well enough. He always wanted to meet you. I think he might even have been jealous of you, a little. You knew his uncle better than he ever did, thanks to his family. And now he'll never get the chance to make up for that."

"Who?" Shilly felt the gears of her thoughts seize up. "Kail—what?"

"Was Lodo's nephew. Didn't he tell you? I thought he would have when you met. Perhaps he meant to later."

Shilly fumbled for her memories of that first meeting in the Broken Lands with the wardens stranded in the Homunculus's wake. Kail had come to join her and Sal in the buggy, and talked about how Lodo's family had spurned him for rebelling against tradition. He had said that Marmion was Lodo's nephew—or so she'd taken his words to mean.

Looking back on it now, the conversation had a very different cast. Marmion, Kail had actually said, *is a hapless peacock who would rather die than admit any disloyalty to the Alcaide. Look all you like, but I doubt you'll see any family resemblance.*

All true.

But: *These days, Lodo's nephew likes to think he's leading this expedition. There are, however, plenty who disagree.*

Marmion was *in charge* of the expedition. Habryn Kail was leading it, or trying to. Kail the outsider, the loner, the tracker.

Not Marmion. *Kail.*

Blood rushed to her cheeks. Her embarrassment couldn't have been more profound. All those times she'd wished Marmion could be more like Lodo, and not once had Kail corrected her mistake. Had it been a case of simple misconception on her part, or deliberate misdirection on his? Either way, he had let it persist.

Embarrassment turned to anger. Why hadn't he told her the truth? Had he been laughing at her expense? Enjoying her foolishness? Secretly betting on how long it would take her to make the connection?

And now he was gone. He had left the last laugh too late.

Serves him right, she thought, even as she came to the understanding that he hadn't been laughing at her at all. He had been watching her and relating with her in a way that wouldn't have been possible if she *had* known the truth. She would have been evaluating him, judging him right back—just as she had been with Marmion. Her expectations would have got in the way of any genuine communication.

He had, perhaps, wanted her to like him for who he was, not who she wanted him to be. That, after all, was what everyone deserved.

"Thank you," she said to Marmion, "for telling me the truth. I think I earned that much, at least."

Marmion—free of the burden of her expectations, which he hadn't even known he was bearing—didn't answer. His mouth hung half-open. The sound of his breathing had deepened.

She told herself that an apology wasn't worth waking him for, and felt relief.

Someone knocked at the door behind her. She opened it. Warden Banner stuck her head through the gap. Her eyes took in the entire room with one sweep. Marmion didn't stir.

"It's gone awfully quiet," Banner observed.

"He's asleep. I'll leave now."

Banner opened the door wider and Shilly stepped through. "It's good that you two talked. The tension has been putting the rest of us on edge."

"I don't think that'll be a problem any more." Shilly took the woman's arm before she could slip past. "Were you listening?"

"Not enough to hear actual words."

"Good." Shilly took a moment to gather herself outside the room, then went downstairs. A stiff drink, she hoped, would be just the thing to get the taste of sand out of her mouth—assuming Chu hadn't drunk the bar dry first.

THE MOTHER

". . . except, perhaps, one's heart."
THE BOOK OF TOWERS, EXEGESIS 4:18

*P*_{ain.}

Skender tried to open his eyes and failed on the first attempt. Every movement, no matter how slight, sent agony spiking through his skull. It was worse than being in the cage with Rattails poking him, worse than Pirelius's dirty fingers squeezing his windpipe shut, worse even than seeing the ground come up at him when he and Chu crashed her wing.

How had he got in such a situation? What had happened to him?

The last thing he remembered was arguing with Chu. Had she hit him? That didn't seem likely, but it wasn't impossible. How else to explain the utter nothingness that connected that moment to the present?

A dreadful suspicion began to creep over him, made only worse as he prised his eyelids open a crack and took in his surroundings. He was in his room in the Black Galah, sprawled face up on the bed, wearing nothing but his shirt. He didn't remember coming up to his room after the argument; he didn't remember getting undressed. He didn't remember anything after Chu yelling at him, and him yelling back. The content of even that conversation was hazy.

He didn't *remember*!

The mental breakdown he had suffered was worse than any merely physical pain. He hauled himself upright, appalled at the taste in his mouth. The world spun violently around him, and he supported himself with one hand against the bedpost while his stomach roiled. His new robe lay splayed across the floor. Putting it on required a supreme effort.

The void in his memory gnawed at him. He had to find out what had happened. The thought of not knowing was unbearable. Staggering slightly, he wound his way along the empty corridor of the hostel's top floor to the bathroom, where he was mortified to discover that the strange smell in his nostrils really did come from him.

Urtagh informed him that everyone had gone to inspect the waters in the Divide from the vantage point of the Wall. The landlord also offered him breakfast, which he quickly and firmly declined. The sun was halfway across the sky when he left the hostel. Squinting through the light, still feeling as though someone had hammered nails into his head, he hailed a cab. He collapsed into the back with a groan, and tried his best to ignore the rocking motion of the seat beneath him.

Flashes of the previous night came back to him, disconnected and confused like images from a dream. There had been singing, laughter, shouting, and a lot of drinking. There had also been accusations and hurt and Chu's face before him, mouth moving but words lost in a roar of forgetfulness. The fragments wouldn't fit together, no matter how he tried to force them. How had the argument ended? He needed to know.

The cab let him out at the checkpoint, and the redhead who had been fooled by Gwil Flintham saluted him through. He barely acknowledged her, focusing instead on putting one foot in front of the other. A cool wind blew from the direction of the Divide, carrying with it the sound of voices. Someone called out to him.

It was Kemp. The big albino occupied a spot on the far side of the right-hand guardrail, his throat bandaged and legs dangling over what had once been empty space. Now a drop of about six metres led to the surface of swirling, muddy water. Skender took in the mind-boggling view in small pieces, unable to credit the change all at once. The last time he had stood in that spot, the Divide had been exactly as it always had been—a dry, dangerous desert with no reason to recommend it whatsoever.

Now he could have been standing on the bank of an enormous river. The water stretched almost the entire distance across the canyon. He could see strong currents swirling under the surface, coalescing into eddies and whirlpools and fading again as he watched. A flood line—several metres above the water's present level—revealed just how torrential the surge had been. The exposed rock had a scoured, raw finish.

"You don't look so good." Kemp tugged on a makeshift fishing line, surely the only one for hundreds of kilometres.

Skender shook his head, not trusting his balance enough to approach any nearer the edge than the guardrail.

A flock of white cockatoos with yellow crests flew overhead, calling raucously.

"I don't feel so good," he admitted.

"Here." Kemp pressed a flask of water into his hand. "Drink. You'll feel better eventually."

He swigged carefully from it, lest his stomach revolt. "What did I do last night?"

Kemp chuckled. "Boy, you must have got it bad, if even *you* don't remember."

Skender felt a flash of irritation. There was no point stating the obvious. "I just want to know, no matter how bad it is."

"Well, the last time I saw you, we were talking about old times with Chu. She wanted to hear the story of how we were caught by the Sky Wardens in the Haunted City. She seems a good sort, that one. Enjoys a good laugh, anyway."

Several pieces fell into place. He did recall boasting to someone about his adventures. It could have been Chu.

"What came after that?"

"I don't know. You wandered off to get some more of those delicious koftas and didn't come back. Chu went after you."

"She did?" That he couldn't remember. The thought of food made him queasy. "Was she mad at me?"

"Not that I could tell. You seemed to be getting on fine."

"Do you know where she is now?"

"No. Sorry." Kemp's eyes drifted back out over the water, where his float bobbed fruitlessly among the debris. "Look at that! There's a whole tree in there! Where on Earth does it all come from?"

The water had a sound to it that reminded him of lizards slithering. Skender remembered the old creek beds in the bottom of the Divide, and wondered if there had been a river there once, ages ago. Perhaps something had stopped it up, dammed it, and now that dam had burst. He couldn't imagine the scale of such a dam, and for the moment he didn't care.

Thanking Kemp, he headed further out along the Wall, to the next people in line.

Sal and Shilly were arguing about who had said sorry to whom and why. Skender didn't know what they were talking about, and they didn't know what he and Chu had fought over the previous night, since they had retired early.

"Do you think Kail might still be alive?" Shilly asked him out of nowhere. "You were down there. You saw him better than Sal did."

"I don't know," he said, "but he's a tough old bird. I wouldn't put anything past him, if he set his mind to it."

Skender couldn't tell whether that news saddened or gladdened them. None the wiser on any count, he wandered off.

More birds glided by, and he followed their trajectory into the sky. A low-flying heavy lifter caught his eye. Tom and Banner and several of the wardens were hanging over its edge, waving as they headed out across the Divide. Now that water had returned to the centre of the world, the Sky Wardens were able to exercise their powers again. He idly wondered what his father and the other Stone Mages would think of that.

A snippet of information came to him in a flash.

Stone and air don't mix.

The phrase was a simple one, frequently heard in his training. Fire and water didn't mix either, and the lesson was one drummed into every Sky Warden or Stone Mage raised in their respective countries— summarising the difference between the divergent philosophies. He had heard the phrase on the lips of the quartermaster, when he had offered to help fix Chu's wing, six days earlier. Something told him that he had heard it even more recently than that.

Again he saw Chu's face before him, angry and hurt. He was stone, and she was air. What had Shilly said about him being like his father? *Now you're flirting with a flyer from the other side of the Interior. It's a recipe for exactly the same disaster.*

A hole seemed to open up beneath him. He sincerely hoped he hadn't said what he thought he might have . . .

"You look like you're about to either throw up or fall down," said a familiar voice. He focused on the world around him and saw his mother watching him, concerned. She had changed into new robes; her many scrapes and bruises stood out against her pale skin.

"Or both," he said, putting a hand over his face. Cold sweat prickled in the breeze. "What have I done?"

"Drank far too much, that's all," she said, ruffling his hair. "Come and sit down. There are seats along here."

He followed her towards an impromptu viewing area where someone had had the forethought to provide benches for spectators. His mother walked with the assistance of crutches, favouring her right leg, but she still managed to outpace him. His entire body felt like it needed a crutch.

When the weight came off his legs, he sighed with intense relief.

"I think I've been unbelievably stupid," he said. "Again."

She laughed, revealing a cracked tooth on her upper jaw. Combined with a bandaged eye and short-hewn hair, it made her look like one of Pirelius's bandits. "So you've got a hangover. It's not the end of the world—although it might feel like it for a while."

"No, not that." He explained the situation to her: his lack of memory and a growing fear that he might have told Chu something he didn't mean. "I think I told her it wouldn't work between us."

"Was she interested in trying, do you think?"

"I don't know." Normally he would have been blushing to talk about something so intimate with his mother, but his cheeks were cold in the wind and he didn't know who else to turn to. "I can't remember."

"Well, if that is what happened, you should take some comfort from the knowledge that your father did exactly the same thing to me when we first met. It's nothing to be ashamed of."

"What isn't?"

"Fear, of course."

"Goddess." Now Chu thought he was *frightened*? His day was deteriorating fast. "I can't imagine Dad turning you down." He wasn't sure he wanted to think about it in any detail.

His mother seemed to understand that much, at least. "It's a long story. I'll tell you one day, when all this is over. But it worked out for the best, I think." She put a hand on his arm, where one of the bruises from Pirelius's whip lay.

"Ouch."

"Sorry." She laughed. "You Van Haasterens are a fragile lot. If only you'd taken after me."

He couldn't help a bad-tempered scowl. Fragility, it seemed, was something else he had inherited from his father. Why couldn't Skender be tall like him, too, to make up for it?

"What are you going to do now?" he asked, to turn the subject back to her. "Go back home to Dad?"

"Not just yet." She flexed her injured leg and winced. "The Aad is flooded, but I'm hoping the tunnels might still be clear. The Caduceus is in there somewhere. It's just a matter of fishing it out."

"Why?"

"Why not?"

He didn't have a good answer to that, just a bad one. "You know it won't be complete. Kail took a piece of it with him."

"I do know that, but it's still an important find. And who knows where Kail will reappear again? Alive or dead, he might still have the fragment on him." She ran a hand across her close-cropped hair, reaching for the braids that weren't there any more. "What about you? You've found me, so you're free to go back to the Keep, to your father. Is that what you're going to do?"

"I don't know." The Sky Wardens intended to keep looking for the twins, if they were still alive. At the same time they would investigate the source of the flood and the mysterious Angel that appeared to be driving the man'kin migration. Something was going on in the Hanging Mountains, and it was important to know what that was, in case it spread.

Just because Skender could follow Marmion's reasoning, that didn't mean he had to be part of it. He could leave in good conscience and begin the long trek home that very moment, if he wanted to. He simply wasn't sure, yet, what he would be leaving behind if he did.

Out on the water, the heavy lifter had stopped and lowered ropes tipped with grapnels and hooks. Its stern dipped low under the weight of something it had snared. Skender could just make out Tom and Banner gesticulating and calling instructions to the yadachi crew. The two Engineers would probably be happy in Laure for months, trawling the water for arcane finds. How was Marmion intending to travel upstream anyway? There were no boats in Laure, and buses could only go so far over the increasingly mountainous terrain. He doubted Marmion would get within a kilometre of a heavy lifter again.

It was a fool's errand. He had no part to play in it.

"Chu was here earlier," said his mother.

"Really? Why didn't you tell me?"

"I thought I'd hear your side of the story first."

"There's a story? What did she say?"

"I think you need to ask her that, not me."

"How did she look? Where is she now?"

"She looked pretty happy, actually. Her licence has been renewed."

"Did she say where she was going?"

"No."

Skender knew anyway. If she had her licence again, there was only one possible place. "Thanks, Mum." He levered himself upright. "I'll see you later."

"No doubt."

He hurried along the Wall, retracing his steps. As he passed Sal and Shilly, they had stopped talking and were watching the heavy lifter's progress.

"Look!" Shilly said. "It's the body of a hullfish, like the one *Os* is carved from!"

He barely glanced to his left. Noting the enormous white carcass dangling from the rear of the heavy lifter, but not immediately making the connection with the Alcaide's charmed ship, he simply waved and kept going.

Her licence. Skender's heart beat fast as the cab wound its way to the armoury. It seemed to take an inordinately long time to get anywhere.

A new fear had struck him. What if his interpretation of the argument was wrong? What if the hurt and anger had been on *his* side, not hers? What if he had misunderstood the situation completely, and he was the rejected one, not her?

He remembered the Magister saying to Chu, earlier that week: *The moment I give you your licence back, you will abandon this young man to his fate. Your intentions are transparent to me.*

The taxi driver turned around to ask him a question, and for an instant Skender was certain he was the same one he'd charmed three days earlier. His heart tripped a beat and he swore that he would make amends on that score the very next day. But it wasn't the same man.

This driver's head was full of grey hair, and his ears hung low under the weight of several gold hoops.

Skender stammered an answer. Yes, he was from out of town; no, he wasn't interested in a good price on Ruin fragments.

"Hasn't Magister Considine frozen trade in artefacts until the flood situation is clarified?" he asked.

The driver took the hint and went back to driving in silence.

Skender stewed all the way to the armoury, wondering how people without his perfect memory coped under the burden of so much uncertainty. It was devouring him from within. He knew he should be deciding what he was going to do in the coming days, but until he had filled the void in his mind he couldn't contemplate anything else. A builder wouldn't begin walls or a roof without finishing the foundations first. How could he move into the future without a rock-solid guarantee of the past behind him?

Part of him was aware that he might be overreacting. He couldn't help it. He had to know where he stood with Chu. That particular mystery was more alarming than anything to do with Laure, the Divide, the twins, his parents—or anything else that came to mind.

The cab jerked to a halt at the base of the armoury, and he paid the fare. As he stepped out onto the familiar streets, he began to feel nervous. Finding out could be worse than being left in the dark. Perhaps some things were better left forgotten.

"Hey, stone-boy!"

Skender looked up to see Kazzo Niclais sauntering out of the armoury entrance, a folded wing slung under his arm like a plank of wood. Inwardly, he groaned.

"What do you want?"

"Just saw you standing out here, looking lost. You need directions?"

"That's okay. I know where I am."

"Right, then." The handsome flyer waved cockily and went to continue on his way.

"Wait," said Skender, ignoring the throbbing in his head. "Have you seen Chu today?"

"Sure have, stone-boy. She took to the air a quarter-hour ago. Testing out her new licence."

Distrusting Kazzo's word, Skender looked up and around him, seeking her out among the many wings in the air that afternoon. He did recognise her, swooping and gliding like an eagle over the Wall. Part of him ached to be up there, too, but that wasn't likely to happen soon. His licence, last seen flying off into a sandstorm with the quartermaster, had been most firmly revoked by the yadachi.

"Will she be up there long?"

"I wouldn't stand out here waiting for her, if that's what you're wondering. It's been a long time since she got to go solo. No offence, but flying with you just wasn't the same."

Kazzo smirked. Skender didn't have the energy for resentment. "Thanks."

"No problems, stone-boy." Kazzo sauntered off a second time, then stopped himself with an afterthought. "Hey, look, just to show there are no hard feelings, why don't you meet us at the Crown and Sceptre tonight. You look like you could use a drink."

Skender couldn't think of a single use for alcohol at that moment except as an emetic. He squinted up at the brawny flyer, wondering if he was hearing a peace offering or charity.

"Who's we?" he asked, imagining a room full of cocky types like Kazzo, overwhelming with their good looks and scraggly beards and coarse humour.

"Me and Chu, of course. You can talk to her then. I'm sure that'd be okay."

"You and—?" He stopped, hearing the subtle inflection in Kazzo's voice. Not charity *or* peace, but an excuse to use the phrase. "*What?*"

"You look surprised. Didn't she tell you?"

"Tell me what exactly?"

Holding the wing vertically in his muscular arms, Kazzo came back to Skender.

"Look, don't take this too hard, stone-boy, but you've been led down a bit of a merry path. Chu never wanted to be with you. She was just looking out for herself. And who can blame her for that? Things were pretty tough for a while there. She needed someone to help her out, and she was too wretchedly proud to ask me to take her back. You came along at just the right time. You helped her get her licence back. She needed the confidence boost." A big hand clapped down on Skender's shoulder. "You did the right thing, man, and you've got a right to feel ripped off. I'm sorry."

Kazzo did his best to feign sympathy, but there was no hiding a certain amount of gloating. Skender didn't know what to say. He felt as though the box containing all his Chu-related suspicion and paranoia had been torn open and its contents laid bare for the world to see. Every niggling doubt took on a new significance in the light of this possibility. She had made it clear right from the beginning that she hadn't been helping him out of the goodness of her heart; he had been under no illusions on that score, although later he had come to wonder. Now it seemed as if her motives had been even more self-centred than he could have imagined.

Chu had everything back. Not just her licence, but the respect of the other miners as well, and Kazzo. She didn't need Skender any more, and certainly wouldn't leave Laure in a screaming blue fit. Any romantic notions he might have entertained about her testing the updrafts of the Keep's cliff faces were just nonsense.

Some people might say that like should stick with like, she herself had said, *or else you're asking for disaster.*

He didn't wonder for longer than a second if Kazzo was lying. It all fitted together too well.

All I care about is my own skin . . .

"Are you all right?"

Skender was sick of people asking him that. "I'm fine, thanks." He swore he would be, just to spite them all, as he looked around for another cab.

"Sorry you had to find out from me. She should really have told you before she went flying."

"Right." *Perhaps she did it last night*, Skender thought hopelessly to himself.

"Don't forget that drink, stone-boy."

"I won't." That was guaranteed. He had no intention of going, though. He'd rather tear out his heart and eat it raw.

"Okay, see you." Kazzo rotated his wing smoothly back to horizontal and strode off down the street.

Skender decided to give up on the day. It was unlikely to improve, and he could think of several ways in which it could get worse. He went back to the Black Galah and locked the door to his room behind him. Pulling the curtains, he collapsed on the bed and closed his eyes. He felt like a complete, utter idiot. The pain in his head was nothing compared to the ache in his heart. If he didn't wake up until the Divide was dry again, that would be fine by him.

In his nightmare, the man'kin who had fled into Laure thudded heavily through the streets, searching for something. The amnesty the Magister had offered them was forgotten and they had burst through the walls of the boneyards where they had been living, waving human femurs like clubs. Skender walked among them, unnoticed, until he came face to face with the one who had raised him above its head on top of the Wall to show him the approaching flood. It blocked the road ahead of him, arms spread wide and low so he couldn't pass.

"*ANGEL*," it said.

"Listen to it, rabbit," hissed another voice from the shadows. "This is important."

Skender twisted to see Rattails lying half in and half out of a garbage bin, his face permanently locked in a rictus of pain.

"Thought you'd got rid of me—didn't you, rabbit?"

"What are you doing in there?" Skender backed away, but the alley had closed shut behind him. He was trapped in a dead end with the grimacing bandit.

"I'm waiting for the rubbish collectors," Rattails whispered, sitting up and crawling forward with slow, careful movements. Wilted lettuce leaves fell from his scars. "The time has come to sweep out the new and bring back the old."

"Don't you mean—?"

"*ANGEL WAITS*," boomed the giant man'kin.

Skender looked up in confusion. "Angel waits for what?"

"The end, of course." Rattails lunged for Skender with twisted, clawlike hands, his teeth bared in a vengeful snarl. "You left me behind, rabbit!"

Skender leapt over the man'kin's giant arms and fled without looking back. Slapping footsteps followed him, and the sound of maniacal, pained laughter. His heart pounded as he tried to find his way back to the hostel. The streets had shifted, become those of the Aad. The ground was as dry as bone. Giant cracks appeared in the road and buildings, and the Wall protecting the city from the Divide suddenly split and peeled away. Instead of water, a tide of yellow sand poured forth in a giant wave to bury everything and everyone forever.

A key turned in the lock to his room. He sat up straight on the bed and blinked at the door as it opened.

"Oh, it's you," said Chu, struggling under the bulk of her wing. Her head was still bound but the dressing was clean. "What are you doing here?"

"What are *you* doing here?"

"I asked first. I waited half an hour, but you didn't show up." She looked around her in disbelief. "Have you been asleep the whole time?"

He stared at her. His headache had eased but the confusion in his thoughts was undiminished. Was she talking about the drinks with Kazzo? Why would she have wanted him there? And what was she doing *here*? How had she got in?

He had been dreaming about man'kin, and something about an endless yellow desert.

"What?" was the best he could manage as she manoeuvred the wing into one corner. A key tinkled onto the floor beside it.

"This is my room, remember? I moved in here while you were in the Aad."

"As a matter of fact, I *don't* remember. I don't remember anything since last night."

"Oh, sure. That's the lamest excuse I've ever heard for standing a girl up—especially coming from you." She unzipped her patched leather top and stretched.

"But it's true!" He groaned and fell back onto the bed—and jerked back upright with a start. The bed had somehow become hers without him knowing. The Goddess only knew what she thought he was doing there.

Chu studied him with the beginnings of a frown. "Just how much did you drink last night?"

"I don't know." He rubbed his temples. "Too much, obviously."

"Do you remember being carried up here after we found you lying on the floor of bar, out cold?"

Horror gripped him. She had to be joking.

She laughed at the expression on his face. "You really don't remember a thing. This is hysterical."

"It's not!" Some of his earlier frustration returned. He backed away from her, taking the covers with him, until he was leaning against the wall behind the bed. The bruises on his arms and chest stood out starkly on his pale skin.

"All right," she said, sobering. "No, it's not. What's the last thing you remember?"

"Drinking. Then we argued. I thought—I don't know what I

thought. And then I saw Kazzo. He told me that you two were meeting for a drink."

It was her turn to look horrified. "When did you see *him?*"

"I went to the armoury to find you after Mum said you had your licence back. He invited me along."

"What else did he say?"

"He said that you two were back together." His mouth wanted to close shut on the terrible words and the vulnerability they would reveal. He forced them out. "That you were using me."

"We were using each other. Wouldn't you say?"

He didn't know how to answer that question. It was hard enough just meeting her eyes.

"Let me tell you something," she said, her expression very serious. "That day I found you in the tunnels, I *did* think of screwing you over. You were practically begging to be taken advantage of. And me? I really needed something to go right for a change. My Dad didn't leave much when he died, and that went when he was blamed for the crash. I could keep a roof over my head while I had my licence but when I lost that I had to move in with Kazzo for a bit. It soon became clear that he was only after one thing, and then I was out on the street, selling blood to survive—and that wasn't going to go well if it went on much longer." She held out her arm and showed him the line of old cuts he had already noticed. "When I heard about this gormless Stone Mage looking for help, I knew you were an opportunity too good to pass up."

"I'm sorry things didn't go according to plan."

"They didn't, but that's not your fault. First the Magister screwed things up by giving you a licence, not me. Then we crashed and I was stuck with the Sky Wardens on the wrong side of the Divide. Things got really messy then. The further they waded into the shit the less likely it was I'd ever fly again. I still can't quite believe it's worked out so well, that I'm not in jail and I'm free to do whatever I want." Her eyes didn't leave his. "And you know what? What I want isn't so obvious any more. If I've learned one thing in the last week, it's that the licence isn't as important as I thought it was. Sure, I'm happier with it than without it, but maybe it wasn't what I was really missing. Maybe I was looking for something else all along and not knowing it."

A faint memory stirred, and with it his hopes. "Did we talk about this last night?"

"You bet," she said. "You think I'm crazy, but it'll take more than that to change my mind."

"About what?"

"Going with the wardens, of course. What else? They're heading for the Hanging Mountains—for the fog forests and the balloon cities. This is my big chance to see where my family comes from. I'm not going to turn that down."

"I guess not," he said, his stomach doing a gentle backflip. He didn't know whether to be relieved or appalled. "I guess that's what we argued about."

"Not at all." The beginnings of a smile returned. "That was about who would win a wrestling match between Kemp and the quarter-master. I think you're overestimating your white friend's reach, but would you listen? Pfft. For someone who professes to like girls, you're rather smitten with Kemp's form."

"I am?" he squeaked.

She laughed again, and he felt his face burn.

"So what about Kazzo?" he asked. "If you're not staying in Laure, what gave him the impression that you were? Was he just lying?"

"Why does it matter what that jerk says? Sure, I said I'd meet him for a drink. I even hinted that I might spend the night with him if he'd ditch that slutty Liris. But now he'll sit in the bar for a while and get bored. Then he'll give up and go home alone, feeling like an idiot. Serves him right, the shit."

A knot of tension loosened inside him. "And me? Where do I stand in all this?"

"Well, that's up to you. When you've decided which you'd rather do—go back to your father's safe little nest, or come with us to the Hanging Mountains—you let me know."

That wasn't entirely what he'd meant, but he supposed the answer served either way.

He shook his aching head. "I can't believe I slept on the bar floor. Did you really have to carry me up here?"

"Yes, and you *do* snore. I can tell you that for a fact."

"I—what?"

"This is my room now, as well as yours. Where do you think I slept last night?"

He stared at her, not sure exactly which part of this new development horrified him more.

"Are you pulling my leg?"

"Maybe I am, maybe I'm not. After all the drinking and the carousing . . ." She hesitated, studying him with her gracefully curved eyes. Her expression was one he hadn't seen before: almost wistful, almost wounded; almost a lot of things, but not quite. "You *really* don't remember?"

He shook his head.

"Then I guess, my friend, you'll never know."

THE SAVED

"On the beach, on the brink of death, on the Divide, and on the cliff; on the boundary between one state and another—from the edge of things we see most clearly and lose ourselves most readily."

THE BOOK OF TOWERS, FRAGMENT 99

Habryn Kail sat in his undergarments as the rest of his clothes dried by the fire. The night was deep and dark and as empty of the Change as the heart of the Aad had been. The shadow watching him from the far side of the fire was darker and emptier still.

"You must have rescued me for a reason," he said over the crackling flames.

"We need your help," said the Homunculus.

"I've already helped you by stopping Pirelius from killing you. On that score, I figure we're even."

"Yes. We're asking, not demanding."

"For what, exactly?"

The creature's eyes glittered. "Understanding. We must understand each other or all will end in disaster. That's obvious, now. We tried to do it alone and it didn't work. We were pursued and attacked and imprisoned, almost killed. If we die, everything will come undone. It will all have been for nothing. We need you to help keep us alive long enough to achieve what we came here for. Then you will be free. We will *all* be released."

Kail took several slow, measured breaths. The sense of tumbling and drowning in the flood returned, making him feel disoriented and nauseous. Then, he had thought he would die. He had been willing enough to accept his fate, under the circumstances, until two pairs of strong hands working in unison caught his wrists and hauled him to the surface, setting him on an entirely new path. Now, he thought he might just lose his grip on himself.

The taste of spiderbush leaf was bitter in his mouth. The leaves took the edge off his appetite, but little else.

"The place you're headed," he said, "it must be in the Hanging Mountains. I've studied the maps of the plains between here and the foothills, and there's nothing else to speak of. The occasional Ruin, the odd struggling town. Laure is the last outpost until you hit the mountains, and there my knowledge ends."

"How far are they?"

"Hundreds of kilometres. I don't know exactly. It depends on how far downstream we've been swept. By tomorrow morning, I'll be able to tell you."

The Homunculus slowly nodded. "It's a long way. But the mountains sound . . . plausible. There is a connection between our previous lives and this one."

"What sort of connection?"

"That'll be hard to explain."

"Well, I'm not going anywhere until my clothes are dry."

"We mean that it will be hard for us as well as you. Much remains unclear in our own minds. It's been a long time since we last had to think of such things."

"How long?"

"You tell us. When did the giant cities die? When did electricity stop working? When did the world end?"

"No one knows for sure. 'A thousand years ago' is what the stories say, but that's like 'once upon a time.' People say it because they don't know for certain."

"However long it's been, that's how long we've been in the Void. We're only just beginning to remember parts of what happened. You'll have to be patient with us."

"But you *will* tell me?"

"In return for helping us survive our journey, yes. We'll owe you that much, at least."

Kail thought of Eisak Marmion and his mission to destroy the unnatural interloper, for reasons he kept carefully to himself. He thought of Shilly insisting that the Homunculus deserved to live, and the promise he had made to her, to prevent the Homunculus from being killed out of hand. He thought of Highson Sparre, who had inadvertently given it a route back among the living. And he thought of himself, a tracker who had disobeyed orders and now had to work out where he stood. Everything had seemed so simple in the moments before the flood.

One thing he was sure of was that few things deserved automatic obliteration. Nature was about coexistence, even among hunter and hunted. Predators could be avoided, just as he would avoid dangerous insects and snakes, and the need to flee kept prey vigorous and vital. He didn't know which class of being he belonged to at that moment, but he knew the world would be diminished if he chose to kill the Homunculus without understanding it first.

If he even *could* kill it. The wound Pirelius had inflicted in its shoulder was gone, as though it had never existed.

What would Lodo do? he wondered, as he had so often in his life.

"All right," he said, "I'll help you of my own free will. I'll guide you across the plains to the mountains and keep you out of trouble. It doesn't take me too far into the Interior, and I can manage well enough without the Change. In return you'll tell me about where you come from and why you're here. Does that sound fair to you?"

"We need to know about *your* world, too," the Homunculus responded. "There's a lot we don't understand."

"We'll teach each other." Kail wondered if he should go around the fire to shake the creature's hands. It made no move to come to him, so he stayed where he was. "There's something else I need from you, if we're to cooperate."

"And that is?"

"Your names."

The dark figure didn't move for a long moment. Although the features of the physical vessel were shadowed, he sensed a fierce internal struggle taking place between the minds it contained. Its posture was rigid. Its skin shivered from more than just the shifting of the firelight.

Then it relaxed. "I am Hadrian Castillo," it said.

"And I am Seth Castillo," said a second voice, one similar to the first but not identical.

Kail waited a moment, but nothing else was forthcoming.

"My name is Habryn Kail," he said, "and I guess we have a deal."

The twins nodded, then froze again.

They said nothing more that night. When his clothes were dry, Kail put them back on and lay down by the fading flames. The fragment of the Change-sink, secure in a pouch normally reserved for coins, dug into his side, and he adjusted it to a more comfortable position. He was exhausted from his trials in the Aad and the Divide, and hungry, too, despite the spiderbush he had found growing on the edge of the flood-filled canyon. Foraging in earnest would have to wait until morning. He needed to take what rest he could before they set out on their long journey.

The Homunculus watched him, sleepless and silent beyond the fire. Its thoughts were unknown to him. When he slept, he dreamed of those four gleaming eyes staring at him all night long, and he shifted uneasily on the cold, hard ground.

The time has come. It has always been. You are there. We are there with you.

You weren't there! You couldn't possibly know! We are alone!

The stone shadows knew. That much was obvious. They used words the twins hadn't heard for eons, words that had presaged the death of one of them and the end for everyone.

Tiden har kommit. The time has come.

In that moment, the twins understood that they couldn't walk through the world like a ghost any longer. It might feel nebulous and strange to them, but it was powerfully real. For all that they might want to rush headlong to their fate, those around them might have different ideas. They needed to see things more clearly, lest they lose their way.

The time for thinking is over. If you won't kill it, I will!

So much violence. So much anger.

You! You have destroyed me!

All directed away from the thing that really mattered . . .

You must have rescued me for a reason.

The fire crackled and popped like a living creature. It was the first truly vivid thing the twins had seen since entering the world. Its manifold golds and crimsons blended in a superb alchemical mix that told them they had made the right decision. They were connecting, slowly but surely. They had taken a step that was at least as important as any physical journey.

It's the right thing to do, said Hadrian. *You know it as well as I.*

Yes, but I'm the one who remembers dying, Seth replied. *That's what we're risking now.*

Have to risk all to gain all.

There's no "all" for us. I know that as well as you do.

They looked out at the world through their strange, alien skin. New puzzlements greeted them. They could see the stars now, but they looked wrong, somehow—brighter and sparser, as though there were fewer of them, and closer to the Earth than they remembered. The horizon was less distinct, although that could have been the immensity of the desert around them, confusing their eyes. Sunrises and sunsets looked strange.

The precise nature of the world eluded them still. Where did the Change fit in? What happened after death with the First and Second Realms so closely aligned? Who was the Goddess?

Instead of answers, the questions raised names from the distant past. Kybele. Agatha. Barbelo. Simapesiel. Ana. Meg. Horva. Ellis.

Yod.

As the strange stars slid westward across the sky, the twins thought they saw something fly overhead, like a distant golden bird, catching the light of an invisible sun. It reminded them of someone or something they had once known. Another name: Pukje. Another voice from the past . . .

Would you believe me if I told you it was a dragon?

A real *dragon?*

Is there any other sort?

The golden speck circled once, then angled off to meet the darkness looming in the northeast, urging them to hurry.

To be continued in
The Hanging Mountains
Books of the Cataclysm: Three

GLOSSARY

Alcaide—The position of Alcaide is equivalent to grand chancellor or highest judge of the Strand, and is currently held by Dragan Braham.

Book of Towers—A collection of tales and commentaries concerning the Cataclysm and related matters, gathered down the centuries. It contains legends and fables from the times before and immediately after the Cataclysm, and maps of the changing world. Scholars invariably disagree over what is real and what is imagined. The argument will no doubt rage for centuries to come.

Broken Lands—Regions of fractured landscape left over from the Cataclysm. Such regions are scattered apparently at random across the world, but may be subtly connected. One of the five great ancient cities moves between various Broken Lands, changing location every few years. The relocation has never been witnessed by human eyes.

Cataclysm—The catastrophe that marked the beginning of the world as understood by Sky Warden and Stone Mage, and other chroniclers of human events. The cause of the Cataclysm, along with knowledge of the times that preceded it, is lost. Much has been said about it, and such stories, along with speculation concerning their veracity, have been collected in the multiauthor account known as *The Book of Towers*.

Conclave—The term used to refer to the Sky Warden community as a whole. The Conclave maintains a strict hierarchical structure within itself, dominated by three family lines: Air, Cloud, and Water.

Divide—A vast, jagged, human-made canyon that separates the Interior from the Strand. Its origins stretch back to the days shortly after the Cataclysm, when the world was rife with the Change and the chaos it brought. Some say it was created to keep Stone Mage and Sky Warden teachings separate, others that it served as a repository for the new and dangerous creatures that walked the Earth. Whatever purpose it serves, bridges cross it at only two points, Tintenbar and the Lookout, and both are heavily charmed against hostile use of the Change.

Fundelry—A small but locally important fishing village on the section of the Strand known as Gooron.

Ghost—The common name for the bodiless minds imprisoned in the Haunted City. On two occasions in recent times, a ghost or ghosts contacted human residents of the island and used them to facilitate a bid for freedom. On both occasions, the ghosts turned on their liberators, with lethal results.

Golem—When a Change-worker overexerts themselves, they run the risk of vanishing into the Void Beneath and becoming the opposite of a ghost: a body without a mind. Such empty bodies can be inhabited by golems, fleshless minds with a hunger for experience. Such inhabitation is invariably fatal in the end, for the golem's human host.

Haunted City—The capital of the Strand. A mysterious place, which humans inhabit only by default, its crystalline towers are cages for ancient ghosts who seek forever to escape.

Interior—The vast inland state to the north of the Divide, dominated by large, underground cities and people with light-coloured skin.

Keep—A prestigious school for Stone Mages situated in a cliff-face retreat connected to the city of Ulum by a space-bending Way. The Van Haasteren family, with their hereditary recall, has administered the school for generations. The current principal is the ninth in the line.

Man'kin—One of the many castes of intelligent beings to walk the world since the Cataclysm. Animated, self-aware statues with an ability to see all times as one, the man'kin have occasionally been tricked into acting as advisers for their human "masters." Rogue man'kin are feared everywhere, as their strength and indifference to human affairs make them capricious and formidable foes.

Nine Stars—The ancient, arcane city deep in the desert of the Interior where the Stone Mage Conclave meets every full moon to make decisions and cast judgments.

Novitiate—The training ground for those with talent in the Strand. It is situated on the same island as the Haunted City and currently overseen by Master Warden Risa Atilde.

Ruin—A location, usually rich or poor in the Change to some notable degree, with close ties to the past. These may include cities, isolated buildings, mine shafts, roads, harbours, and other relics of ancient civilisation. They are often places of great danger, to be approached with caution.

Selection—The process by which those with innate talent or strong Change-sensitivity are discovered in the Strand. Selectors visit every village at least once a year, testing candidates and taking the successful to attend the Novitiate in the Haunted City.

Sky Warden—Those trained in the Change who rule the Strand. They traditionally wear blue robes and crystal torcs. Their charms often involve feathers and wood, and have efficacy over water and air. They claim to draw their powers from the deep reservoirs of the open ocean, so they are most puissant near the coast.

Stone Mage—Those trained in the Change who rule the Interior. They traditionally wear red robes and tattoo signs of rank on their skin. Their charms often involve stone and metal, and are effective over fire and earth. They claim to draw their powers from the red heart of the desert, near the site of the ancient city known as the Nine Stars.

Strand—The nation known as the Strand encompasses one vast stretch of uninterrupted coastline along which are scattered numerous villages. Each village is run by a group of ten elected Alders, who in turn elect a Mayor. The Mayors then elect Regional Governors who meet once every four years in the Haunted City with representatives of the Sky Wardens to discuss governance of their nation. The highest rank obtainable in the Strand is the Alcaide, closely followed by the Syndic.

Surveyor—A member of the multidisciplinary and bipartisan corps dedicated to research and exploration of the historically active sites known as Ruins. To be a Surveyor is to be regarded as both supremely talented and foolhardy, and perhaps a little reckless.

Syndic—The Syndic is the Alcaide's chief administrator, a position currently held by Nu Zanshin, aunt of Highson Sparre and great-aunt of Sal Hrvati.

Synod—The body of select, high-ranking Stone Mages that cast judgments every month from the city of the Nine Stars.

Ulum—One of the great cities of the Interior, in the Desert Port Region.

Void Beneath—The emptiness connecting all things, and into which the minds of Change-workers might disappear if they exert themselves too greatly. Even partial exposure to the Void may irreversibly corrode memory.

Author's Note

The world of Sal, Shilly, and Skender owes much to my upbringing in South Australia and the Northern Territory. I am grateful to those readers who noted the source of this inspiration in the Books of the Change and encouraged me to continue mining. I've always maintained that it's a rich vein, and I'm certain now that it won't run out any time soon.

Specific thanks to: Julia Gosling, Sara Henschke, and Robin Potanin for wanting more; Rebekah Clarkson and K*m Mann for encouraging me to write from the heart; Kirsty Brooks for lessons in sassiness; Greg Bridges for another window into wonder; my niece Jessica for a simple misspelling; my mother, Heather Williams, and my family in Cowell and Mt. Ghearty for their patience; Richard Curtis for persistence and continued friendship; Stephanie Smith for, well, the usual (and no less wonderful it is for being so!); and everyone at HarperCollins for doing all the hard work.

The quotes in the second interlude and "The Wall" come from "The Charge of the Light Brigade" by Alfred, Lord Tennyson, while the quote in "The Wake" is an excerpt from Edgar Allen Poe's "Eldorado." I owe the former, and a great deal of inspiration, to Kim Selling, to whom this book is dedicated, with love.

Sean Williams
Adelaide, September 2004

ABOUT
THE AUTHOR

A delaide author (and occasional DJ) SEAN WILLIAMS has published twenty-one novels and over sixty short stories. A multiple winner of Australia's speculative fiction awards, recipient of the "SA Great" Literature Award, and *New York Times* bestseller, he has also written a sci-fi musical and the odd piece of bad haiku. You can visit his Web site at www.seanwilliams.com.